THE SEVENTH SOUL

The ParaNormal Series:

Book One

M.L. Harveland

This is a work of fiction. Names, characters, places, and incidents either are the product of the author's imagination or are used fictitiously, and any resemblance to actual persons, living or dead, business establishments, events, or locals is entirely coincidental.

THE SEVENTH SOUL
Copyright © 2011 by M.L. Harveland
Cover design by Mark Sorgaard

Published in the United States of America

ISBN-10: 1492393584
ISBN-13: 9781492393580

For Dan, always…

Deep into that darkness peering, long I stood there wondering, fearing,
Doubting, dreaming dreams no mortal ever dared to dream before;
But the silence was unbroken, and the stillness gave no token,
And the only word there spoken was the whispered word, "Lenore"
This I whispered, and an echo murmured back the word, "Lenore!"—
Merely this and nothing more.

EDGAR ALLAN POE
"The Raven"

Prelude

The dark figure straightened – she had finally arrived.

He stood watching, unmoving, behind the tree, as she took a seat on the park bench—her bench. She was here at the same time every day.

He admired her punctuality.

Most days, he watched from afar, waiting until she left so he could touch the bench planks and feel her warm impression.

Today would be different.

She was in a moment of quiet reflection, unaware of his presence. He could nearly taste the deliciousness of the moment – her soft movement … a wisp of hair in a gentle breeze, hand gracing a soft cheek, eyelashes batting, eyes flashing in the sunlight, the curve of her knee… such a delectable feast for the eyes.

But the real deliciousness would come later.

He smiled and breathed deeply the hint of her perfume that blended with the warm breeze. Tonight's plan swirled in his head, making him feel dizzy, almost numb. He closed his eyes and sighed surprisingly loud. His body tensed as he opened his eyes to see if she had noticed.

She had not.

Instant relief washed over him. He must be more careful. She was the chosen one – any stupid mistakes would ruin his plan.

He steeled himself and walked toward the bench, sitting in the empty spot next to her. He nearly fainted when his hand grazed hers. She blushed, moving her hand away without even a glance.

She was mesmerizing, particularly her eyes, which were the color of deep aqua, like pools of cold springs melting in the warm sun. No one had the right to possess such beauty.

Her brow creased deeply. His eyes lingered too long. He repositioned himself away from her, opened a newspaper, and pretended to read.

His heart fluttered nervously—being so close to her was thrilling. He afforded only momentary glances at her—the pearlescent skin, supple lips, her dainty hands, the curve of her waist…her youth.

She was so *alive*.

He glanced at his watch; time was drawing near.

She closed her book, set it gently in her bag, and rose from the bench.

His heart thudded loudly as he followed her to Silver Street Bridge. Her habits were like clockwork: reading for thirty minutes in the park, followed by a stroll to the bridge, where she stood for several minutes, glancing into the river in reverie. He imagined that this was a way of allowing her mind to absorb the book, of letting the author's world become part of her. The thought made him want her all the more. He loved smart girls.

Now, she moved away from the bridge and walked toward Market Square. She always window shopped, but never bought. After several minutes, she started toward home. He watched as she walked languidly down the alley toward her building, and marveled at her nimble fingers as they maneuvered the key into the lock and opened the door.

This door was always locked. But, several days ago, he stole her key when she wasn't looking and duplicated it. The process took mere seconds.

He'd done it before.

He waited several seconds before quietly entering the building. The faint sound of heels clicking against stone told him that she was still making her assent. His heart quickened along with his pace.

Once behind her, he checked quickly to make sure no one was around. He moved swiftly behind her and put a hand firmly on the door. She froze and then slowly turned around.

Bright aqua eyes revealed her frightened state. The expression immediately softened in recognition.

"Oh, it's just you," she said, putting a hand to her heart, smiling in relief. "You scared me!" She looked up at him expectantly, smile fading as he offered no response. Then, she frowned. "Wait, how did you get in here?"

Without hesitation, he lurched forward and placed a handkerchief soaked in chloroform over her mouth and nose. She struggled, but quietly – he had taken her by surprise. It took mere seconds for the drug to take effect. One last struggle for breath, and then she slumped forward.

She was his now.

He dragged the limp body into her small room, closing the door softly behind them. He was well aware that no one would hear him. It was Saturday; all the resident girls would either be working late or out with gentlemen callers.

Nevertheless, he had to work quickly.

He gently laid her on the bed, pulling a blanket over her shoulders to keep her warm. He removed a needle from his pocket, injecting a stronger drug into her system, one that would keep her sleeping comfortably for several hours.

When the sky turned dark, he rolled her into a large floor rug. He hauled the rug over his shoulder and then carried his prize out of the building. He worked his way around the alleys he knew so well—alleyways that typically housed tradesman. No one would suspect a man carrying a rolled-up rug, especially a man wearing a painter's cap.

Upon arrival to his flat, he carried her to a special room and lay her down upon the daybed. He quickly tied straps to her arms and legs so she couldn't escape.

Suddenly, he felt dizzy, as if outside of himself. The room looked hazy, surreal. His blood sugar was lowering—he needed to eat. He stuffed a cloth into her mouth and shut the door, lest she should awake and make noise.

Of course, he knew no one would hear her. He made sure of that.

After dinner, he opened the secret door, only to find her stirring quietly. It wouldn't be long before she woke. He eased into the wingback chair next to her, pulse racing in anticipation.

Impatiently, he sighed, refocusing his attention on the room he built – *her* room.

He blessed the day that he found this room, just weeks ago. He was hanging artwork with the intention of inviting her over—an attempt to impress her. The hammer went straight through the wall, creating a gaping hole, revealing a secret room within. That's when his plans had changed.

He stomped his foot loudly, smiling proudly at the solid reverberation.

The room was sound proof.

Extra insulation in the ceiling and under the floorboards ensured undisturbed privacy. An oddly-shaped room at the end of an oddly-shaped building, this room was situated above nothing but an infrequently-used entrance. The room was surrounded only by his apartment and the open air of a vacant alley.

It was perfect.

It was for her.

A quiet murmur broke his reverie. He quickly rose and removed the cloth from her mouth, hovering inches above her face, feeling her warm breath. He kissed her gently on the lips before backing into the shadows to watch, unseen, her awakening.

Her delicate eyelashes fluttered and then opened, revealing intense aqua pools of light—the windows into her soul.

Disoriented, she frowned, slowly glancing around the room, trying to gain her bearings. Her eyes flew open in astonishment as confusion turned to realization—she was in a strange place. She tried moving her arms and legs, but they were strapped in. Horrified, she began wrenching her arms to free them, but realizing her effort was to no avail, she stopped and sobbed in frustration.

A quiet squeal came from her dry throat.

He quickly covered his mouth to stifle an amused chuckle. Though he felt some sympathy for her, he felt an indescribable deliciousness in the moment.

She tried to scream, but the drugs had made her throat so dry that it only came out as a hoarse croak.

He needed to move before she found her voice.

He slowly moved toward her, trying to look empathetic, kind. However, his amusement contorted the expression, making him appear crazed.

Her eyes grew wide with terror at his approach. She screamed, thrashing her limbs in an attempt to escape the approaching madman.

He smiled, putting a finger to his lips. "Shh," he shushed her soothingly, "I won't hurt you."

She stopped thrashing, and frowned in momentary consideration. A silver light glinted off her face, redirecting her gaze to the sharp instrument in his hand. She screamed in terror.

He looked at his hand, his heart lurching in dread as he noticed her source of fear: it was the awl that he used on her wrist straps. Her wrists were so tiny that he needed to make a new hole in the leather strap so that he could secure her.

"Oh, no—you see, this isn't meant for you," he opened his hand, offering to show her the tool. "It's just an awl, you see. I needed to make a new hole in your wrist strap, that's all!" He smiled, trying to look amiable, non-threatening. But, it wasn't working—she began thrashing about more aggressively.

He threw the awl aside and held his hands out, walking slowly toward her. "See? I threw it away! Don't panic, it's alright—I'm going to take care of you. I'm *not* going to hurt you!" His voice shook as he tried talking soothingly, taking careful steps closer.

The sound of cracking wood stopped him in his tracks.

He looked down and noticed that the daybed's legs were cracking and splintering under her violent thrashing.

She was stronger than he thought.

He lunged forward to help steady the bed, but it began to wobble and the cracking grew more pronounced.

"No!" He screamed. "Stop moving! You're going to ruin everything!" He lunged at her just as the bed toppled over on its side and then rolled completely over, pinning her underneath, facedown. He flew in the air, hitting his head hard on the wall, causing him to black out.

He slowly opened his eyes, glancing around in a daze. His hand moved to his head; he winced in pain as he touched the lump forming on the top of his head.

How long had he been out?

Glancing over to his side, he saw the upturned daybed and frowned.

Sudden realization forced him up off the floor. He ran over to the daybed, where she was still pinned underneath.

"No!" he screamed, clawing at the legs, trying to raise the heavy bed off the floor.

"See what happens when you don't listen?" he screamed at her. He gasped for breath and paused to gain his composure. Then, he froze, listening for her breath in the room's stillness.

Oh, please, no!

He picked up the edge of the bed and pushed it over. Her head lolled unnaturally to the side. He kneeled next to her, gently raising her head in his hands. Her eyes were wide open, but the expression was blank.

Panicking, he placed a finger under her nose to feel for breath. He checked for a pulse. He felt nothing.

Then he saw it: a little silver glint protruding from her chest...a red stain spreading across the front of her dress.

He raised the chest strap and shuddered—the awl he had so carelessly tossed aside was lodged in her chest.

Tears streamed down his face at the realization that his plan had failed…all the hours planning, building the room…all for naught.

He wept uncontrollably, the deep anguish eventually culminating into a continuous, piercing scream.

Finally, he collapsed in an exhausted heap, his head resting on her chest. Warm blood seeped from her wound, covering his cheek and coating his hair. Her beauty was still mesmerizing; he ran a hand along her pearlescent cheek, traced a finger down her neck and along her collar bone. Then, he raised himself on one arm and gazed into those aqua eyes.

Those beautiful pools of light, extinguished forevermore. He anguished at the thought that those eyes would never gaze upon him again—never look upon him with the love he longed for.

Angry tears flowed. He pounded his fist into the floor as memories of her flooded his mind. He tore at his hair and scratched his eyes, screaming her name. He would surely die without her.

Then, as if flicking a switch, he stopped.

A voice within quelled his sorrow, soothed him, comforted him, told him what to do.

He nodded, acknowledging the invisible command, and then gazed once more upon her eyes before closing them.

No more time to waste; he had work to do.

ONE

L enora bolted upright, looking in confusion around the darkened room.

That dream was so bizarre.

The window next to her bed was open, letting in a cool evening
breeze. The moon illuminated her room so brightly that it almost
appeared daylight.

Unable to sleep, Lenora got out of bed and crept over to her
desk, switching on the lamp. She glanced around her new room.
Most of her things were unpacked, except for a couple of boxes—
those went under her bed for another time.

This room was smaller than the one she had back in Ann Arbor,
but all of her things were in it. Crammed into the tiny space were
her bed, nightstand, dresser, and the desk that Grandpa Kelley built.
Even the mirror with the ornate frame that her mother gave her was
hung carefully above the desk, just as she had it back home. The
walls were freshly painted a deep violet, which stood stark against
the white furniture, and her favorite blue and black fleur-de-lis com-
forter added texture, comfort. Her dad worked hard to make sure
she felt at home here.

Home.

Her *real* home felt light years away. When her dad announced
that he got a job as Professor of Psychology at the University of
Cambridge, Lenora thought it meant they were moving to Cambridge,
Massachusetts—not Cambridge, England. And, it couldn't have
come at a worst time. In three months, she would be starting her last

year of high school. She hoped to be spending it making memories with her friends. Now, she had to make new ones.

And, it was so soon after her mother's death—only four months.

Her dad said it was just the change they both needed. She didn't need change—she needed to be close to her friends and grandparents…she needed her mom.

Looking for something to read, Lenora shifted books and magazines around on the desk, when something caught her eye. It was a picture of her mom. She picked it up, studying her mom's face in an effort to remember what she looked like. But, she didn't have far to look to remember—she only need look in a mirror. Apart from the dark auburn hair, she was a near mirror image of her mom— right down to the deep emerald green eyes. Tears coursed down her cheek as she remembered how beautiful her mom was…and so young. Lenora thought of all the things her mom would miss out on: giggling over her first boyfriend, cheering her on at graduation, seeing her get married and have children.

It just wasn't fair.

Lenora shook her head, refusing to dwell on it. She inserted the picture into the mirror's frame.

Now, I can see you every day, she thought with a sad smile.

A movement in the mirror caught her eye. She glanced up, noticing that her breath misted, as if she were outside on a cold winter morning. The temperature in the room quickly plummeted. She started to shiver. She walked over to the window and frowned as the June breeze warmed her arm.

The air conditioner must be on the fritz. She looked at the clock, which read 3:17 a.m.—not a good time to wake dad. *I'll just tell dad about it in the morning.*

She tiptoed out to the hallway closet and removed thick winter blankets, threw them on her bed, and dove in.

The next morning, Lenora woke up in a pool of sweat. She threw off the covers and gasped—the room was stifling hot and stuffy. Her chest felt heavy as she struggled to open the window next to the bed. The window pane appeared to be swollen, as it slowly slid open. The cool morning breeze drifted into the sweltering room. She leaned out onto the window and gulped in the cool air.

Though the breeze helped, her clothes clung to her body like wet paper. Grimacing, she peeled the shirt away from her chest and fanned it to cool down. A cool shower was in order.

Her dad was reading a newspaper when she walked into the living room.

"Late night?" Tom grinned at her over the top of the newspaper.

Lenora frowned and looked at the clock. *Eleven-thirty?* She couldn't believe how late it was. "Dad, why did you let me sleep so long?"

Tom's eyebrows rose in astonishment. "Len, you're old enough to wake yourself. It's not my fault that you were up late and slept in, now, is it?"

"No," she sighed. He was always too reasonable. She dropped into the chair next to him and secured her long auburn locks into a ponytail before leafing through sections of the paper, finally settling on the comics.

"It's a bit late for breakfast, but maybe we could go out for lunch?"

"Yes," she agreed, "I'm starving." She studied her dad for a moment, remembering the temperature anomaly from the previous night. "Hey, before I forget. A strange thing happened last night." She explained how her room grew so frigid that she could see her breath, that she needed winter blankets to stay warm, and how stifling her room was when she woke.

Tom looked incredulous. "Lenora, it's the first week of June. That's a little impossible. Could you have been dreaming?"

"No, dad, I was perfectly awake."

Tom frowned. "Well, the air conditioner is probably not working. If it happens again, let me know, and I'll get someone to look into it. Okay?" He patted her on the head with the newspaper. "Let's go eat—you're starving."

TWO

It happened again…and again. And, when Tom finally noticed the change in temperature and saw his breath, he called a technician to fix the air conditioner.

The repairman installed a new thermostat, but informed them that nothing was wrong with the air conditioning—that maybe they needed to turn the temperature up at night. Lenora couldn't help but notice the strange looks he gave them on the way out.

On a positive note, Lenora got a really cool necklace out of the deal.

When the repairman was removing the old thermostat, he found a perfectly round, amber-colored stone lodged in the wall. Tom examined it with skepticism, and despite his assertions that it had no value, immediately took it to a jeweler, who verified that it was indeed a precious gemstone. Tom had the stone polished and set inside a sterling silver, filigree heart pendant, which he gave to his daughter.

Lenora stretched out on her bed and held the pendant up, twirling it in the sunlight. She peered, mesmerized, inside the little heart as the stone's deep amber and bronze flecks glimmered in the light. This was probably the first gift her dad had given her since her mom died. Lenora looked at the pendant thoughtfully for several minutes and then let it softly drop to the end of the long chain.

She swung her legs over the bed and stared lazily into the room. It was raining out—check that—pouring, and she couldn't go any-where. She was in the flat…alone…with nothing to do. She finished one of her books several hours ago, cleaned the entire flat, put dinner in the oven, and tried to take a nap. There was nothing left to do, and she felt trapped.

Lenora felt that way a lot lately, and was having mixed feelings about moving here. Being so far from friends and family left her feeling lonely. However, she knew it was the new start that her dad needed—the job opportunity of a lifetime.

Consequently, she decided to make the best of what she could and tried to acclimate to her new surroundings. She toured the museums and strolled through the many beautiful gardens Cambridge had to offer. Early mornings before dawn, she rose to walk along the city's narrow streets, reflecting on its antiquity, reveling in the history. Afternoons were spent browsing her already favorite bookstore, Barton's Books, and then taking her new purchase and lazing alongside the River Cam, reading and watching as the punters drifted idly by.

Her dad's position at the university allotted her access to the many bridges along the Cam that only students and faculty were allowed to enjoy. Lenora particularly enjoyed standing quietly atop the bridges on a misty morning right before dawn, when the black swans glided smoothly through the water. She found serenity in the eerie silence, when the river was tranquil and the fog slid its milky fingers along the embankments and disappeared behind the mossy trees. She felt as if in another world, apart from all civilization, at peace and utterly alone.

Often, when the university was particularly quiet in the early twilight, she sat on the rocks beneath Trinity Bridge, along the embankment, and wrote in her journal or read. As time drew on, she began to feel a certain connection with her new home—as if she were meant to be here.

Today, however, she was stuck in the apartment and felt homesick—missing her friends, grandparents, and the familiarity of the creaky floorboards in her old room. She missed the smells, the sights, the sounds of everything familiar.

That's it! I'm telling Dad that I'm moving back to Ann Arbor before school starts. She groaned in frustrated boredom.

She lounged on the couch with a soda and opened another book. She loved to read—it was like living someone else's life, sharing in another's adventures, living vicariously through the author's vision. Disappearing into someone else's life appealed to her.

Goose bumps formed on her arms as the temperature slightly dipped. Frowning, she got up from the couch and looked at the thermometer. It was set for 70 degrees, but the temperature reading said 60…now 55…now 50…now 45. The temperature kept lowering bit-by-bit.

Bert the Technician never fixed the air conditioning, she thought angrily.

She grabbed the quilt off the couch, wrapping herself in it before delving back into her book. She was reading Anne Rice's "The Witching Hour," and it was getting good. Tom didn't particularly like that Lenora read so much gothic literature, but she loved it—loved how it made her heart race. Tom thought that reading gothic literature somehow lead to dark thoughts. Lenora thought his reasoning unsound, and told him so. Dark and mysterious was attractive to her—maudlin and formulaic romance just wasn't her thing.

Her nose felt cold. She let the blanket fall from her head and shoulders. The room was getting colder. Her brows furrowed—how could it be getting this cold in here? She leaned forward to take a sip of her soda, when she felt an icy coldness behind her. She touched the back of her neck and felt the coldness. The iciness met her fingers, as if someone touched the back of her neck and left their icy imprints. She shivered.

She moved her hand and proceeded to lean forward again, when she felt hot breath on her neck. At first, she thought it was a brief return of the heat, but then checked herself when the breath returned—this time with an exhaling sound and vapor. Eyes wide, she froze.

"Ahhhhhhh…….lennnnn….." something behind her breathed, followed by a quiet chuckle.

Horrified, she shot up from the couch, hitting her leg on the coffee table and sending the glass of soda spilling to the ground. She spun around and looked at the space behind her. No one was there. A lump formed in the back of her throat.

"Dad?" She looked around, still feeling frozen to the spot. When no reply came, she briskly walked through the apartment to see if her dad was home and playing a trick on her. Maybe this was his poor attempt to convince her not to read so much gothic horror. But, Tom was nowhere to be found, and the front door was locked.

Lenora sprinted into the living room, grabbed her book, and then ran out the apartment door. She sat on the top step and tried to catch her breath, heart racing, lump still in her throat.

What just happened?

"Hey, Len! What are you doing out here?"

Lenora jumped, her heart beating furiously in her chest. "Ach, Dad, don't do that!"

"Do what?" Tom asked, looking amused.

"Sneak up on a person like that!"

"I would hardly call that sneaking, Len." Tom chuckled. He glanced at the book she was reading and raised an eyebrow. "Reading gothic again?"

Lenora rolled her eyes, choosing not to answer him. "So, what are you doing home so early?" She rose from the step to let her dad into the apartment.

"Well, I have great news and couldn't wait to share it!" Tom smiled widely, his hazel eyes sparkling. "Guess what happened to me today?" he asked sheepishly.

"Let me guess," she added with a sigh, disinterested in playing. "You got a better job offer back home?" A sarcastic grin played across her face.

"Cute, but not even close." He chuckled, noting her sarcasm. "Not interested in playing today?" Lenora shrugged her shoulders apologetically. Tom smiled at her. "Okay, I'll just tell you then. I was offered the job of Professorial Fellow and Director of Studies in Psychology! And, after a summer of mentoring with the current director, I will take over a special research group in the department. That's quite the promotion!"

Lenora forced a smile. "After only three weeks? You'd think they'd at least give you a year or two." She walked into the apartment, shoulders slumped.

Tom frowned as he watched his daughter collapse onto the couch, a sullen look on her face. "Hey, what's the deal?"

Lenora sighed heavily. She hesitated telling him that she wanted to go home. She didn't want to disappoint him, or worse, ruin his chances for success…for happiness.

Tom plopped into the chair next to her. "Hey, what's going on?" he asked, grasping her hands in his, looking puzzled. "Come on, Len, you can tell me. We have to be honest with each other—you're all I've got in this world. So whatever it is, please tell me."

Lenora softened. "It's just that…" she hesitated. She had inwardly vowed never to complain about the move. Her dad had been through too much in the last few months to have yet another disappointment on his hands.

"Come on," he pressed, "you can tell me."

"It's just that…it's so boring here!" She lied. She knew that telling him how homesick she was would cause him too much anxiety, and she just couldn't do that to him…not now.

"*Boring?*" Tom huffed, exasperated. "How can you say that? Len, there's tons to do here."

"Like what?" she questioned, crossing her arms in defiance.

"Like what?" he echoed in irritation. "Okay, like punting down the Cam."

"Done that."

"Okay," he nodded, folding his arms. "How about museums? You love history."

"Check. I've been to the museums already."

Tom sighed. "Alright. There are parks, beautiful gardens, punting tours, walking tours…there's even a ghost tour!" He leveled a gaze at her. "Before we left, I told you to research the area—to find somewhere new to explore every day. The purpose was to help you get to know the area better. You love architecture and history, I would think even walking around would be interesting for you."

"Well, a person can walk around only so much before going insane with boredom." She tried a look of sincere annoyance.

Tom narrowed his eyes incredulously. "Hmm, I see." He leaned in, capturing her gaze. "You know what I think? I don't think this is about boredom. I think you're lonely. You're homesick for friends and family, and have no one to hang out with here."

Lenora gaped. Sometimes his perception drove her crazy. He was a good psychologist. She pursed her lips, shrugged her shoulders, and looked away from him.

"That's what I thought," he chuckled softly. "Isn't there anyone your age in this building?"

"No."

"Have you even checked?"

"Yes, I checked," she retorted.

"Why am I having a hard time believing that?" Tom asked, visibly amused.

"Think what you want, it's the truth," she replied indignantly. "The other day, I asked the little boy down the hall if anyone my age lived here. Do you know what he said? He told me that no one 'old' lives in the building." She scowled.

Tom laughed heartily. "Old, huh? Well, that's new for you!"

"Thanks. Not funny," she replied angrily.

"Look," Tom responded, still visibly amused, "I can't help that there's no one your age in this building—I guess you'll just have to wait for school to start. Until then, I can help your boredom by offering you a job."

"What, more shopping and cooking?" she answered sardonically, instantly feeling terrible.

Lenora recalled memories of cooking and baking with her parents. Some of her best memories involved snowy days in a warm kitchen, a hot plate of chocolate chip cookies, and listening to her mom's stories about her childhood. Tom was happier then. He stopped cooking the day after Bessie died. Now, it was simply a chore that Lenora took on so that Tom didn't have to. A chore she sometimes begrudged.

"No," Tom replied dryly, "I was thinking that I could find you a job at the university."

Lenora sat up. "A paid job?"

"Yes, paid. It wouldn't be much, but it would be play money and something to do until school starts."

Lenora thought for a moment. "Okay," she agreed, "I'll try it out."

"Good!" Tom rose from the chair. "Now that we have that settled, what's for dinner, old lady?" He winked and then smiled at her. She was about to protest, when she noticed his gaze shift to the floor. He frowned. "What in the world…" he pointed at the floor, where a puddle of sticky brown liquid had congealed into the carpet. "… is *that?*"

"Oh. Forgot about that. I spilled earlier."

He raised an eyebrow. "And…you couldn't clean it up right away because…?"

Lenora nodded. "Just forgot, that's all. I'll clean it up."

"Thanks, Len. Let me know when dinner's ready—I'll be in my study."

Lenora got a rag from the kitchen and wondered if she should have told Tom about her recent scare. When she returned to the living room, she froze. The glass was sitting atop the table.

"Dad? Did you pick the glass up off the floor?"

"What glass?"

Lenora's heart lurched into her throat. *It's nothing, you probably set it on the table and just spaced it out.*

She knelt to clean the stain, when a sliding sound startled her. She glanced up to the coffee table. The glass slid slowly across the table...on its own. She pushed back into the couch, heart hammering in her chest. The glass slowed down and came to a stop right in front of her. She swallowed hard, staring at the glass as it quivered and shook. Suddenly, the glass flew at her, just grazing the side of her head. She swatted at the glass, sending it crashing to the floor.

"Hey, what's going on out there?" Tom shouted from the den.

"Nothing," Lenora replied, barely able to speak, "I just broke a glass, that's all."

"Did you get hurt?"

"No," she replied with a heavy sigh.

I'm just scared out of my mind.

THREE

"Lenora? Are you listening?"

She started at the sound of her name and looked up in time to see her father's disapproving look.

"Uh, sorry Dad," she said apologetically, "I was just....well, this place is really..."

"I know," Tom responded, assuming her meaning. "Architecturally, this building is amazing, and the history is amazing too," Tom explained. "Perhaps when you have a break, you might go over to the archives and research the history of the place."

What Lenora meant to say was that the place was creepy. The hair stood up on her arms as she wound her way through the dark maze in the bowels of St. Catharine's. It was like a dungeon, and she felt uncomfortable, like something was watching her. But, she didn't want to interrupt her father in his moment. Tom loved that his daughter was so interested in architecture, and she was—this place was amazing. But it gave her the creeps. So, for now, she just nodded her head in agreement, and traced her fingers along the cold stone walls.

Lenora crossed her arms from the chill in the air. She was still cold from last night—her room was like a virtual deep-freeze, and no matter how many blankets she piled on top of her, the room seemed to get chillier and chillier. Apparently, the air conditioning was not fixed.

Tom nodded his head at her. "Yes, these buildings can get really cold, particularly here in the basement."

Lenora nodded, shivered, and then hugged herself for warmth.

Tom led Lenora to a little room at the end of a dark hallway. File cabinets lined one side of the room, and the rest of the space contained several boxes that were stacked to the ceiling. In the middle of the boxes stood a miniscule desk, a small table lamp glowing like a spotlight in the center. "This," Tom said, pointing to the desk, "will be your work station."

His patronizing excitement irritated her. Maybe it was her lack of sleep.

Noticing the scowl on his daughter's face, Tom smiled. "I know, not the best place to work in the world, but you'll be on your own, away from everyone else. You can listen to music while you work… and as loud as you want…within reason, of course."

Lenora forced a smile and gave her dad the thumbs-up.

Super.

"Basically," he explained, "you will be helping with archived files. My assistant, Judith, is too busy to work on these, but she has taken the time to put a date and description on the individual files for you."

Tom walked over to a stack of boxes and tapped one. "These are boxes from my department." Then he pointed over to the file cabinets. "Those are empty file cabinets. Your job will be to go through all of the boxes, categorize the files, and then organize them according to category and date in the file cabinets—earliest dates in the back, most recent ones in the front."

Lenora nodded in understanding. It seemed simple enough. She glanced at the boxes, mentally counting them. The boxes were stacked four deep, five up, and ten across.

"Holy crap, there's like 200 boxes here, Dad!"

"You're correct. There are exactly 200 boxes. And, don't say 'crap' here, Len."

"What, they don't say 'crap' in England?"

Tom shook his head and chuckled. "Yes, I'm sure they say 'crap' here in England too. But, this is a professional environment and you should use professional language."

"What, like Jumping Jehoshaphat? Or, how about Good Golly....
or...bloody hell? We're in England, and I've heard that a lot."

"You're incorrigible." Tom shook his head, grinning.

"You raised me," she teased.

"I know," he said in a mockingly disappointed tone. "I blame
your mother." He smiled widely, then a dark look swept across his
face and his smile faded. He cleared his throat. "Well, that's it, in a
nutshell. Do you have any questions?"

*You just still can't bring yourself to talk about Mom without becoming
incredibly sad, can you?*

Lenora wanted to tell Tom that it was okay to talk about Mom,
to laugh about her eccentricities. She wanted to talk about her mom
with him...and remember her. She missed her mom every day, and
not being able to talk about it left her feeling alone and sad. But she
didn't say any of that.

"No, I think it's pretty self-explanatory."

"Good," he nodded, "I'll leave you to your work then." He smiled
at her and then turned to walk out.

"Dad?" she blurted out.

He turned and looked at her expectantly. "Yes?"

*Why can't we talk about Mom? Why won't you let me talk about her?
I'm forgetting the sound of her voice, her laugh, her smile...everything*, she
thought, looking down at her feet, losing her nerve. "Ah," she was
reaching, "when's lunch?"

"Oh," he responded, "I forgot about that. I'll come and get you
at eleven-thirty and we'll head over to the hall."

"Cool," she replied, upset that she chickened out.

He nodded and then turned to leave, but then suddenly spun
back around. "Hey, before I forget. Please just organize the files
from what you read on the tabs. Do not–under *any* circumstances–
open and read those files. Understand? They're private and you
would be violating the privacy of the university's clients and
research. Okay?"

She nodded her assent and then watched as he left the room.

Lenora stood in the middle of the room for what felt like ages. The room was cold and damp, and she thought she could hear the drip or trickle of water somewhere. No windows let in any light, and the walls and floor were a mixture of dark grey rock and concrete. She was certain that at one time it had to be a prison or a room meant to torture someone. The flickering of the desk lamp shook her out of her stupor.

Well, I guess I should start going through this maze of boxes. She looked at the piles of boxes and felt overwhelmed. *Where do I even start?*

"Start at the end."

The voice startled her and she screamed.

"Hey, hey," the voice said from the doorway, chuckling "Sorry I scared you!" A figure walked toward her, arms stretched out toward her. She backed into the desk and tripped on the table leg, which sent her reeling backward. On the way down, she hit her head on the corner of a file cabinet.

She lay on the ground, head throbbing, eyesight growing hazy. She blinked as the light faded. The figure hovered over her.

"Are you okay?" he asked, sounding worried.

She blinked again, and a face came into view—a nice face. "Yeah, well sort of. My head hurts."

The figure extended a hand to help her up. He guided her over to the chair and helped her sit down.

"Sit here, I'll be right back," he said as he ran out of the room.

Feeling foolish, Lenora wasn't sure she wanted him to come back. But then again, she really did.

He came back into the room, carrying a towel. He sat down on the desk, swiveled her chair around so that her back was to him, and pressed a cool, wet towel to the back of her head and then examined it. "Well, there's no blood. I felt a significant bump though, so you might want to hold this cool towel to your head to reduce swelling."

Lenora swiveled the chair back around so that she could see her rescuer. She looked up into his face and felt dizzy all over again. She felt as if she were losing consciousness and started leaning away from the chair.

"Hey, maybe you need to go home for the day," he said as he steadied the chair, leaning so close to her that she could feel his breath.

"No," she argued breathlessly, "I think I'm okay. I just felt a little dizzy for a second."

"Yes, and the reason why you might want to go home. Let me call my director."

He reached over and grabbed the phone at the edge of the desk and dialed. "Hello? Dr. Kelley?"

Oh, crap, Dad!

She listened as he recounted the entire embarrassing episode. *Ugh, I can't believe this.*

He stopped talking and listened to what her dad was saying on the other end. He smiled and looked at Lenora. "Aha. Okay, I'll do that." He smirked and handed her the phone. "Your dad wants to speak with you."

Embarrassed, she gingerly took the phone and eyed the man as he walked around to the other side of the desk and lounged back in the rickety, metal chair. "Thanks," she muttered. "Hello?"

"Hi, Len." She could hear the amusement in her dad's voice. "Are you okay? Do you need to go to the hospital?"

Lenora's heart dropped. "Geez, Dad. No, I don't need..." she looked up at the man and blushed. "...a hospital," she whispered. A small chuckle was heard across the desk.

How embarrassing.

"Well, I instructed Ian to stay there and keep you company until he's sure you're alright."

She looked up at the man, who grinned and waved, confirming he must be the "Ian" her dad was referring to. So, that was his name. Ian. She liked it.

"Uh, thanks Dad."

"Ian's a grad student here and knows a lot about the files you're going through, so he might be able to help you get a head start on the project at least."

"Sure, thanks Dad." She looked over at Ian and rolled her eyes, and he chuckled quietly. Encouraged, she pointed to the phone and shook her head and smiled. Ian nodded and smirked.

"Well, give me a call if you have any questions. My extension is written on the phone." Lenora looked at the phone. His number *was* written on the phone's extension list...with the name "Dad" next to it. She closed her eyes, mortified. She hung up the phone and then smiled at Ian uncomfortably, lowered her eyes, and then shifted in the chair.

Ian cleared his throat, got up from the chair, and walked toward her. Lenora straightened, heart thudding. What was he doing?

He smiled at her and then extended his hand. "I should really introduce myself." He sat on the edge of the desk at an intimately close range. Lenora could feel the blush rising in her cheeks. "I'm Ian, and I'm a grad student here at Cambridge. Actually, I'm getting a doctorate in psychology. Your dad will be my mentor this year, so I'm pleased to meet you."

Lenora nodded. "Nice to meet you too. I'm..."

"Lenora, yeah, I know."

"How did you..." She regretted the question the minute it left her lips. *He must think I'm a moron!*

He smiled, his silence acknowledging the redundancy of her question. "Oh, before I forget." He opened his satchel. "Your dad told me to bring this to you. It's from the lost and found." He held out a pink, cotton cardigan sweater.

"Oh." She took the sweater. Pink. She hated that color more than anything in the world. She scowled as she put it on. Warmth won over color any day.

"Does your head hurt?"

"A little, but it's not bad." It was actually throbbing now, but she didn't want to tell him that.

"Does the sweater smell badly?"

Confused, Lenora smelled the sweater—it smelled nice, like lilac. Whoever the previous owner was might not have very good taste in color, but she certainly smelled good. "No, the sweater smells fine."

"Well, I'm sorry for all the questions, but you made a face when you put that sweater on. I thought it might be pain from your head injury. That, or the sweater didn't smell very good."

She felt a new wave of embarrassment flood within her. *Falling, head injury, stupid comments—I'm just batting a thousand.* She felt like wrapping herself up in the ugly sweater and hiding in the corner.

He waved a hand in front of her face. "Hey, are you sure you're okay? You just checked out for a minute."

Ah! Now he thinks I'm a space cadet!

"I'm fine...just thinking about something else." She paused. "No, the sweater smells fine, and my head is fine—I just hate the color pink."

Ian laughed heartily. "Oh, is that it, then? A color snob?"

Lenora blushed and giggled. She looked down at the desk, embarrassed.

"Well." Ian broke the silence. "Since you seem to be fine, I'll leave you to your work."

"No!" Lenora yelled loudly, and then stood frozen. *I can't believe I just shouted at him.*

"Okay," Ian stopped, frowning. "So, I shouldn't go?"

Think, Lenora, think!

"S-sorry, that didn't come out right. It's just that..." she stalled, stooping in pretense of picking a pen up off the floor. She looked over to the stack of boxes and got an idea. "I just thought...since you were familiar with this stuff...maybe you could lend me a hand?" She motioned over to the stack of boxes and tried her best to look desperate.

Ian frowned and then looked at the boxes. "I suppose this seems a bit daunting, doesn't it?" He looked at his watch.

"Oh, if you have to go..."

"No," Ian shook his head, "I have a seminar in two hours, but I have time to at least help you categorize the mess."

"If you don't mind...I'd..."

"No worries." Ian walked over to the boxes, knelt down, and inspected the labels on the side. He grabbed a chair and rolled it over to the stack. Lenora's heart raced as he grinned handsomely at her and then motioned for her to join him. "Bring that notepad and a pen. I'll read through the labels and you write them down."

Lenora grabbed the notepad and pen and joined Ian by the boxes. He patted the back of the chair with his hand and said "Sit down. You hit your head, so you need to stay off your feet."

She sat down immediately and then watched as he opened the boxes, one after the other, and read through the labels. She couldn't tell what color his eyes were, the room was so dark. But, she did notice that his hair was flaxen, wavy, and a bit unkempt. He wore it long, and often had to brush a lock out of his eyes, his jaw line flexing as he read through the files. Occasionally, he caught her looking at him and would flash a bright smile, lighting up his whole face.

She wished she knew what color his eyes were.

He talked too fast, and she wasn't familiar with his accent, so it was tough at first to keep up. Eventually, they developed a method, and got through twelve boxes in a little over an hour.

Ian leaned on one of the stacks and wiped fake sweat off his forehead. "Phew! What a job! Now I'm glad I helped you—that was a lot to go through." Lenora didn't speak, but nodded in agreement. Ian looked at his watch. "Look at that—we went through twelve boxes in a little over an hour and I still have time to take a little break before my seminar." He smiled at her. "Would you like a cola?"

Lenora nodded enthusiastically. "Yes, that sounds good." It did sound good—she was suddenly very thirsty. Ian nodded and instantly left the room.

She couldn't believe this—he wanted to stay and spend the last bit of time he had left with *her*. This was, by far, the coolest thing that had ever happened to her. She spun around in her chair and pumped her fists in the air in excitement.

"What are you doing?" Ian interrupted her, laughing.

Lenora stopped spinning. *How close is that soda machine?* She closed her eyes. *This can't be happening. Just when I think I've made progress, he catches me acting like a moron.* She turned and looked at him, feeling completely humiliated. "Sorry, I was just…being a moron." It was best to speak the truth in a moment like this.

Ian laughed quietly as he walked toward her. "It's okay to celebrate getting through all of those boxes," he continued, handing her the ice-cold can of soda, "but you really should take it easy, considering the knock on the head you've suffered today."

"Oh, yeah, I forgot about that," she agreed. *Note to self: stop acting like a moron when someone can walk in on you.*

Ian brought a box over to her chair and sat down. Lenora felt out of breath.

"So," he said thoughtfully, "do you go by Lenora or do you have a nickname?"

"My dad calls me Len sometimes, but mostly I go by my full name. My mom always got mad when people shortened it. She said that I was named Lenora, and people should call me that." She shrugged her shoulders. "I sort of found it ironic, though—her full name was Elizabeth, but she went by Bessie." She half laughed and took a drink. The iciness raced down her throat, causing her to shiver.

Ian sat there for some time, not talking. Lenora shifted in her chair, feeling uncomfortable, when he finally spoke. "So, when you referenced your mom, you used past-tense. Is she…"

"Dead? Yeah." Lenora looked down at her feet.

"Sorry." Ian said sympathetically. "When did she die? How? That is, if you don't mind me asking."

"No, it's okay." Lenora squeezed her eyes shut for a second and exhaled. "She died four months ago…" she paused. She hated talking about how her mom died, and she usually didn't talk about it, but Ian just seemed to genuinely care. Most people were simply prying, and she knew it. "She accidentally killed herself."

"Accidentally…" Ian interrupted, frowning. "How?"

"She took a sleeping pill with another pill that counteracted it, but she didn't know. She didn't read the labels."

"Ah." Ian muttered, as if he understood. "That really stinks."

"It sucks," she responded firmly.

"Yeah, indeed it does….suck," he agreed, smiling. "Do you miss her?"

"Every day," she said pensively.

The two sat in silence in the musty, dimly lit room—she, slouched in the chair, head tilted toward the ceiling, and Ian, staring in front of him. Tired of the quiet, she lifted her head and cleared her throat. She was about to say something lame about the weather, but he interrupted her by getting up off the box, putting it back, and then throwing his empty can of soda in the trash next to the desk.

"I really have to get going," he said almost apologetically. "I have to go back to my flat, get my books, and walk all the way back here again."

Lenora shrugged her shoulders feigning indifference. "Okay. Thanks for the help." She smiled at him half-heartedly.

"Any time," Ian responded, lifting her hand and kissing it gently. "It was nice to meet you, Lenora. I hope our paths cross again sometime soon."

"Sure," she said, breathless. No one ever kissed the back of her hand before. It was an old-fashioned gesture that none of the boys she knew bothered with. In fact, the only thing remotely "romantic" a boy had ever done was punch her in the arm to thank her for going to the movies with him. Of course, she and the boy were only ten years old.

She looked up at Ian and wanted badly to ask if she could go with him to the seminar—and then everywhere after that. But she just smiled at him and stupidly let him walk out the door.

As he got to the door, he stopped short and turned around. "You know," he said, waving a finger at her, "Edgar Allan Poe wrote a poem with the name Lenore in it, I think."

"I know. It's called 'The Raven'," she answered.

He smiled. "Yeah, that's it. Best poem in the world. I love Poe's work." He stood in the doorway, his shape outlined by the warm light in the hall. He smiled at her and held his arms out dramatically, "'A rare and radiant maiden, whom the angels named Lenore.'"

Lenora's smile faded. That was the line her mother often recited. "That doesn't really apply to me," she said, the melancholy choking the words from her.

Ian dropped his hands and tilted his head to the side. "Oh, it applies. More than you know."

She looked up to protest, but he was already gone.

FOUR

"Ow, Dad, quit touching it, you're making it worse!" Lenora waved her hand at her dad, who was examining the large bump that had formed on the back of her head.

"I'm barely touching it, Lenora. Besides, I need to look at it to see if I should take you to the doctor."

"Ugh." Lenora rolled her eyes. "I'm fine, Dad. It hurts when I touch it, but I'm not dizzy or seeing double, so I think I'm okay."

"Regardless," he explained, "head injuries are not to be fooled around with." He tilted her head forward to examine it more closely. Lenora glanced around in embarrassment at the people in the cafeteria, who were now staring at her rather than eating their meals. Thankfully, classes hadn't yet started, so most of the people in the room were faculty, and she didn't care what they thought.

"Is her head broken?" asked a familiar voice.

Lenora was mortified to see Ian sitting across from them, smiling broadly. She moved away from her dad, shooting a look of irritation.

"No, my dad just thinks he needs to conduct a full head exam while I try to eat my lunch," she complained, stabbing her fork into her salad. She shoved food in her mouth as if in a race against time and then swallowed loudly.

Ian, visibly amused, smirked at Lenora. "Better slow down there... you don't want to choke, do you?" Lenora's shoulders dropped. She put her fork down and smiled nervously. Ian frowned and then pointed at her. "You have lettuce stuck to your teeth."

Horrified, Lenora quickly grabbed a napkin. *Could this **get** any worse?*

Ian turned his focus to Tom. "So, is it serious? Will she need to go to the doctor? If you want, I can fetch Dr. Stevens and he can put a head brace on her in the meantime—just in case." He gave her a sidelong glance and then grinned. "We can't be too careful...it being a head injury and all."

"Don't you dare!" Lenora retorted, spitting out a large piece of lettuce.

Tom smiled and chuckled. "No, it's not serious, but I do think she needs to go home."

"No!" she argued, trying to ignore the chewed-up piece of lettuce that landed in her dad's water glass. "I don't need to go home. I still have a lot of work to do."

"Work that can wait until tomorrow," Tom replied sternly, grimacing as he pushed his glass to the side.

"But...."

"No arguments. You will go home after lunch and that's the final word." Tom softly insisted.

Ian sat up. "You know, Dr. Kelley, I have the entire afternoon off. I can walk her home and then stay until you get back."

Lenora straightened, suddenly feeling elated. She stared eagerly at Tom, crossing her fingers under the table. *Please, please, please, oh please let him!*

Tom considered Ian for a moment. "Thanks for the offer, Ian, but I wouldn't feel right if I couldn't watch her myself."

Lenora frowned, pushing the plate from her. *This sucks. He treats me like a baby.*

"Oh, no worries." Ian looked over at Lenora and smiled. "Just thought I'd be neighborly."

"Oy, Roberts!" A male voice shouted from the back of the hall.

Ian waved at a group of boys in the corner of the room. "Well, I guess I'm being flagged." He nodded to both of them. "Dr. Kelley... Lenora." He winked at her and then left to join his friends.

Lenora felt a sour mood coming on.

"Dad, seriously, I want to stay here and get some work done. I made great headway this morning."

Tom nodded thoughtfully while he listened to her explain about the productive morning. When she finished, he patted her hand. "Well, though I'm glad you had a productive morning, I still think it best to take you home for the day. The work will still be there tomorrow."

Lenora exhaled loudly, and waited impatiently for Tom to finish his meal. Occasionally, she stole glances at Ian, who was in the middle of telling an animated story. At one point, he caught her staring at him, and stopped momentarily to smile and wink at her. Her cheeks instantly flushed, and she quickly turned toward her dad, feigning interest in the conversation he was having with a colleague. Then, she heard uproarious laughter coming from Ian's general direction. She shifted her gaze just in time to see him mimic her head hitting the file cabinet.

He's making fun of me! Horrified, she turned to Tom and poked his arm.

"What?" he asked, irritated at the interruption.

"Can we go now?"

"In a minute. I need to finish my conversation." He frowned and then lowered his voice. "And, you know how I feel about being interrupted."

She nodded. *This is the worst day ever.*

The laughter from the corner of the room stopped completely. Thinking that Ian was through parodying her, she glanced in their direction. They were all staring at her. And, once she made eye contact, they all snickered as if she was the new private joke shared between friends.

Lenora glanced at Ian, who was also laughing. She felt the tears burning her eyes.

I have to get out of here.

What happened next was a complete blur.

Lenora moved to get up, and in her haste, got her jeans caught on the bench. Her body jerked forward and she lost balance, falling sideways off the bench. On the way down, she grabbed at the table behind her to catch her fall. Instead, she only gripped the tablecloth, which she took—food and all—down with her in a loud crash. She landed, splayed out, between her table and the buffet table, food and trays scattered everywhere.

Instant and raucous laughter shook the room. Humiliated, Lenora glanced at her dad, who was glowering at her as if she did this on purpose. Lenora immediately scrambled to get up, and in doing so, fell again to the floor, smearing her clothes with food, and causing another outburst of laughter.

Lenora struggled back onto her feet and ran out of the hall. She paused briefly in the doorway to see if her dad was coming, and caught a glimpse of Ian, who was standing up at his table. He wasn't laughing. In fact, he wasn't smiling at all.

After listening patiently to her mortified sobs and helping her wipe the food stains from her clothes, Tom took Lenora to Barton's Books to help lighten her mood.

They were greeted enthusiastically by the store owner, Percy Barton, who instantly shook Tom's hand. "Your daughter is becoming quite the fixture here already," Percy remarked, beaming at Lenora.

"Already?" Tom looked at Lenora, one eyebrow raised. "A fixture, eh? We've only been here three weeks. Just how many books have you bought, Len?"

"Oh, she's bought only two, I assure you," Mr. Barton insisted, "She mostly just browses, that one. Browses, and dreams, I daresay." He glanced at Lenora and winked. "I think it a grand thing when youngsters enjoy reading."

Tom nodded and gave Lenora a cautionary look. "Alright, browse, and find two or three." He looked at the price on the back of a book and winced. "Maybe just two."

Lenora left the bookstore with two books: Radcliffe's "The Mysteries of Udolpho" and Lewis's "The Monk," two classic gothic novels.

After telling Mr. Barton of her love for gothic literature, he quickly wrote a list, insisting that she begin with the classics. "A good summer's goal, if you ask me—partaking in a survey of classic gothic literature. After all, you can't appreciate the contemporary without first delving into the classics."

Lenora agreed and was thrilled with the notion. Tom was not as enthusiastic.

Sweat dripped from her forehead and splashed like a giant rain drop onto the page. The room was sweltering, and though the window was wide open, there was no breeze. The heat was trapped in the room, and she felt like she was suffocating. Tom was mystified. The rest of the apartment was cool and pleasant. He offered to let her sleep on the couch, but after what happened that afternoon, she just wanted to be alone.

Tired of the heat, Lenora put her book on the nightstand, rose from the bed, and took a new pair of pajamas out of her dresser, setting them out on the bed.

Times like these, I'm glad I have my own bathroom.

She trudged into her bathroom and took yet another cool shower, which made her feel briefly refreshed—that is, until she walked back into her sweltering room. Lenora reached for her pajamas on the bed, but they weren't there—they were on the floor. She bent to pick them up and discovered her book lying on the floor as well.

What the...?

She shrugged her shoulders. *I probably knocked them over when I put my robe on.*

At least she could be thankful for the fact that her pajamas were lying near the air conditioning vent—they felt cool and fresh against her skin. She flopped back down on the bed and resumed reading, hoping that soon, drowsiness would take over.

Lenora knew it was late—the clock read 3:15 a.m.—but the heat prevented her from relaxing to the point of sleepiness. She thumbed through the book—only 60 pages left. Her other book was on the kitchen table, which meant she would have to leave her room to get it.

She sighed. *No way—Dad would freak if he knew I was still awake.*

Floorboards creaked outside her door. *Dad must be checking in on me.* She put the book down and stared at the door, waiting for Tom to peek his head in. But nothing happened.

Stupid old wood floors, she thought, shrugging her shoulders and returning to the book.

The sound of footsteps approached her door. The doorknob slowly turned. Lenora waited, preparing for her dad's reprimand. But the door didn't open. She found herself growing more irritated by the minute.

If he does this again, I'm going to open that door and tell him I'll go to sleep already.

Suddenly, a prickly sensation ran down her arm. She looked down just as the hairs on her arm slowly stood on end, as if electrically charged. She shivered as the temperature grew progressively chilly and the air misted with her warm breath.

Well, I guess the air conditioning is back—

Something interrupted her thought. She sat motionless as she felt movement on the surface of her skin, as if something was touching her.

Long, frosty fingers crept along the small of her back, inching their way up her spine, touching her shoulder, lingering on her neck. She shrugged her shoulder, as if to ward off the coldness. Moist, hot breath on her neck…unintelligible whispers…a soft laugh.

Lenora jumped, a small whimper escaping her throat. She started feeling disoriented, dizzy. Terrified, she looked slowly over her shoulder. Nothing was there. She closed her eyes and shook her head.

It's late, and my mind's playing tricks on me.

She glanced at the clock—3:22 a.m.—definitely late. Reaching to turn off the lamp, she noticed her book on the nightstand and then laughed nervously. Perhaps there was something in her dad's theory—reading dark fiction so late at night was definitely wreaking havoc on her sensibilities. Chuckling at her irrationality, she switched off the light and settled in.

Tonight, the moon's absence made her room black as pitch. She couldn't see. And though she dismissed her little episode as self-induced, she still had the willies.

She jumped again as floorboards creaked outside her door. The doorknob twisted quickly, and then turned slowly. Her body trembled uncontrollably as the door slowly creaked open and then closed with a silent click. The sound of footsteps coming toward the bed caused her to shriek and pull the covers over the top of her head.

The footsteps stopped, and she waited, holding her breath. When nothing happened, she slowly removed the covers from her face and looked around. No one was there. Then, the covers were jerked out of her hand and slowly fell down her body, landing on the floor. Her heart thudded heavily, and little bubbles formed in her throat, catching it as she tried to make a sound—any sound.

She was frozen in place as icy fingers ran up along her ankle, her calf, thigh, and then briefly stopped on her hip. Heavy breathing came from a vacant place in front of her—she could see the mist that mysterious breath made. Her body shook in fear. The breath came closer, hot on her neck.

"*Lenoooorahhhh...*"

Chilling terror ran through her body, and she issued a blood-curdling scream. "Who's there? Go away! Go away!"

Tom burst into the room and flicked on the light. "Lenora! What's going on?"

"Dad!" she screamed, "Someone's in my room!"

Tom rushed across the room, grabbed his daughter, and carried her into the living room. "Stay here!" He ran into her bedroom, and she could hear him rummaging around, opening doors, scouring through the apartment. Finally, he emerged, looking perturbed. "Len, I looked, and there's no one here. What happened?"

Lenora told him what happened. He raked his hands through his hair. "Look, Len, I checked everywhere—the front door is deadbolted, there is no sign of anyone…anywhere. Are you sure?"

Lenora started to cry. "Dad, he said my name! I'm so scared!"

Tom came over to her and put an arm around her shoulders. "I don't know what to tell you. But, if you would like, I'll stay with you in your room tonight. Would you like that?" Lenora nodded, wiping tears from her cheeks. "Okay, I'll grab a pillow and blanket, and will be right in."

Lenora was hesitant to go back into her bedroom, but she crept back in and waited for her dad, who came around the corner quickly. He laid his blanket and pillow on the floor and then helped her into bed, tucking her in.

Tom smoothed the hair around his daughter's face and smiled affectionately. "I'm here now," he said in a soothing voice. "If anything scares you in the middle of the night, you just wake me—" He trailed off, frowning. He reached over to her nightstand, picked up the book, and then looked at her angrily. "This is the problem right here," he waved the book in front of her. "What have I told you about reading this before bed?"

Lenora, having no response, lowered her eyes.

Tom sighed. "Well, you know what I said. I'll stay here with you tonight. But, from now on, you have got to quit reading gothic horror before bed. Got it?" Lenora nodded. "Good. It's late. Go to sleep." He reached up, turned her light off, and then grunted as he settled in for an uncomfortable sleep on her hardwood floor.

She, on the other hand, didn't sleep at all.

FIVE

"**T**ime to wake up, Peanut."

Lenora opened her eyes. Tom was hovering over her, coffee cup and a plate of toast in hand. "I made you breakfast." He set the coffee and toast on the nightstand and then kissed the top of her head.

Lenora sat up, rubbed her eyes, and then stared at the covers, confused. "Thanks," she mumbled, feeling a sour mood creeping in.

"Well, grumpy girl, eat your breakfast and then hit the shower—we leave in…" he glanced at his watch, "thirty minutes."

Thirty minutes!

Lenora looked at the clock and frowned. "That's hardly enough time for me to—"

"Come on, Len," Tom said in an exasperated tone. "I slept on your floor last night and am not in the mood to dilly-dally—I have a lot of work to do."

"You go ahead," she offered, "I'm not going back there–not after what happened yesterday!"

Tom smiled softly. "You need to go back. It shows that you are brave and mature enough to appreciate the humor of the moment."

"But I didn't think it was funny."

"No, and it wasn't. But, you have to be mature about it so they don't think otherwise." He ruffled her hair. "Now, eat your breakfast."

Lenora begrudgingly sat up and took a sip of coffee. "I'll hurry."

"Thanks." Tom smiled, winked, and closed her bedroom door.

Lenora finished her toast and coffee and then walked over to the bathroom. She looked at her face in the mirror; it was puffy from a night of little sleep. She hoped no one saw her today—especially Ian. She thought of yesterday's events and winced. How could she show her face there again?

A cool shower helped the puffiness go away, and she felt more wide awake. She towel-dried her hair, put on a minimal amount of makeup, slipped into jeans and a simple white t-shirt, and then walked out into the kitchen.

"Feel better after the shower?" Tom asked, smiling.

"Yeah," she shrugged.

"Well, you'll see that I'm right about going back in today. People will think you're brave."

Or a glutton for punishment, she mused glumly.

On the way down to the car, Lenora noticed that she had stains down the front of her shirt. She sighed heavily and rolled her eyes in frustration. "Dad, I have to run back upstairs."

"Why?"

She pointed at the front of her shirt and exhaled loudly.

"Oh. Well, hurry because we're already running late."

"I won't be long – I'm just going to change my shirt. I'll be right out."

Lenora ran into the building and up the long flight of steps to their apartment. She hurried into her room, and knowing that she didn't have any clean t-shirts, dug a black t-shirt out of the dirty clothes basket. *I only wore this for two hours, it should be fine.* She sniffed it, and thinking it was okay, pulled it on.

Ugly Pink Sweater was draped on the back of her bed; she hurried over and grabbed it, thinking she'd need it while working in that dungeon of an office.

Lenora ran to the apartment door, but hesitated, thinking that the stains needed to be treated. She quickly ran into her room, dug the white t-shirt out of the basket, and ran to the hallway closet to get out the stain remover.

In her haste, she forgot to turn the sprayer to ON, and continued to spray frantically while nothing came out.

"Damn it!" she yelled, frustrated. Lenora turned the nozzle so it would spray, and then stilled as the hairs on the back of her neck bristled. She had an eerie feeling...like she was being watched. She shook her head and returned to the task at hand.

A long, exhaling breath came from behind her left ear. The warm dampness of the breath on her neck made her motionless. Goose bumps rose on her skin and the hair on her arms stood on end. Afraid to move, Lenora slowly turned her head. Nothing was there.

She grabbed the spray bottle, quickly sprayed the stain, grabbed her sweater and ran out the door.

Lenora nearly fell down the stairs, she was running so fast, and was completely out of breath when she got to the car.

Tom was visibly angry. "What took you so long?"

Lenora recounted what had happened in the apartment up until now, from the glass moving on its own, to the icy fingers running along her body, to what just happened. "Dad, don't freak out, but I think someone...some *thing*...is in the apartment."

Tom took a deep breath. "Stay here, Len, I'll go check it out."

He got out of the car and walked up to the apartment. Not wanting anything to happen to her dad, Lenora got out of the car. She rummaged in the back seat for the jug of window washing fluid and stood in the doorway–just in case her dad needed help, and she needed a weapon.

Tom emerged from the apartment, shaking his head. "No one's up there, Len. It was probably your imagination." He laughed and shook his head at her holding up the jug defensively. "You're more likely to injure yourself more than someone else with that."

Lenora nodded, handing him the jug.

She followed her dad to the car in silence. She didn't know how to tell him that it wasn't just her imagination. There was someone in the apartment. She could feel it.

When they arrived at St. Catherine's, she went straight to the dungeon and to her work. Lenora breathed a sigh of relief when Ian was a no-show for the day, and for the rest of the week, much to her chagrin.

But, the nightmares and odd voices made continual appearances. She didn't tell Tom.

It wasn't until the following Wednesday—as Lenora began to relax in the comfort of predictability—when Ian finally decided to waltz back into her life.

"Hey lovely."

Papers flew from Lenora's hands as she glanced, startled, at the doorway. Ian was leaning against the frame, grinning charmingly at her. The sound of his voice made her heart flutter and the color rise to her cheeks.

"Oh, it's you. What do you want?" She tried sounding annoyed.

"Well, what kind of greeting is that?" he asked, sauntering over to her, still grinning.

"It's the greeting you get," she retorted, eyes narrowed in an attempt at looking irritated.

The smile faded from Ian's face and he nodded slowly. "I know—you should be quite peeved at me. My friends are—"

"Jerks," Lenora finished, glaring at him.

"Yes, but it's my fault. I thought it was just a funny story. I didn't expect—" he hesitated.

"You didn't expect what? That I would fall all over the place and humiliate myself? That was really embarrassing, Ian!"

"I didn't know…it was a freak accident! What I did was—"

"Mean…and cruel," she finished, glowering.

Ian lowered his head and sighed deeply. "I'm so sorry, Lenora. If I could make up for it…anything…" he trailed off, looking at her earnestly.

Lenora fixed an angry stare at him for a moment and then softened. "You could help me with this." She pointed behind him to the new stack of boxes that were brought in over the weekend. Last week, she was able to get through almost half of the boxes, but was horrified upon her return Monday morning to four new stacks.

"What in the world?" Ian gaped. "Where did all of these come from?"

"The Psychology department," she explained. "I guess there's a big conference room up there that, until now, has been used as a place for everyone to dump their junk. They want to restore the room to its original purpose. Now I get the pleasure of sorting through everything. They even gave me more file cabinets." She pointed to the other side of the room, where three new file cabinets were placed.

"Wow," Ian uttered, dumbstruck, scratching his head, "this is crazy...too much for just one person." He grinned at her. "So, I guess I'm yours for the day!"

Her heart palpitated and sweat formed on her brow. She opened her mouth to say something witty, when her dad peered around the corner.

"Hey, Len," Tom said, glancing to her right, "oh, hello Ian."

"Dr. Kelley," Ian nodded.

"Len, I forgot to tell you that I have a meeting that runs until seven tonight."

"But, Dad," Lenora protested, "this is the fourth time in the past week! I'm sick of staying late every night!"

Tom shrugged his shoulders unapologetically. "Sorry, but these meetings are situational and I need to attend them." He sighed. "I'll take you out to dinner tonight, if it helps."

Lenora shrugged her shoulders, feeling the urge to cry. These late-night meetings were tiring, especially since they didn't eat until nearly nine o'clock every night, a circumstance, she was sure, that was contributing to her nightmares of late.

Ian, seeing the troubled look on Lenora's face interceded. "Hey, I have no plans tonight, Dr. Kelley, and Lenora clearly needs help here." He motioned to the fresh stack of boxes. "How about if I run and get us a pizza, and then help Lenora until you're finished?"

Lenora perked up. The idea sounded great to her, and she couldn't help smiling.

Tom pursed his lips together and looked at Lenora. Her enthusiasm caused him to raise his eyebrows in a cautionary look. "That's fine, if my daughter agrees." Lenora nodded her head and shrugged her shoulders noncommittally. "Thanks, Ian."

"No worries, Dr. Kelley!" Ian smiled at Lenora. "I'll be right back!"

Lenora and Tom watched as Ian sprinted out of the office. Tom turned his attention to Lenora and gave her a reproachful look.

"What?" she asked, feeling the color rise to her cheeks.

"He's too old for you," Tom cautioned.

"Ugh, Dad!" Lenora felt embarrassed. "I don't like him…*that* way. We're just friends."

Tom raised one eyebrow. "Uh huh. Well, just make sure you keep it that way. And, I'll be having a chat with Ian to make sure that it does."

"Don't you dare!" Lenora was now mortified. "Dad, that's really… embarrassing. Please, don't."

Tom nodded. "Alright. But, I'm keeping an eye on him."

Lenora rolled her eyes. "Go to your meeting already."

Tom chuckled, giving her one last look of reproach, and then left. Lenora stood there, staring at the door in disbelief.

Parents.

Lenora and Ian demolished a large pizza in less than fifteen minutes, and then proceeded to work. But, it didn't feel like work to Lenora, who was having the time of her life. Ian was fun and witty, and she enjoyed his stories.

They fell into a comfortable silence, working diligently through the files. Occasionally, Lenora stole a glance at Ian, who was quick to catch her and return a handsome smile or a wink. Her eyes fell to his nimble hands as they flipped through the files, and noticed that he wasn't working as quickly as he was before—he was reading.

"Hey, Ian? We're not supposed to read these, you know. My dad said this is sensitive stuff."

Ian didn't bother looking at her. "This is good stuff—really, really, interesting…" he trailed off in distraction.

"Seriously, Ian, I could get in trouble—"

Ian looked up at her and frowned. "I really don't think it's a big deal, Lenora. These files are from 1970 and earlier—more than likely, these people are either dead or far away from the university by now."

"Still—" Lenora felt uncomfortable. "These are confidential, and I don't think they would like it if we were snooping through their personal lives like that."

"I understand, but if your dad catches us, I'll tell him it was only me that read the files, and that you were completely against it and tried to stop me."

"No, you don't understand," Lenora said more firmly, walking over to him, "I could lose my job."

Ian looked up at her, disappointed, and sighed. "These files give me a glimpse into past diagnoses and treatments—information that could really help me in my field, Lenora."

Lenora pursed her lips together and nodded her head in defeat. "Fine. But, if we get caught, you're taking the blame." She couldn't believe how quickly she caved.

"No worries!"

Ian saluted her and winked, flashing a smile that she felt was a bit patronizing. She returned to her seat and resumed her work.

"Get a load of this case," Ian suddenly exclaimed. "This patient had…it says here…forty-five documented personalities. One of the personalities—"

"Stop!" Lenora clapped her hands over her ears. Once she had Ian's attention, she uncovered her ears. "Don't read the files off to me! I said it would get me into trouble!"

"Not if I omit the names," Ian said in a conspiratorial way. "I'll just tell you the interesting bits and leave off names, dates—the identifying stuff." He raised his eyebrows, silently entreating her. "Seriously, Lenora, this is fascinating!"

Lenora inhaled deeply and sat in careful consideration. "Alright," she finally acquiesced, "but you have to leave out the identifications. I *really* don't want to get in trouble. Okay?"

"Yes!" Ian did a fist pump and then proceeded. "One of the patient's personalities was a little girl, who insisted on carrying around a teddy for comfort; another personality was a homeless man; and yet another was a…butcher? Strange." Ian studied the file for a moment in silence and then read off the rest of the file—the other personalities, the psychologist's diagnosis and treatment recommendations. The file went cold, however, after the patient was sent to an insane asylum.

Ian then read off file after file, reading aloud the interesting parts. The more intrigued Lenora became, the closer Ian sat, until he pulled a box up next to her and leaned against her while he read. Frequently, he stopped to answer some of her questions and offer his own diagnoses—either concurring with the psychologist, or offering a contemporary approach. Lenora found it all fascinating, but more so because Ian became more animated, and she enjoyed watching him in his element.

In the middle of listening to Ian read another case study, a box toppled over, grazing the top of Lenora's head. She fell backward and cracked her head on the concrete floor. Ian ran over, picking her up off the ground.

"Are you alright?"

"Y-yeah, I think so," Lenora muttered, groaning.

Ian frowned while examining her head. He winced. "Awe, you hit the same place as before—and a new lump is growing there. Your poor head!" He placed his hands gently alongside her face and kissed her forehead. He looked into her eyes and smiled affectionately. "Well, there's no blood—just the lump." He shook his head and chuckled. "Good grief, girl! I'm starting to think you're accident prone!"

Lenora nodded her head. She was in a total daze, but wasn't sure if it was from the bump on her head or from Ian's surprising kiss.

"That box seemed to come out of nowhere," she commented after recovering a bit. "Strange how it just suddenly fell."

Ian contemplated for a moment and then shook his head. "Not really—the dampness down here causes cardboard to become flimsy. So, I'm not surprised."

Lenora nodded, accepting his explanation. She got up from the chair and joined Ian, who was picking up the files that had spilled out of the box and were now splayed all over the floor.

"We're really going to have to look through these now," Ian observed, sounding frustrated. "Papers are everywhere, and none that go together."

Lenora picked up a bunch of files and searched through the papers. "Well, it shouldn't be too difficult," she remarked, "all of the papers have case numbers on them."

"Oh, brilliant girl!" Ian exclaimed. "We'll just organize per file number—that shouldn't take too long."

Lenora began sorting the piles into case numbers, when she saw in her peripherals, one file that strayed farther than the others. The file lay open on the floor, and she immediately made out the words "He had been sentenced to death by hanging." Intrigued, she sat on one of the boxes, file spread open on her lap. A newspaper article fell from between the pages, landing on the floor. She bent to pick it up, and noticed the words "...her Body having been stabbed in the chest, and the Eyes were missing."

Suddenly, her head exploded in pain. A series of bright flashes blinded her, followed by flashes of images that were not of her own memory.

He closed in on her...kissing forcibly on the lips...horrible taste, like rotten flesh...

...eyes open...a man hovering above her...

...sweat pouring down his forehead...sweat staining his shirt...

...sickening smile...breath hot and foul on her face...

...feeling of sickened revulsion...can't move...chest, arms, legs bound...

Oh God, no....please....no....

Can't move....can't scream...

He reaches for her...she flinches, feeling of disgust...waves of nausea...

...he smiles...eyes wild....he laughs....tries to grab her arm...his hand passes through...

...confusion, anger in his eyes...spittle flies from his mouth...

...determination in mad eyes...he reaches and grabs hold, this time hard and firm...

It hurts...oh, please, let go...

...pressure...feeling pulled...he is tugging her right arm, looking angry....pulling from her left...

Lenoooooora! The man whispered, laughing...pulling...

She looks to her left...Ian, terrified, shouting... wrenching her arm...

Ian, help me!

A loud snap in her head. Everything turns to black.

"Lenora! Come on, Lenora!"

Lenora woke to Ian hovering above her, worried expression on his face. She felt a sharp pain in her arm—it was scratched and bleeding.

"What just happened?" She asked, confused.

"I was just about to ask you the same thing," he said, concerned. Lenora relayed what she saw in those flashes of images. When she finished, Ian had a stunned look on his face. "Do you know what it is...I mean what happened?"

"No, not a clue. And, this isn't the first problem I've had like this." She told him about the temperature changes in her room, the breathing, voices, and objects moving on their own.

Ian looked deeply troubled. He took the file from her and closed it. "I think we're done for the night. Let's pack up and then go up to your dad's office."

"He's in a meeting right now."

"I don't bloody care," Ian said in an angry tone.

"I'll get in trouble. I'm not supposed to disturb him."

"Too bad, Love. This is more important."

"What do you think just happened?"

He studied her face for a moment. "Not sure. I might have an idea, but want to run it by Tom."

SIX

Lenora watched through Tom's office window as he and Ian talked. It was an animated discussion on Ian's part, with her dad sitting on the edge of the desk, calm expression on his face. She warned Ian about interrupting her dad's meeting, but he didn't seem to care, as he barged into the room and demanded that Tom finish his meeting immediately. Lenora thought she was done for when Tom peered around Ian to look at her, and then asked "What has she done now?"

Lenora wilted—she knew she was in trouble.

But, after Ian whispered something in her dad's ear, he immediately got up, ended the meeting, and then came out to see her. Tom held her chin, tilting her head up to his face. He looked warmly at her and asked if she was alright. When she nodded, he told her to wait outside his office while he and Ian chatted.

That was an hour ago. Now, she was fidgeting uncomfortably in her seat and wishing she could just go home.

The door to Tom's office opened, and he walked past her without even a glance. Ian was still standing in Tom's office, visibly angry. Lenora caught his attention and shrugged her shoulders with inquiry. He shook his head and held up his hand, motioning that she should just stay where she was. She turned around in her chair, irritated.

This is about me, but I can't be there? Yeah…seems fair.

Tom reappeared around the corner with another man. He let the man into his office and then motioned for Lenora to come in.

Tom closed the door behind her. "Lenora, take a seat." She sat in a chair next to her dad's desk. "This is Dr. Walter Steel—he's a professor of Psychology and the current director of the CSP group."

"The what?" Lenora was confused—her dad always had these weird acronyms he threw at her.

"Never mind that," Tom responded. "Just tell Dr. Steel what happened tonight…and last night. And don't leave anything out." He raised his eyebrows, leveling a gaze at her. "I mean it."

Confused, Lenora took a minute to gather her wits and then glanced at Dr. Steel, who was looking at her with sincere interest.

Dr. Steel grabbed a chair and positioned it so they were facing each other. "You can call me Walter, sweetheart." He said reassuringly. "Please, do tell your story, I am sincerely interested. Perhaps I can help you."

Lenora gazed at Dr. Steel, who looked friendly—perfectly harmless. He had salt-and-pepper hair, kind blue eyes, and a warm smile. He seemed almost grandfatherly, reminding her of Grandpa Kelley. She began to relax and felt comfortable as she looked into his warm eyes. She cleared her throat and related the past experiences, starting with the previous night, working her way to the strange "dream" she had a little over an hour ago. Walter never interrupted her, but continued looking at her with deep interest, urging her to continue when she thought she couldn't.

When she finished, Walter studied her, a hand resting on his chin. After several minutes in silence, he nodded his head and rubbed his eyes. "You know, Tom, no better time like the present." He looked over at Tom, eyebrows raised knowingly.

"I couldn't disagree more." Tom shook his head and crossed his arms in front of his chest. "She's not ready for that kind of information."

Walter chuckled. "They're never ready to hear it, are they, son?" Walter directed the question at Ian, who flicked his eyes at Lenora and then shook his head. "No, they're never ready. And, when the parents are in denial, it makes the situation worse." Walter rose from the chair and walked toward Tom, patting Ian on the shoulder on the way. "No, I say tell her now." Tom opened his mouth to protest, but Walter stopped him. "She's young—it will give her plenty of time to hone her gifts—to learn to accept them. It's the best gift you could give her, Tom."

Tom lowered his head and rubbed his eyes. He sighed deeply and nodded his head. "I just wish—"

"What? That you had more time?" Walter asked. "There's never enough of that, my friend. She needs to know." He touched Tom's shoulder. "She has a *right* to know."

Tom exhaled and wiped a tear that escaped from his left eye. Lenora was shocked to see her dad cry—she had only seen that once—and now, she feared what he was about to tell her.

Tom sat in the chair across from her and took her hands. "What I'm about to tell you will be shocking," he admitted, "and all will be revealed to you—as we know it." He gave Ian a sidelong glance and then squeezed his daughter's hands. Tom drew in a long breath, shaking his head. Lenora knew he was telling her against his will, and was uncertain she wanted to know now—she had a feeling what he had to tell her was going to change her somehow…change their relationship…change everything.

SEVEN

"Your mother was a special person, Lenora—and not just in the way she was special to us." Tom shifted in his seat and glanced uncertainly at Walter and shook his head. "I just don't...I can't...what if I lose—"

Walter gave a quick nod of encouragement. "Go on, Tom. She needs to know...must know...if she's going to survive."

Tom took another slow breath and then regained composure. "Your mother had special abilities—we refer to them as 'gifts' in our field," he explained. "Your mother...she was...a medium, Lenora."

Lenora frowned, she had no idea what that meant.

Tom, acknowledging her confusion, explained. "A medium is a person who can communicate with spirits. Bessie was born with it, and discovered it at an early age. Her parents weren't very open-minded about it, so they sent her away to live at a mental institution. Thankfully, they sent her to the right place. Someone on staff at the hospital spent enough time with her to discover her abilities. That person was Dr. Steele." Tom nodded appreciatively at Walter, who smiled sadly.

"Yes, your mother was certainly a special case," Walter remarked. "She not only communicated with spirits—hearing them and speaking with them—but she also saw them frequently. They tormented her sometimes."

Tom nodded in agreement. "Because people at that time weren't open to mediumship or paranormal abilities, she was looked upon as a freak. She was keenly aware of this. To top it off, consistently seeing and hearing spirits made her feel like she was going crazy."

"So, to tame those spirits, I prescribed her medication so that it would lessen the occurrence…so she could live a normal life," Walter explained.

"After a while," Tom continued, "she seemed to return to normal. She went to live with her grandmother—in a town where no one knew her—and went to high school, and then off to college, where she met me." Tom smiled in remembrance. "I was a newly-minted professor, and new to the field of paranormal research. Your mother intrigued me. After much cajoling and pursuit, I finally convinced her to work with me…to study and hone her abilities."

"We were able to tame her ability and found gifted people from around the world to help her hone those talents. We were hoping that at some point, she would use her gift for paranormal research," Walter explained.

"But, she wasn't interested," Tom added. "All Bessie wanted was a 'normal' life—a husband, children, and a home—nothing more. So, she fought her ability on a daily basis. Our intensive studies wore her down, I'm afraid." Tom's eyes welled with tears.

Walter reached out and touched Tom's shoulder. "We were all devastated by her loss—she was loved and well-respected." He glanced at Lenora, who was also fighting tears. "Like your mother, Lenora, you too possess abilities. We weren't entirely sure what they would be until after your mother died and the ability began to surface."

"What are you talking about?" Lenora turned to Tom, completely confused.

Tom smiled weakly and nodded. "A couple of weeks after your mom died, you and I went to see one of Bessie's friends. Remember Mrs. Kavanaugh?"

Lenora nodded. She did remember Mrs. Kavanaugh—Mrs. K, she called her. She was a sweet lady that her mom visited often. Occasionally, Lenora was allowed to join her on these visits. Mrs. K and Bessie drank tea and visited on the front porch while Lenora played, usually in a different room. On rainy days, Mrs. K permitted Lenora to play in the little schoolroom she had set up in the attic for her granddaughters.

"Yes, I remember her—mom said a couple of times that Mrs. K was the mother she never had. I never really got that since she already had a mom."

"Yes, well, Aileen was the one that had Bessie committed; they became estranged after that," Tom admitted. "Well, there are some things you don't know about Mrs. Kavanaugh, Lenora. One thing you were never told is that she is your grandmother Aileen's sister."

"So she's my—"

"Great aunt," Tom finished.

"But why didn't mom tell me—"

"Because the family didn't acknowledge her," Tom explained. "Your great-grandparents were embarrassed of her. She was a medium too, Len."

Lenora gaped. "Okay, but that still doesn't explain why I didn't know she was my aunt."

"That was Mrs. K...Loraine's idea. She didn't want to dredge up old memories...and she didn't want you asking questions." Tom grasped her hands firmly. "No one on your mother's side understood the supernatural—Loraine's abilities weren't recognized as gifts, but as a curse. She was treated like a freak of nature and ostracized by her own family. But, Loraine was a strong woman and sought help from various paranormal societies, eventually finding someone to help her hone her gift. She helped your mother come to terms with her own abilities, and helped her learn to control them."

"After your mother died," he continued, "I brought you to Loraine's—at her request. She told me it was because she simply wanted to see how you were doing. However, it was for another reason." He paused and sighed, looking drained. "She suspected you had gifts too, and she wanted to try you out. One day, while Loraine and I talked, you walked over to the piano and picked at the keys. I was going to tell you to stop, but you stopped on your own and seemed to go into some kind of trance. You started speaking indirectly to Loraine about her husband, Seamus, who had been a concert pianist. I assumed that either your mom or Loraine had shared that information with you. However, you talked about concert dates, places, and people I didn't know. Then, you played actual tunes—you don't know how to play piano, Len—and you started talking in a Scottish brogue and calling Loraine 'lassie,' just like her husband did."

"Loraine immediately shouted at me, telling me to yell your name as loud as I could. I was absolutely terrified. I ran over and held you and shouted your name. She just put her hands on your head and closed her eyes. Finally, you woke up from your dream state. It was quite frightening."

Lenora frowned, "I sort of remember that....you told me that I passed out."

"Yes," Tom answered, "because I didn't want to alarm you. The next day, I went to visit Loraine, and she told me of her suspicions that you had retro-cognition abilities, but she was uncertain until your episode the day before. She said that because the spirit of Mr. Kavanaugh was able to possess you, that it was also a strong possibility that you have additional abilities. After a lot of coaxing, she finally convinced me to allow her to examine you more closely."

Realization dawned on Lenora's face. "Our Tuesday teas! I thought that was just so we could stay connected to Mom!"

Tom nodded. "Loraine didn't want to tell you—just in case she was wrong. And, if she was wrong, then at least the two of you had special time together."

"So, I assume she found out that I had abilities?" Lenora felt dismayed—this was the first she heard about her supposed ability, and it was irritating that no one told her until now.

"Yes," Tom answered, "after many trials, she was able to prove that you do have paranormal abilities."

Tears spilled down Lenora's cheeks. Ian ran over to the desk and handed her a box of tissues, which she instantly pushed aside. "No thank you, Ian. I'm not sad…just really…angry! Why didn't anyone tell me? I mean, I'm not a baby, Dad!"

"Sweetheart," Tom tried taking her hand in his, but she pushed him away. "Mrs. K said that your abilities were too much for her to handle—that you needed more help than she could give. Besides, I wasn't quite ready to go there with you. Your mom just died, and I wanted you to have time to mourn her." He exhaled deeply. "Hell, I needed time to mourn her without worrying about all of this."

He squeezed her hand despite her resistance. "I only meant to protect you and let you have a normal childhood. Your mother's childhood was very tough on her—I wanted to help you avoid that, if I could…while I could. The intention was to let you grow up, be a normal teenager. I planned to tell you after you graduated from high school—*after* I could assemble the proper support system for you."

"What do you mean, 'support system'?"

"I wanted to bring you here—to Cambridge."

"But I thought you got the job on chance…that this was one of several applications you sent out…that you wanted to move because being in Ann Arbor reminded you too much of mom."

Tom shook his head. "No, not exactly. I didn't apply here at all. I contacted Walter immediately after your episode at Mrs. K's."

"And, it was great timing, if you ask me," Walter joined. "I had just decided that this was my last year as head of the Parapsychology department—no one is better qualified than Tom to replace me."

"Parapsychology department?" Lenora's head started to ache.

"My position at the university isn't exactly what you think. I'm a parapsychologist—I specialize in the study of psychological phenomena such as clairvoyance, mediumship, and telepathy. Walter has been my mentor since graduate school."

"When Tom called," Walter added, "I immediately convinced him to take a professorship in the Psychology department. What he didn't know was that I planned to retire before classes began in the fall. My full intention was to groom him for my position as head of the Parapsychology Department and Director of the Cambridge Society of the Paranormal."

"Cambridge Society of...?" Lenora was thoroughly confused.

"We call it CSP here," Walter answered, "it's a secret society that studies and investigates paranormal activity around the world. Our team is world-renowned and made up of the best of the best."

"If you're so *world-renowned*, how is it that you're a 'secret' society?" Lenora asked sardonically.

A collective chuckle rang out around the room.

"You're very perceptive, Lenora," Walter answered, bemused. "We're considered a 'secret' society because the university cannot gain funding for it because parapsychology is an unrecognized science. However, the university founders staunchly believed in the paranormal, a belief that is still upheld today. So, the university does not *recognize* it as a legitimate department, but *supports* its endeavors to gain knowledge through research. Our reputation precedes us only by word of mouth. Does that make sense?"

"So, who are these 'best of the best' you talk about?" Lenora knew the tone was snarky, but she got that way when irritated.

"Well," Walter answered, his blue eyes twinkling with amusement, "your dad is one of them – he's the best paranormal researcher in the world...he has surmounted my research, and I was at one time considered the best in my field."

Lenora looked over at her dad, who smiled and nodded at her, as if to concur with Walter's assertions.

"We also have some of the top paranormal investigators, scientists, and engineers," continued Walter. "Then, we have people like this guy over here," Walter nodded his head at Ian, "who is one of the most talented mediums in the world."

Lenora shot a surprised glance at Ian. "Medium? Just like Aunt Loraine...like Mom?"

"Yes, I see, hear, and speak to dead people, Lenora," Ian explained with a grin.

Lenora couldn't believe what she was hearing. This wasn't possible…it was the kind of thing that happened only in movies.

"Are you okay, Lenora?" Tom asked his daughter, shooting an annoyed look at Ian. "You know, you could have explained that with a bit more sensitivity."

"The girl has to learn somehow, Tom," Ian retorted. "And, she's not going to learn with a bunch of technical mumbo-jumbo. She needs simple explanations."

"Well, perhaps, but a little more compassion would be nice. This is a lot of information to take in," Tom responded angrily.

Ian stood up and walked toward Tom. "Look, I'm sorry, I only wanted to…"

"Stop!" Lenora shouted and then looked at Tom. "Ian's right, Dad! I'm not a baby. You should have trusted me enough to tell me the truth. From now on, I expect full honesty from you, understand?"

Tom, taken aback, just nodded.

Ian chuckled, to which Lenora turned and pointed a finger in his face. "And as for you. Give my dad a break—he did what he thought was best for me." She glanced briefly at Tom. "Even though it wasn't."

The smile left Ian's face and was replaced with a half-serious smirk. "Okay, you're the boss." He saluted her.

"Stop being an ass," Lenora cautioned. She turned to Walter. "So, what happens from here?"

Walter raised his eyebrows. "You're taking this quite well…I'm impressed. Your dad underestimated you, I think." He gave Tom a look of reproof and then shifted his gaze back to Lenora. "What I'd like to do is to immediately run some tests, with your permission. Then, I'd like to introduce you to the CSP team and begin training."

"Now Walter, I don't think she's ready to—"

Walter held a hand up, cutting Tom off. "No one is ever ready, and the sooner she starts, the better. But, you know this." He gazed sternly at Tom. "I think becoming involved with CSP now will help her learn how to control her ability—it will help her feel less frightened and overwhelmed." He looked at Lenora. "We have the world's best here, and everyone will be able to help you, in one way or another, to learn about your ability. What do you say?"

"What kind of tests are they?" Lenora asked, swallowing hard. "Are they painful?"

Walter laughed. "No, bless you, the tests are not painful – they're simple tests that help us zero in on what your abilities might be."

"Will I have to give blood?" She hated the thought of big needles in her veins. *Yuck.*

"A small sample for our records, but that's it," Walter explained.

"Alright, I'll do it," she agreed. "When do I begin?"

Walter beamed. "Tomorrow, if you like."

EIGHT

Lenora sat on her bed, knees curled to her chest, reflecting on what had just happened. So much information whirled about in her mind, and it was difficult taking it all in. Mrs. K was her aunt… her mom was a medium…she had abilities too. It was a shock to the system.

Ian said he would explain exactly what all this meant later. She was going to take him up on that.

Before everyone left Tom's office, Walter suggested that since touching things caused the visions, she should avoid touching anything with her bare hands. He wanted Lenora to wait until she met with someone named Rose, who could help Lenora learn about her ability.

According to Walter, she was also in danger of being entrapped by a spirit while in a trance. And, until she learned how to control her ability, she was in danger whenever someone like Ian wasn't around to help her out of it. Walter explained that sometimes, entities liked to grab the souls of the living either to gain strength or possess them.

Lenora wondered aloud how she was supposed to manage not touching anything. Walter immediately ran to the janitorial closet and pulled out a box of yellow cleaning gloves. Apparently, she was to wear them at all times—inside and outside the apartment.

Lenora glanced down at her hands, which donned the ugly, rubbery gloves. They were too big for her hands, and she felt clumsy in them. Wearing these gloves at all times would be embarrassing, not to mention annoying. She grabbed her headphones and then closed her eyes to let the music drown out the thick, disturbing quiet that enveloped her and left her feeling on edge.

He couldn't believe how easy this was. Here she was, in his room, and he only had to open the door for her to enter.

He watched eagerly as she walked over to the bookshelf and ran a finger over the spines of the books, gasping quietly at a few of the titles, giving him a smile of approval. He was glad—little did she know that he bought them for her. She walked over to the desk and felt the soft texture of the chair's cushion.

"Go ahead, take a seat," he said, feeling a lump in his throat and a rapid pulse. His hands started to shake, and cool sweat dripped from his palms. He tried taking deep breaths to calm himself, but the anticipation was too overwhelming.

"No, I couldn't." She gazed coyly at him. He pulled the chair out for her. She took a seat and ran her hands along the smooth surface of the desktop. She examined the stationary and opened the little envelope drawer in the ink stand.

"That was my father's," he offered.

"It's beautiful," she whispered. "It's full of ink. Do you use— "

He thrust the needle into her neck, injecting the drug into her system. She instantly slumped over in the chair. He picked her up and carried her to the settee. This time, he chose a piece of furniture that was too heavy to move, and one that had a head and foot rest so that if she were to topple over, she would be protected against any accidents that may occur.

He didn't want what happened with the last girl to happen again...

He strapped her in and then collapsed in the wingback chair. This one was so much easier than the last. It was a good omen.

Exhausted, he rested his head against the side of the chair, letting his gaze wander to the corner of the room, where Lenora sat watching, a terrified expression on her face.

He met her gaze, smiled, and then waved her off dismissively.

"Don't worry, Love, your turn soon," he said, chuckling lazily to himself.

Lenora jolted up in bed, clutching her neck, a feeling of dread washing through her. She glanced around, realizing that she was in her own room, and it was morning.

Though an entire night had passed, she woke up feeling like she hadn't slept at all.

And that dream…

She wasn't sure what it meant, and who that creepy man was, but it was deeply disturbing, and parts of her mind felt hazy, as if she was still in the dream.

A cool breeze drifted past her, fluttering a piece of paper on her nightstand. She glanced at it—it was a note from her dad saying he wanted to take her out for breakfast.

Great.

She looked down at her yellow gloves and scowled; she didn't feel much like venturing out in those ugly things. What would people think?

She was like a zombie through her shower, even while fighting with those stupid yellow gloves. Flashes of her dream kept wavering in and out of her consciousness—she wanted the images out of her mind.

Once out of the shower, Lenora walked over to her desk and sat down to do her makeup. Images of the woman in her dream flashed before her—the woman sitting at a desk…her neck being punctured by the syringe. Lenora squeezed her eyes shut—it was just too much. She grabbed her little mirror and instantly went into the kitchen to finish getting ready.

Tom was already sitting at the dinette, reading a newspaper. He looked up over the top of the paper at her. "Good morning, Len." He frowned. "Getting ready in the kitchen? Is your room too warm—"

Lenora held a hand up, stopping Tom in mid-sentence. "I just feel like getting ready out here, is that okay?"

"Sure, no problem," he replied gingerly, raising the newspaper to continue reading.

Lenora's heart sunk. She hated being rude to her dad.

Once she finished getting ready and zipped her cosmetic bag, Tom glanced up from the paper. "Ready to go?"

Wow. Amazing how he can act as if nothing has happened. "Sure," she shrugged, "I'll just go get my…"

"Sweater?" Tom interrupted. "Got it." He nodded to the back of the chair next to him, where Ugly Pink Sweater was draped. She also noticed that her purse and book bag were sitting on the chair. He thought of everything this morning.

Irritated, she walked over to the chair, threw on the sweater, and then picked up her purse and book bag. "Well, let's go, then," she snapped.

Tom smiled, grabbed the newspaper and keys, and chuckled. "Okay, whatever you say, sunshine!"

Lenora was glad that Tom was so engrossed in reading the newspaper—she was too grouchy to carry on a conversation today. When they arrived at the restaurant, she couldn't help but notice the stares that her giant yellow gloves attracted. Thoroughly embarrassed, she convinced Tom to let her take the gloves off while she was at the restaurant—telling him that she wouldn't touch anything, that her hands needed air.

She removed the gloves and inspected her hands; they were wrinkled and pruney. Lenora quickly glanced at Tom to ensure that he was still occupied with his newspaper, and then grabbed her fork to see what would happen. Nothing enticed visions, except that she got brief flashes of someone washing it, or yellowed teeth scraping across the fork. She scowled and shook her head to try and get rid of the image. It didn't work, and by the time her food arrived, she had lost her appetite.

She picked up her toast, spread jelly on it, and then tore it into tiny pieces on her plate.

"You really shouldn't pick at your food."

Lenora looked up at her dad to protest. But, it wasn't her dad who spoke—it was Ian, who stood beside the table, grinning at her. She eyed her toast as if it were the most interesting thing in the world.

"Hello, Ian." Tom put his newspaper down. "How did you know to find us here?"

"Your car is out front," Ian smiled, as if impressed with his detective skills.

"Oh, I suppose so." Tom didn't look at Ian, but glanced at his daughter, frowning. "Lenora? I know you're grumpy today, but can you please move over so Ian can join us?"

"Sure." Lenora said, color rising to her cheeks.

Ian jumped into the seat next to Lenora, put his arm around her, and squeezed. "So, how's our little girl this morning?"

He sounds chipper. "I'm not a little girl, Ian."

"Oh, sorry—I beg your pardon," he responded, still in good spirits. He removed his arm from around Lenora and placed a small package on the table in front of her. The package was wrapped in light pink matte paper with a metallic, dark fuchsia bow.

She looked at Ian and frowned in confusion. He smiled and pushed it at her. "Here, I bought you a present."

Damn it. He knows I hate pink. She stared at it, being in no mood to be teased today.

"Well, don't just stare at it, open it!"

Lenora sighed heavily, grabbed the package, and slowly peeled the paper. However, when she touched the package, flashes of Ian ran through her mind—him buying the wrapping paper, laughing as he put the fuchsia bow atop the small box, carrying the package to the restaurant. She set the package down and looked over at Ian, trying to smile appreciatively. "I'll open it later." She tried sounding dismissive—as if she was more interested in finishing her breakfast.

"Oh for God's sake...." Ian made an irritated grunt and grabbed the package and started ripping the paper.

Lenora, surprised by Ian's boldness, grabbed the package back. "This is *my* present, thank you very much." She quickly ripped through the paper, trying to ignore the flashes. She removed the wrapping, crumpled it up, tossed it at Ian, and then opened the box. Her shoulders slumped out of confusion. It was a box full of gloves. She looked up at Ian, disconcerted.

"I didn't think you would enjoy wearing those big, yellow, clunky things." He explained, nodding at the cleaning gloves. "So, I solicited a friend's help last night, and we picked out every kind of fashionable glove that a girl your age might like."

Lenora examined the box's contents. There were crocheted gloves in black, white, and cream, a pair of black leather gloves, and matte cotton gloves of different colors. At the bottom of the box were two more pairs: a pair of black satin gloves with fur trim, and the other, a pair of burgundy satin gloves with sequined trim. She frowned and looked at Ian, questioning his judgment on those.

"Oh, those are for *fancy* times," he said, grinning proudly.

"Fancy? I don't do anything fancy," Lenora replied.

"Regardless," Tom said, putting a hand on hers, "this was very thoughtful of Ian, don't you think?"

"Oh!" Lenora was still too stunned. "Yes, thank you, Ian. This *was* very nice of you. A lot better than the cleaning gloves, that's for sure." She smiled warmly at Ian, who grabbed her around the shoulders and squeezed enthusiastically. She giggled.

Ian beamed. "You're welcome. And, I also know someone that does beautiful crocheting work. She told me that if you wanted, she would make a pair in every color for you."

"Oh, wow," Lenora didn't know what to say. "That's...nice...of her," she said, instantly wondering who this girl was, and if she and Ian were an item. She felt a pang of jealousy and was instantly certain she wouldn't like this person.

"Her name is Tabitha," Ian explained, as if he could hear her thoughts, "and she has abilities too. She sees auras, and as a result, is a very colorful person. You will like her—she's eternally positive and fun to talk to."

Lenora smiled wanly, nervous to meet someone else with abilities, and uncertain about meeting her, considering how enthusiastic Ian was.

Ian excitedly sifted through the gloves and picked out the cream-colored crocheted pair. "Here," he thrust them at her, "these will match UPS." He grinned sarcastically and winked.

"UPS?" Tom asked.

"Uh…Ugly Pink Sweater," Lenora responded distractedly, taking the gloves from Ian and sliding them on. She glanced at Ian appreciatively. "Thanks."

"Don't think of it – I'm just happy to help," he smiled. "Oh, and after you're done with the tests today, maybe I'll stop by and take you to meet Tabitha." He looked up at Tom. "Would that be alright, Dr. Kelley?"

Lenora was about to protest, when her dad spoke for her. "That would be nice, Ian, thank you."

"But, I have a lot of work to do today," Lenora argued.

"Don't worry about that," Tom reassured her, "it will still be there when you go back in tomorrow. In fact, you can take the rest of the week off and start back on Monday morning, if you would like."

"Well, I…."

"Excellent!" interrupted Ian. "I only have one seminar this morning, and then the rest of the week is off for me, so I can take you around and introduce you to everyone on the CSP team this week."

"Actually, I don't…" Lenora began.

"Lenora, I thought you should know that Walter has appointed Ian as your guide," Tom interrupted her. "Ian is the only member of our group with the strength to help you when you're in a trance. He will also be helping Rose teach you how to control your ability. You'll need to get used to him being around."

"Oh," Lenora said, trying to hide her delight in the idea that she would be "forced" to spend more time with Ian.

Ian jabbed her in the side with his elbow. "Hey, it's not going to be that bad. I got you presents, you should be happy to have me as a mentor. Mine never gave me gifts."

"Who was your mentor?" Lenora asked.

"I'll have to tell you another time," Ian answered, looking at his watch and gasping. "I'm late!" He got up from his seat and nodded at them. "Catch you later!"

Lenora watched Ian leave and then turned to Tom. "Who is Rose?"

A dark look passed over Tom's expression, and he exhaled. "Rose is a talented clairvoyant who has worked with the CSP team for several years…since she was your age, I think. She can help you learn to use your gifts—she'll be a good teacher."

"Have you met her?" Lenora asked.

Tom studied her for a moment. "Yes. I met her many years ago."

"When?" Lenora was intrigued—it stunned her that her dad knew these people and had never once mentioned them.

Tom threw her a cautionary look and shook his head. "Not now, Len. Eat your breakfast." He rustled the paper and continued reading.

Lenora didn't press him—she knew better.

NINE

"**N**ow, you're going to feel a little sting, and then you can relax."

Lenora squeezed her eyes shut as the technician took blood from her arm.

Only 20 seconds of my life, just a little bit of time, this isn't a big deal.

The mantra was meant to help her through it, but she was still feeling squeamish, like she was going to pass out.

Lenora felt slightly disturbed by the pleasant look on the technician's face. She turned her face—she couldn't watch someone gleaning so much pleasure from draining blood from someone's arm.

This is so disgusting!

"There!" The technician placed a piece of cotton gauze on Lenora's arm. "You're all done." Lenora looked apprehensively out of the corner of her eye as a bandage was affixed to what—she thought—appeared to be the gaping, gushing, throbbing hole in her arm. Her whole body shuddered and she felt weak, dizzy.

"Are you alright, miss?" the technician asked, concerned.

"Yeah," Lenora responded. *No! I'm going to pass out! This was so disgusting!* She looked down at her arm as she rolled her sweater sleeve down and spotted the bandage—it had a cartoon character on it.

When will people quit treating me like a baby?

She got up off the table and walked out of the room.

"Wait!" The technician came running after her, holding a sucker out in front of her. "Take this, it will help."

Lenora looked at the sucker and thought of telling her to shove it "you-know-where," but thought otherwise. No one should refuse free candy. She took the sucker from the technician. "Hey, thanks," she muttered.

"You're welcome! Have a great…"

Lenora was too far away to hear her finish the sentence, and was certain she didn't want to.

She walked over to her dad's office and looked in his window. Tom was busy on the phone, and just motioned for her to come in and take a seat. She walked in and sat down in a chair across from him. His office was still stacked with boxes from his office at the University of Michigan. She reached over and picked up a picture that was sticking out of a nearby box—it was the entire U-Mich psychology department, her dad standing in the back row, smiling broadly. Standing next to him was Dr. John Gruber, Tom's best friend.

Lenora smiled as she recalled the many visits that Dr. John had made to their home, particularly after her mom died. John always brought Lenora little presents; he and his wife couldn't have children, so they spoiled her like she was their own.

Standing next to John in the picture was Dr. Lucretia Morton, and next to her was KrisAnn Jorby, Tom's favorite grad student. Lenora looked at all the faces she knew so well. They all looked so happy. Seeing them made her feel homesick for Ann Arbor. She missed everything—the trees, gardens, buildings, the smell of her Grandpa Kelley's lilacs.

She inhaled deeply and sighed.

Tom got off the phone and gave Lenora a mildly curious look. "Something the matter?" Lenora shook her head, not wanting to go into detail about her homesickness. "Alright then. Walter said that they're ready for you, so I'll take you down to the lab. Ready?"

Lenora nodded gingerly. "I guess."

"Don't be afraid," Tom soothed, "the tests will be painless…I assure you."

When they got to the lab, Walter was waiting for them, smiling cheerfully. "Welcome, Lenora!" He put an arm around her shoulder and signaled to Tom. "I've got it from here, Tom. You go on back to your office—I'll send our girl up to you when we're finished."

Tom exhaled loudly, nodded, and then left reluctantly. Lenora felt a pang in her chest as she watched her dad slowly walk out of the room, quietly closing the door behind him.

"Now, now, look lively my dear—we're going to have a fun afternoon together!" Walter squeezed her shoulders and led her into a room that looked like a den. The muted lighting, accompanied with the overstuffed couches and chairs, created a cozy environment. Lenora thought to herself that the only thing missing was a fireplace. Walter brought her over to the seating area and smiled. "Take a seat—anywhere you like—and I'll go get us some tea."

Lenora waited until Walter left the room and then sat down in one of the overstuffed chairs. Her entire body sunk into the chair, making her feel small, like a little girl. Her feet were barely touching the floor, and just as she thought of switching to another chair, Walter came in, carrying a tray.

Walter set the tray down on the table in front of Lenora and poured two cups of tea. He set a cup in front of her and then held out a plate of cookies. "Biscuit?" Lenora took what looked like a shortbread cookie and set in on her little plate.

"Is this your office, Walter?" she asked, hoping that chitchat would help quell her rising nerves.

"Oh, no," Walter chuckled, "my office isn't nearly this nice. This is the therapy room. This is where students come for therapy—either with a seasoned psychologist like your dad or me, or with a novice. It's a great place for PhD candidates to practice their field."

"Practice? That sounds sort of...wrong...to practice on someone who needs help."

Walter laughed, cookie crumbs flying out of his mouth. "You're so refreshingly honest—like your mother!" He laughed while taking a sip of tea and brushing the wayward crumbs off his chest. "Well, the PhD candidates need to practice *somewhere*. How else would they gain experience? No, we assign minor cases to only the thoroughly trained student; all the others must practice with a professor in the room. They are *all* monitored."

"Oh." Lenora hoped that she didn't insult him.

But, he didn't seem fazed as he continued with a line of small talk that took them through tea and cookies. When they finished, Walter clapped his hands together. "Well, are you ready?"

"No...I mean, yes...I think so..." Lenora's stomach tightened into a knot as she felt nervous waves surge through her body. Her legs bounced uncontrollably, and she fidgeted with her hands.

Perceiving her anxiety, Walter leaned in and touched her jumpy leg. "Nothing to be nervous about." Her leg stopped bouncing for a minute while Walter produced a bag from beside the chair. He dumped out a series of items: a red crayon, a hair brush, a pen, a pair of glasses, a children's book, and an action figure.

Though the items were strangely random, the last item surprised her the most. An action figure? She opened her mouth to ask, but Walter held his hand up. "No questions. Only talk when I ask you to. Okay?" He smiled warmly at her. "Now, I'm going to hand an item to you, and you will tell me what you see in your mind. Simple enough?" Lenora nodded, feeling more at ease. "You'll have to remove your gloves first, though." He winked at her.

Lenora removed her gloves and set them beside her.

"Very nice of Ian to get those for you," Walter observed as he held the crayon out to her on a tray.

Lenora nodded and took the crayon. The second she touched it, bright flashes blinded her. She closed her eyes and strained to see the images in her mind.

"Tell me what you see," Walter prompted.

"A hand...a small hand...coloring a picture."

"Do you see the picture?" Walter asked.

Lenora strained, leaning forward, as if it would help her see more clearly. The image appeared in broken bits, finally emerging to a fuzzy, yet discernable form. "It's...a fire engine...the hand is coloring it red..."

"Good. What else can you see?"

Lenora squeezed her eyes harder. "I think...it might be...the person coloring...yes, it's a little boy." Lenora smiled as she saw a small boy with brown hair and big brown eyes as he concentrated on his picture. Suddenly, the picture left as quickly as it came to her. She opened her eyes and noticed that Walter had the crayon in his hand.

"Good job, my dear."

"I'm done?"

"With the crayon you are." Walter handed over each item individually, taking her through the same exercise. Each time, she saw something rather similar. With the hairbrush, it was a blonde-haired girl combing her hair. She saw a different little girl—this one in brown, curly pigtails—holding the pen. The glasses were worn by a small red-haired boy, whom she sensed suffered from some sort of ailment, and it was the same child that she saw reading the children's book. The action figure seemed to belong to the boy who colored the fire engine.

When they finished with the series of objects, Lenora opened her eyes. "Was I right?"

Walter nodded, writing in his notebook. "Yes, you were right on all counts."

"These were all items owned by children?"

"Yes." Walter seemed pleased. "You are right about the theme as well."

"Are they—" Lenora couldn't bring herself to say it.

"Dead?" Walter finished the question for her. "Heavens no!" His blue eyes twinkled as he chuckled. "They are all alive and very well, thank you!" He sat forward and whispered conspiratorially. "They're all actually my grandchildren."

"Oh!" Lenora was pleasantly surprised. "So, why children?"

"I wanted to test your ability on innocuous items. Children have very limited past experiences, which helps you practice your ability without the problems that adults...living or dead...can bring. In this case, I bought brand new items, and then had my grandchildren work with them, thereafter placing each item in the paper sack so that I didn't contaminate anything by touching the items myself."

"One of the children," Lenora began, unsure of whether she wanted to breach a potential touchy subject, "the red-haired boy...I sensed that he might be sick?"

Walter nodded, a sad expression darkened his face. "Yes. His name is Toby, and he is fine." Walter smiled with affection. "He was born with cystic fibrosis. However, he does as well as he can." Walter's eyes welled up with tears. He sniffed and cleared his throat in an attempt to hide his sadness. "He's tough, though, don't you know. Plans on being an astronaut." He chuckled quietly.

Lenora smiled, feeling a touch of sadness. "Well, I'm sure he'll make a great one, someday," she offered cheerfully.

"Yes, I look forward to that—very much." Walter considered her for a moment. "You know, you look very much like your mother. She was a lovely woman." He rose from his seat and helped her up. Walter placed Lenora's hand in his arm as he walked her out. "I consider myself to be among the few that were honored to call her friend." He turned and gazed at her. "If there is anything that you need...ever... don't hesitate to call." He patted her hand and opened the door. "It's been a pleasure."

"Thank you, Walter," Lenora said as Walter gently closed the door. She stood in the hallway for several seconds, staring at the door. An odd sadness lingered, and her heart felt heavy as she thought of Walter's grandson.

Lenora walked up to her dad's office where Judith, Tom's secretary, was organizing files on his desk. "Well, hello Lenora! Tom said you had the day off. So, what are you doing here?"

"I don't know," Lenora replied, "I guess I'm a glutton for punishment." She collapsed in a chair across from Tom's desk.

"Oh, no you don't." Judith came round the desk, picked up Lenora's book bag, and grabbed her arm. She escorted Lenora out into the main office and plopped the book bag onto the floor next to her desk. "You're not going to sit in that musty old office and wait for your dad—you're going to sit out here and help me sort mail and eat candy." She laughed merrily. Lenora liked Judith—she was a somewhat younger version of Nana Noreen, Tom's mother. Nana Noreen was silly, dynamic, and prone to gossip, much like Judith.

Lenora sat with Judith for the next hour, sorting mail, eating candy, and listening to gossip. She didn't know the people that Judith was talking about, so the gossip may not have been as interesting to her, but Judith's liveliness was infectious and it got Lenora out of her gloomy mood.

Judith was in the middle of telling Lenora about a particularly interesting love triangle between three professors in the English Department, when Ian peeked his head around the door.

"What gossip are you poisoning Lenora's mind with now?" he asked, a sarcastic grin on his face.

Judith looked up, startled. "Oh, it's you." She gave him a sidelong glance and then leaned in toward Lenora. "There are some juicy little tidbits I could tell you about that one." She motioned toward Ian.

"Be quiet, woman!" Ian ran over and grabbed Judith around the waist and held her close to him. "I told you not to tell anyone about our love affair. I don't like scandal." He kissed Judith on both cheeks and whirled her about the room.

Judith initially feigned struggle, which eventually lapsed into a fit of giggles. "Oh, Ian Roberts, what am I to do with you?"

"Love me forever," he said, twirling her around one more time before allowing her to collapse in her chair.

Ian grabbed a piece of candy and plopped down next to Lenora, poking her with his elbow. "So, how'd it go?"

Lenora glanced briefly at Judith. "Okay," she shrugged her shoulders.

"How'd what go?" Judith leaned in, placing a hand on her chin, appearing intrigued and slightly flushed.

"N-nothing," Lenora replied, flicking a nervous gaze at Ian.

"Oh, you mean the psychic tests with Walter?" Judith smiled.

"Oh, um, well…" Lenora didn't know what to say…what she was allowed to say.

Judith waved a hand at her. "Don't fret darling, I know all about those." She laughed at the look of shock on Lenora's face. "Oh, please. I am the eyes and ears of this university—I know everything that goes on here. Everything." She gave Ian a stern look. "Eyes. And. Ears." She pointed to herself and then smiled at Lenora. "You'll either tell me in good time, or I'll find out in my own way." She winked.

Ian laughed hysterically. "Well, Lenora, are you ready to get out of here?"

"Like you wouldn't believe," Lenora responded, grabbing her book bag. She thanked Judith for the talk and the candy and then followed Ian out the door.

TEN

"**W**here are we going?"

Ian didn't answer, but grabbed her hand and led her through the campus. They went into the library and wound around several corners, until they came to a brightly-lit room. Ian knocked briefly on the closed door before waltzing in. The room was full of people, who were talking amongst themselves until Ian barged in. Lenora felt like pulling the sweater over her head and running away…really fast.

"Everyone, this is Lenora…finally!" Ian motioned to Lenora, who tried to hide behind his back. Ian grabbed her arm and pulled her out from behind him. "Good grief, Len, don't be such a coward!" He pushed her in front of him. "As I was saying, everyone, this is Lenora—I know you've all been anxiously waiting to meet her!"

The people in the room stopped what they were doing and smiled at her, which made Lenora all the more nervous.

Who are these people?

Apparently, she said that out loud, because everyone laughed.

"Who are these people?" Ian repeated. "Well, I'll tell you. These are the leads for the CSP team." Ian pointed to one side of the table at a girl with cropped red hair and a bright smile. "That over there is Amelia, and there," he pointed toward a good-looking man with black hair and piercing blue eyes, "is Phil—they're the team documentarians." Amelia chirped an enthusiastic hello, while Phil simply nodded.

"Over there," Ian motioned to the back corner, "are Joe and Maggie—they're our technical specialists." Joe and Maggie waved before turning back to their computer screens. "And here," Ian turned to his left, "is Emily—she's our occultist."

Emily rose from her chair and shook Lenora's hand. "Pleased to meet you," she responded, turning her focus to Ian. "I have something I need to talk to you about."

"Ah, should we leave?" Ian asked, glancing briefly at Lenora.

Emily eyed Lenora for a bit and then shook her head. "No—what I have to ask can be said in front of the group…and Lenora won't understand anyway."

Ian nodded and listened to Emily as she expounded upon a problem with a current case they were apparently working on. Lenora didn't understand any of the terminology, so she just stood to the side, listening to the languid and articulated tone of Emily's voice. She surveyed Emily's appearance and came to the quick conclusion that she was not your average girl.

Emily wore her black hair long, with bangs that went past her eyebrows and fluttered whenever she batted an eyelash. She wore a good deal of dark eye makeup (much more than Tom would ever allow Lenora to wear, though she thought it looked super cool). Emily's lips were polished with a deep shade of burgundy, and on her neck hung some sort of silver talisman on the end of a short leather string. Her clothing was entirely black: a tight, long sleeved shirt, black pants, and lacy boots with big, chunky heels.

Emily caught her staring and returned her gaze with a sarcastic grin. "Again, it was lovely meeting you, Lenora."

"You too," was all Lenora got out before Emily walked out the door. Lenora's shoulders slumped—she feared that she may have insulted Emily before she had a chance to get to know her.

"Don't worry," Ian said, reading her response. "Emily's got thick skin, and she doesn't rightly care about what people think about her."

"Yeah, but I think she looks pretty...cool." Lenora said, feeling sick to her stomach.

"I know—it was written all over your face. I'm positive Emily caught that."

"Oh." Lenora felt a modicum of relief. "Hope I can remember everyone's names."

"You'll have plenty of time for that, Len. Besides, you haven't met everyone yet."

"There's more?" Lenora's stomach turned.

"Yeah," Ian replied with a sly grin, "you haven't met Rose or Tabitha yet."

"When do I get to meet them?" Lenora asked, hoping it wasn't today—she was already exhausted.

Ian opened his mouth to respond, when he looked up at the clock. "Oh! We're late! Come on," he said, tugging at Lenora's sleeve. "We have to catch the 12:43 train."

"Where are we going?"

But Ian didn't hear her. He pulled her silently through the library, and then they raced to the train station.

"How much longer?" Lenora asked Ian, who was reading what looked like a romance novel.

"Not long."

He didn't even look up from his book. Lenora glanced at the front cover of the book he was reading—it had a muscular man embracing a busty blond. She giggled. "Are you reading a romance novel?"

"Yes," Ian answered distractedly, "and I'm at the good part, so no more questions."

Lenora rolled her eyes and huffed in irritation. They had been on the train now for nearly two hours and Ian didn't tell her where they were going—in fact, he had spoken very little to her since they got on the train. She removed the crocheted gloves and pressed her fingers in between the stitches, wondering how a person could make something so intricate.

"Don't do that—you'll stretch them out and then they won't fit." Ian closed his book and looked at her like she was a petulant child. "Do I need to give you something to do?"

Lenora glared at him. "No, but you could at least talk to me—I mean, we've been on this train for nearly two hours and you have barely said two words to me."

Ian tilted his head in reflection. "No, I think I've said more than two words, Lenora." He grinned sarcastically.

"You know what I mean," she grumbled, crossing her arms in front of her. "It's boring, just sitting here."

"Look at the scenery. It's beautiful this time of year."

"What, the scenery changes from grass, trees, and more grass?" Lenora quipped. "Oh, look, a hill!"

"My, my, aren't we the child this afternoon." Ian grinned.

Lenora turned her back on him and looked out the window. "Read your clichéd romance."

"Clichéd, huh?" Ian chuckled and then rested his shoulder on her back, reopening his book with an amused grin. "Okay then."

They walked in silence along the streets of a small village called Clacton-on-Sea, Ian walking a few steps ahead of Lenora. Initially, Lenora had to practically run to keep up, but she gave up after a while, and followed Ian, who acted as if he were on a mapped course with little time. She felt almost invisible, and wondered if he was angry with her.

Lenora felt a lump in her throat and tried distracting herself with the view. Small cottages dotted the streets—most with their own little gate—all adorned with beautiful natural gardens. The little Victorian village was like a picture book—picturesque and charming. The village seemed incredibly peaceful. She took a deep breath of the fresh sea air and began to relax.

"It's quite beautiful here," she observed.

"Yes, it is…quite," Ian replied matter-of-fact, "I'll have to bring you here again some time when we aren't busy—it's lovely here, and the pier is glorious at sunset." Lenora opened her mouth to reply, but Ian interrupted. "Come on, Len, keep up!"

Well, there went the mood.

She glowered at him and started walking faster, despite her initial feeling to turn on her heels and catch the train back to Cambridge.

Ian stopped in his tracks, and Lenora ran into the back of him.

"Hey, look where you're walking!" He huffed.

"Well, geez, I'm sorry for not being able to read your mind and know that you were going to stop," Lenora said caustically. She gave him a hostile look—there was no way she was apologizing.

Ian tilted his head to the side and considered her expression for a moment. "Sorry, Lenora," he sighed, "I guess I was lost in thought and you stepped on my heels. It hurt a bit." He leaned over and bent his head so that he could gain eye contact. "Forgive me?" he pleaded.

"I suppose," she said, unwilling to give in. "Where are we?"

"We, my little apprentice, are at the home of a lovely, talented, and gifted woman—I absolutely *adore* her, and I know you will too." He smiled warmly, seeming lost in reminiscence.

Excellent – she's probably really beautiful and he's in love with her.

Her mood was turning more disagreeable as the day went on.

"One thing I would like to say, however," Ian continued, "is that she is a little ….odd. But, she is kindhearted and a great friend." Ian smiled broadly, opened the gate, and motioned for her to go in.

The path to the little cottage was odd in and of itself—multi-colored stones on a curving path that twisted and turned the length of the front yard. To her, it resembled a "Candyland" board.

Couldn't she have designed a straight path? This is a little beyond juvenile. Lenora was quickly becoming frustrated.

The footpath started at the gate and immediately turned left, went all the way to the one end of the yard, a right turn, then all the way to the other end. Lenora looked ahead and the rest of the path was similar – winding around the yard, some sections with multiple curves. She shook her head in disbelief. *What a waste.*

"Why couldn't she just have a straight path like everyone else? Why couldn't we have just cut through? This is silly," Lenora objected, more to herself than to anyone in particular.

Ian stopped and spun around, frowning at her. "The path is exactly how she wants it. Tabitha feels that taking the path to least resistance is bad karma, and an indication of her visitor's true nature. I take the path as it is laid, out of respect for her. Besides, it's fun!" He smiled and then continued his journey. Lenora silently followed Ian and pouted—she felt like he was mocking her as he skipped the final length of the walkway.

They finally took the last turn that lead to the doorway. The plain wood door was adorned with a simple wrought iron door knocker in a fleur-de-lis pattern, simplicity that contradicted the odd shape and décor of the cottage. Ian lifted the door knocker and looked at her. "Be prepared for a fun afternoon," he said enigmatically, wiggling his eyebrows. Lenora wasn't sure how to feel about that.

Ian vigorously wrapped the door knocker several times until a lyrical voice chirped, "I'll be right there!"

Lenora glanced at Ian, who was absolutely beaming. *Wow, can he get any more excited?*

The door opened swiftly, and standing there was the tiniest person Lenora had ever seen. Though she appeared to be in her late twenties, she had snow white hair in a spiked pixie cut. Two luminous eyes peered through thick glasses, making the eyes appear bulbous. A dark purple cardigan with multiple-colored buttons draped her shoulders, beneath which hung a long, burgundy velvet dress, white tights, and a royal blue silk scarf topped the ensemble. Everything she wore appeared to be three sizes too large.

Ian smiled and laughed heartily as he hugged the tiny woman in the doorway. "Tabitha, I am glad to see you!"

"Of course you are," Tabitha cooed, "you're yellow."

She looked over at Lenora, who was mesmerized by the woman's piercing black eyes.

Tabitha gasped and smiled in surprise. "Oh!" She gazed at Lenora's form and then turned to Ian. "She's angry with you."

Ian appeared surprised, and then glanced at Lenora. "Really?"

"Most undoubtedly," Tabitha remarked.

Several seconds of uncomfortable silence passed, when Ian finally recovered. "Oh, where are my manners," Ian laughed, "Tabitha Tibbits, meet Lenora Kelley."

The corners of Lenora's mouth twitched in an attempt to smile, but it looked more like she bit into something sour. She had this over-whelming feeling as if the woman were staring straight through her. No matter how hard she tried, Lenora couldn't look away. It was unnerving.

Tabitha smiled and nodded. She shifted her eyes from Lenora and went back to Ian. A small, knowing smile played across her lips. "Do come in—I was just about to make a spot of tea."

Ian gestured for Lenora to walk in ahead of him and she shook her head vigorously. She was a little afraid of this woman, and she wasn't sure why. Ian frowned at her, wagged a finger in warning, and then entered the cottage.

The cottage was small and simple: a living room, kitchen, two bedrooms, and a bathroom—all on one floor. But that was the only thing simple about it. Colorful was definitely an understatement. Lenora gazed in awe at the multitude of colors around the living room. The walls were a soft lavender, all enhanced with beautiful seascape watercolors. Plush, red velvet furniture stood stark against the soft color on the walls, and several pillows were propped on each piece, all various shades of purple, blue, and turquoise. Panels of soft, flowing curtains in shades of deep purple, blue, and turquoise framed the windows and fluttered in the breeze. Plants were scattered about the room, and strategically-placed seashells adorned the ornate tables and bookcases. Paper lanterns were strung around the room along the outside edges of each wall—every lantern a different shape and arranged according to the rainbow.

Noticing Lenora's expression, Tabitha beamed. "I decorate only in positive colors." She motioned to the living room and instructed them to sit while she fixed a pot of tea.

Ian bounded across the room and plopped animatedly upon a large red velvet settee. He appeared quite at home as he stretched his legs and glanced around the room. "Have you switched things around, Tabby?"

"Yes, I did!" Tabitha chirruped from the kitchen. "I'm glad you noticed!" She peered around the corner at Ian. "I added the water-color above the fireplace. Painted it myself."

Ian studied the colorful painting positioned on the mantle. Two dolphins stood on a sandy beach beside one another, holding hands, looking out into the sea—except that the sea wasn't comprised of water, but of humans, laying prone, as if they were themselves the water. Ian's eyebrows rose in astonishment. "Wow," Ian said, heading over to the painting for a closer look. "Fine attention to detail," he said, head leaning sideways. "What do you call it?"

"Pollution," came the answer from the kitchen.

"Ah, lovely, lovely," said Ian as he strolled back to the settee, frowning and shaking his head in disbelief. He flopped back into the sofa, and was just about to recline, when he noticed that Lenora was still standing in the doorway.

"Get in here," he hissed. She walked gingerly toward him, and he pointed in irritation at a chair across from him. "Now, sit down, behave yourself, and be nice," he whispered authoritatively. "She's a lovely person, and I won't have you treating her otherwise." He frowned at her and Lenora hung her head, humiliated.

As soon as Lenora sat down, Tabitha came in carrying a tray with a teapot, three cups, and a plate of cookies. She eyed Ian, who instantly removed his feet from the ottoman, upon which she set the tray.

Lenora wasn't a big fan of tea, but she took some anyway to be polite. She didn't want to get Ian riled up any more than he already was.

She took a sip of tea and closed her eyes. It was good. It tasted like sugary lemon drops. She took a cookie off the tray and took a bite—it was a thick, crispy shortbread with hints of vanilla and lemon. She sat in silence as she savored every bite of the cookie and sipped the wonderfully warm tea. It was almost magical.

"Well," Ian said as he beamed at Lenora, "it looks like our girl likes your tea and biscuits, Tabby."

Tabitha turned toward Lenora. "Indeed she does!"

"What color is she?" Ian asked enthusiastically.

"She's a pale yellow," answered Tabitha. "Good. This means we can have an open conversation now. I was almost concerned—when I came in, she was a mustard color." She pinned Ian with a stern look. "Someone must have said something unpleasant to make her uncomfortable."

Ian lowered his eyes. "I may have said a thing or two, yes, but nothing that didn't need to be said." He glanced at Lenora and gave her a strained smile. "Your biscuits have made her better, I just know it."

Lenora frowned and looked at Tabitha. "What did you mean when you said I'm a 'pale yellow'?"

"That's the color of your aura," replied Tabitha. "Pale yellow often signifies that someone feels optimistic, positive, and open to new ideas."

"Oh," Lenora responded as if she understood completely. She took another bite of the cookie and closed her eyes. "These are the best cookies that I've ever….wait a minute," she turned back to Tabitha, "what do you mean by 'aura'?"

"An aura is a luminous, colorful energy that surrounds a body," Tabitha explained. "All living things in the universe have auras— even the trees, flowers, and animals—everything. An aura reader, such as myself, can see the auras of every living being—we can discern emotions or moods, personalities, or even health." She smiled warmly at Lenora. "For instance, Ian's aura is generally yellow, which indicates a person who is intelligent, creative, playful, and full of life. Sometimes, his aura is full of silver metallic flecks that sparkle like little diamonds–that's how I know he is in tune with his ability, that he's speaking with or hearing others from the spiritual plane."

"Does he have the silvery flecks now?" Lenora asked, completely enthralled.

"No, he's just yellow," laughed Tabitha.

"And, so I'm a pale yellow?"

"Now you are," responded Tabitha, "however, when you arrived, your aura was fluctuating between a dark gray and forest green, which tells me that you were full of fear and insecurity. In that state, I cannot trust what I would hear from you. Now that you are feeling more optimistic and open, we can communicate better. And, once I've gotten to know you, I will be able to discern your aura more clearly."

Lenora nodded her head and took another bite of cookie. Her eyes shifted slightly in Ian's direction and then quickly focused back on her cookie, which she felt certain was magical—she felt so relaxed.

Tabitha sighed and shifted her attention to Ian. "Would you be a dear and go make another pot of tea?"

"Oh, absolutely!" Ian took the tray and went into the kitchen.

As soon as he was out of sight, Tabitha turned to Lenora, and took both of her hands. "There is one color that I didn't say in front of Ian," she whispered. "I will share that only with you alone: a very pale pink. This is the mark of someone in love."

Lenora dropped her cookie on the floor. She quickly put it back on the plate and then tried not to meet Tabitha's penetrating gaze.

Tabitha scrutinized her closely—it was as if she were staring right into Lenora's mind. "Forest green is also indicative jealousy." She smiled at Lenora, who began feeling uncomfortable. She looked toward the kitchen and could hear Ian messing around, whistling.

"Ian and I have been friends for a long time," Tabitha continued warmly, "but I'm too whimsical for him, and he's too…young for me." She smiled, released Lenora's hands and patted them. Lenora opened her mouth to say that she was absolutely *not* in love with Ian, but Tabitha put up a hand to stop her. "No need to argue—you know I'm right." Then, she pointed to the kitchen, put a finger to her lips, and gently shook her head as if to say this was their little secret.

Ian came in and set the tea pot and a plate of fresh cookies down on the tray. He sat down and looked at the two ladies nervously. "So, what have you two been talking about?"

"I was telling Lenora about the meaning of some colors," Tabitha quickly responded.

"Which ones?" Ian started to ask, but Lenora interrupted him.

"What are your colors, Tabitha?"

"Oh!" she uttered excitedly, "they are green and a soft blue. Standard green is related to the love of people and animals, and also for one who teaches."

"You're a teacher?"

"Yes," Tabitha beamed, "I teach art at a secondary school and belong to the Clacton Art Club. On Tuesdays, I teach knitting and crocheting. Both are very rewarding—I love to teach."

"So, I suppose you see lots of different auras." Lenora's interest in Tabitha was growing.

"Yes, many," Tabitha answered, "Mostly good, bright colors. There is darkness surrounding some beings, however."

"Can you tell if a person is bad?"

"No, but I can tell if someone going to *do* something bad in the moment."

"Yeah," Ian interrupted excitedly, "one time, Tabby reported a bank robbery before it even happened. And, she saved the life of a woman in her knitting group."

"I didn't save her life," corrected Tabitha, "I just informed her that she should really go to the doctor."

"You're too modest, Tabby," Ian responded and turned to Lenora, "one of the ladies' auras had a dark color in it. I forget the color. Tabby?"

"It was a muddy gray." Tabitha answered unaffectedly.

"Yeah, a muddy gray," continued Ian, "but not just waves of color, the gray was clustered near her stomach. The lady went to the doctor and after some blood work, discovered that she needed emergency gall bladder surgery. She got it removed, and now she's perfectly healthy!"

"Wow, that's cool!" Lenora was impressed. "You saved someone's life!"

"Hardly," Tabitha answered, subdued. She looked at Ian and raised an eyebrow. "I merely suggested. Mathilda did the rest herself. You're being dramatic, as usual."

Ian smiled and then waved a hand at her, dismissing her inability to see the situation as positively amazing as he did.

The conversation continued for another two hours, and Lenora found herself completely engrossed with Tabitha and her abilities.

Ian looked at his watch. "Oh! We have to get back to Cambridge—I have a paper to write."

"Well, thank you for coming to visit," Tabitha replied. "But before you leave, I wanted to tell you, Lenora, what your true aura colors are now that I've been able to see them clearly."

"Oh! You can see them now?" Lenora asked enthusiastically.

"Yes, they've been prevalent for the past hour or more, so I know these are your true colors. Your aura begins as a bright royal blue, which signifies someone who is highly spiritual and generous. Then, the color begins to fade into an indigo, which means that you're very intuitive and sensitive—excellent colors, if you ask me," Tabitha said encouragingly.

Lenora was speechless. She wasn't altogether certain about what auras were or what they meant, but she was excited about learning more about them. "Thanks, Tabitha, it was great meeting you."

"Likewise," Tabitha responded.

"Yes," Ian added, "thank you for the tea and biscuits. We'll definitely be back soon."

Tabitha nodded and followed them to the door. Lenora walked out and waved at Tabitha, who waved and smiled back.

"Ian," Tabitha said, "may I speak with you quickly on the last case we worked on?"

"Sure." Ian sounded confused. "Lenora, could you wait for me at the gate?"

Lenora nodded, continuing along the path that she considered ridiculous just two hours ago. Near the end of the path, she sat down on a bench under an arbor. The arbor was painted a bright white, with lush ivy weaving through it. A rose bush was behind her with the biggest blooms she had ever seen. Lenora took off her glove to touch the rose and brought it to her face, closing her eyes as she was enveloped with its sweet scent. Small, colorful flashes came before her eyes, and she was soon seeing Tabitha in her mind, tending to her flowers, humming a pleasant tune. Lenora let go of the flower and smiled. The first real pleasant vision she had on her own.

The air was cool for mid-June, so she buttoned up her sweater and crossed her arms for warmth. Lenora surveyed Tabitha's front yard. Along each turn of the path was a separate little "garden," each with a white arbor over a bench, and each seeming to have its own floral theme. One had nothing but buttercups and black-eyed Susan, another had pink tulips and lilies, and another had deep blue irises and sweet William. Suddenly, she got it – Tabitha decorated in auras. Lenora smiled at her personal revelation.

Lenora examined the bench she was sitting on and saw what seemed like paint peeling from the wood. She leaned over to get a closer look. The paint was not peeling, but appeared to be scratched off. Looking more closely, Lenora soon realized that the scratches were happening as she watched—they seemed to come out of thin air, and eventually spelled out a name: Bartholomew Booth. Terrified, she jumped off the bench and uttered a small whimper.

Without thinking, she leaned over the bench and traced the writing to determine if it was real.

Lenora's hand froze to the spot, as if someone were holding it there. Spots formed in front of her eyes, and her eyesight wavered as the corner images blackened. She was losing consciousness.

Eleven

Her body spiraled downward in a thick blackness. Something prevented her movement—it was as if her limbs were suspended in heavy tar. She opened her eyes, trying to discern where she was, but the blackness clouded her vision, made her feel disoriented, trapped.

A sinister laugh.

She strained to see who it was, but saw nothing. Warm, hot breath on her neck made her body quake in fear. The breath drew near, hovered over her face. A pungent odor permeated her nose. She cringed in revulsion.

"Lenoooooorah...." it breathed.

"No, please," she murmured, starting to sob.

"Seeeee meeeee...." Lenora squeezed her eyes tight, refusing to look. "See me!" it hissed insistently.

"No, please...just let me go," she shook her head violently from side-to-side.

It laughed. "Never!"

"No!" Lenora felt something cold sliding its way up her body, reaching her face, touching her eyelids. She tried shaking her head, but it was held fast by invisible hands. Cold fingers pried her eyelids open and she saw it. His face was twisted in a menacing grin, his eyes were sunken, black, and fierce. She tried wrenching from its grip, but the hold grew tighter, painful. She winced as bony fingers dug into her arms and knees ground into her thighs.

"Please, no! Ian! Help me!" No matter how hard she tried, the screams just came out muffled.

Pressure on her legs and arms grew more intense as the thing leaned in closer.

Cracked, cold lips on hers.

She whimpered, her body shook.

"Lenora!"

Her head turned—someone shouted her name. The thing was startled and grabbed onto her with more force, looking angrily into the thick blackness as if it saw what shouted at them.

"Lenora!"

The shouting grew louder. She recognized the voice—it was Ian!

"Ian! Help me!"

A sharp pain on her cheek caused the blackness to dissipate, but only just. She screamed for help. An intense pain seared her cheek—this time from the other side. She struggled against the weight of the thing holding her down. Its grip eventually loosened; she twisted her arm free, reaching out to the abyss.

"Ian!"

Another sharp blow. This time, her head wrenched heavily to the side and the darkness faded...

"Lenora!"

Lenora woke to see Ian and Tabitha hovering above her, worried expressions on their faces. Feeling disoriented, she sat up, shook her head, and rubbed her eyes. She was on the ground. Apparently, she fell backward off the bench, nearly missing the rose bush behind her.

"What happened?"

"I was going to ask you the same," Ian returned, sounding out of breath.

Lenora frowned, trying to recall what had happened. "Well, I was sitting here...looking around the garden..." Her eyes grew wide as she recalled what happened. Tears streamed down her face as she recounted the details of her vision to Ian and Tabitha. When she finished, both stared at her in quiet dismay.

Tabitha traced her finger over the scrawled name.

"Do you know who that is, Tabitha?" Ian didn't take his eyes off of Lenora.

"No, the name doesn't sound familiar," Tabitha responded, sounding distant.

Ian frowned. "Do you know who it is, Lenora?"

Lenora shook her head. "No, I don't. But, it's the same voice that talks to me in my apartment—the same one that keeps bothering me at night."

Ian's eyes widened. "Are you certain?"

"Yes, I'm certain," Lenora replied. "The same voice, the same awful smells, the same touches..." she trailed off, shaking her head, trying to eliminate the image from her mind.

Tabitha shifted her gaze to Ian. "Can entities follow?"

Ian nodded. "Yes, they can." He gave Tabitha a serious look. "Remember Thaddeus?"

"Oh...yes." Tabitha appeared to recall.

"Who's Thaddeus?" Lenora inquired, feeling left out.

"I'll explain later," Ian responded. "But first, we need to get you home." Ian helped Lenora get up and brushed her off. "Thank you, Tabby, for a lovely visit."

"It was my pleasure," Tabitha responded, still looking concerned. "I'm just sorry that it ended so...disagreeably." Lenora heard a note of caution in Tabitha's reply, which told her that the vision she had today, and the fact that it connected to the entity in her apartment, was not good.

When they got to the train station, Ian led Lenora to a bench and sat her down. "Wait for me here—I'll only be a minute." He turned to leave and then stopped. "Oh, and for the love of God, please, *please* don't touch anything." Lenora nodded, curling her body into itself and resting her head on her knees.

Lenora's body shivered uncontrollably as if she had just plunged into icy water. No matter how much she tried, she just couldn't warm her body—she was cold to the core.

Ian returned quickly and then grabbed her arm and gently helped her to her feet. "Come on, we need to board now." He looked at her gravely. "Say nothing, understand?" When Lenora agreed, he led her to a man standing at the platform near the train.

"Hello, miss, my name is Nigel Watersby and I am the Station Operator." He offered his hand and she shook it, smiling weakly. "Follow me." He led Ian and Lenora to the front of the train and they boarded. "No one has reserved the quiet coach, so you can have it for the entirety of your return trip. Dave will be at your service." Nigel motioned toward a thin uniformed man in the corner, who nodded at them both. "At that, I will leave you." Nigel shook Ian's hand and then left promptly.

Ian led Lenora to a seat near the window and then approached Dave. "Could I please have two blankets and some hot tea? She's freezing." Dave nodded and left immediately. Ian returned to Lenora, taking a seat next to her. She looked up at him in confusion, teeth still chattering. He shook his head. "Not yet. Once Dave leaves, we can talk."

Dave returned with two blankets and a tea service. "I'll be right outside the doors if you need me," he informed them, giving Lenora a warm look of sympathy.

"Thank you, we appreciate it," Ian responded somberly. Once Dave left, Ian wrapped the blankets around Lenora's shoulders and handed her a cup of tea.

"So," Lenora asked after taking a sip of the hot tea, "how did you convince them to give us the private cabin?"

Ian checked the doors to make sure they were closed. "I told them you were my sister and that you were gravely ill." He grinned awkwardly. "I'm a bit ashamed of myself, but it's imperative that we're alone."

"What did you say I was sick from?"

Ian glanced at her, embarrassed. "I'd rather not say. Let's just say it's a serious, yet non-contagious condition that requires medical professionals."

Lenora straightened up. "Ian, what did you say?"

Ian shook his head regrettably. "Sorry, not for you to know."

Lenora sank down in her seat. "You're unbelievable."

"Yep." Ian took a sip of his tea.

"So, tell me this," Lenora said, glaring at him, "next time I board the train, will people go running from me?"

Ian chuckled. "No…" he gave her a sidelong glance and smirked. "But, you'll get plenty looks of sympathy and free stuff…"

"Ugh!" Lenora couldn't believe his audacity. She slunk down in the seat, faced away from Ian, and sipped her tea in silence.

The tea helped warm Lenora and eventually she was able to remove the blankets. She gazed at Ian, who tried distracting himself with "All Aboard!" magazine. Lenora cleared her throat, which caught Ian's attention, but he simply tried to appear mesmerized by his reading. She cleared her throat again and he set the magazine down, looking at her expectantly.

"Yes?"

"Oh, I'm sorry, am I taking you way from a riveting article?"

"Yes, you were," he admitted, an insincere expression on his face.

"What was the article about?"

"Um…" Ian's eyes shifted about, and he reached for the magazine. Lenora clapped her hand over the top and shook her head, raising her eyebrows. Ian chuckled. "Yes, well…um…it was about… trains."

"Duh," Lenora responded impatiently. She tilted her head to the side and crossed her arms. "Are you going to actually talk to me about what happened back at Tabitha's? Or, are you going to keep me in the dark like everyone else does?" The annoyed expression on her face turned crestfallen.

He softened, nodding. "Yeah. People do keep you in the dark, don't they?"

"Yes, they do," she replied. "I'm not fragile—I won't break. I just want to know what's going on with me, why, and what I need to do to handle it. This is so frustrating! Whatever is going on with this… ability, if that's what it can be called…is scary. I've been through a lot in my life, and I think I can handle whatever life throws my way.

People don't give me credit for being strong enough. But, when my mom died, I had to be strong for me and my dad—he was completely crushed. All I want is for someone to have enough faith that I'll be strong," she hesitated, "and someone who can trust me with the truth."

Ian sighed heavily and touched her arm. "I'm sorry. You're right—no one is giving you the benefit of the doubt, and no one has trusted you with the truth. But, from here on, you can count on me to tell you the truth…even if it hurts."

"Promise?" Lenora still didn't believe him.

"Promise." He noted the apprehension in her face. "I'm serious. I know what it's like to have people keep things from you."

She nodded in appreciation. "Thanks."

Ian smiled warmly. "Now, I can tell you what I *saw* in Tabitha's garden. It was a man pinning you down to the ground. He held your arms down and pressed his knees into your thighs." He paused as Lenora became visibly shaken.

"Go on, *please*," Lenora begged.

Ian exhaled and shook his head. "This isn't easy for me, you know, recounting that horrible scene." He squeezed her hand. "But, you lived it—I just don't want you to relive it, that's all."

"I *need* you to go on," Lenora insisted.

Ian continued, his eyes clouded with self-doubt. "I saw him… touching you." He scowled. "He…touched you…and kissed you…" he shook his head as if to ward off the memory. "It was…disgusting…dreadful. I don't care if I ever see that again."

He took a minute to regain composure. "What originally caught my attention was your screaming. We saw you in a struggle—I saw the man; Tabitha saw his aura—and your screams were…frightening. I ran to you and called your name, but you were so in his grip that you didn't hear me at first. I grabbed you and struggled against the man, who just held on tighter—I could see you wincing in pain. I had to do something, so I slapped your face…hard….several times." Lenora put her hand to her cheek, still feeling the sting. "Finally, you became coherent—in the present—and I was able to free you from his clutches. You know the rest."

Lenora sat, shivering, in silence for several seconds. "I can't believe you actually *saw* him."

"Yes," Ian replied with regret. "I can't stop seeing it, actually." A horrified expression crossed Lenora's face as she glanced nervously around the room, whimpering. Ian grabbed her and held her close. "No, he's not here now—I just meant that I can't get the image out of my mind, that's all." When Lenora began to relax, he released his hold. "He knows I can protect you, so I doubt he'll bother you while I'm around now. And believe me, when I'm with you, I will never leave your side again."

"What about when you can't be with me?" Lenora questioned fearfully.

"We'll figure it out. Don't worry."

"Why is this…*thing*…bothering me?"

"I can't be certain exactly *why* this happened to you," he responded, noticing Lenora's eyes narrowing. He held his hand up in his defense. "But, I *can* guess. Now, this is just a guess—we'll need to bring Walter and Tom, and perhaps some others on the team, to get to the bottom of it all." He looked to see if she believed him, and then continued. "What Tabitha and I think, is that the entity that has been bothering you at your flat is following you."

"F-following me? But, how…?" Lenora shook her head in disbelief. She trembled as waves of fear engulfed her.

Ian immediately threw the blankets around her shoulders. "This is what we in the paranormal business call an intelligent haunting. It's a rare occurrence, and generally happens to spirits that died traumatically, had unfinished business, are still emotionally connected to loved ones and can't move on, suffered injustice, or had a simple fear of the beyond. It might also be that the entity is haunting a specific *person* rather than place, which can happen, I'm afraid."

"Why me? Why do you think he chose me?"

"That, I truly don't know—we'll have to conduct research on the spirit, who fortunately scratched its human name on the bench. That will at least give us a benchmark from where to start. The CSP team will then conduct background research—on your flat and on the name. When they come up with this background information, the team can figure out how to proceed."

"Proceed? With what?"

"Getting rid of it…for good."

"You can do that?"

"That's our specialty, Love—that's why we're considered the best in the world." Lenora relaxed a bit, the trembling began to subside, and she sighed in relief. Ian's expression hardened. "I'm glad you're feeling better, but I will tell you that we're not talking about an overnight fix—this could take several weeks."

"Weeks? But, I can't take it anymore, Ian!" Lenora, frustrated, felt the color rise to her cheeks.

Ian grabbed her arms gently. "You need to calm down. There is a process and we *will* follow it. No one can afford mistakes…particularly where an intelligent haunting is concerned. This *has* to be done right, which means you have to be patient. Can you do that for me?" Lenora lowered her head, tears now freely flowing, and conceded. "Good. I'll find a way to protect you while the investigation continues so that the haunting either ceases, or it becomes relatively innocuous."

They sat in silence for several minutes while Lenora wiped away her tears. A myriad of emotions swept through her at different intervals: fear, anger, then self-pity, then disparity, and then fear again. The thoughts churned in her mind until she finally came to the conclusion that she had to face this thing head-on—and the only way to do it was to learn to control her ability, to fight the entity, to stand strong.

She looked at Ian, a new resolve on her face. "Okay, I'm ready to face it…whatever it takes."

Ian chuckled. "Well, Lenora, I don't blame you for feeling a bit of despair—this is a lot to take in and handle. You will have plenty of opportunity to become accustomed to your abilities. Don't rush it."

"I'm not—what I'm saying is that I'm tired of feeling sorry for myself...of being a victim."

"You might be tired of it," Ian grinned, "but it'll happen against your will many more times."

"Maybe," Lenora agreed, "but not for the rest of today." She gave Ian a steady look. He nodded and beamed at her as she changed the subject. "So, tell me about the other types of hauntings—you said that an intelligent haunting is only one type. How many are there?"

"Well, there are several," Ian admitted. "You'll learn about these over time—mostly through your own experiences. However, CSP has lumped them into three categories: intelligent, residual, and portal." He shrugged his shoulders indifferently. "I believe there are many more categories than that, but this will help keep it simple for you."

"A residual haunting," he continued, "is a recurrence of actions—whether mundane or tragic—that happened in the past and left a sort of imprint in that particular environment. For example, Civil War era soldiers continuously set up for battle on a hill. Another example would be miners continuing to dig at a site that collapsed a hundred years ago. Residual activity is often reported as phantom footsteps, scents, perhaps sounds like music playing in the background or digging."

"But, I can hear footsteps, the door open, and I can smell his breath."

Ian shook his head. "No. If your haunting was residual, the door wouldn't actually open, and the breath wouldn't actually appear as mist—they would simply be sounds."

Lenora nodded, disappointed. "What about the other haunting... portals?"

"Yes, these are controversial. The theory is that there are doorways to other dimensions or worlds through which spirits travel."

"Do you believe this theory?"

"Yes, I happen to be one of the few mediums in the world who have witnessed them."

"That's...kinda cool," Lenora whispered, in awe.

"Not really," Ian frowned. "It's rather frightening, especially knowing that the spirit can drag you along, if you aren't careful."

Lenora started feeling concerned. "Do you think—"

"No," Ian interrupted, knowing where she was going. "Your entity does *not* use a portal. No worries there."

Lenora was just about to ask how certain he was, when the train stopped. They had arrived at Cambridge.

Ian helped Lenora off the train, took her hand in his, and led her from the station. They walked several blocks before Lenora stopped. "Ian," she began, "aren't you going to introduce me to Rose?"

Ian pursed his lips together and shook his head. "No, sorry, not today, Love. You've been through too much."

"I don't mind," Lenora responded, uncertain she was ready to go home yet. "If her house is on the way, we can stop by—"

"No, not today," Ian replied emphatically. "Besides, Rose lives in Colchester—we'd have to get back on the train."

"Colchester?" Lenora was still unfamiliar with England's geography.

"It's the halfway stop between Cambridge and Clacton-on-Sea. My plan was to first visit Tabitha, and then head to Colchester to have dinner with Rose—she makes the best shepherd's pie I've ever had."

"I don't have anywhere to go," Lenora offered, hoping Ian would catch on to the hint that she'd rather go back on the train to see Rose than go home.

Ian chuckled. "You're certainly persistent!" He steadied a gaze at her. "Seriously, Len, you need to rest. I'll take you to see Rose some other time. The trip is worth taking the time for, believe me. Rose is a lovely woman…and incredibly gifted. And, you would love Colchester—it's the oldest recorded town in Britain. And I *know* how you love history." He smiled slyly at her.

Lenora returned the smile and nodded, gingerly taking Ian's hand to resume their walk.

"Besides," Ian mentioned, after they had walked another block, "I want to call an emergency CSP meeting once we get back. Everyone needs to hear what happened to you, and we need to come up with a plan to investigate this entity that's been following you."

"What?" Lenora was incredulous, stopping in her tracks. She wanted the entity gone more than anything, but wasn't quite ready to face the CSP group and relive the horrible details of her vision.

"Aw, come on! It won't be that bad!" Ian exclaimed, throwing an arm around Lenora's shoulder and urging her forward.

Lenora groaned as a knot twisted in her stomach.

TWELVE

Later that night, Ian called an emergency meeting, and nearly the entire CSP team showed up—the only ones missing were Tabitha and Rose. For some odd reason, Lenora felt relief when she saw Emily, who gave Lenora a look of quiet assurance.

Ian spoke for Lenora, at her request, and told them everything—from her experiences in the flat to this afternoon at Tabitha's. While Ian explained what happened, Tom held his daughter tight against him. Everyone else sat in silence, occasionally stealing worried glances at Lenora.

"That's not all," Ian said, looking at Lenora, a guilty expression on his face. "After I left you with your dad, I went immediately to Walter and Emily to tell them what I didn't tell you."

"What do you mean?" Lenora sat up, terrified. "What didn't you tell me?"

"Well," Ian sighed, "not only did I see what the entity was doing to you, I could hear his thoughts. But, I didn't want to tell you what these were before I had talked to Walter and Emily first." Noticing Lenora's angry stare, he continued. "I'm sorry to have kept this from you, considering our agreement, but these thoughts were so… frightening that they have me really worried."

Ian stopped briefly, exchanging a worried glance with Emily, who nodded and handed him a drawing from her sketch book. Ian took it and sighed. "I was able to glean some information from the entity, but it's still a bit ambiguous." He glanced at Lenora. "I saw what it is that he wants," Ian said hesitantly. "For some reason, he wants your soul—not just to take it, but to possess it."

"Why? Why me?" Lenora asked, shaking.

Ian shook his head sadly. "That, Love, I couldn't figure out." He turned to Tom. "He's taken others before, and is intent on fulfilling…something…I don't know what. He failed in his last attempt." Ian hesitated, his eyes quickly darting in Lenora's direction.

"And?" Tom seemed impatient, angry.

"The last girl…she took her own life." Ian whispered, almost inaudibly. He paused for several seconds before continuing. "The entity went after her. She committed suicide. That's how she escaped."

"So, what does that mean?" Tom asked, sounding exasperated.

"The entity showed me in a vision that Lenora is his next victim. He will do everything in his power to possess her soul. The only way for escape is to take her own life. But—" Ian stopped, pursing his lips together in hesitation.

"But what?" Tom shouted. "Spit it out, Ian!"

"But, if she takes her own life," Ian explained, "the entity will go after another. He'll keep on until he's fulfilled his plan."

"So, let him take someone else!" Tom shouted.

Ian shook his head and gave Tom the sketch. "I had Emily make this sketch for me—it's a rendering of his next victim should Lenora refuse him."

Tom glanced at the sketch and shook his head. "I don't know who this is." He showed the sketch to Lenora. "Do you recognize her?"

Lenora glanced at the drawing and shook her head slowly. "N-no, I don't know her."

"She's the same age as Lenora," Emily said, interrupting the thick silence. "When Ian described her to me, she was wearing the current uniform from Lenora's school."

"He's getting more powerful, Tom." Ian explained. "Lenora's psychic sensibilities have helped him regain the strength he needs to sustain. He won't quit. Not until he's fulfilled his quest." Ian put a hand on Tom's shoulder. "This girl...she's someone's daughter. Do you wish this kind of pain on another father?"

Tom shook his head and exhaled. "No, I don't. But, I don't want to lose Lenora either. Do you see my predicament, Ian?"

"Yes, I do!" Ian exclaimed. "But, who better than Lenora to battle this entity? She has our backing and resources. She might be the one to stop him before he takes another innocent life."

The room grew heavy with silence.

Lenora started to shiver. A lump formed in her throat and hot tears streamed down her face. "S-so, no matter what we do, I'm going to *die*?"

"No!" Tom nearly shouted. "That is not going to happen." He glanced at Walter. "We'll figure it out, right?"

Walter nodded slowly. "We'll work around the clock to figure this out. I promise."

"We all promise," Ian added firmly.

"So, what do you all think? What needs to be done here?" Walter glanced around the room solemnly at his team. They had been working for four hours, trying to come up with a plausible plan to help Lenora—it was nearing two o'clock in the morning, and the crew looked haggard.

"Amelia and I can start right away on the research—we can research the entity's name and the historical information about their flat," Phil offered immediately.

"Good, thanks Phillip. We'll start with that." Walter turned toward Tom. "Lenora needs to keep those gloves on at *all* times." He fixed a stern gaze on her. "I mean it—only remove those gloves when around someone who can help you, like Ian or Rose—but no one else. Is that clear?" Lenora nodded. "Excellent. I will contact Rose and ask her to come to town immediately."

"How are we to protect her against the entity becoming more physical, Walter?" Ian asked.

"Well, we can't know what she's up against until Phillip and Amelia come back with their research," Walter stated plainly.

"What if the entity…" Ian glanced worriedly at Lenora, "injures her, or worse, drags her in?"

Lenora was stunned. "I thought you said it wasn't a portal haunting."

Ian flicked his eyes at her and then back to Walter. "It isn't a portal haunting—but the entity is interested in keeping her in the spiritual realm."

"What does that mean?" Lenora shouted, now becoming agitated.

"Some entities," Walter explained, shooting a warning glance at Ian, "gain power from their anger, enabling them to capture the spirit of the living person and keep it. In light of that, you will need constant supervision until we can figure out how to keep you safe," Walter admitted.

Lenora wilted. "Well, that's just great."

"It would only be for a little while," Emily soothed. "It's better than the alternative, now, isn't it?"

Lenora nodded. "So? Do I follow my dad around all day?"

Tom shook his head. "I don't have paranormal abilities. It would have to be Ian, or Rose, I suspect."

"Yes, you're correct," Walter agreed. He glanced at Ian.

Ian shook his head. "I would love to be on constant protective duty," he issued a sly sidelong glance at Lenora that made her blush and Tom clear his throat in irritation. "But, I also have classes, papers to write…I can't be with her constantly."

"There is a way," Walter suggested, "that you could be with her without being…present."

Ian shook his head. "No, not him. It's not a good idea." He glanced at Lenora and exhaled, defeated. "Let me think about it." Ian nodded at the group and then left abruptly. Lenora felt crushed that Ian was hesitant about spending so much time with her.

Taking Ian's cue, Walter dismissed the CSP group.

Lenora and Tom walked home, each lost in the darkness of their own thoughts.

When they got home, they sat in the living room in utter silence. Occasionally, Lenora stole glances at Tom and noticed his furrowed brow.

"Dad?" Tom glanced at her—he appeared to be holding back tears. Lenora's heart lurched. She steeled herself, thinking about her former resolve to be strong. "Obviously neither one of us is taking this well, and I really don't think either one of us is going to sleep well tonight, so what do you suggest we do?"

"Well, we really need to wait for Phil and—"

"No," Lenora shook her head, "I mean tonight. What's the plan for the rest of the night?"

"Right," he swallowed hard and looked at his watch. "Well, it's almost three o'clock in the morning...I think we can agree that sleep is a moot point." He glanced at his daughter and smiled weakly. "You know what? I think we pull an all-nighter. What do you think?"

"We haven't done that for a long time," she smiled. Lenora recalled the last all-nighter they pulled, and it was when her mom was still alive. They decided to ring in the New Year proper, and pulled sleeping bags into the living room, popped corn, and watched movies all night. Lenora, of course, didn't last, but it was exciting nonetheless.

"No, and I think we're about due," Tom replied, his eyes shrouded in melancholy. "I'll get out the sleeping bags and movies, you pop the corn."

Tom had the sleeping bags spread out on the floor, a movie ready to go, when Lenora came in with the giant popcorn bowl. Her smile faded once she saw that Tom already had his pajamas on, a reminder that she needed hers. This meant she had to go in her room...alone.

Noticing her expression, Tom smiled. "Already thought of that." He pointed to the couch, where he had laid out a pair of pajamas, thick wooly socks, her favorite blanket, and even a new pair of gloves. She gaped. "I'm sorry for going through your personal space, but I thought it would…help."

"No, that's great, Dad! I was a little…scared…to go back into my room." She set the popcorn bowl down and then withdrew to the kitchen to change. Lenora slipped into her sleeping bag and propped her head on Tom's shoulder, and despite their pact to stay up all night, she quickly drifted into dizzying slumber.

The woman woke up with a gag in her mouth and her limbs strapped to the legs of a large settee. She looked around the room, confused for a bit, but then soon realized where she was. She turned her head and noticed **him** *in the chair next to her, asleep. Trying not to panic, she jostled her legs and hands to get free of the tethers. He left the room open, and if she could just get these straps loose, she could run out before he woke up.*

His snoring helped while she tried to wrestle one arm from the straps that he tied too loosely. Once she wiggled one arm free, she was able to loosen the strap enough to free her other arm and leg. She sat up to get her bearings. The room was now darkening as twilight drew near. She knew she needed to get out of there quickly. Standing up, she nearly stumbled, her legs stiff from being strapped in so long. She walked quietly past **him**, *whose snoring was long and steady, so she knew he was sleeping soundly. Hope filled her, propelled her toward the door.*

She tiptoed to the doorway and looked back in disbelief—what could have led him to drug her and tie her up like he did? She looked about the flat, trying to adjust her eyesight in the darkness. Her previous walk about the flat was now going to help in her endeavor to find the door. She felt her way along the wall until she came upon the table near the door—the one with the picture of Tuscany above it. She knew the door was near, so continued to feel against the wall until she found the doorknob. She gasped in quiet triumph and then turned the knob. It was locked from the inside!

She tried the door again, this time looking for the lock. She felt above the doorknob, but couldn't find it. Now panicking, she tried the doorknob again, thinking it was just difficult to turn, and then stopped. She strained to listen—she could no longer hear the snoring. She held her breath and stood perfectly still. Nothing stirred in the darkness, so she reached out for the doorknob again, feeling along the top for the lock, when she felt a warm breath on her neck.

"Going somewhere?"

She turned around and saw a dark figure standing there. She started to scream, when he placed a cloth over her mouth. Her struggle soon gave in to tiredness—her body grew limp. She tried fighting the blackness that was coming to her eyes, but it wouldn't stop, and she faded.

THIRTEEN

Lenora looked across the table at her dad's haggard face. His usually bright hazel eyes were dull and heavy, and his normally well-groomed hair was disheveled. She was startled at the new crop of white along his temples, which stood stark against his deep copper hair. Stubble lined his jawbone, and there were coffee stains on his shirt.

Her dad was a mess, and it was her fault. If she hadn't fallen asleep last night and had that hideous dream, Tom wouldn't have had to stay up with her, trying to calm her down. What got to her the most was the frightened expression on his face when he shook her awake. She never wanted to see that again.

"Dad?" Tom looked up wearily from the newspaper, black circles darkening his eyes. "I'm really sorry you lost sleep. Maybe we can figure something out so you don't have to stay up with me all the time."

Tom grinned and reached a hand across to her. "I don't mind—it's only temporary."

Lenora squeezed her eyes tightly, feeling wretched. "You can't keep losing sleep, Dad, you have classes to teach—"

"Well, not today," he interrupted, "it's Saturday." He smiled warmly, trying to cheer her. "We'll figure it out. Until then, don't you worry about your old man—I'll be just fine." He smiled optimistically and then resumed reading the newspaper while Lenora picked at the food on her plate.

Later that morning, Tom took Lenora to Market Square for a bit of browsing and then out to lunch. At one point in the afternoon, Lenora was able to get away from her dad and slipped into a drug store, where she purchased a mild sedative. She reasoned that the sedative could lull her mind and ward off the haunting enough so that she might just sleep; then, perhaps her dad could actually get some sleep as well. She felt so guilty and he looked so tired.

After lunch, Tom took Lenora up to his office.

"Do you have some work to do?" Lenora asked.

"No, actually, you do," Tom responded enigmatically.

"I do?"

Tom saw the confusion on Lenora's face and chuckled. "Yes, I have a fun project for you." He led her down a long hallway in the Psychology Department and then unlocked a room at the far end. She coughed as a moldy breeze wafted into the hall. She grimaced at Tom, who was covering his nose. "Yes, the air in here is quite stale—the room has been used as a junkyard of sorts for years, I've been told."

Lenora entered the enormous room. It was difficult to tell just how large the room was because it was piled high with various boxes, books, and junk piles. Windows at the far end of the room let in little light, the boxes were stacked so high. A long table situated in the center of the room was currently being used to store boxes, various stacks of books, and numerous files. The floor was riddled with paper waste and badly needed vacuuming. Book shelves were filled to their capacity, many shelves bowing from books being crammed in and doubled up.

"I just received permission from the department to use this for the CSP staff room," Tom explained. "The CSP group often meets at various locations around campus—we have no real place to meet regularly, and there's a desperate need for it." He glanced at Lenora and grinned. "That's where you come in."

"Me? How?" Lenora didn't like the sound of this.

"Your new job for the next couple of weeks is to clean this place out—going through and removing all the boxes, sorting through the junk piles, and finding a new place for the books."

Lenora sighed heavily. "Why me? This is such a…big job. Don't you want someone who knows psychology to go through all this stuff?"

"Not necessary," Tom replied, shaking his head. "None of this is really important. If you don't know what to do with something, ask Judith." Tom poked his overwhelmed daughter with his elbow. "When you're done cleaning, you also get full permission to decorate…" he eyed her, "tastefully and professionally, of course."

Lenora brightened—now it didn't seem so daunting, particularly since she got to decorate. "Paint? New furniture?"

Tom nodded. "Anything you want—within reason, of course, there is a budget," he reminded her.

"I can handle that," Lenora responded confidently.

"I know—that's why we all voted to have you do it," Tom beamed.

Lenora spent the better part of the following week sifting through boxes, hauling massive piles of books and donating them to local libraries, removing junk piles, and doing lots of cleaning. Judith lent a hand when she could, voicing her irritation at all the junk that was allowed to pile in the room. Lenora sniggered at the expletives that came from Judith—it was unexpected.

Lenora met most of the professors in the psychology department that week, as most peered in and often offered their help, which Lenora took willingly. She enjoyed meeting her dad's colleagues, and was fascinated at how many different personalities could fit together in one department.

Tom decided that sleeping in their apartment for the time being wasn't the best idea, so every night before she left, Judith set up three cots in Tom's office—one each for Lenora and Tom, and then another for a guest. Tom and Walter felt that there was safety in numbers, so the CSP team took turns staying with them at night. It was like an interminable slumber party to Lenora, so it was mostly fun for her.

Almost everyone from the CSP team came to stay with them— Emily, Tabitha, Phillip and Amelia, Maggie, Joe—everyone, except for Rose, who lived several miles away from Cambridge, and Ian, who seemed to fall off the face of the earth. He was nowhere to be seen, and never once stopped by to even say hello. Lenora was beginning to wonder what had happened to him. Even Tom was thoroughly confused, but less concerned than his daughter, who looked for Ian every day with great expectation and ended the day disheartened.

Other than the incredible disappointment of missing Ian, Lenora felt that the best part of the arrangement was that the entity left her alone that week, much as Walter and Tom had predicted. She slept well—mostly from sheer exhaustion—and felt energized. Even Tom seemed much better. But, she knew they couldn't do that forever—she had to go home some time. And, they did occasionally go home to refill their overnight bags, wash clothes, or simply hang out during the day. But, they never stayed too long or too late, and Lenora was never left alone.

Over the weekend, Tom took Lenora to flea markets and yard sales to buy furniture for the conference room. Except for the long conference table, the rest of the furniture was too dilapidated to use and needed replacement. They purchased new chairs, a plush cream sofa with two matching high-backed wing chairs, book shelves, and small work station tables. They also got a microwave and a mini fridge, which she stocked full of soda and water.

While vacuuming the floors, she discovered unblemished, beautiful hardwood flooring, so ripped up the carpet and then polished the floor. The next two days was reserved for painting and redecorating—she had a deadline to have everything completed by Thursday, when they were hosting an open-house for the new CSP headquarters. The entire psychology department was to come, and of course, everyone from the CSP team.

Lenora's stomach knotted in nervous anticipation—this was the unveiling of her hard work, and the first open house she was throwing. Additionally, she knew that Ian didn't have class on Thursday evenings, so was nervously anticipating his attendance; it had been nearly two weeks since she had seen or heard from him.

Thursday night arrived, and Lenora couldn't be more excited. The conference room looked clean and fresh, various appetizers were spread out on the polished table, which was adorned with a bouquet of red painted daisies, and she borrowed Judith's records to have some jazz playing quietly in the background. Everything seemed perfect.

She was so excited to see Ian that she bought a new sundress of a soft butter yellow and had her hair done special.

Tabitha was the first to show and excitedly complemented her on the lovely décor (Lenora consulted her on the colors, so decorated in various shades of green to influence a restful energy, and blue for balance—per Tabitha's suggestion).

Emily was the next to arrive, who glanced about and nodded in appreciation. "You did good, girl," she commented while hugging Lenora. "Though, it's entirely too bright for my taste," she whispered, grinning. Lenora smiled and giggled.

Tom entered soon after, with a mesmerizingly beautiful woman in tow. She was tall, graceful, and sophisticated. She wore a stylish, grey tailored suit, a burgundy shell, and pearls hung luminous against her alabaster skin. A carefully manicured hand held a glass of deep red wine, which sparkled against the rich burgundy of her polished fingernails. Honey blonde hair cascaded silkily down her back and was pinned softly away from her face. She appeared absorbed in an intense conversation with Tom, who didn't return her concentrated gaze, but glanced uncomfortably around the room.

Tom spotted Lenora staring at them and waved her over. Lenora gingerly approached, feeling incredibly nervous. She nodded at Tom. "You wanted to see me?"

"Yes," Tom replied sternly. "I want to introduce you to Rose."

Rose nodded without smiling, her penetrating ice-blue eyes causing Lenora to blush self-consciously and look away. Rose chuckled softly at Lenora's awkwardness.

Unsure of what to do, Lenora began to excuse herself, but when she tried to pull away, Tom grabbed her arm.

"Don't be rude, Len." He frowned at his daughter and flashed an embarrassed glance at Rose.

"Oh, Tom, she's fine," Rose returned softly, turning to Lenora and smiling warmly. Lenora was taken aback by how warm the smile was, considering the cold gaze of her piercing eyes. "You're not interested in talking to us old folk anyway, are you?" She fixed her cold gaze on Lenora, who felt instant goose bumps forming on her arms.

"Well…I…I—" Lenora stammered. She felt flustered. Rose's stare was deep, penetrating, and it left Lenora feeling uncomfortable…as if Rose could infiltrate her mind and know her every thought.

"It's alright, Lenora," Rose uttered, placing a hand on Lenora's arm. Lenora couldn't get over how creamy and lustrous Rose's skin looked against her own imperfect, slightly freckled arm. "This must be overwhelming." Lenora nodded. "Well, I must commend you on your decorating sensibilities—the room looks lovely." Rose flashed an anemic smile and then returned her attention to Tom. "You were saying?"

"Oh," Tom faltered, surprised at the sudden turn in conversation. "Ah…oh, yes…I was talking about the paper I presented at the parapsychologist convention…"

Lenora took this as her cue to inch quietly away from Tom and Rose and work her way toward the door to see if Ian was coming.

Before she was able to peer out the door, Phillip and Amelia entered—the former offering his subdued comments about Lenora's efforts, and the latter, her enthusiastic applause for a job well-done. Maggie and Joe soon followed, each seeming equally pleased, as did the rest of the department, who sporadically filed in.

The only person missing was Ian, and every time someone moved by the door, Lenora strained to see if it was Ian, only to slump in disappointment. Where was he? Despite the success of the night and the festive environment, Lenora found that without Ian there, she just couldn't enjoy it completely.

Noticing Lenora's disheartened spirits, Tabitha sidled in beside her. "Lovely party, Lenora—it's quite the success!"

"Thanks," Lenora responded with an unconvincing smile.

"The colors are perfectly complimentary," Tabitha remarked, "and the music…well, it's fabulous. Wonderful job, my dear!"

Lenora nodded and gave her an appreciative look. "Thanks, Tabitha. Coming from you, it's a real compliment—I worked really hard at this." The disappointment in her tone was apparent.

"Yet, not everyone is here to laud your success," Tabitha astutely observed. She eyed Lenora, who knew she couldn't hide her feelings from Tabitha. "No one knows where he is," she confided, "but my guess is that he is off trying to solve your case."

Lenora brightened somewhat and then nodded. "I'm sure…it would just—" she couldn't finish, a lump forming in her throat.

"It would have been nice for him to show," Tabitha finished. "Well, you'll just have to give him a private showing later!" Tabitha grinned and winked at Lenora.

Color immediately rose to Lenora's cheeks and she smiled despite herself. "Tabitha, you're bad!"

"Naughty, naughty me," Tabitha sang as she walked away, giving Lenora one last playful glance.

Lenora grinned as she watched Tabitha flit about, chatting with everyone—her infectious laughter ringing through the room.

"Where's party boy?" someone asked from behind Lenora.

Lenora turned to see Emily standing next to her, scrutinizing the crowd. "I don't know," she replied, trying not to sound as disappointed as she felt.

"Well, I'm shocked he's not here—he's always one for a party."

"Maybe this isn't his type of party," Lenora offered.

Emily chuckled. "Oh darling, every party is his type. Just like every girl is his type." She rolled her eyes and popped an appetizer in her mouth. "What chaps my hide is that he left you in the lurch," she said with her mouth full, shaking her head. "He's supposed to be your mentor—that means that he doesn't leave you." The tone in her voice betrayed excessive disapproval.

"You don't like Ian, do you?" Lenora observed, beginning to feel defensive.

Emily's eyebrows raised in surprise. "Of course I like him—he's a hell of a guy…when he's around. He'll do anything for anyone, he's highly intelligent and talented, and a great friend. But he's undependable." She gave Lenora a sidelong glance. "And…a playboy."

"A playboy?" Lenora asked anxiously. The thought of Ian with another girl made her stomach twist in a knot.

"Yes. He dates a different woman every week, it seems," Emily scoffed. "We all refer to them as Ian's flavor of the week."

"Did…you…ever date Ian?" Lenora was afraid of the answer.

"Oh, God no!" Emily stated emphatically, laughing and choking on her drink. "I'm thirty-six, Lenora. He's way too young for me— chronologically *and* mentally. His mental age is more like fifteen," she murmured. "Besides, he's not my type."

"Who's *your* type?" Lenora asked, now intrigued at what kind of man piqued Emily's interest.

"I like them intellectual, dark, brooding, unavailable…emotionally, that is. I find marriage—relationships—boring and an unnecessary waste of time and energy. I just want to enjoy someone's company without all the baggage a relationship brings." She flashed a tight smile and then put a hand on Lenora's arm, her expression turning serious. "Don't allow him to break your heart." She patted Lenora's arm and walked off, helping herself to another handful of pretzels.

Lenora sighed heavily and looked around the empty room—the night just wasn't what she had hoped. She cleaned up the post-party mess, unaided since her dad was meeting with Rose and Emily in his office.

Someone sighed behind her.

Lenora whirled around excitedly. "Ian?" Nothing was there. She shook her head and continued tossing paper cups into the waste basket.

Now I'm imagining him. Excellent.

Hot breath swept her neck.

Lenora froze. The hair rose on her neck and arms. A bolt of fear shot through her and her limbs grew cold. She shivered and closed her eyes, hoping it was just her imagination.

"*Lenooooorah....*" it breathed. Warm, fetid vapors permeated her nostrils, making her stomach churn.

"Please, leave me alone," she whimpered.

"*You can't escape me, Lenora.*" The voice was now more apparent, clearer. An ominous laugh sounded behind her.

A brutal blow to her back sent Lenora lurching forward, causing her to lose balance and fall to the floor. In shock, she lay there, motionless, disoriented. After several seconds, she shook her head and tried to sit up, only to have something heavy strike her on the back of the head, forcing her to the ground.

She felt a slow, sharp pain on the back of her neck. Warm fluid coursed from the back of her neck to the front. She touched the liquid and surveyed her hand—it was blood. Her body trembled, a faint whine issued from her throat. She forced her body up off the ground and started a feeble run. But, she wasn't quick enough—something tripped her, sending her flying across the room, and she knocked her head against a table.

Lenora lay in a heap on the floor, sharp white flashes of pain in her head. She turned her body over, her eyesight hazy as she weaved in and out of consciousness. Her body felt heavy, weak, and she was unable to move. A jolt ran through her body as icy fingers touched her ankle, a sinewy finger slowly tracing the curve of her leg, stopping on her thigh.

Lenora started to cry, her body now shaking uncontrollably. Head bursting in pain, she tried raising herself and crawling away from its touch, but an invisible hand grabbed her, and she could feel an acute sting as a deep, jagged scratch formed on her thigh. She watched as the scratches became letters: B, then A, then R...

"Leave me alone!" she screamed, kicking her legs into the void. She managed to scramble to her feet, and despite the dizziness, ran toward the door.

A sinister laugh rang from behind her. "You are mine!"

Lenora stopped, noticing now that the voice was distinct, deep, foreboding —near.

"LEAVE ME ALONE!" she shrieked, now in full panic. As she turned to run out of the room, a hand grabbed her wrist and held her. She struggled in the grip, only to feel another hand clamp icily around her arm, holding her secure. The entity pulled her away from the door. She fought, trying to wrench from its grip, but to no avail—she was fighting air.

Tom and Emily burst into the room—just in time to see Lenora hurled into mid-air, her head bashing into the wall, her body falling into a crumpled heap on the floor. As Lenora drifted in and out of consciousness, she heard Emily chanting in a strange language, throwing some sort of white powder into the air. Lenora moaned as prickly darkness enveloped her eyes and the room grew black.

White hot flashes of pain surged through her head as she tried to open her eyes. She heard the moan escaping her dry lips, but felt apart from her own body. Her eyes fluttered open, little white and grey spots floating in her line of sight—everything was blurry.

Once she regained focus, she saw Tom hovering above her, brows deeply creased in worry. "Are you okay, sweetheart?" Tom asked, eyes welling with tears.

Emily appeared beside her with a cool rag and some bandages. Lenora watched in silence as Emily tended to her wounds. She carefully lifted Lenora's skirt, surveying the gashes in her leg that spelled "B-A-R in giant scrawl. Emily and Tom exchanged glances.

"Well, you might not like it now, but it'll be good fun at the pub." Emily smirked, but when the amusement wasn't returned she shrugged. "You could always have a tattooist cover this with something pretty." Tom shot Emily a look of disapproval and she giggled.

This was the first time Lenora caught a close glimpse of Emily's eyes, which were a brilliant lime green. A silver amulet on Emily's neck resembled an iron cross with Celtic knot work connecting the four large arms, each adorned with a curious symbol at the end. Lenora squinted to make out the symbols, when Emily loudly cleared her throat.

"You know, sweetheart, it's not nice to stare."

How embarrassing.

Lenora felt the blood rushing to her cheeks. "I'm sorry, it's just that…" she hesitated, reaching for the right words – she didn't want to insult her. "…your necklace—it's cool….different."

"Ah," Emily said knowingly, "it's a Celtic cross. The four symbols on either end represent the four elements—air, earth, fire, water." Emily's eyes flashed toward Tom and then back at Lenora. "I'll explain that at some other time."

Since she was on a roll in the embarrassment department, she thought of asking about Emily's heavy brogue. "Are you from Ireland or Scotland?"

"Ireland," Emily responded with a proud smile. "How perceptive of you."

"Do you have any…abilities?"

"Yes, actually," Emily admitted, "I'm telepathic."

"What does that mean?" Lenora sat up, curious.

"Simplistically? I hear people's thoughts," Emily informed her.

"You can hear my thoughts?" Lenora instantly felt uncomfortable.

Emily chuckled. "Don't worry—I can turn it off when I wish… which is most of the time." She grinned and flashed Lenora an amused grin. "And, I keep private thoughts to myself," she whispered, giving her a knowing glance.

Lenora nodded, going over in her mind what she was thinking at the party.

"There," Emily said with finality, "you're all bandaged up." She rose, leaning in to meet Lenora's gaze. "I will always be here for you, if you need me." She smiled warmly and then sat in the chair next to Lenora.

"Can you tell us what happened here?" Tom asked, brushing the hair from Lenora's face while she explained what happened to her. Tom and Emily exchanged worried looks. "Could you *see* who it was?"

"No, but it's the same entity that's been haunting me at the apartment—that much I do know. His voice was…familiar."

"I need to call Ian, get his butt in here," Tom said in an irritated tone. He turned to Emily. "Can you stay with her so that I can try to find him?"

"Absolutely," Emily answered with a firm nod.

"Thanks," Tom muttered as he walked out of the room. Lenora could hear him faintly mutter "Where the hell is that little…" before he shut the door. She didn't hear the last word, but could guess at what it might be.

She turned to Emily. "So, what do you do at CSP?"

"I am an expert on the occult, or an occultist," Emily explained, smiling.

"The occult?" Lenora frowned and then shook her head in confusion.

"It's the study of the unseen, the unknown—hidden wisdom. It can involve magic, astrology, numerology, spiritualism, alchemy, the supernatural."

"And, you're an expert on it? I mean, you know how to do magic?"

"Well," Emily explained, smiling, "I'm an expert in as much as others deem me."

"I don't know what that means," Lenora answered honestly.

Emily laughed heartily. "It means that I dabble, but I'm not the best. I'm better at small spells, but need help with the bigger ones. I'm more book-smart than street-smart…I can 'talk the talk' but not necessarily 'walk the walk,' but for some reason, people think I know more than I do. Know what I mean?"

"You are being too modest, Emily." Tom interrupted as he walked back into the room. "Emily is the world's foremost expert on the occult. She graduated with a PhD in Psychology and a PhD in Religion, with a special focus on the occult—all before she turned 28. Since then, Emily has published six bestsellers on the occult, and she's world-renowned for her knowledge. I'm happy to have her as part of the team."

"You sound like you're making a pitch for a product," Emily remarked and then rolled her eyes.

"Well," Tom explained, "you are talented, and though you don't like talking about it, I certainly don't mind." He walked over to the fridge and grabbed a coke.

Emily immediately changed the subject. "Did you get Ian?"

"No, I can't find him. It's a total mystery—he's been a no-show all week, and I found out from his professors that he hasn't been in class either, which is entirely unlike him."

"He'll show up. He's probably at a pub, snogging with some tart." She smirked and then winked at Lenora, who was not amused. She looked up at the clock. "Hey, I've got to get going—I've a séance to attend at midnight."

Lenora giggled again and then looked at Emily, who was not smiling, but was frowning in confusion.

Oh, she's being serious.

"Sorry, I thought you were joking," Lenora said apologetically. "I'll learn...eventually."

"Don't worry, I'm used to it," Emily replied, and then looked at Tom. "That charm should last any time she's in this room. She's protected here, but nowhere else, so you will need to find a way to keep her safe until you've found Ian."

"Well," Tom replied, smiling at Lenora. "looks like we'll be camping out in here tonight rather than my office."

"Call me if you have problems," Emily said as she walked toward the door without looking in their direction. "Ta-ta," she murmured, waving nonchalantly as she walked out the door.

Lenora was sad to see her go. She thought it would be much more fun to go to the séance than to camp out in the Psychology Department...again.

FOURTEEN

Lenora stared up at the ceiling, unable to sleep. The night's events and her dad's snoring were keeping her up.

The white twinkle lights that she strung around the ceiling for the party were still lit, creating a soft amber glow. The lights had the appearance of stars, as if she and Tom were sleeping under a celestial canopy. She closed her eyes and tried to imagine that they were out camping under the stars, a soft, cool evening breeze blowing through the tall evergreens. But, no matter how serene the scene played in her mind, she still struggled for sleep.

She looked down at the bruises and scrapes that had formed on her arms and legs. A finger absentmindedly traced the letters that were scratched in her leg. A tear trickled down her cheek and she angrily swiped it away.

I don't get it. Why me? Why now? Dad and I were just trying to get our lives back in order.

She rolled over on her side, thoughts of her mom flooding her mind. She wanted her mom here, even if just for a moment…if only to ask her what to do. This entity, for some reason, chose her. And, now the only choice she had was to have her soul possessed by a vile entity or to die?

I don't want to die! I have so much more to do, so much to see! This isn't fair!

A heavy feeling pressed upon her chest, and the tears flowed more steadily. She buried her head in the pillow and cried softly, internally mourning the places she'd never see, the people she'd never meet, and the man she'd never fall in love with.

Then she thought of Ian—his handsome face, his wit, those stunning blue-grey eyes. Fresh tears streamed down her face at the thought that she'd never have the chance to tell him how she felt.

But then, why would he care? He hasn't been around at all. Where has he been the past couple of weeks? He should have been here—helping me!

Newly angry, Lenora sat up, dried her eyes, and looked around the room she worked so hard on. She thought of the people who had come here tonight—for her—and a new sense of encouragement washed over her. Walter said they would help her—she had no reason to think their plans couldn't work.

Since when, Lenora Kelley, have you let a boy ruin your life? Stop feeling sorry for yourself!

Lenora looked over at her dad, who was sound asleep, and smiled. She felt safer with her dad in the room, but still had the creeps. Leaning over the side of her cot, she picked up her book and book light. Sleep may elude her tonight, but she wasn't going to just lie there, wallowing in self-pity. She opened the book and flipped on the book light.

A door creaked…the sound of footsteps.

Chills ran up her spine; goose bumps rose on her arms and legs, and her heart beat furiously.

Oh please, no, not again. She trembled, clapping a hand over her mouth to stifle a cry.

Paralyzed with fear, Lenora couldn't move to wake Tom. What if it was nothing? What if it was her imagination? She didn't want to disturb her dad—he had already been through enough tonight.

Something approached the door; the knob wiggled. Lenora held her breath. Maybe it was the night cleaning staff.

This time, the door knob jiggled vigorously, followed by an audible grunt coming from the other side of the door. Lenora felt a lump in her throat, her limps growing numb. She was afraid to move.

"Bugger!" a familiar voice sounded outside the door.

Ian?

Lenora immediately got up and peered in the door's eyehole. It was Ian, messing around with a long, metal object. Lenora quickly opened the door, just as Ian moved to strike the door.

"*Ian!*" Lenora half whispered. "What are you *doing?*"

"Trying to get in," Ian replied plainly.

Lenora grimaced. Ian smelled like he had been drinking. She put a finger up to her lips and ushered him into the hall, away from the conference room, where her dad was still loudly snoring. Once they were a safe distance, she pinned him with an angry glare. "You could have called—you scared me to death!"

Ian puckered his lips in a pout. "S-sorry…I loss my phooone." He wavered to the side and then belched wetly.

"Ugh." Lenora waved a hand in front of her nose. "Have you been *drinking?*"

Ian snickered and pinched his thumb and forefinger together. "Juss a little," he slurred, smiling. Then, he turned serious, "I'm not pissed, just happy." He started laughing and then leaned sideways, nearly toppling over.

Lenora exhaled, thoroughly irritated. She tugged at Ian's sleeve. "Come on." She pulled Ian into Tom's office and locked the door. Ian laughed and she poked him hard and put her finger to her lips. "Quiet! My dad is trying to sleep!"

Ian tiptoed animatedly to the desk and then pointed at the extra cot that sat in the corner. "Wha's that? Your dad sleeping in the office now?"

"We've been sleeping here a while now," she whispered, annoyed.

"What for?" Ian asked loudly.

Lenora shushed him again. "I'm going to make you a pot of coffee." She looked at him sternly. "You will stay here…and be *quiet.* Got it?" she hissed. Ian saluted her and sniggered. Lenora rolled her eyes and quickly left to make the coffee. When she returned, he was lounging on the cot, singing some sort of drinking song.

She poured a cup for both of them, handed a cup to Ian, and then took a seat in her dad's office chair. Ian sat up and glanced at her with a smirk. He patted the space on the cot next to him and gave her a sly look.

Lenora sighed, got up, and stood in front of him, looking cross. "Just what do you think you're doing? You disappear for two weeks, with not even a clue as to where you're going. You miss the party, and then you just show up, unannounced? What's wrong with you?"

Ian's face turned serious. "Well, I went to talk to….wait," he tilted his head in curiosity, "did you say party?"

"Yes," she snapped, "we had a party to celebrate the new CSP room tonight. I worked hard to plan it, and you didn't even show."

"Well," Ian said with exaggerated concern, "I would have, if I had known. I'm sorry you went through all the trouble to plan the party and I didn't show." He looked at her and smiled. "Was it a success?"

"Yes, it was, until…" she hesitated, not wanting to tell him about what happened to her. She wasn't sure he'd remember in the morning.

"Until what?" He asked.

"I don't know if I want to tell you," she said.

"You can tell me anything – you can trust me," Ian responded.

"I know I can *trust* you, it's just that you're drunk, Ian. I really don't want to repeat it."

"Oh, well, I assure you that I'm not drunk—just happy," he hiccupped and then giggled.

"Ugh." Lenora rolled her eyes in disbelief, sat on the opposite side of the cot, and looked out the window. She crossed her arms to ward off the cold and shivered. Ian slid over to her side of the cot and put his coat around her shoulders.

"Lenora, please tell me what happened," Ian begged.

She looked over at him. His expression was earnest. "Fine. But if you forget, I'm not repeating it, and I will never let you in when you're drunk again." She took a deep breath and then made a face. "Ah, you *stink!*"

Ian smelled himself and then smiled. "It's the pub, not me. Tell your story!"

Lenora nodded and explained what happened over the past couple of nights, ending with tonight's horror show. While she related her story, Ian paced the room agitatedly. The moonlight shone so brightly in the room that it barely needed a light—she could see the look of confusion on his face—he looked disoriented.

*He's too drunk—he'll never comprehend...or remember **any** of this*, she thought, shaking her head.

Ian walked over to the desk and studied the pictures Tom had on display. He chose the one of thirteen-year-old Lenora, her best friend Kristine, and her parents at the beach—one of their happier moments.

He pointed at the picture. "Is this you?"

She walked over and took the picture from him. "No, that's my best friend Kristine from back home. The homely one here," she pointed to her image, "is me." She replaced the picture on the desk.

"Oh. Sorry. She sort of looks like you."

"Hardly," Lenora said, frowning, "she has short black hair. I have long, auburn hair. Her eyes are a nice chocolate brown, mine are..."

"A beautiful shade of emerald green," Ian finished, a faraway look on his face. He touched her cheek tenderly, gazed intently into her eyes, and then walked back over to the cot. He unfolded a blanket, pulled himself close to the wall, grabbed a pillow, and propped his head up. Then, he opened the covers next to him and patted the cot. "You need to try to sleep now."

Lenora felt dizzy, like she was going to pass out. She walked over to the cot and climbed in. Ian situated a pillow on his chest and leaned her into him. Lenora laid her head on the pillow and Ian covered her up and then caressed her hair. "Go to sleep now, my fair and radiant maiden named Lenora."

"Did you even hear a word I just said?" She waited for a response, but all she got was the sound of his head thumping softly against the wall, and then light snoring.

She shook her head in disbelief. It was nearly an hour before she finally drifted....in Ian's arms.

Lenora stood near the edge of the water, looking at the dark pier that loomed before her. The air was thick, murky, the waves breaking along the shore nearby. She strained her eyes, but couldn't see the water. A strong urge compelled her to walk onto the pier—the fog growing ever more dense.

A patch of fog cleared in the distance. A figure in black appeared. A long black cloak shrouded his figure, while black, flowing hair framed a pale, strikingly handsome face.

He smiled lovingly at her. "Hello, Lenora."

She started, not expecting him to know her name. She felt unafraid—a soothing calm enveloped her as she walked toward the man, who stood at the end of the pier, arms outstretched.

"I have waited for you all my life," he said. His voice was enticing, calming.

Inexplicably drawn, she walked toward him, feeling an overwhelming need to be near him. She held her arms out and quickened her pace—she must get to him! He smiled, beckoning to her, calling her name.

"Lenora!"

"I'm coming, my love!" she shouted, running faster.

However, no matter how quickly she ran, it seemed as if the pier grew in length—the distance between them growing. He was getting further and further away. His arms lowered and the smile faltered. Head hung in despair, he turned from her, waved a sad goodbye, and then disappeared into the mist.

"No!" she shouted, running toward him, the edge of the pier coming quickly. She lost balance and fell, grabbing the edge just at the last minute. She held on for dear life, until her dad's face appeared above her.

"Lenora! Grab my hand!"

She tried to grab his hand, but her fingers were slick from the sea water roiling beneath her. She tried again, but this time, her grasp failed and sent her careening into the cold sea.

The last thing she heard before disappearing into the briny darkness was her father's desperate call. "Lenora!"

FIFTEEN

"Lenora! What the *hell* is going on here?"

Lenora opened her eyes, feeling groggy and remote. Her dad stood in the doorway, visibly angry. She looked around, confused for a moment, forgetting where she was. Her dream's residue still lingered, and in her mind, she was still standing in the mist. Movement near her head released her from the stupor, and she looked up to see Ian.

Oh. Crap.

"Good morning, Dad," she said sleepily.

Tom grunted, walked over to the cot, and shook Ian's foot. "Get up, Ian."

Ian began to stir. "Oh, hi Dr. Kelley."

"Don't 'hi Dr. Kelley' me, Ian. What the hell are you doing here…in *my* office…with my *daughter*?"

Lenora interrupted immediately, explaining what happened the previous night to her father, leaving out the part about Ian being drunk. Tom glared at Ian, his face becoming redder by the minute. Lenora sat up and touched her dad's hand. "I told Ian what happened…he stayed only to help me sleep. That's *all*."

"Well, you need to get up now anyway," Tom responded, anger still in his voice. He stepped away from the cot, crossed his arms, and stared at Ian. Lenora got up and poked Ian in the side. He climbed out of the cot, and then stood up to stretch.

"Not the best night's sleep I've ever had," he said cheerfully.

Tom wasn't amused. "You need to get out of my office now."
He looked at his watch. "People start arriving for work in a couple
of hours." He nodded toward the door. Ian grinned and started
walking out, but then turned around and looked at Lenora with an
amused grin.

"Nice pajamas," he commented sarcastically. "What are those,
puppies?" Lenora looked down at her blue pajama bottoms, which
were dotted with puppies, and then flushed.

"Get out, Ian." Tom pointed toward the hallway and then watched
as Ian made his way down the hall toward the department kitchen.
Tom looked at his daughter. "Go get dressed. I have some things to
discuss with Ian, and then we can go have breakfast."

"Can Ian have breakfast with us, Dad?" Lenora asked gingerly.

Tom stared at his daughter, the room feeling heavy with tension.
"Yes, I suppose so," he sighed. He shook his head and closed the
door.

Lenora's heart pounded as she padded down to the conference
room to change. Nothing happened between her and Ian, but she
felt guilty nonetheless. She also felt utterly excited—the man of her
dreams just stayed overnight, holding her! She twirled around the
room and giggled softly.

"Nothing happened, Tom, really."

Lenora sat outside of Tom's office as he and Ian had a discussion. She could hear Ian explaining last night's events to her father.
Tom didn't bother closing the door, which Lenora took as his way
of telling her he wanted her to hear his grievances without having to
repeat them.

"I hear what you're saying, Ian, but you have to appreciate
how I feel as a father, walking in on some guy—who's much too
old for my daughter, by the way—sleeping with my daughter. It's
upsetting!"

Lenora winced—her dad made it sound like they were carrying
on a tawdry affair.

"I understand, Dr. Kelley," Ian explained, "but I was only here to protect your daughter, and you know that I'm the only one who can do it." He hesitated. "Besides, you're right, Lenora is far too young for me. She's just a girl—like a little sister to me—and all I want is to protect her."

Lenora withered. *Just a girl? A little sister? I'm only six years younger than him. I'll be eighteen in five months. And we're **not** related!* She felt the color rise in her cheeks—she felt like crying.

Her stomach growled. She rose from her chair, steeled herself, and walked into her dad's office. She folded her arms and frowned at the two men, who stared at each other—a silent tension enveloping the room. "Hey, can you two talk about this stuff later? I'm starving. Also, Dad, we need to eat, get to the apartment, shower and change. It's Friday, which means that you have class at nine." She looked up at the clock. "It's six-fifteen. If we hurry, we'll make it."

Tom paused in uncertainty and then nodded. "Shall we go, then?"

"I think I'll go home," Ian said.

"Don't you want breakfast?" Tom asked, betraying a pleased tone.

"I do, but not like this," he gestured to himself with a grimace. "I stink and look terrible. I want a shower and change." He looked over at Lenora as if he had something to say, but then checked himself. "Maybe I can catch up with you later today."

He got up from his seat and walked toward Lenora. "Bye, then. See you later?"

"Maybe…whatever," Lenora shrugged, trying to appear indifferent.

"Okay, then." Ian said slowly, perplexed. "Thanks, Dr. Kelley. See you later." He waved and then walked out of the office. They didn't see him the rest of the day, or that night.

The following morning, Lenora and Tom walked around Market Square. She loved going to the market on Saturdays—the fresh fruits and vegetables, fresh-cut flowers, and general festive atmosphere made her feel energetic...*normal.* Tom picked out some vegetables, and Lenora strolled about the booths, looking at the custom jewelry and munching on a fresh apple.

Distracted, she walked around one of the booths and crashed into someone. "Ow!" she shouted. Her head now seared with fresh, hot pain from ramming into someone's hard chest. She looked up and saw Ian, who held a bouquet of flowers.

"Fancy meeting you here!" He said cheerfully, and then extended the flowers out to her. "Here, these are for you."

"What are those for?" She asked, wincing from the pain, which just added to Thursday night's bumps and bruises.

"No reason, just because, I guess," he said, offering the flowers again.

"Thanks," she said, taking the flowers and smiling appreciatively.

"So, shopping for anything particular?" he asked, looking amused.

"I was just looking at jewelry," she responded.

"Be careful so you don't get taken in by a scam artist, my young friend," he offered.

"Okay, I will," Lenora replied sarcastically.

"Seriously," Ian retorted, "you're just the sort of person these people are looking for."

"These people?" Lenora asked, incredulous. "These are hard-working merchants, and I don't think they're out to get me." Irritated, Lenora took a bite of her apple and glanced around the market.

"Okay, okay," Ian replied defensively. "You're right—but there are some that will target you. They like to target the young and naïve. You're the perfect target." He paused, noting the annoyed look on her face. "I'm just telling you to watch out, that's all."

"Ugh! You can be so...annoying!" Lenora exclaimed in irritation. Maybe he was right, but this was the thousandth time he referred to her by her age—it was irritating...and disconcerting. The color rose in her cheeks.

"Testy!" Ian held out his hands in surrender and laughed.

"Why do you act like that?" Lenora asked, annoyed.

"Like what?"

"Like you know everything? Like I'm just some stupid kid that doesn't know anything?"

"Well," Ian mused, "because I *do* know everything." He laughed heartily. "And, since you *are* a kid," he touched the tip of her nose with his index finger, "it's my job as your newly-appointed big brother to teach you about the world." He looked at her and wagged a finger. "You are still young and naïve—and you could use some instruction from someone who knows better."

Aggravated, Lenora huffed loudly and pushed past him, throwing the flowers in a trash bin on her way by. She didn't feel like dealing with this...not today.

"Hey, wait!" Ian ran next to her and grabbed her shoulder. "What's the deal?"

"Nothing, except that you're a jerk," she replied angrily.

"Why am I a jerk?" Ian asked confused.

"Because..." He broke her heart a little...calling her a little girl... referring to himself as her brother. She thought it insulting that he put such little faith in her common sense.

"Because is not a reason, Lenora," Ian persisted, giving her a patronizing smile.

"Just...leave me alone," Lenora started to walk away, but Ian grabbed her arm.

"I can't—not until you tell me why you're acting this way," he said, this time with irritation in his voice.

Lenora looked down at her feet and sighed. *Because I totally love you and you treat me like a baby, that's why.* "Because, you think I'm 'too young' and 'just a little girl'–because you treat me like one. I'm not a little girl, Ian!"

Ian looked surprised, and then realization crossed his face. "You were eavesdropping on my conversation with your dad yesterday, weren't you?" he grinned.

"No, I wasn't *eavesdropping*," she lied. "The door *was* open, you know. And you were talking loudly."

"You *were* eavesdropping!" Ian exclaimed and then laughed. "You know, that's rude," he said mocking a serious tone.

"No, I *wasn't*," she insisted. "What you said hurt my feelings, Ian." She bowed her head, working hard against a frustrated cry.

Ian walked toward her and cupped her chin in his hand, turning her face toward his. "I'm sorry, Lenora, if I hurt your feelings," he said soberly. "I was trying to placate your dad. He thought I was taking advantage of his only daughter, and I was trying to reassure him, that's all." When she didn't reply, he continued. "Don't get me wrong, you are a little girl in some ways."

Lenora frowned and started to say something, but he put his finger up to her lips.

"What I was trying to say was, you are a little girl in ways that are wonderful—you're full of curiosity and vigor—you're adventurous. And, you take things personally and jump to conclusions too quickly." He smiled at her knowingly.

Lenora's shoulders slumped. She knew he was right…sort of.

"However," Ian reassured her, "you are on your way to becoming a fine young lady." He bowed, smiled at her, and then walked toward the trash bin, recovering the flowers she threw. "Think of this as my apology for being an arse."

She took the flowers. "Thank you," she whispered, feeling stupid. Ian was a great guy, and here she was, acting like a total moron.

Ian offered his arm and she took it, smiling weakly. "Now," he said, with a sly smile and a chuckle, "let's go see if we can find you some pajama bottoms with kitties on them!"

SIXTEEN

enora busied herself in the kitchen, chopping the fresh veggies they picked up at the market. She smiled, thinking how nice it was being back in their apartment, even if it was only during the day.

It seemed like a normal Saturday afternoon. Tom was watching cricket on TV—he didn't know a thing about it, but a concentrated frown showed his determination to comprehend it. Lenora shook her head and chuckled.

After Lenora had put dinner in the oven to bake, she flopped down on the couch next to Tom and stared at the TV. She wasn't interested in watching the game, but was satisfied just sitting next to her dad, letting her mind wander eventually to her afternoon with Ian.

Ian.

It surprised Lenora how quickly he came to mind. But, she was basking in the glow of a lovely afternoon with him. After following Lenora and Tom around the market, Ian surprised her with a casual stroll around Cambridge, and then a leisurely punt through the backs. Lenora closed her eyes and breathed in deeply. She could almost feel the cool breeze as it blew her hair, and see Ian's hand dragging through the water as they relaxed on the boat. Occasionally, Ian shared what he knew about the buildings' architecture and history, which she found absolutely fascinating.

Lenora was jolted by a knock at the door. She raised her head and looked at her dad. "Are we expecting company?"

"Yes," Tom answered, "I invited someone over for supper. I hope that's okay with you."

"Sure," Lenora responded, somewhat confused, yet excited about having company—it was a rare occurrence.

Tom tousled her hair "Such the little entertainer." He got up and let the mysterious guest in. Lenora could hear two men talking. Two guests! She got up off the couch and checked herself in the mirror above the fireplace. Her hair was messy, and her cheeks were rosy from too much sun, but otherwise, presentable. She guessed.

She walked toward the kitchen and caught her dad coming around the corner with two bottles of wine. "Can you chill these, please?"

Lenora placed the bottles in the refrigerator, but not before noticing that both were fully-leaded. No wine for her. She rolled her eyes and shut the door, and was shocked to see Walter and Ian, smiling broadly at her.

"I originally only invited Walter," Tom explained, "but after Ian's generosity with you today, I thought we could treat him to a nice dinner as well." The look on his face betrayed a bit of annoyance.

Lenora smiled. "That's fine. I made enough for an army."

"Well, I could eat like one, I'm famished," Ian announced.

Lenora immediately pulled together an appetizer plate and then carried it into the living room, where the three men were watching cricket. "Here," she placed the tray on the table, "dinner won't be ready for another forty-five minutes–this is so you aren't too hungry." She looked over at Ian, who immediately dove into the appetizers.

"Thanks, Lenora," he said enthusiastically through cracker crumbs.

Lenora sat down in a chair opposite Ian and watched him devour most of the appetizer tray. "Geez, Ian, you should really share."

Ian stopped, mid bite, and looked at everyone. "Sorry about that. Cracker, anyone?" he held up a cracker and looked apologetically around the room.

Walter and Tom both indicated they had quite enough. Ian shrugged his shoulders and kept snacking. Lenora sat down next to Ian, pushing him over playfully. Just as he was about to throw a cracker in his mouth, she grabbed it and threw it into hers instead. She smirked at him as she ate his intended cracker.

He smiled and pushed her back. "You know, it's not nice to take food from the hungry."

"I doubt that you're ever hungry," Tom huffed.

After enjoying a good dinner and conversation, everyone went back into the living room. Lenora served coffee and the chocolate cake that Walter had brought.

"Lenora, why don't you come in and sit down. There's something that Ian and I would like to discuss with you two," Walter said. Lenora obeyed and sat down on the couch next to Ian. "Go ahead," Walter nodded at Ian, "tell them what you told me the other day."

Ian nodded. "Okay." He turned to face Lenora and Tom and cleared his throat. "This isn't going to be pleasant, so if you could just refrain from asking any questions until I'm finished, I would be greatly obliged."

Lenora stiffened. Chills ran down her arms as nervous energy worked through her. She was nervous to hear what Ian had to say, though she didn't know why.

"Well," Ian began, "I did a lot of thinking after the emergency CSP meeting following Lenora's incident at Tabitha's. That incident, combined with the trance in the dungeon—"

"The *dungeon?*" Tom asked, looking confused.

"Oh, that's what Lenora calls that little office you situated for her in the basement." Ian grinned at Lenora, who could feel the color rise to her cheeks.

She glanced at her dad, who didn't look amused. "Well, it's dark...and dank...and—"

"Well, it's sort of dodgy, really," Ian finished for Lenora and then waved his hand dismissively. "So, the incident at Tabitha's, the trance in the dungeon, all her dreams and physical interactions with entities were weighing heavily on my mind. They also triggered a memory. I had this nagging feeling that I needed to revisit the dungeon," he gave Tom a sidelong glance. "I looked through the files that Lenora and I worked on together until I found the one that caused her to go into the trance."

Ian dug through his satchel and drew out a folder. "Lenora, does this name look familiar to you?"

Lenora took the folder and opened it, gasping. "Bartholomew Booth? That's the name—"

"Yeah, it's the name that was scratched on the bench at Tabitha's. I think this is the name of your entity." Ian paused and drew in a deep breath, focusing now on Tom. "I've been missing the past couple of weeks because I've been neck deep in research. Now, I *know* I could have given this to Phil and Amelia, but this is…" his eyes flitted toward Lenora. "Personal."

Lenora smiled, thrilled that Ian used the word "personal" in reference to her. She glanced at him and noticed that his hands were shaking. "Are you cold, Ian?"

"No," he answered, a notable change in his tone. "I'm terrified, Len." He drew in another breath and turned to Tom. "I've discovered terrible things about this entity—about his human life—and I don't think Lenora's safe…at all. I took the file to a friend of mine, who has been a medium for over forty years, and when I told him all that's happened, he said to remove Lenora from the apartment immediately."

"Yes, but we've done that, Ian, and it appears to be following her," Tom offered. "Did you tell your friend that?"

"Yes," Ian replied, noting Tom's tone. "You can trust this friend of mine—he's been a mentor for most of my life. Without him, I'd be…" he paused, melancholy clouding his eyes. "Well, let's just say he helped me a lot."

"Who is this man?" Walter asked, looking intrigued.

"I'd rather keep that to myself, if you please," Ian responded.

THE SEVENTH SOUL

"But, if he's helped you, then he could be of help to us," Walter suggested.

"I understand, but he doesn't want to be known," Ian replied, his hands tensing. "Can we move on please?" Walter nodded, brows furrowed. "Thank you. As I was saying, it was highly recommended that you choose a new place to live that Lenora's never been. My mentor explained that Lenora leaves her energy everywhere she goes. The entity is connected to her; therefore, her energy invites him in."

"So, no matter where I go, it can follow me?" Lenora felt the fear coursing through her body. She shivered.

"Yes," Ian replied quietly. "But, it can't go where there's protection. First thing, you need to find a place to stay for now. Then, have Emily place her protection spell on the temporary residence—*before* you move in."

"Emily placed a protection spell on the conference room already, but after Lenora had already been there. So, what does that mean— will the spell not work there, then?" Tom sounded as perplexed as he looked.

"The spell will work," Ian responded with a nod, "but only to a certain extent. The entity has already made contact with her in the conference room, which means it can still get to her there." Lenora's chest hitched as she started to panic. Ian knelt in front of her, taking her hands in his. "But, it can only do non-harmful things—like talk to you, appear to you in dreams, or scratch its name in the furniture. Emily's spell protects you from harm—the entity cannot breathe on, touch, or cause you any *physical* harm."

"Why doesn't that make me feel any better?" Lenora's panic attack was subdued, but she still felt short of breath.

Ian laughed softly. "Because you want it to go away completely."

"I'm tired of it! I don't want it to talk to me. I don't want to dream about it—I don't even want it to write on the walls!" Hot tears coursed down her cheeks.

137

"Rose and I will teach you how to block the sound of the entity's voice. We can't do anything about the writing…maybe not even the dreams…but the voices we can."

"When?"

"As soon as we can set it up with Rose," Tom answered. "I'll contact her tomorrow morning right away."

"But, what am I to do until then? I need to know how to block it now!"

Ian nodded. "While I'm here, the entity won't bother you—it can sense my strong energy…that I'm protecting you…and it will stay away. And, I've someone else to look after you when I'm not around." He pursed his lips, pausing. "Emily called me and we had a long talk. She and I both agreed that it would be best if I sent Thaddeus to look after you. Walter was right—he is the best option for your protection right now, Len."

"Thaddeus?" both Tom and Lenora said simultaneously. Tom glanced at Lenora and then spoke for both of them. "*Who* is Thaddeus?"

Ian sighed, sat into a chair, and then looked at them thoughtfully. "Thaddeus is my little brother."

"Your little broth…" Lenora began, "but, I didn't know you had…"

"Of course you didn't. He's been dead for eight years."

"*What?* Dead?" Lenora felt like she was going to faint.

"He died when he was twelve–I was fifteen and wasn't there when he died." Ian's expression turned to grief. "We were best buds—me and Thad—and we usually went everywhere together. But, I was getting to an age when hanging around your little brother wasn't considered 'cool.' One night, I went out with my friends and he followed. Even though he kept a good distance, my friends started to bug me about him, so I told him to leave—in not such nice terms. He left, and that was the last time I saw him alive. If I hadn't…" Ian stopped talking and looked around his shoulder as if he heard a noise.

Lenora turned her head, hearing a faint whisper. "I heard that," Lenora said, almost fearfully. "That voice…it said that it wasn't your fault."

Ian looked up at Lenora, startled. "You heard that?"

Lenora nodded. "Yes, but barely. It was faint, but I heard it clear as a bell."

"That was Thaddeus you heard. He always says that it wasn't my fault…that he died. He says that he was destined to die that night, whether I was with him or not."

"Do you believe that?" asked Lenora.

"I don't know," Ian shook his head sadly. "All I know is that he was alone, and I have never been able to forgive myself for that."

"Is that why he's still here with you," Lenora asked, "because you carry this guilt and he is unable to cross over because of that?"

"You're so perceptive," Ian said, chuckling softly. "But no, he stuck around because he wanted to. He said he will be with me, by my side, for the rest of my life—as my protector."

"That's nice….I think. But a dead person following you around is a little creepy, if you ask me," Lenora said, still feeling a bit frightened.

Ian laughed. "Yes, I know. That's why I don't go around telling everyone. Well, one reason, anyway. My girlfriends would be appalled if they knew…"

Lenora laughed and then stopped, clapping a hand over her mouth. "I'm sorry," she uttered apologetically.

Tom frowned at his daughter. "What are you sorry for?"

"Thaddeus just said something funny about one of Ian's girl-friends," Lenora said, snickering. She smirked at Ian, who shot Lenora a warning glance.

"Oh." Tom said, appearing skeptical. "So," he addressed Ian, "what does it mean, then, when you say that you sent Thaddeus to watch over Lenora?"

"I asked Thad to come to your apartment and look after Lenora—to make sure nothing bad happened. And, if it did, to come to me immediately so that I could help."

"How does he communicate with you? How can he get to you on time?" Tom still sounded utterly confused.

"Well, he's a spirit, isn't he?" Ian grinned sarcastically. "He can appear in one place and then another in no time."

"So, he was with me these past two weeks?" Lenora asked sheepishly, and then heard a faint chuckle from behind Ian. Realization dawned on her face, and she felt instantly embarrassed. "Oh! That little....did you watch me undress?" Lenora said through clenched teeth, glancing angrily at the space behind Ian. "If I could see you, I would..."

"You would *what?*" Ian asked, amused. "He's already dead, what are you going to do to him?" He shook his head. "I told him to watch strictly when you were decent, and not to invade your privacy. As far as I know, he obeyed."

Lenora didn't believe him, particularly after the whispered laughter increased. She crossed her arms and huffed. "Right. Well, I don't think he listened to you." Louder laughter came from behind Ian. Lenora pursed her lips and glanced at Ian, mortified.

Tom got up and raked a hand through his hair. "Okay, this is a little much for me to take in right now." He looked over at Ian. "First, you tell me that you sent your dead brother's spirit to watch after my daughter. Then, my daughter can hear him. This is a little much—even for me—right now." He walked over to the cupboard and took out a bottle, pouring himself a stronger drink.

Ian got up, poured himself a glass of the amber liquid, and then downed it. "I know, but you better get used to it. Your daughter's not only a retro-cog, she has clairaudience capabilities. A real powerhouse, if you ask me."

"What?" Lenora asked, confused. "What are you talking about, Ian?"

Ian ignored her. "You knew she had abilities, Tom—you've known for some time."

Tom nodded. "I just didn't know what we were facing until now."

"Well, you will...if you let Rose talk to her."

Tom shook his head. "No. I don't think she's ready."

"Dr. Kelley, you came here to learn about her abilities—it's time we learn. It's time *she* learns."

"I know!" Tom's raised voice betrayed his growing frustration, which put a halt to the conversation.

Walter slapped his leg and rose from his chair. "Well! Time is getting away from us here." He turned to Tom. "Since your daughter made us such a lovely meal, I think it only fitting that we do the dishes. Tom?" Tom nodded and rose to follow, Ian in tow. Walter stopped Ian. "No, not you—you can stay with our girl and keep her company."

Ian and Lenora engaged in small talk while they waited for Walter and Tom to finish the dishes. Walter said his goodbyes, and then Ian stayed behind to escort Tom and Lenora back to the psychology department and its accommodating conference room.

Lenora got situated on her cot in the conference room and then reflected on the evening. "What's a 'retro-cog'?" Lenora finally asked Tom, who had just closed the book he was reading.

"It's short for retro-cognition."

"Oh, what Mrs. K thought I had? Do I have it…whatever it is? And, what about that Claire-something-or-other?" Lenora asked, propping herself up.

"Can we talk about this in the morning?" Tom asked, yawning.

"Well, sure, but I'd really like to know."

"I know, but I'm exhausted. We need to get some rest, okay?"

Lenora reluctantly agreed and leaned back on her cot. It was late, and Ian was already snoring on his cot on the other side of her. On the way back to the university, Ian confessed that he thought he should stay with them until they got everything cleared up–until the entity stopped bothering Lenora. Tom agreed–much quicker than Lenora had anticipated. However, she thought that might have had more to do with the fact that the spirit of a dead boy was lurking about his daughter's personal space.

Lenora glanced about the dimly-lit room, squinting for a chance to see Thaddeus, but came up with nothing. "Are you there, Thaddeus?" she whispered.

Lenora waited for an answer, surveying the darkened room. When no answer came, she opened her book and turned on the book light. She took a sip of water and began to read, instantly absorbed in her novel's dark world. Suddenly, the book cover slammed down on her fingers. She held back a squeal and nearly dropped her glass.

Get it together, Lenora—you just have the willies because of tonight's conversation and your stupid book.

She opened the book again and set her glass down on the floor beside her. This time, though the book stayed open, her glass started to slide across the floor below her—on its own. The hair on the back of her neck stood up; chills ran down her spine. She froze.

Then she heard a giggle. Thaddeus.

She looked toward the sound. "Thaddeus, stop that," she demanded quietly. She waited for a reply, but when one didn't come, resumed reading. Before she read a second word, the book slammed shut again. This time, she didn't scream, but became agitated.

"Very funny, Thaddeus. Now, please, let me read!"

"Sorry," a soft whispery voice apologized.

"Don't apologize," she said, "just know when to tease. This is not the time—and that's just the kind of thing the entity has been doing to me, by the way." She sat there for a minute, as if she expected some sort of response. "Thaddeus?" she whispered.

"Yes," a soft answer came.

"Thanks."

"Welcome," a murmured reply returned.

Lenora opened her mouth to say something else, but she heard a muffled grumble to her right. Tom was looking at her with a mixture of confusion and concern.

She smiled at him reassuringly. "It'll be okay, Dad. At least I have someone...something... looking after me when you're not able to."

"I know," Tom replied hesitantly, "this is just a bit much, that's all."

"But this was the hand we were dealt, right?" She asked, using one of his frequent adages.

He half-smiled, eyes tired and sunken. "Yes, it is. Good night, Len."

"G'night, dad," Lenora responded. She closed her book, turned off the book light, and instantly succumbed to darkness.

His preparations took little time, and when the day arrived, he could barely concentrate on his work. The time ticked by slowly, as he looked at the clock every five minutes. The wait was nerve-wracking. Finally, when six o'clock came, he threw on his coat and nearly ran home. He sat at his dinner table and ate a bowl of hot broth and a piece of stale bread—he didn't want to get too full. Then, he saturated a cloth with chloroform and put the sleeping draught in the syringe.

He took a carriage toward her new residence; there was no sense for him to be out of breath when he arrived. He needed all the strength he could get—this girl was strong, but a challenge he was looking forward to taking. The carriage dropped him off three blocks away to avoid suspicion, though he doubted there would be any; most had already retired for the evening, so the streets were quiet.

He walked around to the back of the house and watched as the girl...his girl...cleaned the dinner plates and swept the kitchen. She made quick work of it, her body working effortlessly at her tasks. He admired the sinewy muscles in her arms and lean athletic build. She had her hair swept up away from her face; he preferred it long and loose, her coppery curls spiraling down her back. It was sensual....lovely...like glowing embers over creamy silk.

Once she had finished, he knew the time had come. Soon, she would open the back door and throw out the trash—that was when he would grab her. He knew no one would hear since the family usually retired early and their bedrooms were at the opposite end of the house. The house was the last on the corner, and the nearest neighbor was nearly an entire house length away. He knew there was little risk.

The back door creaked open and he could see her silhouette in the doorway. He stepped back into the shadow so she couldn't see him. She walked over to the canister, threw in today's trash, and then closed the lid. She never saw him coming.

Darkness fell upon her...

The image drifted into the darkness as Lenora felt her body spiraling into a deep, cavernous hole. Her limbs moved in slow motion though she tried desperately to grasp for any foothold. After endlessly falling, she finally landed, bouncing onto the soft ground as if it were covered in miles of down. Darkness enveloped her, as she tried to discern where she was. She opened her mouth to scream, but no sound came forth. Suddenly, the ground began to quake and she reached out, hoping to find something to break her fall. She grabbed hold, but the ground continued to quake...she lost her foothold and began another dizzying descent.

SEVENTEEN

"**W**akey, wakey!" Ian exclaimed in a loud whisper, violently shaking her cot.

Lenora opened her eyes. Ian hovered above her, wildly grinning. Realizing she was just coming out of another dream, she noticed that her arms were outstretched, hands tightly grasping Ian's shirt. She instantly let go and then looked at the clock. It was six-thirty in the morning. Lenora groaned and then mumbled an expletive in Ian's general direction, which he found intensely amusing.

"Ian, leave me alone! It's Sunday—I get to sleep in!"

"Not today!" Ian said, too cheerfully, pulling the covers off her head.

"Why not?" Lenora pulled the covers back over her head.

"Because," he whispered, peering over the top of the covers, "I need breakfast, and you're coming with me to get it."

"No," Lenora grumbled, "let's wait until Dad wakes up." She opened her eyes enough to see that Tom was still fast asleep—snoring loudly.

Ian rose from the cot, threw the covers off of Lenora, and then lifted her out of bed. "Come on, it's time to get up!" He looked at Lenora's grumpy face and messy hair and laughed.

"Agh! Don't laugh at me!" Lenora was annoyed.

"You're cute in the morning!" Ian exclaimed, and then ruffled her hair, studying her features. "Maybe I've changed my mind," Ian said seriously, "perhaps I'd like a cuddle with you." Lenora froze, eyes wide. Ian smiled widely and hugged her to him. "I've never cuddled with the bride of Frankenstein before!"

"OUT!" Lenora whispered loudly, pushing him away. "I need to change, you...creep." Ian laughed hysterically and then left the room. After several attempts at getting Ian to quit peeking into the room, she was finally able to get herself dressed. They walked to the patisserie in a serene quiet, both lost in thought.

Lenora enjoyed walking beside Ian and imagined that they were married, the two walking together in quiet married bliss, on their way to enjoy an early morning coffee and pastry together. The only thing that was missing, in her mind, was them walking hand-in-hand. She gave him a sidelong glance. He had a determined look on his face, like he was all business. She sighed. Here she was fostering romantic notions, and he was probably thinking about today's CSP meeting.

"Anything the matter?" Ian asked, hearing Lenora's sigh.

"No, just tired," Lenora half lied. Ian reached out and put an arm around her shoulders and squeezed, kissing her temple. He released her and then held her hand along the rest of their journey. Lenora's heart skipped a beat while she looked in the shop windows to hide her exquisite delight.

They brought coffee and pastries back to a surprised Tom, who appeared as if he could have slept longer. Ian bought a newspaper at the patisserie, so he and Tom swapped sections, enjoying their breakfast in silence. Lenora wasn't interested in the paper, but held a section up in front of her anyway, taking several opportune moments to peer at a distracted Ian.

Eventually, Ian caught on and seized the paper from her hands. "You're not reading this—you've been on the same page for about an hour now." He eyed her suspiciously, mocking a serious tone. "What secrets are you hiding behind that paper?"

Lenora sighed, feigning annoyance. "Nothing—I just wanted to eat my breakfast in peace."

"Oh! I see!" Ian grabbed the paper from her and wrapped her in an embrace, nuzzling her neck until she burst into laughter. "That'll teach you...think you're too good for us, do you?" He grinned charmingly at her while taking the unread section. He pushed her aside and forced her to share the cot with him. Lenora leaned into Ian, his arm around her while he read the paper.

Tom cleared his throat and gave her a stern look and then shook his head. Lenora wilted—she felt like she had been caught doing something wrong. She sat up and looked out the window at the early morning campus—it was peaceful this early on a Sunday morning. She inwardly hoped that something would happen to force the CSP meeting to cancel. She just wanted to spend the day with Ian.

She glanced at Ian, who looked cozy in the warm morning sunlight. Then, despite her dad's silent admonition, she leaned her head on Ian's shoulder and closed her eyes, taking long sips of the aromatic coffee, drinking in the moment.

The new conference room was filled with CSP people. Lenora tried desperately to remember who they were. She had met them all—in what felt like ages ago—but hardly recalled their names, let alone what they do. Of course, she knew Ian, Tabitha, Emily, Walter, and her dad. She was really interested in discovering more of what Emily did. Lenora found her fascinating in so many ways.

Emily was currently engaged in a conversation with Tabitha and Rose. Everyone else in the room appeared occupied with fascinating conversations that didn't involve her. Even Tom, Walter, and Ian were huddled in a group in the far corner, looking at documents she was not allowed to see (as Ian rudely told her when she tried talking to them earlier).

Lenora felt out of place and uncomfortable.

Finally, Walter summoned everyone to order. Lenora just kept her seat near the door, unsure of where she fit in to this group.

"Len, take a seat at the table, please," Tom said with a note of irritation.

Walter started the meeting, reintroducing everyone, and then asking for all to reiterate their plan of action on Tom and Lenora's apartment haunting.

Amelia and Phillip, the lead investigators, took over Ian's research and agreed to conduct further inquiries into the building history and the history of Bartholomew Booth. The electronic specialists, Joe and Maggie, planned on setting up video and audio equipment in the apartment. The rest—Ian, Rose, Emily, and Tabitha—were going to enter the apartment separately to determine what type of entity they were up against.

In the last point of business, Walter tasked Ian and Rose with developing a schedule to help Lenora hone her ability. Lenora sat tall in her chair, excited to finally be part of the meeting, but the moment was fleeting. Disappointed, she put her head in her hand and sulked.

Walter ended the meeting by asking if anyone had questions. This was Lenora's cue.

"Is there anything I can do? I mean…aren't I part of the group? Can't I be of help somewhere?" She slunk in her chair as silence descended the room, scrutinizing eyes upon her. "It…it can be any-thing…" she whispered, immediately lamenting that she had said anything at all.

Tom shook his head. "Sorry, Len, but since the case is about us, we can't participate." Lenora nodded, trying not to look at anyone. She felt like a giant spotlight was shining on her.

Walter took the cue and immediately changed the subject. He gave everyone a schedule and then dismissed the meeting, stating that they would reconvene after he heard back from the separate teams. Finally excused, everyone resumed talking amongst them-selves and left without saying a word to Lenora. Ian came over and sat with Lenora, poking her in the side playfully, but Lenora wasn't in the mood.

"Dr. Spencer Harvey, a friend of mine who works in the Sociology Department, is on sabbatical," Walter explained once everyone had left. "He's going to the U.S. on a research grant and won't be back until autumn…next year. I called him yesterday and explained the situation. He said you could stay in his flat on campus until the investigation is over."

Tom breathed a sigh of relief. "You just don't know what a relief that is Walter, thank you!"

"I think I can grasp the immediacy," Walter replied, blue eyes sparkling. "Living in the department's conference room doesn't sound overly appealing." He chuckled. "Emily already put a protection spell around the flat, so it's ready to be moved into whenever you're ready. I have the keys with me, and I can help the three of you move in, if you like."

"Three?" Tom looked confused.

"Ian has agreed to move in with you for the duration of your stay," Walter clarified.

Tom nodded, shooting Lenora a quick glance. "I'm sure that should be a treat."

"It'll be a blast!" Ian responded, clapping Tom on the back, unaware of his insinuation.

While they moved their things into the new flat, Tom took Lenora aside and had an embarrassing conversation with her about keeping her distance from Ian. He revealed his awareness that she "had a crush on" and "felt puppy love" for Ian (phrases that made her cringe and color in mortification). He then commenced on a lengthy soliloquy about how Ian was too old for her, and that it invited trouble.

The conversation left her with a myriad of feelings, the least of which was embarrassment. She felt like she had been interrogated for three days in a dingy, windowless, and stuffy room for a crime she didn't commit. In the end, she placated him by admitting that while she thought Ian was "cute," that dating him was not a probability—reiterating that she also felt Ian was too old for her, that he was more like a big brother.

Lenora thought that Tom's point on the age difference was ridiculous—Tom was thirteen years older than Bessie when they got married, a point she wanted to bring up, but refrained from out of fear that he would ship her off to another country.

Walter saved her from further humiliating conversation by showing up with pizza. She loved Walter.

The new apartment had two bedrooms. Lenora and Tom took the rooms, while Ian happily agreed to take the couch, claiming that the sofa-sleeper was much more comfortable than what he slept on in his flat (which made Lenora wonder what *exactly* he did sleep on). He also admitted that since he was a night owl, it would be best so that he didn't disturb anyone else.

And, true to his word, Ian went out late that night. He poked his head in the door to her bedroom to say good night on his way out. Lenora barely uttered the word "bye," before he walked out the door. She wondered how his being out late was supposed to help keep her safe from the entity—because that's when she had the most problems.

She paused in thought, remembering Thaddeus. "Thaddeus? Are you here?" Lenora held her breath, waiting for the faint reply—talking to a dead kid still made her hair stand on end.

"Yes," came a murmured voice from beside her.

"I wish I could see you," she sighed.

"Me too," he replied quietly.

"Isn't this boring?" she asked. "Watching me, I mean?"

"No. Lonely."

Lenora's heart dropped. She felt badly for him. "You're lonely for Ian, I know," she sympathized.

"Yes…and no."

Lenora was confused. "Do you only miss Ian sometimes, or…?"

"Miss brother, yes. Lenora doesn't talk."

That was the most she'd heard from him. She frowned, considering what he had said, and then suddenly, she got it. "Oh! So, you're lonely when you're with me because I don't talk to you?"

"Yes," he answered, firmly this time.

"Well, you don't say much, so I figured you didn't want to talk."

"Conserving energy."

Lenora nodded. "Okay, so from now on, I'll talk to you more." She paused, curious. "And, you're conserving energy because—"

"Save Ian's arse," he replied with a chuckle.

Startled, Lenora laughed out loud—something she hadn't done in a long time. Finally, when she regained composure, she wiped the tears from her face. "Thanks for the laugh."

"Welcome."

"Would you like me to read to you? I'm just starting a new gothic novel by Susan Thomas." She showed him the cover. "It's the sundown series about vampires and witches."

"Yes, please."

Lenora thought she heard a note of excitement in his voice. "Cool—it's like we're in a book club. We can go on an adventure together!" She patted the space near her on the bed, as if he could take a seat next to her, and waited for several seconds. "Ready?"

"Yes," the faint reply came from right beside her.

Lenora guessed that he was sitting beside her, as much as a ghost could, anyway. She had been reading for nearly two hours when Tom stuck his head in the door.

"Len? Who are you talking to?"

"I'm not talking, Dad, I'm reading out loud…teachers say it's good for reading comprehension."

Tom studied her for a minute. "Okay, Len, but it's late, and you need to get some rest. Lights out."

Lenora nodded and closed the book. When Tom left, she looked where she thought Thaddeus was and rolled her eyes. "Parents." She heard a faint chuckle as she settled in and turned off the light.

Her slumber that night was dreamless…peaceful.

Eighteen

Lenora glanced up into what appeared to be a promising blue sky and headed out of the borrowed apartment. Her first stop was the music shop, then to her favorite bookstore, ending with a trip to the market to pick up fresh ingredients for tonight's dinner. She was amazed at how easily the three of them melded into a daily routine, as if they had always lived together. Ian even helped her cook most nights, which she enjoyed very much. The living arrangement was so pleasurable that Lenora frequently found herself secretly wishing that the research team took longer than they had planned.

The day was so fine that Lenora spent extra time dawdling in Barton's Books, her favorite bookstore. The store was divided in half: the front part was strictly for new books, and the back was dedicated to used and first editions. She walked along the isles, running her fingers along the spines of the books, breathing in the "new book" smell, which to her came in second only to "old book" smell. She loved the smell of books, the feel of the pages between her fingers, and the worlds they opened to her imagination. Opening a book, for her, was like stepping into another world, as if the characters were inviting her in to share their adventures and forget her troubles. Finishing a book was always depressing for her.

Lenora worked her way to the back of the store where the used, rare, and first-edition books were. She had no intentions to buy a first edition, but liked to hold them in her hand, reveling in their antiquity. Mr. Barton typically didn't like the general public to, as he put it, "molest" the first editions. But, sensing Lenora's appreciation for books, he would often enthusiastically show her a first edition, allowing her to browse through it and trace her fingers along the old leather binding.

As she entered the back of the store, Percy Barton, looked up and smiled. "Well, hello there, young Lenora!" He immediately stepped down from the ladder to rush over and shake Lenora's hand, which made her giggle every time. She liked Percy, and she imagined that if she had to pick a grandfather, he would be the one; he just seemed to fit the bill: wispy white hair, unruly eyebrows, coke-bottle glasses, and twinkling blue eyes.

"A first edition just arrived in the mail today," he said excitedly. "Would you like to be the first to open the box?"

"I would love to!" Lenora was inexpressibly excited.

Percy rushed over to the counter and pulled out a small box, still taped together. He placed it on the counter and then motioned her over. "Come and open it!"

Lenora looked up at Percy in disbelief. "Are you sure?"

"Of course," he nodded enthusiastically. "Open it! I can't stand the suspense!"

Lenora smiled brightly and opened the box. She sifted through the packing peanuts to the bottom, and lifted the book out of the box. The dark green leather binding was cracked and she inhaled the earthy, aged smell. She turned the book over on its side to read the binding and smiled. Percy, who was waiting in eager anticipation, cleared his throat.

"It's a first edition of the complete works of Edgar Allan Poe," she grinned.

Percy gasped and reached a hand toward her. "May I?" Lenora nodded and handed the book to Percy, who turned it over in his hands. He opened the book, leafing carefully through the pages. "This is quite the treasure. I may not want to sell this one." He frowned. "In fact, I wonder who would want to." He went over to the box that the book was shipped in and looked at the return address.

"NS?" he said confused. "That's all that's on here…a couple of initials."

Lenora opened the book to the front and back covers. Sometimes, if the books were family heirlooms, people wrote their family name on the inside covers. Inside the back cover, two letters were neatly scrolled on the bottom left corner: **NS**.

She showed the inscription to Percy, who just shook his head. "Well, I guess it's a complete mystery—"

Lenora looked up at Percy, expecting him to finish his thought, but he was distracted. She followed his gaze to a gentleman standing behind her, looking over her shoulder at the book. She hadn't noticed him until now. In fact, she didn't even hear his approach. But, here he stood, looking over her shoulder so closely that she could now feel his breath on her neck. Suddenly feeling uncomfortable, she stepped aside.

The gentleman smiled at her. "I hope I didn't startle you. I was curious about what you found so exciting."

Lenora dropped her gaze. "That's okay, you just…surprised me."

The man bent in closer to Lenora and she instinctively leaned back. He smirked, reaching for the book. He turned it over in his hands, inspecting the cover and leafing through the pages. "A first-edition copy of Edgar Allan Poe's complete works? Amazing!" He placed the book back on the counter. "The person who buys that copy will be incredibly fortunate." He glanced at Lenora and smiled. She was arrested by his steady, mesmerizing gaze.

"Can I help you with something?" Percy interrupted, with a sternness that surprised Lenora.

"I'm sorry," the man shook his head, "I didn't mean to intrude, but I am new in town and someone recommended this store as the place to look for first editions."

Percy eyed the gentleman and nodded his head. "Well, I guess this would be one place, yes. Is there something particular you're looking for?"

"Yes, I'm looking for a first edition copy of *Jane Eyre*. Do you have anything like that?"

Percy frowned, thinking. "Yes, I do believe I have something like that." He spun on his heels and went to the bookshelves behind the counter. Lenora stood at the counter, wanting to catch a glimpse of the man standing next to her, but she didn't dare.

"Aha!" Percy exclaimed as he removed a book from the shelf. "Here it is." He brought the book to the counter and set it in front of the man, who nodded, as if that was exactly what he was looking for.

Lenora watched as Percy initiated his sales pitch, showing the quality of the cover and explaining the book's history. The man listened intently to Percy's explanation, which gave Lenora a chance to take a better look. He was a lot younger than he at first seemed—the way that he talked and carried himself made him seem much older—but he looked to be about Ian's age, around 23 or 24. He had shoulder-length, black hair in long layers that framed his face in soft waves. He wore a long, black raincoat that was neatly tied at the waist, and his shoes were such a shiny black that they looked as if he just walked out of the store with them. And, though Lenora was average height for a girl, she felt dwarfed next to the man's imposing six-foot-three frame.

Lenora glanced at Percy, who continued his pitch, though she could barely hear what he was saying. She started to feel lightheaded, unbalanced–she grabbed at the counter to steady herself as her head started spinning. Her sight faltered...and then...darkness.

"Lenora? Are you alright?"

Lenora slowly opened her eyes. Percy's blurry face came into focus. She looked around and noticed that she was laying on the floor in the bookstore. Confused, she quickly moved to get up, but Percy stopped her.

"Not so quick, you might lose consciousness again."

"Again?" Lenora was completely confused.

"Yes," another voice uttered, "you fainted. We nearly called for the ambulance."

Lenora followed the sound of the man's voice–it was the mysterious man in black. Embarrassed, she sat up. "I think I'm okay now." Percy helped her up and led her over to a table in the corner.

"Will you look after her while I fetch some water?" Percy asked the man in black.

"Yes," the man nodded and then sat down, looking at Lenora with concern.

Lenora glanced up at the man. "Please don't look at me like that."

"Like what?" he asked, frowning.

"Like you're expecting me to keel over at any minute. I'm fine."

The man laughed heartily. "I'm sorry, but you really took me for a loop there. I apologize. Is this better?" he contorted his face into a false smile, which made Lenora laugh.

Percy brought in a glass of water and set a cookie down in front of her. "I suspect your blood sugar is low, so you may need to eat something."

"You think I passed out because I was hungry?" Lenora asked in disbelief.

"It's not unheard of," the man asserted.

"Oh." Lenora took a sip of water and a bite of cookie.

The bell at the front of the store rang, indicating that a customer had entered. Percy looked up, frowned, and then shot a concerned glance in Lenora's direction.

"It's alright," the man in black assured him, "you go ahead and tend to your customer. I'll stay here with Lenora and we can continue our business later."

Percy nodded, touched Lenora's shoulder, and then walked up to the front of the store. Lenora stole another glance up at the man, quickly averting her eyes when he caught her.

"My name is Nicholas," he said, smiling while extending his hand. Lenora shook his hand and then immediately lowered her head, embarrassed.

He leaned forward and touched her arm. "No need to be embarrassed. Everyone has done that at one time or another. And, if you need to know, I didn't see you fall—one minute, you were standing next to me, the other, you were on the floor. It happened too quickly for you to claim embarrassment."

Lenora gazed into Nicholas's smiling face and grinned. "I suppose so, but I'll just be embarrassed for a while, if that's alright with you."

Nicholas smiled. "Of course it is. You have a right to feel any way you choose." He leaned in and whispered conspiratorially. "However, it would be nice if you got over it. I have a sneaking suspicion that becoming acquainted with you would be good for me."

Lenora looked into his eyes and felt weak. His eyes were so inviting and his face so sincere—she instantly felt herself slipping into that haziness she felt earlier. She broke her gaze and took a bite of cookie.

"I'm really not that exciting to know," Lenora said thoughtfully. "Besides, I think I'm too young for you."

Nicholas laughed loudly and touched her arm. "Perhaps," he said, amused, "but I think friendship knows no boundaries, and I think being friends is okay, is it not?"

Lenora smiled and shrugged her shoulders. "I suppose." She overheard Percy in the front of the store talking to the customer about children's books in a disinterested tone. She suspected that his interest was in the first-editions and rare books, but found that selling new books would keep him in business.

"Listen," Nicholas broke her reverie, "I'm new to town, and would appreciate a tour guide, if you have time."

Lenora thought for a moment. "I don't think that would be a good idea," she said decidedly. The smile left Nicholas's face and was replaced with disappointment. "You see," she explained, "I don't know you very well, and my dad—"

"No need to explain," Nicholas interrupted. "I just thought that—well, it was a thought anyway. Maybe we could meet for tea. Would that be alright?"

"That might be fine. Tea is okay," Lenora responded.

"How about tomorrow afternoon, say 2:30 at Auntie's?"

Lenora thought about tomorrow. It was Saturday, which meant going out for breakfast and then to the market in the early morning with her dad and Ian. Last Saturday, she and Ian went for a punt and then a picnic by the Cam. No, that time was reserved for Ian.

"No, I can't make it tomorrow, I have plans."

"Okay, maybe some other time then," Nicholas responded disappointed.

Percy reappeared around the corner. Nicholas smiled dolefully at Lenora and got up to finish his business with Percy. Lenora's shoulders slumped; she felt awful. Nicholas was genuinely interested in her...and considerate. She turned him down for Ian, who treated her like a sister and didn't appear to notice her at all—at least not in the way she wanted him to.

What is wrong with me? she wondered. Lenora turned around to retract her refusal, and noticed that Nicholas was no longer there.

"Percy? Where did Nicholas go?"

"Nicholas?" Percy asked, visibly confused. "Oh! You mean the gentleman that was just here?"

"Yes, where did he go?"

"Oh, he left already. Bought the *Jane Eyre* first edition and then left. I thought you saw him— he walked right by you."

Lenora put her head in her hands. "No, I didn't see him walk out at all. I wanted to talk to him, to thank him for being so helpful when I...passed out."

"I'm sure he already knows," Percy reassured her.

Lenora thumped her head on the table. "I'm such an *idiot!*"

"He did leave something here for you," Percy interrupted her self-admonishment.

"What?" Lenora asked, puzzled.

Percy tapped a brown package on the counter. "Here, he left this for you."

Lenora got up from her seat and walked to the counter. She couldn't believe that Nicholas bought his own book, left something for her, and then walked out of the store, all without her notice. She picked up the brown paper bag and opened it. There was a book inside. She took the book out and looked at the cover—it was a used copy of *Jane Eyre.*

She shot Percy a confused look. He simply shook his head, and shrugged his shoulders.

A piece of paper stuck out from the middle of the book. She slid the paper out and unfolded it.

A copy for you so we can read together – even if we're apart.
If you change your mind, you know where I'll be.
N~

A note from Nicholas? She felt relief and excitement at the same time. She replaced the note and book in the paper bag, waved good-bye to Percy, and left the store.

At the market, and on the way home, Lenora weighed the pros and cons of meeting Nicholas. But, as she got closer to the apartment, she decided to stick with the plans that were already in place. After all, she didn't know Nicholas. And, seeing the way that Ian's face lit up when she walked in the door solidified her choice.

"Hey you!" Ian shouted. "Where have you been? It's almost time to order the pizza!"

Lenora laughed, feeling almost giddy. *Oh yeah, pizza night.* She looked down at the grocery bag and laughed. "I've been at the market and the bookstore. Did you get the movie?"

"Yep! It's the newest Forrest Brazil action flick 'Grosse Kill.' It's supposed to be good."

Lenora wrinkled her nose.

"What? You don't like action flicks?" Ian asked, noticing her response.

To be honest, she hated action flicks. She told him this last week when he rented the "Hot Cars, Loaded Guns" movie. However, she didn't mind. Ian snuggled with her on the couch for the entire movie, and on the intense parts, whenever she put her face in his chest, he hugged her close to him. She liked to pretended that they were on a date.

"They're not my favorite, but I don't mind," she responded.

"Good, because this one's real intense!" He got up and began karate-chopping the air.

Boys. She sighed and rolled her eyes.

"Hey you two!" Tom shouted from the doorway, "I have hot pizza in my hand and a bag full of sodas. Someone help me!"

Ian rushed over to help unload Tom's burden, and Lenora put plates and napkins on the table.

The three ate until they were near bursting, and then proceeded to move into the living room to watch the movie, when the phone rang. Tom ran to answer the phone and then soon came around the corner. "Ian, it's for you."

Ian got up to answer the phone, ruffling her hair on the way past. Lenora looked at her dad inquisitively, and he shrugged his shoulders in response. She strained to hear Ian's conversation, but all she could hear was his voice, sounding animated and excited... and lots of giggling. It was that ridiculous giggle he got when talking to a pretty girl—she'd heard that before.

Nauseating.

Lenora inwardly groaned. He was probably talking to another girl that he's interested in. She shook her head and slunk down on the couch in disgust.

Ian ended his call and came bounding into the living room. "Hey, I am going to have to take a rain check on movie night. Sue just called. She and some of her mates are down at the pub, so I'm going to join them."

"Who's Sue?" Lenora asked indignantly.

"Just a girl that I met in class the other day," he responded and then kissed the top of her head. "Bye!" He sprinted out of the room—Lenora heard him whistling as he walked down the stairs.

Tom came around the corner, looking confused. "Where's Ian?"

"Went out," Lenora responded irritated.

"Oh," Tom muttered, "well, I guess that just leaves you and me, kid."

"Yeah, I guess so," Lenora responded, crushed.

Tom came over and sat next to her, hugging her shoulders. "It's still going to be fun—your old man's not that bad, is he?"

Lenora looked into her father's bright hazel eyes. Creases formed around the edges as he smiled warmly at her. Her heart sunk. "No, you're fun...I'm just not in the mood to watch 'Grosse Kill' tonight."

"Oh?" Tom asked.

"I really don't like action flicks. Can we watch something else?"

Tom laughed, "Of course we can watch something else. Let me see what we've got."

Tom went over to the cabinet to look through Professor Harvey's collection and finally pulled something out. "Hey, here's 'Lindy's Breakfast Table,' a great classic. Want to watch that?"

"Sure, that sounds much better than 'Grosse Kill,'" Lenora forced a smile.

Tom put the movie in and settled in the chair next to the couch. Lenora turned and pressed her back into the couch's arm rest so she could see better, but mostly because she didn't want her dad to see her disappointment.

They ended up watching two movies. Lenora trudged to her room, dizzy from exhaustion. However, when she got under the covers, she couldn't sleep. She sat in a chair by the window and watched people as they walked along the street below. Couples strolled by, walking hand-in-hand, looking as if they were the only two people on the planet. Groups of college students occasionally stopped somewhere below her window, at which point she eavesdropped on their conversations—who was dating who, which professor was too demanding, post-graduation plans.

The later it got, the more risqué the conversation, and she found herself glued to the window, straining to hear the juicy tidbits, feeling somewhat embarrassed that she was snooping into someone else's private life. Then, she heard someone shout "Roberts!" She quickly glanced out in time to see Ian sauntering down the street with his arm around a girl.

Probably Sue, that bimbo, she thought dejectedly.

Lenora watched, crestfallen, as Ian joked around with his friends—the entire time with his arm around the girl. Once, Lenora noticed that Ian briefly glanced up to her window, causing her to quickly hunker down, hitting her knee on the way down. She winced in pain, clamping a hand over her mouth in case sound traveled.

She sat on the floor for some time, head directly below the window so she could hear the conversation. She didn't want to chance Ian catching her spying on him. Once it sounded like the group was breaking up, she slowly rose just to eye level and peered down into the street. She immediately wished she hadn't. Ian was alone with the girl, and they were locked in an embrace, in the throes of a passionate kiss. Feeling sick to her stomach, Lenora quickly crawled back to her bed and curled into the covers, hot tears streaming down her face.

"He doesn't mean to hurt you." Thaddeus' soft voice tried to soothe her.

"Then why does he do it?" she asked, voice gravely.

"Don't know. Stupid."

Lenora nodded, unable to respond. She couldn't help thinking of the amount of time she'd wasted waiting for Ian to love her. Her time was so limited, and it broke her heart to think that it was spent waiting on the edge of a prayer.

She pressed her eyes closed, letting the tears fall softly upon her pillow as she drifted.

A clear night. Millions of stars twinkled overhead. The bright moon shone as if daylight, illuminating the rolling hillside. She saw a stretch of woods clearly in front of her. A lighted path cut into the dense forest.

Without hesitation, she stepped onto the path, moving slowly and gracefully among the pines, her dress flowing softly behind her like filmy gauze. The earth felt cool and soft beneath her bare feet, and a warm, gentle breeze caressed her skin. She inhaled the sweet scent of pine, and looked into the thick canopy, feeling enveloped within its embrace...protected.

The air hung quiet, but for the sound of the wind in the trees. The tranquility was enticing, urging her to move forward along the path, unafraid... uninhibited.

The snapping of a twig close by caught her attention. Her heart fluttered only a moment before she pressed onward. Rustling movement ahead slowed her step. She paused, waiting. A gust of wind sent leaves whirling into the air around her, like butterflies in the spring. She smiled.

He was coming.

A dark figure stepped out of the shadows and onto the path in front of her. Long, black hair framed a darkened face, his black cloak billowing behind him. He moved toward her, his arms outstretched. She reached for him and quickened her step.

She raced toward him, heart beating, feeling elated. Closer, closer she came toward him...her love. And then, as she grew close enough, she reached out and hit a barrier. Their hands nearly touched—she felt the electricity of their fingers as they brushed, but something prevented them from being together.

She looked with anguish into his face, seeing nothing but his glistening black eyes. Shaking his head with sorrow, he pointed below them. They were both standing opposite each other, each on the very edge of a cliff, merely feet apart. Her balance faltered as she became dizzy looking at the sheer drop beneath her. She took a step back, bewildered, and then looked up in time to see him walking away.

"Come back!" she shouted, but the force of the wind took the breath out of her.

He was gone.

NINETEEN

"**H**ey, where are you going?" Ian asked breathlessly as he ran to catch up to Lenora as she walked through Market Square.

"Nowhere that's any of *your* business," Lenora responded, trying to sound sarcastic though she was still annoyed at Ian for last night.

"Oh-ho!" Ian said in a mocking tone. "Well, I see that *someone* got up on the wrong side of the bed this morning!"

Actually, she barely slept. She spent most of the night drifting in and out of a delicious dream and agonizing over whether she should meet Nicholas for tea or not. The decision was finalized the minute Ian walked in the door that morning. He had been out all night, still wearing yesterday's clothes, and had a stupid grin on his face. She didn't like it. And, he was way too chipper. She spent most of the morning dodging him and his constant whistling. He was getting on her nerves. That's when she decided to take a chance on Nicholas.

"I didn't sleep well last night," she admitted.

"Well," he said conspiratorially, "that makes two of us!" He nudged her arm with his elbow and winked.

"Gross," she rolled her eyes. "That's disgusting. I don't want to hear about it." She didn't. The thought of him touching someone else made her feel sick to her stomach.

"Fine, then, I'll change the subject," he said cheerfully. "Tell me where you're off to!"

"I'm going to meet a friend for tea," she answered.

"A friend, huh? Who?"

The incredulous tone in his voice irritated her. "No one you know. Just a friend."

"I didn't know you had any friends," Ian jested.

Lenora, miffed, glared at him. "Well, you don't know everything about me. For your information—"

Someone shouting Ian's name interrupted her. Ian stood on his tiptoes to look over Lenora's head and scan the market crowd. He smiled and waved the person over. Lenora turned to look, and saw a beautiful brunette making her way through the crowd.

"Who is that?" she asked, already knowing the answer.

"That, my little friend, is Sue. You know, the girl I was with last night?"

"Oh," Lenora sighed disappointedly. "I should go, I have to meet my—"

"No!" Ian protested, "I want you to meet her—you'll love her!"

Doubt it.

She waited in annoyed silence for Sue to make her way through the swarm of people. Once Sue drew nearer, Ian started to laugh in that stupid high-pitched giggle he reserved for girls he dated. Lenora rolled her eyes.

Sue joined them and gave Ian a hug, who returned it with enthusiasm. Lenora stood aside, ignored, as the twosome talked animatedly about the previous night: who had embarrassed themselves, who vomited, who went home with whom.

Crushed, Lenora stood on her tiptoes, looking around the market for Tom—if she could find him, it would be an easy out for her. She spotted him, not too far off, conversing with another professor. After nearly fifteen minutes of exclusion from Ian and Sue's chatter, Lenora couldn't take it anymore. Glancing at her watch, she gaped. She was supposed to meet Nicholas five minutes ago.

"Um," she said timidly interrupting the duo, "Ian? I have to go now."

Neither had seemed to notice that Lenora had spoken, so she cleared her throat loudly. Both stopped and stared at her.

"Oh, hello!" Sue said, feigning amiability. "Who are you?"

"Oh, I'm so sorry!" exclaimed Ian. "I forgot. Lenora, this is Sue. Sue, this is my little sister Lenora."

Little sister? I'm going to kill him!

Lenora was incensed. "Nice to meet you," she said to Sue through gritted teeth.

"Nice to meet you too," Sue said, patronizingly sweet. She then turned to Ian, "I didn't know you had a little sister! It's so nice of you to take her to the market and spend time with her! What a *great* big brother you are!" she cooed at him and then kissed his cheek.

Lenora held her hand out in disagreement. "Well, I'm actually not—"

"Yes," Ian interrupted, patting Lenora on the head, "I *am* a good big brother. Poor girl. Has no friends. In fact, I think she's made one up today just so I don't feel obligated to drag her around with me." Ian looked over at Lenora and winked. "Meeting a 'friend' for tea today?" he jested, air-quoting the word friend. He laughed hysterically.

Lenora glared at Ian, eyes brimming with frustrated tears. "You. Are. A. *Jerk!*" she shouted furiously and then spun on her heels, heading in Tom's direction.

Ian reached toward her, "Aw, come on, Lenora, I was only joking!" He waited for her to turn around, but when she picked up the pace, he started after her. "Lenora!"

Lenora ran faster and caught up to her dad. She looked over in Ian's direction and saw that he was staring after her, looking worried and upset. Sue had a hand on his arm, keeping him from continuing after her.

Lenora tapped Tom on the shoulder. He waved a dismissive hand at her. She knew he was deep in conversation and didn't want to be interrupted. She glanced back at Ian again, who was taking Sue's hand off his arm and heading in their direction. Feeling a sense of urgency, Lenora did something she wasn't allowed to do: interrupt her dad while he was talking with a colleague.

"Dad!" she shouted.

He spun on her. "What?" he asked angrily.

"I was supposed to meet a friend ten minutes ago and I'm late," she said hurriedly.

"Well, you had better get going then," he shrugged indifferently.

"I know, that's why I shouted at you." She glanced at his colleague and nodded apologetically. "I'm sorry for interrupting, but I really needed to tell you where I was going."

"Fine," Tom responded, "Be home by dinner time."

"Yep, I will," Lenora replied as she turned to run toward the tea shop. If she hurried, she would only be twelve minutes late. She hoped that Nicholas would still be there.

When she got to Auntie's Tea Shop, she looked at the tables outside and didn't see any sign of Nicholas. She went into the shop and looked around. In a corner by the window, Nicholas sat reading a book, a pink rose lying on the table across from him. She caught her breath, wiped the sweat off of her brow, and straightened her shirt.

The excitement in meeting Nicholas overshadowed the anger she felt at Ian. With each step, her heart beat faster and harder, the sound thumping loudly in her ears—she was almost sure others could hear it. When she got to the table, Nicholas glanced over the top of his book. He smiled widely and motioned for her to sit down. She took the seat across from him.

"I was hoping you'd change your mind," he grinned. "The flower is for you."

Lenora picked up the rose, inhaled its sweet fragrance, and smiled. "It's beautiful, thank you."

"Not as beautiful as its recipient," he responded softly. Lenora's eyebrows instantly went up in incredulity and she giggled.

Nicholas frowned, confused for a moment, and then understanding dawned his face. "Oh, that sounded corny. Here I am, trying merely to be a gentleman, and I end up spouting a dodgey pick-up line." He smiled apologetically. "Do forgive the tackiness—it's been a while since I've been out with a pretty girl."

Lenora laughed. "That's okay. You're right, though, that was a little corny. But, we can work on that."

"Yes," he beamed, "I would definitely like another go." He studied her face for a moment. "So, have you been able to read any of *Jane Eyre* yet?"

"No," she admitted, "I had a terrible night last night, so reading wasn't an option."

"That's sad news," Nicholas responded, concerned. He waved his hand at the waitress, who immediately came over. "Could you please bring over a pot of Earl Grey, two cups, and a plate of your lemon biscuits?" The waitress nodded, looked longingly at Nicholas, and then walked toward the kitchen.

Nicholas looked surprised at the flash of displeasure in Lenora's expression. "Did I do something wrong?" he asked.

"Well, you ordered for me," Lenora responded. "I really don't like that. It's so 1950s."

"Ah, another mistake," Nicholas nodded, embarrassed. "I apologize. You are a modern woman and prefer to order for yourself. I promise not to do it again…unless you ask. Deal?"

Lenora agreed. "So, it won't hurt your feelings if I don't like what you ordered? I'm not a big fan of biscuits."

"But, I thought most people liked—" his brows furrowed and then he laughed heartily. "I see here that we have a language barrier! You see," he explained, "what you refer to as 'cookies' in America is what we Brits call 'biscuits.' So, I was ordering lemon *cookies*."

"OH!" Lenora exclaimed, almost too loudly. She blushed. "I didn't know that."

"Well, then you and I can help each other," he grinned. "You can teach me about modern women, and I'll teach you how to be properly British!"

Lenora nodded, still blushing. "Does that mean we'll be meeting again, then?"

"I would hope so," he answered softly. "But, that depends on you."

"What do you mean?" Lenora asked nervously. "That it depends on how much I annoy you?"

"No, silly girl," Nicholas chuckled, "it depends on how much I annoy *you*!"

The waitress finally brought the check. Lenora looked at her watch and was surprised that they had spent over two hours eating cookies, drinking tea, and laughing together. Lenora moved to take out her purse, and Nicholas waved her off. "No, I'm paying for this one, since I asked you here." He gave money to the waitress. "Please keep the change."

The waitress beamed. "Thank you!"

Lenora figured by the look on the waitress' face that the tip was excessive. She smiled.

"One must always tip for good service," he explained.

"What year were you born in?" Lenora asked, jesting.

"Why?" Nicholas asked, visibly taken aback by her question.

"You just sound…old-fashioned." Lenora explained, hoping she didn't offend him.

Nicholas chuckled. "Well, you could say I'm a bit of an old soul. Besides, I was raised by my grandfather, and he was determined to make me as much of a gentleman as he was." He looked apologetically at Lenora. "Are you embarrassed?"

"No, absolutely not!" Lenora exclaimed. "I think it's cool. You're different, and I like that."

"Good, because I would like to keep meeting you, if that's alright," he said quietly.

"I would like that," Lenora responded, blushing.

"Very good, then. How about if we meet here Monday at 4:00? That would give you plenty of time to read the first five chapters of *Jane Eyre*. I'm curious to hear your view."

"Oh," Lenora replied, feeling suddenly self-conscious. Was he interested in her romantically, or just as a "book buddy"? She sighed.

Nicholas leaned in, scrutinizing her expression. "Where did you go just then? Your face took a dark turn."

"Nowhere," she began, but decided against lying to him. "Actually, I was just surprised to hear you talk about the book. I wasn't thinking that we were starting a book club."

Nicholas interrupted with a burst of laughter. "A book club! No, I just thought it would break the ice, give us something to talk about, help us become comfortable with each other." He chuckled softly. "I'm not interested in starting a book club with you. I'm interested in getting to know you, and the book is one way to make it easy. Plus," he continued, "I like having intelligent conversations about the books I like, and you're a smart girl."

"Oh," Lenora replied, embarrassed.

"But," Nicholas continued, "if you don't think it's a good idea—"

"No," Lenora interrupted, "you're right, it's a great idea. I'll have the first five chapters done by Monday. See you here at 4:00!"

"Looking forward to it," Nicholas smiled and then bowed. "It was lovely having tea with you." He took hold of her gloved hand, lifted it to his lips, and kissed it gently. He caressed her hand a moment, frowning. "Gloves? Is this a modern woman's fashion?" He gazed at her incredulously.

She withdrew her hand. "No, just my...fashion statement...I guess."

Nicholas smiled, considering her for a moment. "Well, I think it absolutely captivating."

"Aren't you going to ask why I wear them?"

Nicholas' brow furrowed. "No. I don't think anyone should have to explain what they wear—it's an expression of who they are, and no one has the right to judge." He bowed. "Until we meet again."

Lenora responded with a weak laugh and a nod. She felt like she was going to pass out.

TWENTY

Lenora's life ensued along a path of blissful routine. Crossing yesterday's date off on her calendar, she was somewhat shocked that it was already July twelfth.

Because of Emily's protection spell on the new apartment and Thaddeus, Lenora was able to finally sleep. Seldom did the entity bother her—it resorted to what she referred to as simple parlor tricks: moving objects, whispering, and scratching the occasional word into the wall. Though it still terrified her, she tried ignoring it, which worked…for now. The entity left her dreams alone. Now, her dreams were filled with images of the figure in black, who she could never get close to.

Every day, it was the same: mornings working in the dungeon, afternoon teas with Nicholas, dinner with her dad, and falling asleep with a book, which she often read aloud to Thaddeus. Sometimes, she closed the book and talked to Thaddeus for hours. He spent a lot of time with her at night—Ian was mostly unaccounted for since he spent most of his time with Sue. Tom was not thrilled—he felt that since Ian was appointed to protect Lenora, he should at least try to be around. She agreed, but didn't dwell on it—she still felt his absence deeply.

It took Nicholas and Lenora only three days to get through *Jane Eyre*. Nicholas suggested that they continue with the Brontë sisters, so they then moved on to *Villette* and were now reading *Wuthering Heights*. Lenora found the reading engrossing, but enjoyed listening to Nicholas's analysis more. He knew a lot about the Brontës and their works.

Weekends were different now. Saturdays were her favorites because after going to the market with her dad, Lenora met with Nicholas. Frequently, they lounged around by the river Cam, picnicking. She loved to lie in the warm grass while Nicholas read from Shakespeare's sonnets. Sometimes, she closed her eyes, drifting along with the soft melodic tones of his voice. Every now and then, she gazed into his dark eyes, which still made her feel dizzy, they were so mesmerizing.

The more they met, the harder it was to leave him. An overwhelming feeling of dread coursed through her when Nicholas took out his pocket watch and announced that it was time to go. Lenora always made a production of it with a heavy sigh, as he gathered their things and extended a hand to help her up. Then, they would part ways, but not before he kissed her hand and bid her a good evening—that still made her feel light-headed.

Today was Sunday, and the worst day of the week, in her opinion. Sundays were the only days she didn't see Nicholas. He never really told her what he did on that day; only that he had a long-standing appointment that he could not get out of. His answer was a little cryptic, but she didn't spend a lot of time thinking about it. After all, she didn't tell him what her Sunday appointment was, either.

Lenora stretched and yawned and then looked at the clock. It was six o'clock in the morning—she was up a lot earlier than usual, but she couldn't sleep anymore. She contemplated going out to the kitchen and making breakfast, but wasn't in the mood to visit with anyone right at the moment. All she wanted was to bask in the warm sun and think about Nicholas.

She heard the door to the apartment slowly creak open. It was Ian, she was pretty sure. He never stayed overnight anymore, choosing to spend it with Sue. She listened as he tried to quietly shut and lock the door, and heard his shoes thump to the ground as he took them off. The floor squeaked and groaned under his feet, and she heard him catch his breath when the floor cracked loudly in places. She smiled, picturing him stopping short, holding his fists up to his chest, and tightly closing his eyes while he hoped the noise didn't wake anyone.

The footsteps stopped in front of her room. She closed her eyes and held her breath, hoping that he would just pass by. Ever since that day at the market, she tried avoiding him as much as possible. He tried joking around with her, and she noticed his disappointed expression when she refused to participate in his nonsense. He never once offered an apology for the mean way he treated her, which broke her heart a little.

Ian pressed his head against her door, trying to discern if she was awake or not. She hoped her erratic breathing didn't give her away. The doorknob turned slowly and the door opened just a crack. She held still and kept her eyes closed.

Then, her door closed quickly and she heard him walk away. Additional footsteps sounded in the hallway.

"Ian? What are you doing up?" It was Tom's voice.

"Sorry to wake you, Dr. Kelley. I just got home actually."

"Oh, I was already awake, but I heard some footsteps and wanted to check it out. I thought you were already home."

"No, I stayed at Sue's last night," Ian admitted sheepishly.

"Oh, well, no need to explain, Ian. You *are* an adult." Tom said, a note of displeasure in his tone. "What were you doing to Lenora's door just then?"

"Oh," Ian replied, sounding flustered. Lenora listened intently to hear Ian's explanation. "I was just…closing it so that I didn't wake her up."

"Well, that was unnecessary—Lenora sleeps pretty soundly," Tom explained. "But thanks."

"No problem," Ian replied quietly. There was heavy silence that followed. Lenora could almost feel the tension from where she was lying. She imagined the two just standing there, staring uncomfortably into the darkness.

"Well," Tom said, breaking the silence, "I don't want to keep you."

"Right," Ian replied, relief in his voice.

Lenora heard the footsteps as they walked away from her room, and she breathed a sigh of relief. She wasn't quite ready for Ian and one of their early morning chats.

Ian's door closed and she heard her dad clicking on the lamp and sitting back in his recliner. Knowing that it was safe to get up, Lenora got out of bed and took a quick shower. When she entered the living room, her dad was reading the newspaper.

"Oh, hi Lenora! What are you doing up this early?" Tom asked, surprised.

"I heard some noise and then couldn't get back to sleep."

"That was probably Ian that you heard. He was just coming home." He glanced up at her with a disapproving look on his face. "Would you like some breakfast?"

"Actually, I was thinking about going for a walk and then finding a place to read while it's still quiet."

"Oh. Are you sure you don't want to have breakfast first?"

"I have some cash in my pocket. I can just buy a pastry later."

Tom frowned. "Is everything okay?"

"Yeah, I'm fine," Lenora flashed him a reassuring smile. "Maybe we can meet for lunch at Willie's around noon?"

"That sounds great!" Tom smiled at his daughter. "Enjoy your quiet morning, and don't forget that we have CSP this afternoon!"

Lenora nodded, waved goodbye, and then walked out the door. Asking her dad to lunch was a dirty trick to avoid coming back to see Ian. But, she just wanted to get out of there.

Cambridge was completely silent at this early morning hour, and she loved to walk along the bridges and watch the swans elegantly swimming through the water. Mist floated gracefully above the water, hovering as if it dared not touch it. Lenora took a deep breath of the mossy, cool air and sat down on the base of the bridge next to the water's edge. Only students and teachers were allowed on this part of the Cam, so she was certain that she would be alone for as long as she liked.

She took her book out, leaned her back against the cool stone, and closed her eyes.

Quickly, he grabbed her from behind and forced the cloth against her mouth and nose. Her body violently thrashed about and he nearly lost his grip. The only thing that helped him was that her thrashing about caused her to breathe more, taking in the chloroform's fumes. After several seconds, her body grew limp and she slumped in his arms. He took out the syringe and shot the sleeping draught into her neck.

He flung her body onto his shoulder and boldly carried her down the block—out in the open. He didn't expect to be seen since it was a work night and no one would be out at this hour. He took mostly back alley ways, ducking in and out of the shadows to avoid prying eyes—he didn't want to take any chances. There was only one spot where he would have to walk out into the main side streets, but it was near his flat, so if he quickened his pace, he could easily avoid problems.

He ducked into the street and made haste—only a few blocks now. His legs felt rubbery from the extra weight he was carrying and he was becoming winded. He worried whether he could continue. He had yet to carry her up the long flight of narrow stairs to his flat and then get her situated within.

Then, he felt her move.

At first, he thought her body simply readjusted position with his quickened step; however, the movement did not coincide with his step. Growing increasingly nervous, he moved more swiftly, nearly running. Once he accelerated, she began to stir more and then eventually struggled against him, trying to pry herself free of him. Her movement became too much for him to handle, and he dropped her to the ground. At first, she was stunned and simply sat there, looking around in confusion. Then, realization crept to her expression and she quickly tried to get to her feet to run, but he was faster and grabbed her, shaking her violently.

"Lenora! Wake up!"

Lenora screeched in pain, struggling to get free. She opened her eyes to Ian, who looked haggard. She glanced around in confusion — the sun was a little higher in the sky and the fog had already dissipated.

How long had I been asleep? She wondered.

"I've been trying to wake you for a while now," Ian said exasperatedly. "I was almost afraid that you went into a trance and couldn't come out."

Lenora held up her gloved hands to shield the sun. "No, I'm fine…just asleep." She yawned and stretched, then flinched, remembering that she was here to avoid seeing Ian. "What are you doing here?"

"I heard you leave after I came home, so I slipped out and followed you."

"What did you do that for?" Lenora asked, irritated.

"I was just making sure you were okay. It was a little early for you to be out, so I was just making sure you were alright." He looked at her expectantly; Lenora wasn't sure what for…thanks, perhaps? When he didn't get a response, he continued. "I kept my distance," he said defensively. "I've been sitting on the bank, over there." He pointed over his right shoulder, indicating the hill near the beginning of the bridge.

"So, you've been sitting there watching me?" Lenora asked. "That's kind of creepy, you know. Nobody does that…well, except weirdoes."

Ian chuckled. "Hey, your dad asked me to watch over you, and that is exactly what I'm doing."

"Why didn't you just send Thaddeus, like you always do? Not like you've been doing a stellar job watching me anyway," Lenora snapped.

Ian stared at her, slack-jawed. "Do you really feel that way?"

"Yep," she admitted, "and so does my dad." Lenora leveled her gaze. "Look, you were the one who volunteered to help 'protect' me from harm. But, you haven't been around...at all. What kind of protection is that? So, because you aren't interested in babysitting me, you send poor Thaddeus to do your dirty work? If you weren't really interested in doing it, then why did you offer in the first place?"

Ian's shoulders slumped, dumbfounded. "I-I never thought of it as...I wanted to—" he frowned, shaking his head in disbelief, unable to finish his thought. "Thad's been with you at night...he indicated that you're not in danger," Ian explained, "so I thought...oh, I don't know what I thought." He slid down the wall and sat beside her, raking his hand through his hair.

"That's your problem," Lenora uttered, "you weren't thinking at all."

Ian snorted. "You sound like a parent," he smirked. "That's your problem young man, you weren't thinking," pointing his finger, mocking a scolding tone. Lenora's eyes darted toward him in intense fury. Ian's smile faded as he quickly realized his blunder. "Uh...yeah...s-so sorry...I was just trying to lighten...sorry." He tried not making eye contact, in fear of a rebuff.

Lenora stared at him, considering the idea of leaving. He wasn't taking her seriously. One more comment like that, and she was gone. "Anyway," she responded in an irritated tone. "Why did you come here? I mean, if Thaddeus doesn't think I'm in danger, then why come?"

Ian's brow furrowed—he looked troubled, defeated. He slid closer to Lenora, gingerly placing an arm around her shoulder, looking apologetic. Not ready to accept his apology yet, she shrugged his arm off and moved over.

Ian hung his head. "Yep, I thought so."

"You thought so, *what?*" Lenora asked, exasperated.

"You're still mad at me," Ian responded. Lenora feigned not knowing what he was talking about. "Listen, I know that you're still angry with me for what I said that day at the market, and I've been trying...for *days*...to apologize. But, you won't let me. You've been avoiding me for the last two weeks."

He paused, looking to her for affirmation. "I really don't blame you for not wanting to talk to me. But Lenora, when you're mad, you really know how to stick it to a guy. This has been a killer for me, not being able to talk to you. I miss our early morning talks. I miss being your friend." He studied her face, waiting for a reply. When none came, he put his head in his hands. "Lenora, please say something, anything. This ignoring me bit is driving me crazy!"

Lenora felt torn. Something within her wanted to keep being angry. But he always knew how to get under her skin. She sighed and glanced at the swans floating along the river.

"Ian, what you said really hurt me," Lenora admitted. "You say that you're my friend, but you didn't treat me that way. You said mean, hurtful things. You talked about me like I was some stupid little kid that you're stuck babysitting. It was humiliating. Friends don't treat each other that way."

"I know, Lenora, and I'm *so* sorry for that. I acted like a total wanker, and I can't apologize enough for that."

"Well, maybe you should have been more honest about how much of a pain I am. It would have saved a lot of hurt feelings." Tears of frustration brimmed in her eyes, and she swiped them away.

"You're not a pain, Lenora."

"Really? Well, you made it seem that way." Lenora noticed his look of contrition, but she tried to remain strong—he needed to know. "If you can't be honest with me, and if you can't treat me with respect around other people, then I don't want to be your friend."

Ian hung his head. He turned to face Lenora, tears filling his eyes. "I want to be your friend, Lenora. And if you'll give me a second chance, I will promise to never hurt you like that again." He grabbed one of her hands and held it in his. Lenora felt the warmth of his hands radiating through her gloves. Ian lifted her hand up, kissed it, and then held it up to his chest. "Please, Lenora, give me another chance to prove that I can be a good friend to you."

"Well, I –"

"There you two are!" Lenora turned to see Maggie running toward them. "I've been looking all over for you. Amelia and Phillip just got back from their research and have uncovered something. Everyone's waiting at the CSP conference room."

Ian quickly helped Lenora up and they ran behind Maggie toward the university.

When Lenora and Ian walked into the conference room, everyone was already assembled—even her dad and Walter were there. The room grew quiet as they walked in. Lenora felt all eyes on her and she began feeling extremely uncomfortable.

"You both should sit down." Tom motioned to two empty chairs near the center of the table. She and Ian sat down immediately while Tom continued to address the group. "We have asked you all to meet early because Amelia and Phillip have uncovered some interesting information in their latest research trip. This information might enable us to begin a spiritual cleansing of our apartment, allowing us to finally go home."

Lenora perked up. *Go home? That would be fantastic!*

Tom nodded to Amelia and Phillip. "Go ahead and explain what you found."

Phillip got up and looked nervously around the room. Lenora guessed that he wasn't comfortable with public speaking.

"Amelia and I went to the library and spent time in their archives. We uncovered some interesting facts about the past tenants in your apartment, Dr. Kelley, which will help us begin our investigation."

Amelia took a drink of water, and cleared her throat. "One of the tenants that we found particularly interesting was a fellow named

Bartholomew Booth." Lenora gasped. Amelia's eyes darted toward Lenora. "Yes, the entity that haunts you also lived in your apartment."

Lenora felt the scratch on her leg start to burn—the scar still hadn't gone away, and she was afraid she would have BAR inscribed on her leg forever.

"We conducted further research into the tenant and found that he murdered several women back in the early 1900s," Amelia continued. "The file that Ian gave us said very little—it was an initial interview conducted between a tenured professor and a PhD candidate. Bartholomew Booth was the PhD candidate trying to earn his degree in psychology. The professor," she paused to look at her notes, "was a Dr. James Kirkland, who found Mr. Booth ineffectual as a student and practicing therapist, and therefore did not recommend him for a degree."

"That was all that the file offered," Phillip added. "So, we did a bit of digging, or at least, Amelia did the digging." Lenora noticed the warm look that passed between the two of them. "What we found were several police records, newspaper clippings, and another interview between Dr. Kirkland and Mr. Booth after he had been caught. The authorities thought that Mr. Booth would confess to Dr. Kirkland, who was his mentor at university."

"The notes are thorough and telling of what type of entity we may be up against," Amelia offered, passing folders around the room. "Please take a folder and pass it on. This is a compilation of Dr. Kirkland's notes, the newspaper clippings, and police reports— all in order of the events."

"Thank you, Amelia and Phillip, for the detailed notes," Walter nodded at them. "Now, on to the rest of the investigation—"

"Hey, don't I get a folder?" Lenora interrupted, watching the pile of folders stop at each person, passing over her.

"No," Tom said softly, "not this time."

"Well, why not?" Lenora inquired.

"Because the investigation directly involves you," Tom explained. "I've told you this once before."

"But, I think it would be beneficial for me to read it," Lenora insisted. "I'm the one the entity is targeting. Don't you think it would help me to know who it is?"

Tom shook his head. "No, I don't think it's a good idea—"

"Actually, Dr. Kelley," Ian interrupted, "I think it's a great idea. Lenora is right—the entity attacks her, whispers nasty things to her...does things to her. Reading about its history would give her an opportunity to fight back."

"No, Ian," Tom began emphatically, "I think it's a terrible idea, and she's my daughter, so—"

"Okay, enough," Walter intervened. "Tom, I'm going to have to agree with Ian here. Arming Lenora with information will help her deal with the entity head-on."

"I appreciate your observation, Walter, but as her father—"

"But as her employer, I trump your status as father," Walter declared.

"Walter," Tom grinned smugly, "Lenora is not your employee—she's not on your payroll. Therefore, I do trump you as her father."

Walter shook his head. He walked over to Lenora, dug in his pocket, and produced a five pound note, slapping it down on the table in front of her. He flashed Tom a stubborn look and then turned to Lenora. "There, consider this a cash advance for your first paycheck." He glanced over at Judith. "Get her on the payroll tomorrow—starting date as of today—five pounds less."

Judith nodded, looking uncomfortably at Tom.

Tom shook his head, clearly angry at Walter's open boldness. "Walter, I don't like this—she's just a kid..."

"Tough," Walter asserted. "Lenora is nearly eighteen, and this ability of hers forces her to see and hear things that *no one* her age should. Education is her best form of protection." He softened. "Give Lenora what Bessie didn't have—support and education is the best gift you can give her, Tom."

Lenora wilted when she saw the look on Tom's face—he looked completely defeated...and sad. She got up and hugged him. "Dad, let me learn all I can—I need to know. Please don't fight me on this—not knowing what to do is frustrating…and tiring."

Tom nodded and sighed heavily. "I know—it's tough seeing you go through this and not being able to do anything about it."

"But you are," Walter interjected. "You're giving her a chance to learn and grow with her ability. Don't do to her what Bessie's parents did to their own daughter."

Tom acquiesced, handing his folder to Lenora. "I'll have Amelia make me another copy."

"Of course," Amelia offered.

"So," Walter added, breaking the heavy tension, "how about other updates? Joe and Maggie—have you uncovered anything in your initial audio and video surveillance?"

"No, nothing at all," Maggie answered. "There is no movement in the flat at all, and the audio equipment picks up nothing but standard building sounds."

Walter nodded while taking notes. "Thanks, Maggie," he said distractedly, keeping his eyes on the notepad. "I'll expect that you and Joe will re-set the equipment for another round?"

"Yes, we've already started refreshing the equipment," Joe admitted.

"Excellent. Thank you." Walter looked up from his notes, directly at Rose. "What about you? Did you pick up anything?"

Rose shook her head. "No. None of us did. Neither Ian nor I picked up any sense of spiritual presence. Emily tried her dousing rods to no avail. And, since none of us picked up spiritual activity, Tabitha has nothing to report."

Walter frowned and shook his head. "Nothing, huh? Unbelievable. Well, that certainly does not mean there is no spiritual activity—it just means our investigation continues. So, I assume that the four of you will enter the apartment again soon to record your findings."

"Yes," Rose nodded, "we'll reassemble when our schedules allow."

"And, how about a learning plan for Lenora? Have you and Ian come up with one?"

"Yes we have," Ian answered. "Rose and I have come up with a plan that will allow Lenora to practice her abilities in graduated steps."

"It's meant to help ease her into the ability rather than to submerge her in it," Rose added. "I'd rather she not be overwhelmed by her abilities all at once."

"You two would know best how to approach Lenora's learning," Walter commented. "I look forward to hearing about your progress." He gave Lenora a sidelong glance and then continued, addressing the others in the room. "So, I will wait to hear from the technologists and psychic team before calling you to reconvene. In the meantime, everyone is to take your time reading the file that Amelia and Phillip assembled for us. This next part of the investigation might take a bit."

Walter focused his attention on Lenora. "Your task—other than reading the investigation file—is to schedule time with Ian and Rose to hone your ability." He gave her a stern look. "You do everything they tell you—nothing more. Understand?" Lenora nodded. "Good! Then everyone disburse! I'll send notice of the next meeting."

The walk home was quiet. Tom seemed heavy in thought, and Lenora wasn't sure what to say to him. She wanted to say something to ease his mind, but anything she came up with seemed awkward. Ian stayed behind to talk to Rose about their plans for Lenora's training. She couldn't wait for that either.

When they got home, Lenora placed the folder in her room, deciding not to touch it until later. Though she was eager to read it, she felt that showing her enthusiasm would make her dad feel worse. She went into the living room and sat next to her dad, reading a book, while he watched cricket on the television.

Ian arrived soon after and joined them, eventually breaking Tom's mood, engaging him in conversation about cricket. Occasionally, Lenora caught Ian looking at her reflectively, but he didn't attempt ingratiating himself, which she appreciated. They had a quiet dinner in front of the television, after which Lenora cleaned up and then silently retired early—she really didn't feel like talking to anyone.

And, she had some reading to do.

FINAL NARRATIVE OF BARTHOLOMEW BOOTH

PART I

Doctor's Notes:

I, James Theodore Kirkland, doctor of psychology at the University of Cambridge, offer this transcribed narrative from my interview with Bartholomew Booth, convicted murderer. I hereby certify that the notes herein are authentic and in his own words as he spoke them prior to his death by hanging. These words were obtained by me after rendering the patient into an hypnotic state so that I could accurately obtain his full confession and story.

Though under hypnotic state, the patient spoke in third person, as if telling the story of another. This is indicative of one who suffers from intensive psychosis, presumably from events that occurred to him in his past.

Rather than beginning at birth, Bartholomew chose to begin his life story when he first arrived at his aunt's after his mother's death. He almost completely avoided talking of his mother and of her death, as if it was either disappointing to him, or if it was something he nearly completely blocked from memory. This, I will never know.

Mr. Booth has been sentenced to death for his crimes. My time with him is limited. This is day one of my interview.

~~~~~~~~~~~~

Bartholomew remembered the sound that his suitcase made as he set it down on the cold, polished marble floor, the metal on the bottom making a loud clanking sound that echoed through the empty foyer. He looked around at the large entrance hall with a mixed feeling of awe and fear—he had never seen anything so grandiose in his twelve years, which had mostly been spent hiding in the closet of his mother's one-room flat so she could entertain her male guests without being disturbed.

The maid, who escorted him into the hall, walked behind him and silently took his coat off and placed it into a box, which she quickly closed up and carried off. Feeling alone, he gazed wide-eyed at the grand staircase before him, wondering where it led.

A tall, imposing man entered into the hall and stood gazing at him, eyes looking disapproving as they wandered up and down Bartholomew's small frame. After what seemed like several minutes of intense scrutiny from the man, he finally gestured for Bartholomew to follow him.

The man opened the door and held out his hand, signaling that Bartholomew was not yet to enter. "I must announce your entrance first, young sir," he said in a tone that sounded forcibly polite. Bartholomew nodded, standing in complete silence—head bowed, hands held stiffly in front of him—as the man announced his arrival.

"Madame, young master Bartholomew here for you."

"Well, show him in, Graham," a woman's voice sternly replied from within.

"Yes, Madame."

The door opened, and Bartholomew peered in, seeing only the back of a heavily tapestried chair, a tuft of silver hair peering from the top. Graham frowned, giving him yet another disapproving glance. "She'll see you now sir," he said, opening the door wider for Bartholomew to enter. "If that will be all, Madame, I shall retire for the evening."

"No, you will wait beyond the door for further instruction," she asserted. "Leave us." A hand appeared, waving dismissively to Graham, who nodded and, without a word, roughly ushered Bartholomew into the room and closed the door behind him. Bartholomew stood uncomfortably near the door, waiting for the woman to speak.

"Well?" said a stern voice from behind the chair. "Don't just stand there, boy, come here so I can look at you."

Bartholomew slowly moved forward, stepping around the chair, standing with his back to the fireplace. This was the first time he had ever laid eyes on her—even though he had known about her his whole life. He was shocked that, despite her age and silver hair, her facial features seemed almost youthful. Her eyes were almost black, her skin was pale and silky, and wrinkles around her mouth betrayed years of smoking.

His aunt scowled in disapproval at his face and body. She rose agilely from the chair and walked toward him, brusquely taking his hands and inspecting them. He was amazed at how unexpectedly warm her hands were, and how smooth, elegant, and polished they were; he wasn't accustomed to seeing groomed hands—his mother's were rough, and the fingernails always dirty and chewed to the quick.

Bartholomew started as the woman huffed and instantly dropped his hands. She gazed intently at him, making him feel uncomfortable, exposed. "You will learn to keep yourself neatly groomed at all times. Do you understand?"

"Yes ma'am," he replied, shifting his eyes to the ground.

"And," she added sternly, "you will look at me when I talk to you."

"Yes, ma'am," he agreed, nodding, looking up at her in fear.

"Now, you will go with Graham, who will show you to your room and give you a warm meal, after which, you shall retire for the evening." He nodded in agreement as her eyes narrowed. "Your day begins tomorrow before dawn."

Without another word, she returned to her seat and rang a little bell that sat on the table next to her chair. She then picked up her pipe and took a long draw.

The door instantly opened. Graham whisked in and gestured for Bartholomew to leave who, without hesitation, left swiftly.

He followed Graham up the long, winding grand staircase. They passed one floor and then ascended the next. Once they reached the landing of the second floor, Graham stopped and turned to Bartholomew. "Your rooms are in the left wing—never go right; those are the Madame's apartments, and no one is allowed there." Bartholomew nodded quickly. Graham silently led him down a wide hall, which was covered with heavy red tapestry and dark cherry furnishings. On the walls were paintings of ancient-looking figures— none of whom smiled, but wore a heavy, stern countenance.

Once they reached the end of the long, dark hall, Graham opened the last door on the left and motioned for Bartholomew to enter. Graham stepped in after Bartholomew and waved his arm in grand gesture. "This is the parlor, where you will eat your meals— unless Madame summons you for dinner—entertain guests, and see your tutors."

"Tutors?" Bartholomew interrupted and was instantly sorry, for Graham huffed and issued a warning glance.

"To your left," Graham continued, glaring at Bartholomew, "is your bed chamber. To your right, is your nanny's quarters."

Bartholomew started at the word "nanny" – it was a word he only saw in books. He wanted Graham to clarify, but didn't want to interrupt.

"Someone will come to retrieve you in a few moments and escort you to your evening bath, after which, you shall dine in your

chambers and then retire immediately thereafter." Graham nodded, as if validating his statement, and then turned on his heels to
leave.

"Wait!" Bartholomew shouted after Graham, who stopped mid-
stride, lifting his head without looking in Bartholomew's direction.
"Where are my things? My suitcase?"

"Your suitcase will be delivered momentarily," Graham answered
and then quickly left the room.

Bartholomew stood in the center of the parlor, looking around.
The room was decorated in dark blue damask—pictures of wildlife
hung along the walls, the majority of which were deer with large
antlers. In the corner was a small writing desk with paper and pens.
Next to the desk was a large bookshelf, which housed several books,
including one in Latin.

In the opposite corner sat a pianoforte and a music stand. He
sat down at the piano and tinkered with the keys a bit, giggling at
the funny sounds it made, until he heard a loud knock at the door.
A stern-looking woman in stark clothing entered with his suitcase.

He grinned shyly at the woman, who did not return his smile, but
walked immediately toward the bedroom, set the suitcase upon the
bed, and began removing the things within. Bartholomew frowned
and walked swiftly into the room, uncomfortable that a strange
woman was going through his things. He watched as she roughly
handled his photographs and various letters and childhood trinkets.
Anger surged within him.

"What are you doing?" he asked the woman, wanting to rip his
possessions from her hands.

"Putting your things away, sir," she replied without looking at
him.

He took the silver snuff box from her hand. "This was my father's,
and I'd rather put it away myself."

The woman gave him an irritated glance. "It's my job, sir. I won't
mishandle your things—or take them for that matter." She grimaced

as she picked up a moldy, wooden rocking horse figurine from the suitcase.

Disliking the look of disgust on her face, Bartholomew snatched the figurine from her hand. "That was my father's too, and I don't like you going through my things!" He looked into the suitcase and instantly noticed that all of his clothing was missing. "Where are my clothes?"

"They're being burnt," the woman answered nonchalantly.

"Burnt!" he exclaimed, now becoming irate. "But, those are the only clothes I have!"

"Madame will replace them all with new clothing—we are burning them on her orders."

Bartholomew gaped. "What else have you removed from this case?"

"Nothing else, sir—just the clothing," the woman answered, now appearing insulted, "and I don't appreciate what you're insinuating."

Her expression told him that she was telling the truth—he was good at judging character...he had to be. "Sorry, I was just a little...shocked at not seeing my clothes," he replied, trying to sound apologetic.

She removed the rest of his things and then stood by the door. "Now, I am to take you to your evening bath."

Startled, he backed away from her, shaking his head. The woman frowned and then instantly smiled in realization. "Well, I'm not going to bathe you—I'm just taking you there."

She led him down the hall to a room complete with a bathing vessel and sink. The woman handed him towels, soap, and scrub brushes.

"Remove all of your clothing and set them outside the door, where I will collect them. Get into the bathing vessel and use the scrub brushes and soap. The robe hanging on the hook is yours—put it on after your bath and then step out into the hall, where I will inspect your hands and feet."

Bartholomew looked at the various scrub brushes in confusion—he never had to use them before. The woman smiled at him—the first show of kindness since his arrival. He returned her smile. "Thanks....uh?"

"Lottie," she answered.

"Thanks, Lottie."

She chuckled. "Wait to thank me later—you may not be happy with me if you don't wash correctly."

And, she was right—after the fourth inspection, when his skin was red and raw, Lottie finally gave her approval.

Clean bedclothes were already laid upon the bed for him, which felt warm and soft next to his raw, cold skin. He combed his hair, slipped on a pair of wooly socks, and walked out into the parlor, where a meal was waiting.

His mouth began immediately watering. He hadn't eaten for days, and it was more food than he was used to in an entire day: a hearty stew, fresh bread, and a variety of cheeses. He ate ravenously, until feeling almost to burst, and then sat back, looking miserable.

"You need to govern your appetite, Master Bartholomew—you'll not go without now." Bartholomew nodded, issuing forth loud, wet belches. Lottie motioned toward the bedroom. "Come now, it's time to retire—your day begins early, and it's best to keep the lady's schedule."

Bartholomew climbed into the softest bed he had ever felt—it was like a cloud. Lottie tucked the covers in around him and then smiled. "I am your chamber maid." She nodded over to the bedside table at a string that hung directly above the table. "That is connected to my chamber and will call me at any time of day. Now, get some sleep—I'll be here to wake you at the appointed time."

Bartholomew waited until Lottie left before surveying his room. To his right was a fireplace, warming his chamber comfortably. On the left was a clothing wardrobe, which was opened to show clothing and shoes neatly aligned. He wondered whose clothing it was.

Though his bed was comfortable, the events of the day and his unsettled stomach caused him to lay awake for hours. He finally drifted asleep an hour before his appointed waking time.

The next morning, Lottie explained that the clothing inside the wardrobe was his. He never had new clothes before, and was glad— these were itchy and uncomfortable, unlike his old clothing.

Lottie explained that he would have a series of tutors come throughout the day—every day except Sundays, where he would be expected to attend Sunday mass with his aunt. The first tutor was for general subjects, then a Latin tutor, followed by social manners instruction, and then music. He would only have short breaks in between for refreshment.

Bartholomew soon found the schedule grueling, and was often exhausted by day's end. He rarely saw his aunt, so the forthcoming Sunday was looked upon with mixed trepidation and excitement.

When Sunday arrived, Lottie was pleasantly surprised to find Bartholomew dressed and ready to see his aunt.

"The lady will be impressed," she said, beaming.

I hope so, he thought nervously.

Bartholomew did not like mass, but enjoyed tea time with the Donnerhills, who had two sons his age, Eugene and Francis, with whom he played several hands of Speculation. He won most of the hands, and to keep things friendly, played poorly so that Eugene and Francis could win occasionally. He suspected that they knew as much, but both appeared to be great sports about it.

Dinner that night at the mansion was quiet. Bartholomew sat at one end of a long table, and his aunt at the other. Having no one to talk to, he counted the number of chairs around the table—twenty-four, including the two that were currently occupied. The paintings on the walls depicted large and intimidating animals; a great stag adorned the wall behind his aunt.

He never felt so lonely in his life.

Tired of the dreadful silence, Bartholomew cleared his throat loudly to gain his aunt's attention, which worked immediately. She instantly stopped chewing and eyed him with brief irritation before setting her fork down and focusing on him. Her eyebrows arched upward as she tilted her head expectantly.

"I was wondering…" he paused, swallowing hard.

"Well, speak up, boy, I haven't all day," his aunt interrupted.

"Might I come closer so that I may speak with you?" he asked timidly. Her eyes narrowed in thought. After several moments of intense silence, she gestured to the seat on her left.

Graham instantly walked over and picked up Bartholomew's place setting and repositioned it at the spot to her left, and then held the chair out for Bartholomew.

His aunt looked at him with mixed annoyance and curiosity. Bartholomew's stomach churned, producing a loud, gurgling sound that echoed loudly through the dining hall. He glanced at his aunt, embarrassed.

"Well?" she asked, irritated. "Are you going to speak, or am I to sit idly while my dinner cools?"

"Oh, sorry!" Bartholomew exclaimed. "I-I only want to ask you a few questions."

"Go on," she said, resuming eating.

"I know you are my aunt, but not sure how…" he trailed off.

"I am your father's sister," she answered blankly.

"My father?"

"Yes, your father," she replied with irritation. "Your mother explained that you have a father, did she not?"

"Y-yes," he answered, "I know his name was Edward and that he died serving England. Mum said he was a good man, and that I resemble him. But, that's it."

Her eyebrows raised and she smiled knowingly. "I guessed as much. She didn't want to have anything to do with this family."

"But, why?" Bartholomew asked.

"Because she thought we were evil people."

"Even my father?"

"No," she replied earnestly, "I'm sure not—she seemed to be very much in love with your father."

"Then, why were they not married? Why wasn't I told about you? Who are the rest of my family?"

"You ask too many questions," she replied, exasperatedly. "You will know, in time, the perplexities of your parents' relationship. Until then, I will tell you a bit about your father." Bartholomew, sat up in his chair excitedly. "Your father's complete name was Edward Henry Bartholomew Fitzhugh."

She smiled—the first he had seen since his arrival, and he liked it—she was a handsome woman.

"Edward was an incredibly intelligent man," she continued, "and should have continued his career at university, rather than enlisting in the military. But, that was not his choice."

"Whose choice was it?"

"Our father's—the Baron," she answered. "He felt that your father was too imprudent in his choices of friends, activities," she paused, "...and lovers. He decided to let the military help straighten him up." She eyed Bartholomew, who was silent, absorbing all the information. "But, alas, Edward was not meant for military service, for it was only weeks into his training that he was killed in a routine drill."

"He was...killed...how?" Bartholomew was still thoroughly engrossed.

"Let's just say that he didn't follow orders and leave it at that," his aunt offered. "Perhaps one day, you can know the full details, but for now, just accept what I tell you." Bartholomew nodded his head. "In time, I will share details, but it's too painful to relive all at once. I loved your father. He was younger than I, and my only brother, and we took care of each other. When he died, a part of me went with him."

His aunt's demeanor changed; tears welled in her eyes, and she looked at him with slight affection. "When I heard about your mother's passing, I immediately took action to adopt you as my own—you are my brother's child, and I see it in your face, eyes, and mannerisms. You are just as inquisitive and willful as he was."

"He was smart?" Bartholomew asked, thrilled to be compared to his unseen hero.

"As a whip," she replied, smiling. "He accelerated beyond any-one his age." Her smile widened as she reminisced. "Oftentimes, our parents would leave on important business, leaving your father and me alone to our own devices." She chuckled. "We spent a lot of time deluding our governesses and tutors—hiding in the attic and playing at pirates or some other adventure your father would dream up. He was very creative." Her smile faded quickly. "After I married, I was so lonely for your father's company that I wrote him several times a day. He wrote back as often, until he met your mother—then I rarely ever heard from him."

"How did he and my mother meet?" Bartholomew asked, imme-diately regretting the question because of the change in his aunt's expression.

"That's enough," she responded sternly. "It's time for you to go to bed now."

Bartholomew swallowed hard and nodded. "Can I ask just one more question?"

Her eyes narrowed. "What is it?"

"I don't know your name," he said matter-of-factly.

She drained her wine, her narrowed expression growing softer. "I suppose that would be important information," she said, plac-ing hands on either side of his arms, squeezing affectionately. Bartholomew's expression betrayed astonishment. "Don't be sur-prised—I'm not a tyrant. I just have…duties and expectations that require me to be strong, dispassionate. I do hope that in time, you and I will share a bond that I once had with your father. Until then, you have duties of your own. I have high expectations of you."

She lowered her arms and leveled her gaze. "While here, it is my expectation that you will study hard, mind your nanny, and learn the manners of a titled person. When I am dead, you shall inherit all that is mine, and was your fathers—but not until you've proven yourself worthy. You will learn shortly what is expected of you—and you will do it without complaint or problem. That is what I expect. In return, I will give you information."

Bartholomew nodded and watched as his aunt walked out of the room, turning to him before going out the door. "Annabelle is my given name. However, you will call me Lady Fitzhugh…or Baroness—whichever you prefer."

She walked out of the room, closing the door softly behind her. Bartholomew felt alone in the dark stillness of the room, until Graham touched his arm.

"It is time for bed, young master Bartholomew."

Bartholomew nodded and walked alone along the silent, dark corridors to his room.

Bartholomew's nanny, Constance, was five years older than he—only seventeen when she came to live with them. And she was pretty—he could see her as clearly in his mind as if she were standing before him today. He recalled how her long, blonde locks shone golden in the sunlit window, and the brightness of her hazel eyes, the specks of orange and golden brown seeming to shift and ripple in the soft twilight. She had a quick, soft laugh and melodic voice that mesmerized him whenever she spoke. And she was smart. He loved how she kept up with his studies, how they would sometimes bounce ideas off of one another and debate issues.

On rainy Saturdays when the Baroness was away, they explored the mansion, sneaking down corridors, making up stories about the people in the paintings. Bartholomew enjoyed watching Constance as she imagined fantastic stories of horror and intrigue, becoming more animated as she delved into her creative imaginings.

One particular afternoon, as they explored the mansion, Constance came upon a door that opened to the attic. Surprisingly, it was open. Most doors in the mansion were locked, so naturally they were excited to find an open door.

Constance gasped when they entered the attic, which was covered in thick layers of dust and cobwebs. Both instantly began investigating the stacks of old books, boxes, clothing racks, old furniture, and paintings. Bartholomew perused an illustrated copy of Homer's "The Odyssey," while Constance explored further into the clutter.

After several minutes of silence, Constance glanced at Bartholomew, frowning. "Barty, what was your father's name?"

"Edward Henry Bartholomew Fitzhugh," he answered distractedly.

"So, his initials were EHBF?" she asked.

Bartholomew looked up from his book. "Yes, why?"

"Because, this old trunk has those initials on them."

Bartholomew put his book down and knelt next to Constance. He ran his fingers over a dusty gold plate. There, in script, were the letters EHBF. Without a word, they tried lifting the lid together, but to no avail—the chest was locked.

"Uh, it's locked!" Constance uttered, exasperated.

"Of course it's locked," said a stern voice from behind them. Constance and Bartholomew exchanging worried glances before looking toward the door. The baroness stood in the open attic door, arms crossed, an angry look on her face.

"Lady Fitzhugh," Constance exclaimed, standing up immediately, and motioning for Bartholomew to do the same, "I...we... didn't see you there."

"Of course not," the baroness replied sourly, "you were skulking about in areas you have no business being in."

"I'm sorry, ma'am, we were just—"

"What? You were what?" the baroness interrupted, disinterested in the explanation. "There is no explanation for what you are doing here. The rooms in this house are off limits—I told you that on your first day here. What part of that did you not understand? And what part of my instructions to keep Bartholomew out of trouble did you not comprehend?"

"It's my fault," Bartholomew interjected, "I asked her to come with me—the door was unlocked, and—"

"A mistake that will soon be corrected," the baroness responded, motioning for them to leave the room. Both quickly moved past the baroness and descended the stairs toward the main hall below.

At the bottom of the steps, Graham was awaiting them, an unsympathetic look on his face. "Stay here and wait for Madame," he said sternly.

They waited for what seemed like an eternity. When the baroness appeared, she took Graham aside and whispered something in his ear before he disappeared up the stairs. The baroness turned toward Constance and Bartholomew, her eyes narrowed. "Bartholomew, go back to your room—I'll talk with you later."

Bartholomew shot a worried glance at Constance, and then did as his aunt instructed. He walked until he was out of sight, and then listened from around the corner. He feared the worst—that his aunt was going to let Constance go. He held his breath and waited.

"Constance, I hired you to perform the duties of a nanny. Pray, tell me, what are those duties?" Bartholomew winced—he hated the way his aunt made Constance's name sound like a dirty word.

"Well...I—"

"Come on, girl, I haven't all day."

"Yes, my lady," Constance replied. "My duties as nanny are to ensure that Barty...Bartholomew wakes and sleeps at appropriate times, that he bathes and maintains a cleanly demeanor at all times, and that he minds his studies, eats nutritiously, and learns manners and behaviors as appropriate for his station."

"And that includes?"

"Ensuring that he behaves himself and stays out of trouble... ma'am." Bartholomew heard the shakiness in Constance's voice and a lump formed in his throat.

"Exactly," the baroness responded crossly. "Duties that you are, I am afraid, neglecting."

"I apologize, wholeheartedly, ma'am, it won't happen again—"

"That's correct, it won't happen again," his aunt responded angrily. Bartholomew felt as if he was going to collapse. "Your tardiness upon arrival on your first day was your first reprimand. Consider this your second warning. Dismissed."

As punishment for their indiscretions, Bartholomew and Constance were restricted to Bartholomew's personal apartments for an entire month. For a while, Constance maintained a level of seriousness that he had never seen—she only attended to her duties as prescribed and was less inclined to adventure.

However, time soon softened Constance's resolve as she once again encouraged creative storytelling. Occasionally, Lottie listened to the stories, seeming enthralled by the adventures they conjured up together. Eventually, the baroness even relaxed as she realized what a great influence Constance was on Bartholomew's well-being. During holidays and his birthdays, the baroness indulged Constance, allowing extravagant celebrations, and participating in the games and fun herself.

Never again, however, did they venture into the attic.

~~~~~~~~~~~~~~

Doctor's Notes:

The patient's aunt often forced him to fraternize with members of her social circle—a task he found arduous, a contributing factor to his changing mental imbalance. One particular family, the Donnerhills, had two boys—Eugene and Frances—who acted amiable around the baroness, but were abusive to Bartholomew when her back was turned. The boys taunted Bartholomew about his parentage, and engaged in physical abuse, kicking and punching Bartholomew until he vomited or blacked out.

Bartholomew endured years of abuse from the Donnerhill boys and their comrades. When Bartholomew was around age fifteen, his nanny Constance noticed the bruises and alerted the baroness.

~~~~~~~~~~~~~

"I've spoken with the Donnerhills," the baroness said somberly the following Sunday. "This will never happen again. They are sending the boys away to military school."

Shocked, Bartholomew sat up in his chair. "Military…?"

"You should expect nothing less." She uttered with guile. "No one harms my family and gets away with it. Everyone knows that—it's about time you do." She took a long drag off of her pipe, a smug expression on her face. "I am not one to contend with."

Bartholomew was stunned. No one had ever defended him before—it felt good, but he also felt oddly ashamed. He sighed, tears springing to his eyes.

"I know you said you didn't want to talk about it, but I think I have a right to know." He hesitated and took a deep breath. "They called me a bastard and a son of a whore. Were they right?"

"Partly," she answered, taking another long drag from her pipe. "Your parents were never married. However, it wasn't for a lack of trying." She sighed heavily and drained her drink. Graham moved quickly to refill the glass. Bartholomew felt dizzy by the mixture of old pipe and strong alcohol aromas.

"Your mother was not a whore…despite what she did in her later years," the baroness continued, staring into the amber liquid in her glass. "That was just to pay for her drinking habit. Your mother was the daughter of a highly respectable merchant. She and your father met at a ball held by a baronet in the village."

She refilled her pipe, lit it, and took another drag, puffing out white, billowy clouds of smoke. He coughed quietly—he hated that pipe.

"Edward said that it was love at first sight—they found out about you almost immediately thereafter." She chuckled. "Our father completely lost it when he found out, especially after Edward confessed to their intended nuptials. Father threatened to ban Edward from the family—that acknowledging the child out of wedlock meant immediate disinheritance."

She considered Bartholomew a moment. "At first, Edward put up quite the fight," she chuckled. "He said he cared nothing for the money, that he loved you and your mother too much. But in the end, our father won, sending Edward off to military service. He didn't have a chance." Her expression grew dark. "He died shortly afterward—the worst day of my life."

She shook her head to ward off the memory. "Thereafter, your grandmamma and I tried, in vain, to convince your mother to let us raise you as a proper Fitzhugh, but she refused. We even offered to pay her—handsomely—but she was too proud. She went into hiding shortly after and your trail went cold." She sighed. "That silver snuff box was the last gift we were allowed to give you. It was your father's. The little wooden pony inside was a gift to you from your grandmamma."

She smiled and placed a hand on top of Bartholomew's. "We loved you—your grandmamma and I. Our father was cold, heartless—and we lost you and Edward because of it." She withdrew her hand and touched Bartholomew on the shoulder before leaving him alone to cry in front of the fire.

The day of Bartholomew's sixteenth birthday was when he began to distinguish a difference in Constance's demeanor. Each year, Constance seemed to mature—replacing youthful vitality for demureness and sensibility—traits that won the baroness' favor. However, it was irritating to Bartholomew, who wished Constance to remain a virtual playmate. This was also when he discovered his romantic feelings for her.

Typically, while Bartholomew studied, Constance sat in the corner sewing or mending. Now and then, Bartholomew stole glances at her, and she would occasionally look up and wink at him. They ate together in the evenings, and then told stories while warming next to the fire. He loved those little moments.

However, lately, Constance went out in the afternoons, returning shortly before his evening meal. She was enigmatic regarding her whereabouts and brushed off Bartholomew's inquiries. She also began dining alone in her room. Often, she seemed distant, and took to staring out the window at length. Bartholomew found the listlessness distracting. His continual search out the window for Constance's return cost him several wrappings on the hands with a ruler by his tutors.

The afternoon of his sixteenth birthday was spent staring out the window, waiting for Constance's return. At quarter past five o'clock in the afternoon, she was still missing. Usually, Saturdays were reserved for fun. He assumed that since today was his birthday, it would be a full day of fun with Constance. But, she was up and gone before he woke up that morning. It just wasn't like her.

A knock at the door startled him. He ran to the door, disappointed that it was only Lottie, informing him that dinner was being served in the main dining hall.

The dining hall was festively decorated and a great feast was spread out upon the table. He glanced at the smiling faces—including his aunt's—and he even had the rare occasion of seeing Graham smile, which was more like a grimace.

His eyes flicked to Constance's setting, and he noticed she was not seated.

His aunt read his expression. "She's not here yet."

"Should we—"

"Wait?" she finished. "Absolutely not! Sit!" Bartholomew obeyed and watched as Graham poured them wine. She raised her glass. "A toast to you, Bartholomew, upon reaching near manhood!" She chuckled and then took a drink.

He took a drink and grimaced—it didn't taste very good.

The meal, however, was delicious: lamb with roasted autumn vegetables, bread, and cheeses. They finished with a chocolate crème cake, his favorite. After the meal, Graham brought over a silver tray adorned with gifts.

The baroness eyed him, smiling. "These were all taken from that trunk you and Miss Brown tried to break into. The trunk was your father's. And, though it's not time for you to inherit it, I felt that you would enjoy some of its treasures."

Bartholomew ripped into the gifts with fervor. The first gift was an inlaid walnut inkstand with double silver inkwells, the tops of which were etched the initials EHBF. The next gift was a sterling silver letter opener and magnifying glass, with matching designs. The **pièce de** résistance was a silver pocket watch adorned with an etching of a train. Bartholomew was thrilled. He surprised his aunt with an enthusiastic hug, as he thanked her several times for the gifts. She chuckled and gently pushed him away.

The Baroness straightened her jacket, gave him a reproachful glance, and then softened. "I'm glad you liked your gifts." She rose, patted his hand, and then left the room.

Apparently, the celebration was over.

When he got back to his personal apartments, Constance was there, sitting quietly by the fire. She rose from her seat when he came in.

"Happy birthday, Barty," she said softly.

"Where were you?" he asked, insistently.

Constance hesitated. "I had things to do today, Barty. I'm sorry that I missed your celebration—I really am—but, I was unavoidably detained."

"What sort of things did *you* have to do?"

His meaning was not lost on Constance. "Barty, though you think otherwise, I *do* have a life outside of these walls."

Bartholomew walked forward, stopping a mere foot in front of her. His closeness and expression startled her; she stepped back. He smirked. "Scared of me?"

"No...I—"

"You should be," he uttered, "because without me, you have no job. One word from me, and you are out on the street." He snapped his fingers to indicate her quick demise. "Now, tell me where you've been, and all is forgiven."

"You listen here, Bartholomew," she said in a tone more severe than he expected, "you are not my employer, and do not secure my position here. Lady Fitzhugh knows where I went. And, if she didn't take issue with it, neither should you." She crossed her arms and frowned. "Honestly, you don't need a nanny anymore—you can take care of yourself. Lady Fitzhugh agrees." Bartholomew flinched, not expecting the statement. "Furthermore, your forgiveness does not come at a price to me—either you forgive me, or you don't."

She set a small package on the seat of her chair. "This is my gift to you. Open it at your leisure." She walked swiftly to her room and locked the door behind her.

Bartholomew stared in disbelief for several minutes. Finally, he examined the small package. He recognized the neat wrapping and carefully tied silk bow as her work. He untied the ribbon and opened the little package, which contained a hand-carved dip pen, five pen nibs, and an embroidered pen pouch with his initials. Feeling a guilty pang as he ran a finger along the precise stitching, he thought of going to her immediately and offering his sincerest apology. But, he knew better.

TWENTY-ONE

"**O**kay, Lenora, close your eyes and take a deep breath."
Lenora stared into eyes that, despite their ice-blue color, were warm, reassuring. Rose seemed to look right through her, like she could see what was in her mind. The thought made Lenora uncomfortable, but Rose's warm disposition offset any uneasiness she might have. Lenora rested her head on the back of the couch, closed her eyes, drew in a deep breath, and waited for Rose's next instruction.

"Now," Rose continued, in a soothing voice, "keeping your eyes closed, I want you to remove your gloves and place your hands—palm side up—on your lap." Lenora did as she was told. "Ian is going to place a piece of cloth in your hand. When the cloth touches your skin, I want you to ignore all the pictures that come to your mind and describe to me what the cloth feels like on your skin…the texture, for example."

Lenora felt something brush her fingertips. Suddenly, light flashed behind her eyelids, as if there were thousands of photographers in the room. Trying to dull the intensity, she squeezed her eyes tightly, but the lights continued getting brighter. She shook her head side-to-side and then tried to open her eyes.

"No, keep your eyes closed," Rose said firmly, yet softly. "Rest your head back on the couch and describe how the cloth's texture feels."

"I can't—" The pressure behind Lenora's eyes was just too much.

"Yes you can, Lenora," Ian uttered. "Just concentrate....you can do it."

Lenora took a deep breath and moved the cloth around in her hand. "It feels bumpy, velvety...like there are ridges," she frowned. "It's like corduroy."

"Good, you're right on! Continue," Rose encouraged.

Lenora felt along the ridges of the fabric, concentrating, and then the brightness of the flashes dulled. Shadowy images of people drifted into her sight.

"Don't stop. Keep describing the cloth, no matter what images come to mind," Rose instructed. "You said the fabric feels velvety, continue from there."

Lenora concentrated again on the texture. "It's velvety soft and I keep picturing a dark color, like navy blue or a deep purple."

"Okay, now connect the texture you feel to the image in your mind."

"I see a dark purple dress...it's corduroy." Lenora squeezed her eyes as if trying to see more clearly. "I see white tights...and a little girl ....she's... *twirling*."

Ian chortled and Lenora began to open her eyes, the picture in her mind fading.

"No, Lenora, keep your eyes closed and concentrate. Ignore the distractions around you." Lenora heard irritation in Rose's tone.

"Sorry," Ian said softly.

"Now," Rose continued, "tell me what the little girl is doing. How old is she? Where is she?"

Lenora shook her head; the image was fading a bit. "I don't know. She might be four or five, but I might be wrong. She's in a room with a fireplace...big, plush chairs...couches, but I can't see—"

Lenora tried harder to concentrate, but the image had completely faded. She opened her eyes in time to see Rose removing the cloth square from her hand. It was a small square of deep purple corduroy. Lenora was intrigued that she was right about the texture, but mostly about the color. Her image seemed right on.

"Am I done?"

"For now, yes," Rose answered.

"But, can't we do this again? I just had the image and it went away," Lenora said, frustrated.

"We will, but next time," Rose answered.

"But why not now?"

"Because, today was about a quick exercise so that I could determine at what pace we need to work."

"And?" Lenora's impatience was transparent.

"We can work at a fairly quick pace," Rose laughed. "However, as the exercises become more difficult, you need to trust that I will know when to stop, and you need to resist fighting me on that. Understood?"

Lenora studied Rose's expression–it was stern, yet there was a kindness in the empathetic way she looked at Lenora. Lenora nodded her head in agreement.

"Good. We'll continue this exercise three days a week. The goal is to help you learn to control your ability. Once you're more adept, I'll help you *hone* your skills." Rose smiled at the look of doubt on Lenora's face. "Yes, my dear, you have skills, and great ones, I might add."

"How do you know? I mean, how can *you* know that?" This was all so difficult to digest.

"Rose is one of the most talented clairvoyants in the world," Ian interjected. "If anyone can figure it out, she can."

Lenora scowled at Ian, still feeling angry at him—he just smirked and winked at her. Her focus returned to Rose. "Is that what you do? You find out what people's abilities are?"

Rose laughed "No, it's not like that. Part of my ability is to see, in my head, events that will happen in the future. For example, a lot of government agencies use my ability to help them find kidnapped or missing children. I can see what will happen to them."

"How do you see it?" Lenora was intrigued.

"Usually in dreams. I dream about the event, and then I report that to the police."

"So, you just dream about random people?"

"No," Rose chuckled, "I need visual stimulation first, such as a picture or piece of clothing, to help the visions materialize."

"Do you find them? The missing children, I mean?"

"She has an accuracy rate of ninety-six percent," Ian interrupted.

Rose smiled warmly at Ian. "So far, I've found most of the children. Most are returned unharmed. Others…" Rose's face grew dark. "well, others are not. That's the frustrating part of my ability—it's subjective. I can only see what *might* happen, not what *will* happen. Sometimes, an event changes direction, and when that happens, their future becomes murky."

"How does an event change direction?"

"If kidnappers discover that the police are on to them," Rose explained, "they will sometimes change their minds and alter plans. That's how the event changes."

"Tell her what else you can do," Ian beamed.

Rose rolled her eyes at Ian and smiled. "My other ability is called claircognizance. It's the ability to obtain psychic knowledge by intrinsically knowing something. It's like a gut feeling, except everything in my mind and body screams that I'm right. It's hard to explain." She noticed Lenora's confusion. "For example, I know that a friend is pregnant before she even knows it."

"I also know if someone is lying or about to commit a crime," Rose continued, "and I know what people's abilities are, even if they don't know about it or intend to use it. My friend Carly is a low-level medium, but she doesn't have any idea. Her psychic self is vehemently against such an idea—it goes against her personal beliefs—so I have never revealed that bit of information to her. Carly frequently tells me about dreams of conversations she's had with her grandmother—who has been dead for over twenty years. I don't tell her that she really did have those conversations—that she wasn't dreaming."

"So, do you know what my ability is?" Lenora asked, still skeptical.

"*Abilities*," Rose corrected. "Yes, I know what they are."

"What are they?"

Rose studied Lenora's face for a minute and then let out a big sigh. She repositioned herself, pulled her long, honey-blonde hair into a ponytail, and then smiled warmly at Lenora. "I'll tell you, in theory, what these abilities are. However, I strongly urge you not to channel these abilities until you've learned to hone your skills with just the one."

"Rose, I don't think it's a good idea—"

Rose put her hand up, stopping Ian in mid-sentence. "No, I think Lenora has the right to know what these abilities are." She turned to Lenora. "I just cannot stress enough, though, how imperative it is that you take these abilities one step at a time. Your mother tried taking it all on at once, and it proved too much for her."

Ian barked out a warning cough that Lenora didn't notice; she was still focused on the fact that Rose knew her mother. "You knew my mom?"

"Yes, I did. We were friends...once. Since I had honed my abilities when I was very young, Walter asked me to help Bessie learn to sharpen her skills. But she was too impatient and headstrong. She decided to take them all on by herself. That was a huge mistake that I implore you not to make. Can you promise me that you will follow my instruction?"

Lenora nodded in assent. "Yes, I promise. Can you tell me more about my mom?"

Rose nodded. "Yes, I will tell you about your mom...in time. For now, if you follow my instruction— exactly as directed—you will be rewarded with information. Deal?"

"Absolutely!" Lenora was shaking out of pure excitement.

"Excellent. Now, about your abilities," Rose cleared her throat and took Lenora's hands in hers. "My dear, you have more ability in you than anyone I've ever met—even your mom. And, if done well, you will be a power beyond reckoning."

Lenora's eyes widened.

"Your first and foremost ability," Rose continued, "is called retro-cognition. It's the ability to see the past in the exact sequence of events as they occurred."

Rose paused to see if Lenora seemed lost and then continued, "Now, as you know, you are only able to see these events if you touch objects or people, and only with your bare hands—hence the gloves. This perception is called clairsentience—you gain insight through touch. And, you also know that by touching the object or person, you are sent into a trance, which sends you back to the place or time in question."

"You also know," Rose explained, "that you are susceptible to spirits that can hold your spirit in that event, thus trapping you in time. That is why Ian is here—to ensure that you are not taken while you learn how to perform your ability. My role is to teach you how to *control* your ability so that eventually, you won't need Ian's help."

Lenora glanced over at Ian, who had a somber, disapproving look on his face.

"This connection to spirits through trance is called trance mediumship," explained Rose. "In addition to your retro-cognition through clairsentience, you have the ability to communicate with the dead through trances."

The hairs rose on the back of Lenora's arms and goose bumps formed on her skin, sending her into an uncontrollable shiver. Ian ran over and draped his coat over her shoulders. He sat behind Lenora and rubbed her arms to help generate heat, but her shivering only increased. She wasn't cold—she was scared.

Rose looked concerned. "Maybe we should continue this discussion some other time—clearly, you are troubled, and this is a lot of information to take in at once."

"No!" Lenora held her hand up. "Please don't stop...I want to know!"

Rose glanced at Ian, took another deep breath, and nodded. "Okay, but if I get any indication from Ian that this needs to stop, I will. You have plenty of time to learn your abilities."

Lenora nodded in agreement.

"Now, where was I?" Rose asked no one in particular. "Oh, yes – communication with the dead. Your other ability is called clairaudience, or the ability to receive auditory impressions from spirits. Basically, you can hear voices, thoughts, sounds, tones, or noises that other humans or recording devices cannot. So, that time you heard someone breathing behind you, and the laugh? That was clairaudience. Hearing Thaddeus? That's also clairaudience."

Lenora sat frozen. Ever since she could remember, she dismissed these eerie, disjointed sounds and voices as figments of her imagination. Now that she knew the sounds were not imagined, it made her skin crawl.

"Can we stop now? I'm getting…tired." She didn't want to admit that she was scared.

"Of course," Rose answered in a concerned tone. "We can continue this discussion another time." She looked over Lenora's shoulder at Ian, who was frantically rubbing Lenora's arms. "Ian? Can I see you in the office for a minute?"

"Sure." Ian squeezed Lenora's arms before following Rose into Tom's office.

When the door clicked closed, Lenora rolled her eyes. She hated it when people talked about her behind closed doors, which was a continual occurrence lately. She was thankful for the window in the office door—it allowed her to see them at least. Currently, Rose appeared to be speaking to Ian in a calm, relaxed manner.

When Rose stopped talking, Ian instantly became animated, his head shaking in vigorous disagreement. Ian gesticulated wildly, while Rose calmly listened, a look of indifference on her face. Lenora chuckled softly. Rose's straightforward and composed nature made Lenora feel safe, relaxed.

After Ian's animated tirade, Rose put her hand on Ian's arm and spoke only a few words that left Ian standing with his head down, a crestfallen expression on his face. Lenora's curiosity was piqued.

Rose walked out of the office and made her way to the coat rack, where she silently put on her raincoat and picked up her briefcase. She looked at her watch and then smiled at Lenora. "It's getting late and I need to go home and prepare tomorrow's lecture. Ian will walk you home." She nodded over to the office, where Ian was still standing with his arms crossed, head down, his expression turned to anger.

"This week, both Ian and I have Tuesday and Thursday open, so we'll meet here again—same time, both nights. Next week, the days might be different, but I would like to try to meet at least three times each week." Rose shot a disapproving look toward Ian and then shook her head. "Ian thinks three days is too aggressive." She nodded at Lenora. "It was lovely meeting you."

"Rose?" Lenora was hesitant to ask the next question, but she knew that Rose would be straight with her. "Why am I just finding out about my abilities now? Why haven't I…felt…them until now?"

Rose forced a smile. "Well, Lenora, you've had these abilities your entire life. However, it sometimes takes a certain event to trigger those abilities—to bring them out. Your event was more than likely your mother's death."

"But, nothing really happened until we moved here."

Rose pursed her lips in hesitation and then nodded, as if making a decision. "You did show signs immediately after your mother's death, as your dad already told you. At Mrs. K's?" Lenora nodded in remembrance. "Immediately after that, Tom called Walter in a state of utter panic. Because your father is not equipped to handle your abilities on his own, Walter instructed him to give you mild sedatives until you moved here."

Lenora frowned. She knew that her dad had her take sedatives, but she thought that it was to help with sleep—not to help keep her abilities at bay.

Rose perceived Lenora's impending anger. "Don't blame your dad. He did what he knew best. It was only meant as a protective measure."

Lenora shook her head. "I'm not mad, it's just…well…I don't know how to explain it."

"Frustrated, perhaps?" Rose offered. Lenora nodded her head. "In time, you'll piece things together and they'll begin to make sense.

But for now, take it slowly—your abilities aren't to be taken lightly. Understand?" Lenora nodded her head again in agreement. "Good, then go and get some rest. And, it is truly wonderful to meet you finally." Rose paused in the doorway. "I did really love Bessie—she and I were best friends once."

Lenora swallowed hard and nodded, speechless. Her heart ached to know the part of her mother that Rose knew.

Once Rose had left, Lenora got up and stood in the office doorway, staring at Ian. "What's wrong with you?"

Ian, startled from his stupor, looked at Lenora and smiled weakly. "Nothing that you need worry about." He put an arm around her shoulder and smiled. "Let's get out of here. I have a hankering for pizza."

Lenora felt utterly exhausted. It was frustrating that the tiniest exercise drained her energy. She hoped it would get better over time. It had to—she couldn't spend her whole life being so tired. Sighing heavily, she slid into her pajamas and fell into bed. She nestled into the covers and reflected on the evening—mostly on the past few hours with Ian.

Dinner with Ian was a bit awkward at first, but they soon fell into an easy conversation and ended the evening as friends again. Lenora felt giddy being this close to Ian again, but apprehensive—she was afraid he would hurt her again. Thoughts of Ian played on her mind as she drifted softly to sleep.

She fought him, throwing punches and kicking his shins. She slapped and clawed at his face, raking into his skin. He winced in pain, feeling the blood running down his face, and strained to gain control of the maniacal woman. He grabbed her body and forcefully swung it around so that her back was pressed against him. He rammed her up against a brick wall so that she was completely pinned. She started to scream, sending a frenzied panic through

him. *He thrust his hand into his pocket and retrieved the cloth, pressing it firmly to her face and waited for her to grow limp.*

He relaxed his tension against her and exhaled in relief. Taking in a deep breath, he lifted her onto his shoulder again. His heart pounded; he perspired heavily from the fight. His cheek throbbed from the deep scratches, and blood still trickled down his face. He rubbed his face on the side of her thigh to wipe off some of the blood, but stopped because it sent sharp bolts of pain through his cheek to his eye. She would regret that mistake.

Close to his flat, he heard footsteps drawing near. Panicking, he looked around for a place to hide—a shadowed doorway or corner that he could press into to avoid being seen, but he found nothing, and it was too late, the man had already seen them.

The man tipped his hat. He nodded nervously in return. "Got some trouble there?" the man asked.

"No..." he said, trying to regain some composure, "it's my wife. She's had too much of the drink."

The man whistled and chuckled. "Do you need assistance, old chap? Can I hail a coach?"

"No, thank you...we're not far now." He shrugged, trying to look mildly amused. "Can't handle her liqueur."

"I know how that goes, my friend." The man chuckled, tipped his hat again, and then walked off.

He watched the man leave, anger and nervousness swelling up inside of him, causing his stomach to churn, making him feel nauseous. He ran the rest of the way, caring not whether she became injured in the process. He carried her up the steps to his flat, and then heaved her body down onto the settee. He ran over to the cupboard and doused another cloth with chloroform—just in case—and filled another syringe. This one was tougher than the others, and he intended to be prepared.

Suddenly, rather than seeing events through the man, Lenora was in the room with them.

She now stood in the corner of a dark room—a room that looked oddly familiar, yet appeared to be from a distant past. Lenora looked in horror as she caught sight of a man standing above a lifeless body, a knife in his hand, arm poised to cut. She gasped in disgust.

He paused, mid-stroke, and turned his head slowly, mechanically. His eyes met hers. Instantly, Lenora glanced behind her, thinking that he was looking at someone else—no way could he see her...this was a dream.

His lips stretched into a menacing sneer, spittle dribbling down his chin and splattering onto the girl's lifeless body. Lenora's stomach churned.

"Welcome, Lenora." His tone was unnerving. Lenora shook her head in disbelief. He laughed. "I can seeeee yoooou!" he sung repulsively. He walked toward her and kneeled.

Lenora cringed as he looked her up and down, assaulting her body with his eyes. He closed his eyes, tilted his head back, and inhaled deeply. As he exhaled, he brought his head back slowly, a terrifying look crossing his face. Lenora felt the bile rise in her throat. She wanted to scream, but was frozen in horror.

"You are a naughty girl, having that protection spell cast against me. Doesn't that stupid witch know that you're mine?" His face contorted into an ugly sneer. "I can't touch you...but give me time." He grinned. "But, I can wait—you'll eventually come to me."

"Never," Lenora said with conviction. "I will never come to you."

"You have no choice." Lenora recoiled as he slaked his tongue over his dry lips. "You're mine—you will bend to my will."

"Never," Lenora repeated, trying to squirm away from him. His hold became stronger. She squeezed her eyes tightly, trying to concentrate on her bed covers, the texture of the material, in hope that it would send her back from his world.

"Look at me," he commanded. Against her will, her head turned and eyes opened. He grinned calmly as he waved the knife over her pants.

"No, please, don't," she sobbed.

He brought the knife down, shredding her pants in swift proficiency. Running the blade along her leg and up to her torso, he sliced a button off the *bottom of her shirt. Lenora whimpered and tried to move, but her body was frozen.*

He moved the knife in slow circles on her stomach, a slow smile spreading across his face, before he quickly sliced two more buttons off her shirt. She felt the sting of the blade as it scraped across her stomach and warm blood trickled down her sides.

He moved the blade up her torso, stopping just below her chin. He leered. "It's time to make you mine."

She screamed.

"Lenora!"

Lenora bolted upright, looking quickly around the room. A heavy feeling pressed upon her—as if she had been asleep for years. It took some time for her to notice Ian sitting on the bed next to her, eyes wide in terror. "Ian?"

"Lenora!" He breathed a sigh of relief. "It took me nearly ten minutes to wake you—" He stopped, looking down at her body, a look of dread and confusion crossing his face.

Lenora propped herself up and looked at her body—her pajamas were torn to shreds and scratches ran along her torso and all across her stomach. She started to cry. "I thought Emily's protection spell…"

"You did this to yourself," Ian said with disbelief. "Look at your hands." Lenora raised her blood-stained hands and whimpered.

"What the hell is going on here…" Tom's voice trailed off as he stared in horror at his daughter. "What the…Lenora? What happened to you? Ian? Her clothes…" He ran over, pushing Ian aside, covering his daughter once he realized just how exposed she really was. He turned to Ian. "Get out!"

"Dr. Kelley…it wasn't me! I-I was just—"

Tom softened. "I know…just leave, okay? I need to be alone with my daughter. You can talk to her when she's…decent."

Ian nodded and left quietly.

Tom threw a robe around Lenora, grabbed hold of his sobbing daughter, and held her for nearly an hour.

They were interrupted with a loud bang and dragging noises in the hall. Lenora's bedroom door flew open and Ian appeared, dragging a mattress along the floor.

"Ian? What are you doing?" Tom asked, sounding exhausted.

Ian refrained from answering until the mattress was fully in the room. He sat down on the mattress and wiped perspiration from his brow. "Heavy bugger. I didn't expect that from a fold-out mattress."

"Ian? Explain?" Tom wasn't interested in small talk.

Ian sighed, nodding. "I'm going to sleep on the floor near Lenora—tonight and every night—until that entity goes away."

"That's nice of you Ian, but maybe you can take my room, and I'll sleep on Lenora's floor."

Ian exhaled loudly. "Look, I know I'm not exactly trustworthy when it comes to women, but that's not the issue here. This *thing* is forcing her to harm herself because it can't. I need to be here to stop it." He paused, gazing at Lenora with concern. "The only reason I knew she was in danger was because Thaddeus got me, and it was nearly too late. I need to be here—there's nothing you can do to help her. You know that, Dr. Kelley. I'm sorry, but this is for her benefit."

Tom nodded in defeat. "You're right." He rose from Lenora's side and kissed the top of her head. "You okay? Do you want me to leave or stay?"

"I'm okay, Dad, you go ahead and try to get some sleep." She wasn't alright, but her dad looked exhausted.

Tom nodded, patting Ian on the shoulder as he walked past. He took one long look at his daughter and sighed heavily before closing the door softly behind him.

Ian made up his bed and then sat next to Lenora. "I'll not leave your side." He kissed her forehead and cheeks, and then paused near her lips. He drew back quickly, looking torn, surprised. Instantly, he got up and walked back to his mattress. He settled in and gave her a weak smile. "Good night. I hope you sleep well."

Lenora waited until Ian fell asleep and then reached to the side of the bed, grabbing the Bartholomew Booth folder. She turned on her book light and settled in.

She didn't sleep a wink the rest of the night.

FINAL NARRATIVE OF BARTHOLOMEW BOOTH

PART II

Constance's days out grew longer, and her arrivals became progressively later, causing her to occasionally neglect her duties. Consequently, the Baroness instigated a curfew. Constance was under strict orders to arrive in the afternoon before high tea. Violation would result in immediate dismissal.

Bartholomew was present during the reprimand and inwardly felt pleased. Though he didn't want her fired, a part of him wanted her punished for staying away so long.

Before the baroness left, she leveled a scrutinizing gaze. "Constance, indeed. You most certainly do not live up to your name." She sneered and left the room, slamming the door.

Constance glanced at Bartholomew, who stared at his untouched meal. "You just had to tattle, didn't you?"

Stunned, Bartholomew shook his head. "I didn't say anything!"

"Oh, come on, Barty! Everyone knows how angry you've become at my increased absence." She removed her scarf and coat. "You're sixteen years old—too old to have someone present at meal times… you can feed yourself, for the love of—"

"It was me, ma'am," Lottie uttered apologetically from the doorway. "I'm sorry, but it's my duty to report any misdoings, and you're breaking the rules. It's…it's my job." Her eyebrows furrowed as she lowered her head.

Constance exhaled. "I know, Lottie—it's not your fault, it's mine. I know better, and you are all paying for my mistake. No harm done, really."

"Thank you," Lottie said quietly, closing the door.

"I'm going to have her fired," Bartholomew said angrily.

"You will do nothing of the sort," Constance uttered, sounding exhausted. She sat in the chair across from Bartholomew. "She was just doing her job, Barty. I am the one disobeying the rules, and I need to face the consequences."

"Well, we'd cover for you if you told us where you were," Bartholomew said sourly.

"Barty," she sighed, resting a hand on her chin, "just eat your supper, please."

Bartholomew opened his mouth to say something else, but decided against it—she looked like she wasn't in the mood for revelations just now. He ate quickly, trying to get through the cold meal so he could just go to bed. A soft hand on his arm stopped him.

"Barty," she said softly and smiled. He liked the way she said his name. "Slow down—you're going to upset your stomach. Why don't you put the fork down and talk to me. How was your day?"

He shrugged. "Fine, I guess. Studies all day, as usual." He eyed her. "Why can't you just stay here? Why don't you spend time with me on Saturdays like you used to?"

Constance lowered her head and sighed in irritation. "Barty, just drop it, please. I'm not going to tell you where I've been—my business is my own."

She rose from her chair and turned to go, when Bartholomew stopped her. "Wait. Please."

"I'm not in the mood for this tonight, Barty."

"Just sit with me...we can talk about something else." He immediately noticed the look of disbelief in her face. "I promise." Constance exhaled and sat down, looking impatient. Bartholomew searched his brain for something...anything...to talk about. "Um..." he began, still searching, "what did my aunt mean when she said you don't 'live up to your name'?"

"My name means steadfastness, unchanging, resolute. It was the closest my parents could come to one of the seven heavenly virtues—they wanted fortitude, but couldn't find a fitting name, so chose something close enough. My parents were great admirers of the virtues. My sisters' names are Charity, Hope, and Prudence."

"What happened...to your family, I mean?" Bartholomew asked tentatively.

"My mother and sister Hope died of scarlet fever shortly before my fifteenth birthday. My father was so distraught that he committed suicide two weeks later, leaving my sisters and me alone."

"How did he—"

"Threw himself in front of a train."

"What happened to you and your sisters?"

"I was sent to St. Adelaide's Almshouse, where your aunt found me." Her expression darkened. "I don't know what became of Charity and Prudence. I fear for them daily. It's my hope that they are somewhere safe and loving." Bartholomew was completely enrapt in her history. "Our parents were loving people—I had a lovely, warm, and happy childhood. Prudence and Charity were ten and eight when we were separated."

"I'm sorry..." Bartholomew was speechless.

"So am I." She rose from her chair. "I'm going to bed now, Barty—it's been a long day and I need my rest." She stopped midway to her room and turned. "That's what I've been doing, you know. A kind person is helping me find my sisters."

"Why didn't you tell me?"

"Because, I have no privacy here, and this is too close to my heart. You understand, don't you?"

Bartholomew nodded. "If you tell my aunt, I'm sure she'll—"

Constance held her hand up and shook her head. "No, she's right, I have a duty. Lady Fitzhugh saved me from a life of obscurity. I owe her my loyalty and commitment…steadfastness." She gave him a stern look. "Can I trust you to keep my secret?"

"Yes," he said, nodding, "you can trust me."

"Thank you." Constance smiled weakly and then closed her door.

The atmosphere changed for a while. Bartholomew was satisfied with Constance's explanation of her outings—he even covered for her when she occasionally ran late. Helping her lent him a deep satisfaction and rising hope that his benevolence would pay off—that she could see him as a giving, loving person and eventually fall in love with him.

Things changed once he realized that the kind person she spoke of was Theodore W. Archer, a young doctoral student at the university.

Bartholomew first noticed that Constance was writing—and receiving—letters, sometimes two or three times a day. Curious, he grabbed one of the letters from Lottie as she walked past to post it for Constance. Lottie tried wrenching the letter free, but Bartholomew was quicker and stronger.

The letter was addressed to Mr. T.W. Archer.

"Who is this?" he asked Lottie, who crossed her arms, refusing to answer. "You are only forcing me to trespass on Constance's privacy, then. I have to read it."

"No, sir, please don't—that's private!"

"Then, tell me who this Archer person is!"

"It's….a family friend."

He saw right through her. "You lie," he said as he pried the letter open. He nearly dropped the letter out of shock.

Dearest Theodore,

As I look out into the gray skies and smell the fresh rain, I think of you and the time we spent under the umbrella at the park. Oh, how I wish I could express how dear our time together has become to me…how dear you are to me now. Never did I dream that the search for my sisters would end in my finding love.

I cannot wait to see you tomorrow – eleven o'clock, sharp, by the old church. And, don't be late—our time is precious and fleeting.

Love and miss you, always,

Your Constance

Bartholomew gaped. He turned to Lottie and thrust the letter at her. "Tell me, now, who is this?"

"I-I don't really know him at all!" Lottie said, shrinking. "All I know is that he is helping to find her sisters…and that they're in love."

Enraged, he lunged at Lottie. "Don't lie to me!"

"I-I'm not lying, really sir!" Her voice faltered.

He scowled at her and huffed. "This never happened, understand? You didn't see me read this letter."

"What? I—"

"Do not tell anyone, especially her, that I know. Do you understand what will happen to you if you tell?"

"Yes, I understand."

"Good. Now, go mail the damn thing."

Lottie slowly took the letter from him and scurried down the hall. Bartholomew waited until she was out of sight and then entered his apartments. Constance was sitting on the window ledge, watching the sun as it set on the horizon, looking content. Bartholomew sneered as he walked toward his bedroom.

"Barty? Is that you?"

He paused, looking blankly ahead. "I need a nap—my head hurts."

"Do you need—"

"No, I just need to be left alone to sleep."

"Please ring if you need me," she replied in a concerned tone.

Bartholomew shut the bedroom door behind him, threw himself down upon the bed, and cried.

Then, he stopped.

A deep, dark voice spoke within. It spoke of dark deeds that terrified and thrilled him. It made him smile.

He slept through to the following morning; Constance had to wake him before the first tutor arrived. He kept an eye on her as she sat in the corner sewing, taking the occasional, longing glance out the window. It made him sick to know she was thinking of *him*.

At half past ten, she left, and he felt a sudden sharp stabbing in his chest.

Once the tutor left, he spent several minutes staring out the window. He wondered which old church they were meeting at. Anger reeled within him at the thought of what Constance might be doing with this Archer person.

"NO!" he screamed, shaking his head violently to rid the thoughts from his mind. He fell to his knees by her favorite chair and lay his head on the soft velvet cushion, crying and pounding his fists until they were numb. At length, he turned and noticed her silver-plated pin cushion. It was her favorite. He turned it over in his hand several times before throwing it across the room.

"Whore!" he shouted, picking up the chair and hitting it continuously against the wall until it broke in several pieces.

Hearing the noise, Lottie ran in and uttered a surprised gasp when she saw the room in disarray.

"Clean this up," Bartholomew uttered without explanation. "Now!"

Lottie moved quickly, holding her breath in fear until Bartholomew left the room.

The following week, the baroness left town for business. Constance took the opportunity to extend her clandestine appointments with Archer. Livid, Bartholomew decided quickly to feign illness to force Constance to stay home to attend his needs.

At first, it was the perfect plan. Constance stayed constantly by his side. Occasionally, he heard Constance weeping outside his door. He knew it was because she missed meeting Archer.

The deep dark within sneered with satisfaction.

On the third day, he was inwardly boasting of his perfect plan, when Lottie entered his room.

"Where's Constance?"

"She's...resting, sir."

"Tell her I need her at once."

"I can tend to you for now, sir. Miss Brown is extremely tired and needs to rest."

"She can rest when I do," he replied with contempt.

Lottie nodded and left the room. He heard Lottie convey his message, and Constance's slow "I see" response. When Constance entered the room, Bartholomew proceeded to sigh and moan.

She placed a cool hand on his head. "You just don't feel feverish," she asserted. "But, you wouldn't carry on so if it weren't serious."

Bartholomew secretly triumphed as she dutifully poured cool water into a vessel, submerged a fresh rag into the water, and wrung it out. He heard a small gasp to his right. Lottie noticed his calculating grin. She narrowed her eyes in a knowing glance, shook her head, and silently left the room.

That afternoon, Lottie threw open the doors. "Since our young master has been so ill, I took it upon myself to call for the doctor."

Bartholomew's eyes flew open in shock as a man entered the room with a medical bag. Bartholomew threw Lottie a menacing leer as the doctor opened his bag and took out examination instruments.

"I'm sorry, master Bartholomew, but it's time you stop being so brave and let us fetch the doctor to help relieve your suffering." She smiled wryly. "Doctor Murray," she began without taking her eyes off of Bartholomew, "will you need our services while attending Bartholomew?"

The doctor shook his head. "Only one of you is necessary. I'll ring if help is needed."

"I'll be right outside the door," Lottie offered, and then turned to Constance. "You're relieved for now, Miss Brown. Go take the rest you need."

"Thank you, Lottie," Constance replied. And, without even a second glance, she left the room.

The doctor could not explain Bartholomew's illness. When he suggested transfusion, Bartholomew jumped up from bed, announcing his sudden revival. The doctor still prescribed rest for the day, yet maintained that Bartholomew could continue the week as scheduled.

Lottie expected Bartholomew's retaliation.

Bartholomew's insistence on reading Constance's letters became relentless. He poured over the letters, growing increasingly agitated the more he read them.

"Why do you insist on torturing yourself?" Lottie asked him one day. "You know that they're in love. She'll never love you that way—you're like a brother to her. Why don't you just let her go? I'm sure there are many girls your own age that would love to have your attentions."

"Shut up, Lottie. What do you know of love? You've been a servant to betters all your life."

"And you know better about love?" She asked, incensed. "You are just a child! I've been married for twenty-five years. I think I know a damn sight more than you."

He sneered at her and then resumed reading the letter from Archer to Miss Brown. The letter oozed of love and tenderness; it made Bartholomew's stomach churn. This man could never love her the way he does. Never.

Ultimately, spying on Constance became his obsession. Confiscating letters, watching her every movement, and listening to her conversations with Lottie became an everyday occurrence. His mind reeled every time Constance arrived looking radiant from her meetings with Archer. Reading the daily letter exchange wore him down physically and mentally. Bartholomew grew more despondent and temperamental with everyone, including his tutors. He became sarcastic and mean to Lottie, often threatening her physically, should she reveal his secret.

One evening, after enduring one of Bartholomew's particularly grueling tirades, Lottie put her foot down. She knew that Bartholomew had no hold over her, so she informed him that no matter how he begged, pleaded, or threatened, she would no longer allow him to see the letters. Furthermore, if he continued the abuse, she would report his behavior to the baroness.

Bartholomew raged, throwing books at Lottie, threatening her bodily harm. But, he knew it would do him no good—and she held true to her word.

For some time thereafter, Bartholomew receded into a quiet reticence. His mood spiraled downward, grades began to falter, and he was sullen with Constance, who was confused by the apparent and sudden change in his countenance.

At dinner one Sunday evening, the baroness leveled a gaze at Bartholomew. "Miss Brown tells me that you've been... morose as of late."

He shot an indignant glance at Constance.

"I'm sorry, Barty…I have just been concerned for you," she responded nervously.

"The staff has also told me," the baroness continued, "that you have been acting like a spoilt child—tossing things about your room, throwing tantrums, and pretending illness." She shook her head. "Care to tell me the problem?"

"I'm sorry, ma'am," Bartholomew said, eyes lowered. "It's just that—"

The baroness never gave him a chance to respond. "The problem is that you're pampered—and you've forgotten what it means to be respectful."

"No, ma'am, I haven't—"

"Don't interrupt me, boy!" The walls echoed with the baroness' piercing shout.

Bartholomew lowered his head meekly, but not before glowering at Constance.

The baroness noticed immediately. "Don't you dare blame Miss Brown! She has been a good, attentive nanny to you, and I'll not have you showing disrespect to her in *my* house." She stared at him for several minutes. "So, what is it that you want to have happen here?"

Bartholomew pondered a moment. He wanted Constance to love him—pure and simple. But, how was he to say that to his aunt? Furthermore, he wanted more information about his father, and to be treated like a man. He glanced at his aunt, who was looking at him expectantly. "I would like to have my father's trunk—I want to see what's inside. I want to know who he was."

"You're not ready to see everything in that trunk. Not just yet."

"When? When will I be ready?"

"When you are older."

"But I *am* older! I'm sixteen and already a man!"

His aunt cackled. "Oh, but you are not yet a man. Age has but little to do with it—there are several qualities one must first have before he is deemed a man, and behaving like a petulant child is not one of them."

Bartholomew slumped in his chair. "I deserve to know who my father was."

"And you think you've acted in a way deserving of that right?"

"No…I mean, yes. I was born, isn't that right enough?"

"Hardly," his aunt chuckled and then sat back and studied him a moment. "I think we're done with this conversation. The several reports I've received from the staff, coupled with Miss Brown's latest testimony, is more than I need to make a decision."

"What are you talking about?"

"Starting tonight, you will begin the transition from boy to young man. I will have Graham move Miss Brown's things from your apartments. She will relocate to a different wing in the house. She will maintain her morning and evening duties, but the rest of the day is her own."

"Thank you, Baroness," Constance whispered appreciatively.

The baroness nodded and then continued. "This will give you time to become less reliant on others." She smiled coolly. "It will also prepare you for next year."

"Next year?" Bartholomew could taste the bile rise in his throat.

"You're going to boarding school, of course."

"No!" Bartholomew shouted. "No, I can behave—please, please give me another chance!"

"No, it's been decided—long before Miss Brown came to me. You were enrolled last week."

"What?" Bartholomew was incredulous. "So, when do I go?"

"At the end of August," she replied. "Miss Brown will be relieved of her duties at that time."

Bartholomew looked pleadingly at Miss Brown, who didn't return his gaze. So, that's it, then, after August, he would never see her again.

After Constance moved to another wing, the relationship between her and Bartholomew changed significantly. Constance seemed distant, cold, as she proficiently tended her morning and evening duties. They no longer ate at meal together. Miss Brown took meals in her room, which Bartholomew discovered was two doors away from his aunt's personal apartments.

When she was around, he still felt that aching bitterness when she glanced yearningly out the window, no doubt thinking of Archer.

The distance between them grew, as did that stirring darkness within him.

The baroness even distanced herself from him. No longer did she make surprise visits to check on his progress, and he found that his place setting was again at the opposite end of the long table for their Sunday dinners.

Loneliness crept upon him like a black shadow, enfolding itself around him. He welcomed the unexpected comfort this loneliness brought—it allowed the darkness to drift within him and grow. An intense resentment grew toward Miss Brown for rejecting his love, and toward his aunt for her coldness and refusal to disclose his father's true history. He became despondent, withdrawing further into himself as the depression deepened.

Then one day, it was like something snapped inside his mind. No longer willing to endure the continual torment, Bartholomew decided to do something about it. Alone in his room, he came up with the perfect plan.

His first task: get the key to the attic.

Graham had keys to every room in the house—including the attic. And, he kept them in his room.

One night, when Graham attended his evening duties, Bartholomew snuck into his room.

Graham's room was small and sparsely furnished, making his task easy. Looking through the dresser and nightstand drawers, Bartholomew found nothing aside from undergarments and personal grooming supplies. The armoire contained Graham's uniforms, both daily wear and special occasion. Bartholomew wondered if he had any regular clothes.

A creaking sound on the stair caught his attention. Bartholomew sprinted to the door, peered out, and gasped. Graham was heading this way! Now in a panic, Bartholomew quickly searched the room for a hiding place. He checked under the bed, but it was so high off the ground that he would be visible from all angles.

Footsteps neared the room.

Quickly, Bartholomew ran across the room, stuffing himself inside the armoire just as Graham entered.

Bartholomew tried to slow his breathing to calm his frantic heart—if he was caught, the baroness would definitely send him away. Looking through the armoire's tiny keyhole, he watched as Graham removed items from his pocket and set them on the dresser. Then, Graham removed his coat and placed it carefully on a chair near the door. He reached to his left, removing a key ring from his belt, hanging it on an iron hook behind the door.

Bartholomew smiled. This would be easier than he thought.

Graham left the room and went down the hall to the water closet. Seeing his opportunity to flee, Bartholomew quickly ran from the room, making it to his own before being discovered.

Once in his room, Bartholomew melted wax into his snuff box. When it was nearly set, he turned it upside down, marveling at the near-perfect wax square that emerged. He placed it in his pocket and then waited.

Sometime after two o'clock in the morning, Bartholomew crept out into the hallway and headed toward Graham's room. He cringed when the door creaked loudly, sure that it would wake Graham. However, he was soon relieved to hear Graham's loud snoring. Quietly, Bartholomew snuck into the room and carefully removed the key ring from the hook. He closed the door to Graham's room and headed toward the attic.

Bartholomew made quick work of trying each key until he found the one that opened the attic door. He lit a lantern near the attic's entrance and then removed the wax square from his pocket. He held the wax over the lantern until it was soft and pliable, and then pushed the key into the wax to make an imprint. Returning the wax mold to his pocket, he snuffed the lantern and relocked the attic door.

Tiptoeing through the hall, he entered Graham's room and returned the key ring without notice. Reaching the end of the hall, he nearly began celebrating, when he stopped short.

Standing in the center of the hall was his aunt, glaring at him.

Bartholomew froze; heart drumming heavily. "G-good evening, aunt," Bartholomew stammered.

The baroness crossed her arms, eyes narrowed. "Nice try, Bartholomew. What are *you* doing up so late, and in this wing of the house? You know you're not allowed."

"I couldn't sleep, so I—"

"Thought you would bother Miss Brown?" A knowing smile played on her face.

"No, actually, I went to Graham's room," he explained, hoping a half-truth would save him.

The baroness frowned. "Graham? Whatever for?"

"To ask him for hot milk…so that it might help me fall asleep." He glanced furtively at his aunt, who looked incredulous. "The last time I couldn't sleep, Graham made me a glass of hot milk with brandy…it helped me sleep. I thought it might help this time, too."

The look on her face made him feel dissected. It was near truth— Graham did make him milk and brandy the last time he suffered from insomnia. The baroness inhaled and nodded. "Yes, Graham's special warm milk is soothing." She raised her eyebrows. "Well? Did you get your milk?"

"No," he responded, "Graham was snoring when I got there. I didn't want to disturb him."

"Well, perhaps you should try reading—it helps me."

"Y-yes, I'll try it," he responded, feeling vastly relieved.

"Good, then. Back to bed, now—you have a long day of study tomorrow."

"Yes, ma'am," he responded, obeying her.

Back in his room, Bartholomew leaned on the door, trying to recover his breath. This sneaking around was perilous, yet thrilling. He walked to his desk, where he took out Miss Brown's silver-plated pincushion and melted it. He poured the molten liquid into the wax mold. Once the metal cooled, he removed the newly made key from the mold and inspected it. It was flawless, and he couldn't wait to try it on the attic door tomorrow night.

Bartholomew opened the door to the attic—he couldn't believe that his key actually worked. Once inside, he lit the lantern and stuffed black cloth in the door crack to avoid light shining through. The tiny, rusted padlock on the outside of his father's trunk was easily broken with a heavy brass candlestick he found on a table nearby.

The trunk contained various awards and metals from Edward's school and athletic events. Silver gilded frames protected pictures of Edward in various stages of life. Bartholomew stood in front of a mirror, holding Edward's university picture at his side. He was tall like his father, but lankier and more awkward looking. Edward stood regal, and had a strong jawline. Bartholomew had his mother's rounder, more feminine facial features. His eyes were dark like Edward's, but he had his mother's small, down-turned mouth.

A small box at the bottom of the trunk caught his attention. The box was deep and heavy, piquing his curiosity. On top was a stack of letters, tied together with a soft blue ribbon. The first name he saw was Adella Elizabeth Booth—his mother, though he only knew her as Addie. Every letter in the bundle was addressed to Edward from Adella. He opened the letters, devouring their accounts of the mundane life of a merchant's daughter, and declarations of her undying devotion to Edward.

One letter contained a miniature portrait of his mother in her youth. She was prettier than he remembered. Her skin was a soft pale pink, and her eyes were bright, happy. This rendering of her was strange to him—he only remembered her leathery skin and worn expression.

The tone in the letters changed quickly from carefree playfulness to one of deep yearning and talk of elopement. Bartholomew held his breath as he read the next letter—the first mention that he was about to enter their lives.

My Dearest Edward,

It is with great elation—and fear, I daresay—that I tell you that I am with child. I am uncertain as to when this little bundle of joy will enter our lives, but I am overwhelmed with happiness.

Please send me word—I am sick with worry for what to do.

Your loving Adella

Bartholomew wished that he had his father's letters so he knew how Edward felt about the news. The next letter in the bundle revealed how Adella's family received the news, immediately banishing her to live with her aunt, several miles away in the country. In her letter, Adella pleaded with Edward to reason with his father again—to ask permission for them to marry before the child was born.

The next letter was dated several months after Bartholomew was born.

My Dearest Edward,

Though you have been gone mere days, I miss you as if it has been months, or even years. How is our little son? Is he well-received with your family? Does he yearn for his mamma?

I am in urgent hope that seeing his grandson will soften your father's resolve and that we may be seen as a legitimate family.

Please write soon, as I long to hear of how our little Bartholomew is doing.

Your loving wife Adella

Wife? Bartholomew stared at the word for several seconds before realization struck him—his parents were married! He put the letter down and sifted through the box until he found what he needed: his birth certificate and his parents' marriage certificate. The latter, showed the date of their marriage being prior to his birth. More shocking was the listing of his last name on the birth certificate—not of Booth, but of Fitzhugh!

He was legitimate after all!

According to Adella's next letter, Edward's family must have become immediately attached to Bartholomew. She expressed great confusion that despite this, Edward's father still refused to recognize Adella as Edward's wife and their son as a legitimate Fitzhugh. Adella encouraged Edward to give up and return home with their son.

The next letter was dated three years later. Bartholomew assumed that he and his parents lived together as a family during this period. He wished he remembered those years—as he imagined them to be happy ones.

The letter was addressed to the mansion. Apparently, Edward traveled alone in another attempt at convincing his father to recognize them as a legitimate family. This was the start of their undoing.

Bartholomew groaned as he read his mother's account. While Edward visited the mansion, his mother and sister made a surprise visit to Adella and Bartholomew. The grandmother and aunt played with Bartholomew, while enjoying Adella's generosity. They wasted little time offering Adella a large sum of money to go away. They tried convincing Adella that leaving was her only option to give Bartholomew a better life and allow Edward the chance to raise their son without scandal.

Evidently, her letter reached Edward, who then spoke to his father about the shocking visit. It seemed as if Edward was successful this time.

My Dearest Edward,

I was overjoyed to read your letter! Please tell your father not to be too angry with your mother and sister—they were just trying to do what they thought best. Tell them I have no hard feelings, and am eagerly anticipating the day we can all become a family once and for all.

Their request of a proper Fitzhugh wedding seems so simple a solution for all. Marrying you again brings such joy to my heart. I would marry you many times over if it were to bring us the bliss we seek.

Bartholomew and I are soon to board the coach, which will take us to you and our new family.

Until then,

Your loving wife Adella

Bartholomew laid the letter down, anticipating another behind it, but found nothing. Instead, he found a confusing letter addressed to Edward from the local constable.

Mr. E. Fitzhugh,

On the twelfth day of August, a coach on route to Cambridge was beset by a band of robbers, who took all possessions inside the coach, murdered all passengers therein, and then set the coach ablaze. We have been hard put to identify the bodies within, but did receive a copy of the travel papers, which indicated that your wife and son were aboard.

I regret to inform you that we were able to identify your wife and son positively through the legible papers on your wife's person.

Your wife's family has come to claim their daughter and your son, so it is to them you should defer. However, should you need further assistance, you may contact our offices.

Regretfully,

Const. Wm. Jefferson

Bartholomew's brow furrowed. This letter did not make sense. He and his mother were obviously not killed on that coach. He sifted through the remaining documents, finding his father's enlistment papers, dated a mere three days after the letter from the constable. Immediately following the enlistment papers was his father's death certificate, dated two weeks after the enlistment.

He looked at the cause of death, and was shocked at what he saw. Written therein were the words "suicide by hanging." His father killed himself? But, his aunt said he died in an accident. Feeling suddenly dizzy, Bartholomew collected the letters and replaced them in the small box.

Back in his room, Bartholomew stared at the box, wondering what to do. He wasn't sure how or when, but he knew that he was going to confront his aunt...with everything. And this time, he was going to get the truth.

TWENTY-TWO

L enora felt frustrated.

The work with Rose and Ian thus far produced few results—Lenora was still only able to faintly distinguish the little girl in the purple dress, and she was starting to see someone's face more clearly, but that was it.

Matters were equally at a dead end with the CSP team. The technical team had spent several days reviewing videos taken in the apartment over the past three weeks, and they had yet to discover anything new.

Lenora missed sleeping in her own bed.

Ian's stay in Lenora's room was short-lived; Tom consulted with Rose, who confirmed that the entity couldn't physically harm Lenora and would only play with her to cause distress and invoke fear. Rose assured Tom that she could show Lenora a technique to fight back. Feeling secure in what Rose told him, Tom said that was enough for Ian to move back into the living room, with the caveat that he be home by midnight so that he could be there when Lenora fell asleep.

Ian immediately moved his mattress back into the living room, and then resumed spending all his waking hours with Sue, waltzing in mere seconds before midnight. And, because he was barely around, poor Thaddeus was forced to spend time with Lenora. Occasionally, she heard bored sighs from the corner of the room when she spent an entire day reading. She was also growing weary of Thad's mocking comments whenever she was with Nicholas.

Nicholas.

Lenora sighed. The past few weeks had been heavenly—long walks in the park, afternoon reading sessions along the Cam, rainy days in the café, and intimate talks into the twilight. She closed her eyes and remembered the first time he held her hand. It was one evening last week, dusk settling over the park, a warm breeze flowing through her hair. Their fingers brushed together as they walked along the path—even her gloves could not mask the electricity she felt in that brief touch. Eventually, he enclosed her hand in the warmth of his own and they walked together in silence, each with an exhilarated smile.

She rolled over, looked at the clock, and sighed. Soon, she would be getting up to start her day, which began with archiving files in the dungeon. Then, it was an afternoon with Nicholas at their tea shop. He said that he had a new book for them to read, and she could hardly wait.

But, she planned on lounging in the little patch of sun on her bed and dreaming about Nicholas' handsome face until her annoying alarm went off.

"Lenora?" Tom interrupted her reverie.

"Yes, Dad?"

"Are you up yet?"

"Yep. Come in!"

Tom slowly opened the door and peered inside. "If you're coming in to work today, you'll need to get ready soon—I have to be in early."

"Oh, I can walk, Dad, it's not that far."

"Are you sure?"

"Yeah. I'm not ready to get up yet."

"Okay," Tom chuckled and then closed the door.

Lenora stretched and yawned, and then quickly caught herself. She heard a strange noise, like a groan. "Who's there?" she asked, not sure she wanted the answer. She pulled herself up in a seated position near the headboard and grabbed her lamp in case she needed a weapon. "Who's there?" she asked more sternly.

"Ack, you don't have to shout, Love!"

Lenora could see a tuft of hair at the end of the bed, its owner slowly rising to reveal a disheveled head of dark brown hair and puffy blue-grey eyes.

"What are you doing, Ian?" Lenora asked, humorlessly.

"Sleeping," he answered matter-of-factly.

"At the end of my bed?" Lenora asked incredulously. "On the floor?"

"Yeah, why not?"

"Why not? Because it's creepy."

"Yeah, seems a bit dodgy of me, doesn't it?" Ian stood up slowly, holding his back and grimacing. "I'm getting too old for this."

"Yeah, well, you do have your own bed, you know." Lenora felt a little invaded.

"Sorry. I didn't make it that far." He frowned, looking confused. "I came in, took my shoes off, fell down—because I was a little pissed—and then decided to come in and say good night, but you were sleeping, and then I guess I must have passed out."

Lenora wasn't sure if she was amused or annoyed. "Maybe you should stop all that drinking, Ian. It's not boding well for you, especially if it makes you do…creepy things. I mean, who just goes into other people's rooms and—"

"I was only trying to say good night. I wasn't being creepy, honest." He gave her his best pouty expression.

"Stop that. It doesn't work on me anymore." She tried not to smile.

"What? Doesn't work? But my pouty look always works! You can always forgive *me*!"

"You overuse the look, Ian. It doesn't even work for Nicholas."

The smile left Ian's face. "Oh. Right. Your boyfriend."

"He's not my boyfriend," Lenora responded, irritated with Ian's tone, yet thrilled to hear Nicholas referred to as her boyfriend. "We haven't made anything official. Besides, what's so wrong with that?"

"Nothing." Ian studied Lenora's face for a few seconds. "Don't you think he's too old for you?"

"Too old? How would you know? You've never even met him!"

Ian smirked slightly. "You forget my extra set of eyes." He nodded to the corner of the room, where Lenora suspected Thaddeus was.

"Oh. Him. Well, I don't need him to spy on me, Ian." She looked over to the corner of the room. "Thanks, Thaddeus, for tattling." She heard a whispered laugh.

"Sorry, love, but he's here to stay—that is, until we've resolved the issues at your flat."

"Which I hope is soon. I'm sick of this."

"What? You don't like living with me?"

"No, I don't," Lenora answered truthfully.

Ian caught the truthfulness in her tone—his shoulders slumped and his mouth went slack. "Oh. I see," he sounded dejected.

Lenora instantly felt sorry. "I'm sorry Ian, it's just that—"

Ian held up his hand to stop her. "That's okay. I can take a hint." He looked over to the corner of the room. "Let's leave the lady alone, Thad." Lenora watched as Ian left the room, shoulders still slumped. He didn't even look at her as he closed the door behind him. She closed her eyes and shook her head. She hurt his feelings this time, and she didn't mean to.

She couldn't have felt any worse about hurting Ian's feelings that morning, that is, until she got to the dungeon and saw a wrapped gift on her desk. It was from Ian. She opened the card first, which read "I miss my girl" (with many exclamation points). She opened the gift—it was a silver charm bracelet, with one charm attached.

Lenora held the charm up to study the tiny enamel globe charm encircled in a ring of silver. She spun the globe inside the silver ring and watched the tiny oceans and continents whirring by. Her eyes shifted to the box that contained the charm and saw a note sitting within. It was from Ian: "So that I can be near you, no matter where you go in the world."

Lenora felt a lump form in her throat and tears stung her eyes. She felt awful.

"Do you like it?"

Lenora started and spun around to see Ian peering in the doorway.

"I love it Ian, but you didn't—"

"Yes, I did."

"But this morning, I shouldn't have—"

"I deserved it. You and Tom took me in and let me live with you—free of charge—for the past few weeks, and how do I show my thanks? I go out and get pissed every night and come home, reeking of booze, at the crack of dawn. Not the best big brother, am I?"

"It's okay, Ian, it's been a little...weird...lately, but I understand," Lenora began to apologize and then cut herself off.

There he goes with that "big brother" crap again.

She withered. Despite better judgment, she still had feelings for Ian, and it stung to hear him refer to himself as her big brother.

Ian, noticing her change in demeanor, sat next to her on the desk. "Don't feel bad, Lenora." He reached across and picked up the charm bracelet, securing it to her wrist. "There. It looks pretty on you!" He smiled at Lenora, put an arm around her shoulders, and squeezed.

Lenora smiled back, trying to look appreciative, though her heart was sinking lower by the minute. "Thanks, Ian. It's pretty."

Ian's smile grew wider. "Good! Now let's see that boyfriend of yours top that!"

Lenora sighed heavily. "It's not a competition, Ian."

"I know...but I was here first," he said, pretending to pout.

Lenora studied Ian's expression. She felt inexplicably drawn to him. Whenever she was with Nicholas, her mind often drifted to Ian, wondering what he was doing, where he was going...who he was with. She felt guilty—when her mind should be wholly invested in Nicholas, it was divided. It wasn't fair to Nicholas...it wasn't fair to her. This was the first real relationship of her life, and she was potentially messing it up by not letting go of her romantic feelings for Ian.

Lenora straightened up in her chair and turned to Ian. "Hey, what are you and Sue doing later this week?"

"Nothing," Ian replied, appearing taken aback, "I don't think so, anyway. I'll have to check. Why?"

"Well, I'll have to check with him, too, but I thought—if you wanted to—that you and Sue could meet Nicholas and me out for dinner?" Perhaps this double-date idea would solidify her relationship with Nicholas…and be a way for her to accept that she and Ian weren't meant to be. She waited as Ian pondered the question, a serious look on his face.

Thinking he may not have heard her, Lenora was about to ask again, when he nodded his head. "Sure, I think that would be nice. I'll check with Sue and get back to you tonight at practice."

Lenora felt a little confused—his words expressed interest, but his faced said otherwise—he didn't appear interested. However, in fear that he might change his mind, she spoke right away. "Great, I'll ask Nicholas and we can make plans from there." She studied Ian's face, which still looked contemplative. "But, you'll need to leave now so I can get my work done. Otherwise, I'll never get out of here."

"Oh, sure." Ian's response was mechanical, distracted. Without looking at Lenora, he slowly walked toward the door. He stopped in the doorway, tapping his fingers on the door jamb, head turned slightly as if he wanted to say something. "See ya, Len," he said quietly and then walked out the door.

Nicholas sat back in his chair, a look of bemusement on his face.

"Why are you looking at me like that?" Lenora felt irritated at Nicholas's inability to take the situation seriously. She had just finished explaining that she invited Ian and Sue to join them for dinner, and admitted her frustration at Ian's apparent disinterest. She confided to Nicholas that she thought Ian still found her boorish and too young.

"Because, you're adorable when confounded with a situation," Nicholas explained, still looking thoroughly amused. He sat up, reached across the table, and caressed her cheek. "You get this absolutely adorable crease in between your brow when you're deep in thought. It makes me smile." Nicholas leaned back in his chair again and studied her face. "Lenora, you need to stop reading so much into this. Ian is just being protective of you. He may be hesitant to meet us for dinner because he doesn't want to give you false hope that he'll accept me."

"I don't need a babysitter," Lenora said, pouting.

"Oh, but sweetheart, if I were your self-appointed 'big brother,' as he puts it, I would feel obliged to protect you too. As a matter of fact," he leaned in closer to her and brushed a strand of hair away from her face, "I *do* feel protective of you. It's just men's way of showing that we care. Don't begrudge him that."

"I know but—"

Nicholas shook his head to quiet her. "No buts, Lenora. It is what it is, and there isn't a whole lot you can do about that." He paused and gazed into her eyes intently. "We care for you. I care for you—deeply. And it's important to me that you are safe. Always."

"Um-hum," Lenora muttered and nodded her head, feeling entranced in his intense gaze.

"Now," Nicholas changed to a more upbeat tone, "just tell me where and when, and I will be there."

Lenora sprawled on the bed, reflecting on her conversation with Nicholas. He was so generous and attentive—just what she needed. Why couldn't she just give in to it? Why did Ian always have to show up in her mind's eye?

Bewildered, she opened Bartholomew Booth's file, immersing herself yet again into someone else's life—maybe it would help her forget about the drama in her own.

FINAL NARRATIVE OF BARTHOLOMEW BOOTH

PART III

Bartholomew was disappointed to discover that his aunt had left on business for the entire week. He had missed her by only thirty minutes. Confronting her would have to wait.

He bided the time obsessively studying Constance's every move—noting when she left and returned each day. Toward the end of that week, Bartholomew decided to venture out. He waited in the corridor for Miss Brown to leave, and immediately followed her. He needed to see Archer for himself—to size up his competition. Once she had reached her destination, he hid behind a pillar so he could watch.

He was so close that he could hear her rapid breath; he could touch her if he wanted to.

Bartholomew surveyed the building—it was the old church she often wrote of in her letters to Archer. The church was nothing special, making him question its significance. The stone church was dilapidated and so small that the other buildings seemed to swallow it whole.

Constance waited alone on the stone step. Bartholomew wanted to reveal himself—to confess his love and carry her away with him. Something inside him was certain she could love him. Her breathing quickened; Archer must be on his way. Bartholomew hid behind the pillar, crouching in the bushes alongside.

"Hello, sweetheart," a deep voice uttered affectionately. Bartholomew peered around the pillar to see a tall, thin man with sparkling blue eyes. Archer smiled lovingly at Constance.

"Hello!" she chirped excitedly.

Bartholomew strained to see them, cringing when he noticed the two leaning into one another. Archer gently put his hand on her neck and kissed her lips. Bartholomew stifled a scream. He felt sick as he watched Archer's hand move down to her waist, resting at the niche below the small of her back.

Bartholomew squeezed his eyes tightly. He couldn't bear to watch him touch her...*her*! His fists clenched tightly, fingernails lacerating his flesh. Warm blood oozed down his hands, trickled down his fingers, and splattered onto the ground.

Archer whispered in her ear. Constance laughed softly, seductively.

What is he saying to her?

Overwrought, Bartholomew slapped a palm to his forehead and ran a hand down his face, smearing blood from forehead to chin and neck.

Constance leaned toward Archer and kissed his cheek. Bartholomew let out an involuntary shriek, which caught their attention. Quickly, he sprung from the pillar, running away from the building.

"Hey! You! Come back here!" Archer yelled, but didn't attempt to follow.

Bartholomew ran all the way home, trying not to notice stares from passersby who balked at the blood smears on his face.

Once in his apartments, he slammed the door and paced about the room in a fit of rage. Spittle flew from his mouth as he shouted obscenities into the empty room. He kicked furniture, breaking one of his toes, and punched walls until his fists bled.

The sun was low in the horizon when Bartholomew woke. He quickly scrambled to his feet to see that it was nearly five o'clock—almost time for Miss Brown's return. He washed the blood from his face and hands, and then changed into a clean shirt.

His apartments were a mess. It looked as if a wind storm had swept through his apartments. Even the books were torn to shreds.

He'd worry about that later.

Rushing to the window, he watched and waited for her arrival, keeping an eye on the clock. At six o'clock, he began to wonder if he had missed her, when she finally arrived at the front gate. She walked slowly and hesitated at the front door, as if not wanting to enter. Bartholomew dashed to the main entrance, stopping at the top of the staircase.

"So, where have you been?" he asked, startling her.

She looked up at him and sighed, putting away her parasol. "Not now, Barty."

"Aren't you supposed to be back by high tea?"

Miss Brown exhaled. "You were there when Lady Fitzhugh said I may come and go as I please, provided I am here when you wake and dine." She glanced at the clock. "You do not dine for another twenty minutes, so I'm punctual." She smiled sardonically.

Bartholomew's blood boiled.

He ran down the stairs at high speed, visibly alarming Miss Brown. She stepped back, pinning herself against the door. He stopped as he drew nearer, walking slowly toward her, his lips stretched into an ominous grin. He stopped mere inches from her face—she turned her head away from him.

He chuckled. "What's wrong? Do I offend you?"

"Barty, you need to step away. I-I'm not comfortable with how close you are." She gently pushed him away from her.

He pushed against her hand, pressing his body tightly into hers.

"Barty, I said back up!" He obeyed, but only took one step back, glaring at her contemptuously. Ignoring his glare, she smoothed her skirt. "Now, what do you want?"

"I want to know where you've been," he answered calmly. "And, not just today, every day."

She shook her head. "No. I've told you many times that it's none of your concern, so stop asking."

He pressed an index finger to her chest. "If you don't tell me now, I'll go to my aunt. She pays you good money to do *what* exactly? Skulking around old churches. Holding clandestine meetings with your lover," he shook his head, tisking. "Not very proper of you, *Constance.*"

She slapped his finger from her chest and pushed him away. "Look, Barty, I—" She stared at him, realization crossing her face. "How do you know where—"

"I followed you," he admitted proudly. "I had to. You're always gone. You leave mid-morning and don't come back until sunset. So I asked myself: what do you do with your time? Where do you go? What do you do that takes so long? I just had to know."

"I didn't want you to know..." she paused. "So, it was you at the church today, wasn't it?" Bartholomew's silence was affirming. She became visibly angrily. "Alright, that's it—this conversation is over." She started walking away, when Bartholomew grabbed her arm. "Let go of my arm, Bartholomew!"

She said his full name. He liked it...and the frightened look on her face. A certain darkness churned within. He smiled at her. "This conversation is over when I say it's over."

She jerked her arm away and walked toward the salon. "No, this conversation is done! I have no more to say to you until the baroness arrives." She slammed the salon door and locked it behind her.

Bartholomew banged his fist on the door several times until someone grabbed his arm from behind.

"Stop it. Now!"

Bartholomew turned to see Graham standing above him, gripping his arm tightly. He let his arm go limp in submission; he didn't want to mess with Graham. Broad, and about a foot taller, Graham was formidable, intimidating. Graham let go of his arm and then moved him away from the door.

"But, I just want to speak to Miss—"

"No, you do not want to *speak* to Miss Brown," Graham corrected him. "If you were interested in speaking with her, you would not behave in this manner. Now, go back to your apartments—your dinner is waiting." Graham gave him a stern, knowing look. "Lottie is cleaning the mess you made. Considering, I think it best that you depart immediately."

Bartholomew obeyed and went back to his apartment. Lottie glared at him the minute he entered the room, and then pointed to the table, where his dinner was waiting. He sighed and then sat down—certainly, he would have explaining to do.

Thankfully, his aunt wouldn't arrive for two days—ample time to come up with a plausible story.

The baroness was not easily fooled. She ordered Constance and Lottie to discontinue attending Bartholomew. Now, it was Graham who woke him, brought his meals, and attended to his needs. When the tutors left in the afternoons, Bartholomew was locked in his apartments. There was no escape for him now.

Bartholomew tried throwing things, breaking glass, tearing books—nothing worked to get attention. Graham simply entered the room, handed him a dust pan, and forced him to clean his mess.

He was prohibited from attending church with his aunt that Sunday morning. So, he spent the day sitting in the windowsill, wondering where Miss Brown went and what she was doing.

Later that afternoon, voices below startled him from his reverie. It was Miss Brown and Archer—they were entering the mansion together!

Bartholomew ran into his room, freshened up, and then waited in his salon for someone to fetch him. But, no one came. After thirty grueling minutes, he couldn't take it anymore. He ran to the door, pounding, kicking, and shouting to get someone's attention. Finally, after his knuckles grew raw and his feet became numb and swollen, he sank down to the floor and sobbed. What could they possibly be doing here...together?

Two agonizing hours had passed when he heard voices outside. He ran to the window in time to see Miss Brown waving farewell to Archer, who walked away in a quick, gamboling step.

What was going on?

Rage surged through his entire body, but rather than becoming violent, Bartholomew began to feel calm, dizzy...almost giddy. A soothing darkness settled over his mind and he fell asleep, smiling.

The click of the lock in his door woke him. He wiped the drool from his mouth, and slowly rose as Graham stepped into the room.

"Madam announces that it is dinner time. You are to join the baroness and Miss Brown directly."

Bartholomew splashed cool water on his face, combed his hair, and then followed Graham to the dining hall. When he entered, his aunt and Miss Brown were already seated. He smiled at Miss Brown and started to speak, when his aunt interrupted.

"Sit, Bartholomew."

He obeyed, taking the chair opposite his aunt, and then gazed at her expectantly. The baroness said nothing, but gave him a stern glance before ringing the bell for meal service.

The entire meal was silent but for the clinking of utensils. Bartholomew felt anxious, as he fidgeted in his chair, stealing fleeting looks at the two women—neither of whom returned his gaze. With either an involuntary or a subconscious effort, Bartholomew cleared his throat, gaining the baroness' attention. She narrowed her eyes, setting her fork down.

"Do you have something to say, Bartholomew?" Her expression conveyed mild annoyance.

"No...I mean...yes, I uh..."

"Well? We haven't all night," she urged impatiently.

"I-I was just wondering," he began apprehensively, "who was here with Miss Brown this afternoon?"

The baroness waved a dismissive hand. "A guest of Miss Brown's. It's none of your concern."

"Why not?" he asked defiantly.

"Because," she answered brusquely, "I said so." She raised her eyebrows, challenging him to press the subject further.

"So what? Who died and made you queen? I live in this house too! I have a right to know!" He slammed his fist into the table.

The baroness sat bolt-upright in her chair, eyes wide in fury. "I will not tolerate this childish behavior at my dinner table!"

Bartholomew sat back in his chair, smiling contemptuously. "I know what you did."

"What do you mean by that?" she challenged.

"You lied to me." He narrowed his eyes, returning her confronting gaze.

"Explain." Annoyed, she sat back in her chair, waiting.

"I broke into my father's trunk and read the letters. My mother and father *were* married." When she didn't reply, he continued. "You said I was illegitimate. That's not true. You lied to me!" He threw his fork to the ground. "You tried to bribe my mother into leaving me...and my father!"

The baroness smiled. "Your mother and father were married? According to *what* or *whom*? A paper you found in his trunk? That document could have been forged by anyone. In the eyes of this family, you are still illegitimate."

Bartholomew gaped. "Then, is it true? You tried to pay my mother off?"

His aunt issued a blank stare. "Perhaps, we had a little...chat with her. Your father would never leave her of his own volition. She was a poor little merchant's daughter—we thought the money sufficient enough to send her packing. Little did we know how... attached she was to Edward." Her mouth pursed into a tight line. "She was a parasite who fed off of your father's good nature. We were just trying to help him realize that before it was too late."

Bartholomew screamed. He stood up, swept his arm across the table, sending his plate crashing to the floor. "You take that back! She was *not* a parasite!"

Miss Brown ran to his side, pressing a hand gently on his arm. "Barty, calm down. She's just trying to provoke you." Bartholomew ignored her, looking instead at the baroness, who stared at him stoically. He felt like slapping her face—he squeezed his fists tightly.

Bartholomew was startled by a squeeze on his arm. He glanced at Constance. Her look of compassion brought tears to his eyes. *She does love me after all!*

"Thank you, my dear Constance." He calmly sat down, inhaling deeply. Constance took the seat next to him, resting a hand on his. This gave him courage, focus. "I disagree with your assertions," he said to his aunt, "my mother was not a parasite. From her letters, I truly believe she loved my father and—"

"Oh, undoubtedly," the baroness interrupted, "she loved your father. However, she also knew his worth. She never stopped pressing Edward to force our family to acknowledge their marriage. As a result, my father became convinced that she was after the family's money. He became rather...stubborn on the matter and therefore refused Edward's request. Mother and I took action to protect Edward and our family heritage."

"But, your plan didn't work."

"Ah, but it did...eventually," the baroness smiled.

"I don't understand—"

"Your mother was difficult to break down, but not impossible. Eventually, we convinced her that it would be better for Edward to let her go. We gave her a sizable amount so she could live comfortably the rest of her life. We even went so far as to promise a monthly report of your progress."

"Everything went according to plan," she continued. "Adella was scheduled to take the coach to Paris alone. She was to leave you in the care of our friends, the Willoghbys, until we came for you." Her expression turned dark. "However, unbeknownst to us, Adella commissioned a separate coach directly to London, where your father was staying. Her plan was to escape with you and tell your father of our schemes. Thankfully, our spies immediately reported her intentions." She chuckled. "Mother was *furious*. She immediately hired a group of thugs—they were to seize the coach and then kidnap you."

Miss Brown uttered a gasp. Bartholomew couldn't believe his ears.

"However," the baroness continued, "the bandits discovered just how wealthy we really were and made other plans. They decided to abscond with you and your mother and request a high ransom. Once the bandits arrived, everything went awry. They took everything of value from the coach and then took the young lady and baby. But, when one of the robbers instructed Adella to come with them and bring young Bartholomew, the young lady corrected them and said that her name was Sarah and that they weren't going anywhere with her baby girl. The thugs, now thinking that we duped them, pushed everyone back into the coach and set it ablaze. The coach driver was all who remained alive."

"How horrible—those poor people!" Constance sobbed quietly, squeezing Bartholomew's hand.

"Shortly thereafter," the baroness resumed, "we received a telegram, informing us that Adella and her little baby were dead. We had no idea what happened. Mother was completely beside herself; she had fallen in love with her grandchild, and felt deep remorse. She confided all to father. He callously told Edward, who went into a massive depression and then shortly committed suicide."

She drained her wine and then refilled the glass. "It was devastating—not only did we lose our beloved Edward, but his son as well. It was a terrible tragedy that mother went to her deathbed grieving for." She shook her head sadly. "Then, several years later, I went to London on business. That's when I saw her—Adella—peddling trinkets to passersby on the street. I shouted her name, and she immediately ran. I had my driver pursue Adella, but we lost sight of her. Thereafter, I was determined to find her. I hired a private investigator, who found her almost instantly. He gave me her address, in addition to a story that she told him."

The baroness walked over to the fireplace and retrieved a small box off the mantle. She removed a single sheet of paper and slid it across to Bartholomew.

When I found Miss Adella, she was in poor straights. She works as a peddler, living with her son Bartholomew in a one-room flat behind a toy shop. I inquired about that day on the coach, and she said that the visit from the Baroness and Miss Annabelle Fitzhugh proved how corrupt the Fitzhughs were. Feeling that their questionable morals were unhealthy for her son, she fled. She bought a ticket for the London coach, but reconsidered at the last minute, giving her seat to a young woman and her infant daughter instead.

In an attempt to get away from the Fitzhughs, Adella secured another coach to Bristol, where she and her son lived for several months. When she thought it safe to travel to London, she and her son boarded another coach. Upon her arrival, she learned that Edward had died while on duty. This news brought a new low. She spent the last of her money and is now destitute, barely able to make enough for her son's bread.

Bartholomew tried ignoring Miss Brown's sobbing. He was completely dumbstruck.

"Adella left with you shortly after the detective saw her. I spent several years searching for both of you. When the detective finally located you, Adella was already reduced to a drunken prostitute, who forced you to hide in a closet while she entertained men. Pathetic."

Bartholomew clenched his fists. "Nevertheless," he said, as calmly as possible, "your actions led to people's deaths. Tomorrow, I'm going to the authorities to report your crimes. You will pay for what you have done!" He brazenly poured himself a glass of wine, and gazed at her derisively.

To his surprise, the baroness laughed heartily. "That would be wholly unwise. But, go ahead and try." Bartholomew's eyes widened. "I've been threatened by far greater men than you, boy, and I destroyed them all singlehandedly. No one contends with me—not even you. Bring this to the authorities, and I will destroy you."

She sauntered toward him and grabbed the glass of wine from his hand. She drained it, wiped her mouth, and gently set the glass on the table. She flicked a glance at Constance, a spiteful grin playing across her face. "Oh, and Miss Brown is getting married this Saturday. Her last day is Thursday." She strolled out of the room, chuckling.

Stunned, Bartholomew quickly glanced at Constance. She didn't return his gaze, but quietly walked out of the room, a hand held over her mouth, tears streaming down her cheeks.

Soon after Bartholomew returned to his room, he found a note underneath the door. It was from Miss Brown.

Dearest Bartholomew,

I planned to tell you privately about my impending nuptials, but in my own way. The way in which Lady Fitzhugh broke the news was unfair and cold-hearted. While I cannot apologize for that, I can apologize for not telling you sooner.

I'm sorry I was unable to do so. I will come to your apartments tomorrow so that we may share breakfast and talk.

Your loving sister,

Constance

Bartholomew could barely read the letter through his tears. "No, no, no!" he cried softly.

He must stop her tonight. She was supposed to marry him, not Archer. He crumpled the letter and threw it to the ground. He sprinted from the room, bumping instantly into Graham.

"Graham, get out of my way!"

"No, I'm afraid not. Madame has given me strict orders not to let you out of this wing."

"But, I've got to talk to Miss Brown! I have something important to tell her."

"You can tell her in the morning," Graham assured him, though Bartholomew knew it was a lie.

Bartholomew tried pushing forward, but Graham was too strong and pushed him back forcefully to the ground. He landed so hard that the air went from his lungs. Bartholomew's expression was one of shock. "I'm sorry to use force on you, young sir, but I must follow orders." He helped Bartholomew to his feet and led him to his apartments, where he shut and locked the door. Bartholomew pounded on the door until his fists were tender and shouted until his throat felt raw. But, no one came to his rescue.

When he woke the next morning, he was laying on the ground near the door. Graham stood over him. "Get up off the floor, young sir. Lady Fitzhugh is joining you for breakfast shortly. You need to get cleaned up."

"I will do nothing of the sort," Bartholomew uttered defiantly.

Graham raised his eyebrows. "Do as you will, but the lady won't like it."

Bartholomew lifted his sore body off the ground and trudged to the bedroom, where he splashed his face with cold water and changed clothes. He sat at the edge of the bed, still feeling groggy, when Graham announced his aunt's arrival. Bartholomew trudged slowly into the salon, where his aunt sat, looking jovial and refreshed. She was even smiling at him.

"Sit down, Bartholomew, we have things to discuss."

"I have nothing to say to you," he mumbled sourly.

"Oh, but you *will* do as I say." She spread jam on her toast and took a bite. She glanced out the window, marveling at the sunrise. "What a beautiful morning!"

Bartholomew frowned. *Was she going senile? Did she forget about what happened last night?*

"Oh, stop being grouchy—things have their way of working out for the best. Take last night for instance." She took a sip of tea. "You learned the truth about your past, found out about Miss Brown's engagement, we had it out. Today's a clean slate!" She took another bite of toast and smiled at him.

Her unusual cheerful disposition made him leery...something was not right. "What are you getting at?"

The baroness smiled serenely, taking another sip of tea. She dabbed at her mouth with the napkin, and then walked over to the window. "Last night's unacceptable behavior led me to decide to send you to boarding school straight away." Without as much as a glance in his direction, she walked toward the door. "You will be leaving at the end of this week." She turned the knob and walked out, closing the door quietly behind her.

Bartholomew was speechless—he expected to be reprimanded, not sent away. He would miss his chance to talk to Constance...to change her mind! Quickly, he rushed to the door, only to find it locked. He pounded on the door for several minutes, until it was opened by a visibly annoyed Graham.

"What do you want?" Graham said, sounding displeased.

"I want out!" The desperation in Bartholomew's tone was apparent. "Please—I'm leaving by the end of the week. I want to say a proper good-bye to Miss Brown!" He looked piteously at Graham.

Graham shook his head sadly. "I'm afraid that's impossible—I am under strict orders to keep you here."

"But, Miss Brown—"

"Miss Brown is scheduled to leave tomorrow morning, you—"

"Tomorrow morning! No! But, why?"

"I'm only told facts, not reasons." Graham's expression softened. "I'm sorry, I know how much she means to you...but I cannot disobey the baroness." Graham patted Bartholomew's shoulder before closing and locking the door. Bartholomew threw himself onto the couch and wept.

"Sir, it's time for your dinner." A gentle hand touched Bartholomew's shoulder. He woke to find Lottie standing over him, a sympathetic look on her face.

"I'm not hungry," he replied, waving his hand dismissively.

"Oh, but I think you'll want to eat your meal tonight," she said in a conspiratorial whisper, which got his attention. "I have a surprise for you, but you must sit at your table to get it."

Bartholomew quickly obeyed, watching as she set his table. Lottie placed a napkin on his lap, slipping an envelope underneath the cloth. "Open it after I've left."

Once Lottie left the room, Bartholomew immediately removed the napkin and examined the envelope. It was Miss Brown's handwriting. He held the envelope to his nose and inhaled her sweet rose water perfume. He ran to his desk, retrieved his father's letter opener, and then opened the envelope.

My Dearest Barty,

This afternoon, Lady Fitzhugh informed me that my services were no longer needed, and I am to leave the premises tomorrow morning. Before leaving, she instructed that I sever all contact with you.

It would be impertinent to disobey her, my dearest Barty. However, I cannot leave without saying good-bye. I am thankful for these years with you, which were blessed with wonder and deep affection.

I grieve that we shall never meet again, and it is with a heavy heart that I must say good-bye to you, my dearest brother.

I wish you much joy and love.

Your sister, always,

Constance

Bartholomew stared at the letter in disbelief.

He mechanically walked to the door with intentions of pounding on it until Graham opened it. He would get to her by force, if need be.

But, when he touched the door knob, it turned. Lottie forgot to lock the door!

Bartholomew threw open the door and sprinted down the hall. His elation was short-lived. Graham caught him, seized Bartholomew's arm, and hauled him back to his apartments.

Bartholomew cried out, struggling in Graham's grip. Realizing that he was still clutching his father's letter opener, he leaned around and plunged it into Graham's throat. Graham released his grip and grabbed at his throat, a shocked expression on his face.

Bartholomew gaped, watching as Graham dropped to the floor, breath gurgling in his throat.

"I'm sorry Graham," Bartholomew muttered. He never meant to kill Graham—he just wanted to get away.

When Graham's breathing ceased, Bartholomew removed the letter opener and wiped it off on Graham's jacket. Then, without further hesitation, he entered the forbidden wing, where his aunt and Miss Brown resided.

A light shone in the crack under Miss Brown's door. She was awake. Bartholomew quickly opened the door to a stunned Miss Brown.

"Barty? How did you—"

"No time," Bartholomew interrupted, closing the door. He took a seat next to Miss Brown near the glowing fire. "I need to talk to you."

The fire's blaze produced a warm glow on her pale skin, and her eyes gleamed near bronze. It was mesmerizing. He wanted to touch her soft hair—to inhale her perfume and kiss her neck. She was the most beautiful woman he had ever seen.

"Barty?"

She broke his reverie. He returned focus to his purpose. "Miss Brown...Constance...I am here to ask you not to marry Archer."

"Why, Barty? I don't understand."

"You're moving too fast with him—you haven't known him long enough to truly love him."

"I've known him for over a year now, Barty. I think that's long enough to love someone."

"No, but you don't understand..." he trailed off. "He can't possibly love *you*."

"And, why not?" she asked, insulted.

"Because he hasn't known you long enough to know the real you." He shook his head, knowing he wasn't getting the point across. "I've known you much longer than he has."

"That goes without saying, but—"

"No, I've known you longer—I know you better than anyone…"

"You've known me longer, yes," she agreed, "but he knows me better."

"No," he shook his head violently. "He couldn't possibly. I'm the one who's known you the longest. *I* love you, Constance."

"I love you too, Barty, but—"

Bartholomew's heart raced. *So, she does love me!*

"Then, run away with me…marry me instead!"

Constance exhaled. "Barty, you don't understand. I love you, but like a brother. I love Theodore like a woman loves a man—like a wife loves her husband."

"But, I love you!" His body trembled. He raked a hand through his hair, grimacing as he tore strands from his scalp.

"I understand that you love me, Barty," she responded, trying to calm him. "But you must understand the difference."

"Run away with me!" he implored, ignoring her. "You love me already. In time, you'll learn to love me like you love him."

She shook her head sadly. "No, I'm sorry, but that's not possible. Theodore is a good man. He's good to me…good *for* me. I love him and want very much to be his wife." She took hold of Bartholomew's hand. "Perhaps after things settle, you and I can find a way to correspond…keep in touch…so that we don't lose one another. I want you in my life, but as my friend, my brother. You understand, don't you?"

A scream was heard in the hall. Bartholomew and Constance exchanged glances.

"What in the world?" Constance rose from her chair, looking concerned.

"They've found him," Bartholomew uttered beneath his breath. "I've no time…"

"What do you mean? Found whom?"

Bartholomew grabbed her hand. "Quickly, we must go!"

"Where are you taking me?" She struggled against his grip.

He tightened his hold and led her toward the door. "We can run away somewhere far from here, get married—no one will know anything."

"No one will know what? What did you do?" She braced against a chair, struggling to loosen his grasp. "Barty, let me go, you're hurting me!"

Ignoring her, he dragged her to the door and peered out. No one was in the hall—a perfect time to leave. He turned to her, a wild expression on his face. "Quick, now, before anyone sees us."

"No! I'm not going anywhere with you!" She broke free. "Not until you explain what is going on!"

Bartholomew appeared to look right through her. "I killed him. It's only a matter of time before—"

"Killed? Who? What's going on?" She teetered, looking as if she were going to faint. Bartholomew grabbed her around the waist to steady her. She put her arms around his neck to gain balance. A look of sheer delight crossed his face. Misreading her intentions, he pulled her to him, forcing his lips upon hers. He tried forcing her into a passionate kiss, but she struggled against him.

"Enough, Barty! What's wrong with you?"

She pushed against his chest, but his grip only tightened. "You're my girl—not his." He reached into his pocket and pulled out the letter opener, pressing it to her chest. She screamed, causing him to push it into her skin. Blood trickled down her chest and she began to sob.

"Please, Barty, don't."

"It's too late," he said, eyes wild. He slowly pushed the edge of the blade into her. "If I can't have you, no one will."

He watched her eyes flit with the pain. With each movement of the blade, her chest hitched as she tried to catch her breath. He gently laid her on the settee, listening as her breath gurgled in her chest, then throat. Her eyes widened as she gasped for a last breath. He kissed her on the mouth as she grew limp in his arms.

"I love you," he said, closing her eyes.

TWENTY-THREE

"So, tomorrow night?" Lenora loudly repeated for the third time. Ian appeared to be ignoring her, but every time she said it, his eyes shifted slightly in her direction. She was getting annoyed. Walking around to face him, she looked at him humorlessly. "I know you heard me, Ian. Give me an answer!"

"Yes, tomorrow is fine," he replied reluctantly.

"Are you sure it's fine with Sue?" Lenora asked, this time not even trying to mask her irritation.

"Yes, she sounded excited to meet Nicholas," he said unenthusiastically.

Lenora frowned, annoyed at his seeming unwillingness to have dinner with her. She was about to reproach him, when she remembered what Nicholas had said earlier that afternoon. "Don't worry, Ian. I'm not asking for your approval of Nicholas—it's just dinner."

Ian glanced at her and grinned. "No worries there—I'm pretty sure I already don't approve."

"Oh, shut up," she said teasing.

"Are you two done?" Rose asked, mocking irritation in her voice. "Because, I have all the time in the world to sit here and wait for you to finish arguing."

"Sorry," Ian and Lenora muttered simultaneously. They looked at each other and snickered like a couple of children sharing a secret.

"You two are pathetic," Rose laughed, rolling her eyes at them. "Let's go." Rose gestured toward the door, indicating that they were leaving the CSP conference room.

"Where are we going?" Lenora asked, intrigued.

"We are going to your flat."

"Why?"

"Because the camera crew isn't catching anything, and I believe it's because you aren't there," Rose explained.

Lenora froze. "You mean, we're going to my *actual* apartment, not Dr. Harvey's…the one we're in now?"

"Yes," Rose answered, smiling. "It's absolutely necessary. The crew isn't picking up anything, and if there isn't any activity, then they'll remove the equipment and use it on another case. This case must be resolved quickly so that you and Tom can get back to normal life. CSP also needs to continue its normal case load. It's generally against policy to utilize money and resources for members' personal use."

Lenora felt the blood drain from her face, a cool trickle of sweat ran down her forehead. "I don't want to go." She started to shiver uncontrollably.

Ian put his arm around Lenora's shoulders. "Rose, maybe we could do this another time. Clearly, she's not ready."

Rose shook her head. "No, Ian, we have to do it now, whether she's scared or not." She turned to face Lenora. "Ian's right, you're not ready. However, you will have us there to protect you, and the cameras will be running at all times to capture any movement. Ian and I need to connect to the entity—it will help us sense its weakness, figure out how to battle it." She lifted Lenora's chin and looked in her eyes. "You need to be brave. Your abilities will not go away, and facing them now and learning how to handle them will only help make you stronger. Do you trust me?" Lenora nodded her head. "Good, then let's go."

The walk to her apartment seemed long. Rose walked a couple of paces ahead; Ian kept pace with Lenora, holding her hand the entire way. Any other time, Lenora would have reveled in the fact that Ian was holding her hand. Now, she was too scared to care. She wished Nicholas was there, he really knew how to calm her down and see the positive side to everything.

They got to the building and then stared at the second-story window of Lenora and Tom's apartment.

"Well, we're not going to get anywhere by standing here, staring at the window," Rose uttered and then gestured toward the stairwell. "After you, Lenora."

Lenora sighed heavily. She didn't want to be the first one to walk up there. "Shouldn't we call my dad and ask him to come and help?"

"No," Rose answered, "your dad would only serve as a distraction right now. Believe me, he wanted to come, but I asked him to stay behind so that we could get an appropriate response from the entity."

"Oh," Lenora muttered under her breath. She turned toward the stairs and slowly trudged upward. As she climbed each step, her anxiety level increased. Beads of sweat formed on her forehead and she started to shiver despite the warm summer night. Someone behind her touched her arm. She looked back to see that it was Ian, a reassuring look on his face.

"We're both right here for you," he said, trying to comfort her.

When they got to the top of the stairs, Lenora paused at the doorknob, not wanting to enter.

"Now," Rose interrupted in a composed voice, "when we get in, I would like you to remove your gloves and hand them to me. Ian and I will be within arm's reach—we won't leave your side. You need to touch something—the wall, a door, anything—and I'll try to keep you focused as you tell me what you see. We'll only stay a few minutes. My goal is to just tempt the entity enough so that it will come out of hiding. We just want it to manifest so that the videographers can capture something worth investigating." Rose looked searchingly into Lenora's eyes. "Are you clear on that, Lenora?"

"Yes," Lenora nodded slowly. She turned toward the door and opened it, the door creaking on its hinges as it slowly opened into the blackness. A breeze blew into Lenora's face and she involuntarily breathed in the arid staleness and then coughed. Ian moved to touch her arm, but Rose intercepted his hand and shook her head at him. He withdrew and watched Lenora carefully, concentrating on her every move.

Lenora took another deep breath, this time inhaling the familiar scent of her home, and took a step into the apartment. She peered around in the blackness and listened for something to break the unnerving stillness. Hearing no sound to still her heart, she took her gloves off and handed them to Rose.

"I don't think you two should be so close to me," she said, unsure of herself. "The entity doesn't talk to me when other people are around."

"We need to be somewhat near you, Lenora," Rose cautioned.

"I know, but maybe I should just go in my room and close the door—that's usually when everything happens." She turned to Ian. "Maybe you could send Thaddeus in with me and he can tell you if I'm in any danger."

Ian's shoulders slumped. "I'm sorry, Love, but I asked Thad to stay away—this is too dangerous for a wayward spirit."

"Oh," Lenora replied nervously. "Then I need to go in by myself."

When neither Rose nor Ian moved to dissuade her, Lenora determinedly entered her room, closing the door behind her. It was still the same way she left it—the blankets were strewn about the unmade bed and dirty clothes lay on the floor. Without turning on the light, Lenora walked over to her bed and sat down.

She looked at the mirror, the moon's reflection casting an eerie glow in her room. Suddenly conscious of the fact that her feet were dangling over the edge of the bed, she curled her legs up so that they were near her body.

Still, after all these years, I'm scared of the "monster under the bed." She chuckled with guarded amusement. However, to satiate her irrational fear, she immediately lowered herself down so she could see under the bed.

Nope, nothing there.

She sat back up on the bed and crossed her arms in front of her. She began to feel a chill in the air. In fact, she noticed that the temperature significantly changed in the last few seconds. She breathed out, her breath creating a frosty mist.

Uh oh.

Lenora closed her eyes and swallowed hard. She felt the hairs on her arm rise, and what felt like icy fingers stroking the back of her neck. A hot, moist air pulsated on her neck and shoulder, as if someone were behind her. A tiny, involuntary squeak came out of her throat and she put a hand over her mouth to stifle the sound.

A gruff, sinister laugh sounded in her ear—it was close and it knew she was terrified. She swallowed hard again, her throat so dry that it made a clicking sound.

This wasn't going to be easy, but she was the only one who could do it. She gathered up what little bit of strength she had and touched the wall above her headboard.

Lenora squinted as strobes of light flashed behind her eyelids. She saw movement behind the light, shadowed arms reaching toward her. She shook her head rapidly, trying to avert the brightness, but no matter how hard she tried or how tightly she closed her eyes, the intensity of the flashes increased. She opened her eyes, searching the blackness of her room, but all she could see were the flashes and images of arms—women's arms—coming out of the blackness, searching.

Concentrate on the textures. She heard whispered echoes of Rose's voice in her head and felt almost instantly relaxed. She took a deep breath. *Okay, concentrate on the texture of the wall. It's bumpy and –*

"Lenora! Yell out the texture!"

Lenora started at Rose's voice—a stern tone she was unaccustomed to hearing.

"It's bumpy and smooth at the same time," she explained aloud. "I can feel cracks in the wall, they're like rivers…" she trailed off, the images becoming clearer in her mind.

An image of a woman lying on a long couch—in the center of this very room—she was naked, except for a white sheet that barely covered her. The sheet was bloody, and the woman was crying and looking at the door. Lenora shifted her gaze toward the door and saw a man's silhouette. She heard a familiar, sickening laugh coming from the doorway. The man moved closer. Lenora shifted to the corner of the bed near the wall.

She saw the woman, heard her whimpering, muttering "No, no, no."

The man slowly approached the bed. Lenora squinted, seeing a shiny object in his hand, but she couldn't tell what it was. Her heart pounded as the man drew nearer—the sound of the woman's pleading becoming more intense.

The moonlight illuminated the figure so that she could almost see his features. The eyes were blackened, a menacing smile played on his face, and a large knife shone in his hand.

A knife.

Lenora's heart leapt and a chill ran through her spine. She froze, even when the woman screamed for him to stop, Lenora couldn't bring herself to move.

The man lifted the knife to the woman's neck and slowly moved his gaze to Lenora, chuckling softly. "You're next," he whispered and then switched focus to the woman on the bed. He brought the knife down, resting it against the woman's neck, blood spilling from the wound as he slowly sliced into her skin. The woman cried uncontrollably, tears mixing with the blood and trickling onto the bed.

"Stop!" Lenora screamed, unable to take her eyes off the scene unfolding before her.

The woman stopped moving, a last fleeting breath escaping her. Lenora trembled uncontrollably, deep waves of revulsion undulating through her body. She felt the bile rise in her throat, and she clapped a hand to her mouth.

The man slowly made his way toward her, his footsteps growing louder at his approach. She tried to look away, but her eyes seemed drawn to his. He smiled at her ominously, crouching down near her. He brought the knife up in front of her face, twisting it around, the blood-stained blade glinting in the dim light. Lenora choked as she involuntarily inhaled the coppery scent of the fresh blood that dripped from the blade.

He brought the blade to her neck. She felt the blade's cold steel as it pressed against her skin. Her heart drummed heavily in her chest. An unintentional squeal escaped her lips.

He chuckled deeply, knowingly.

Lenora moved a hand behind her, willing her mind to concentrate on the texture of the wall—willing her body to escape the clutches of his crazed eyes. Flashes of her room began to distort his figure. He paused, a momentary confusion washing over his expression.

His face filled with a determined rage as the blade pressed deeper into her skin.

She closed her eyes tightly, running a hand along the wall, urging her mind to concentrate—to bring her back to her room.

Again, the vision distorted, the pain numbed.

She fought against the conflicting visions in her head—willing the hazy reality to grasp her, to bring her back.

Suddenly, the door to her room flew open and Ian ran in. His body went through the killer and the woman lying on the bed as he lifted Lenora and ran out of the room.

Lenora heard the whispers coming from the living room of their borrowed apartment.

She knew they were talking about her.

She lay bathed in the bedside lamp's warm amber light. She resisted closing her eyes, fearing that the images from her visions would rematerialize. A tear trickled down her cheek as she recalled the terrified woman on the bed, blood soaking the sheets. The horror in the woman's screams was still vivid in her mind. She sat up and rubbed her eyes to try ridding herself of the images.

The door to her room opened. It was Ian. He forced a smile; she noted its insincerity. Ian sat next to Lenora and stared at her face for what seemed like several minutes. He took a deep breath and ran his hand through his hair. "You know," he said, breaking the silence, "you should really be trying to get some sleep—you went through quite an ordeal back there."

"I can't sleep—the images keep running through my mind," she admitted.

"I wish that I could give you advice on how to remedy that, but I can't," he said apologetically. "I have a hard enough time with my own—" He shook his head and changed the subject. "Rose and I have been arguing with your dad on how to handle this."

"Handle what?" Lenora asked.

"Helping you get through this," replied Ian. "Tom thinks it would be best to give you a sedative—something to help you sleep. But Rose and I disagree. Sedatives will only put you at risk. If you go into a trance state, we risk not being able to rouse you. We—Rose and I—believe that the only way for you to fully control your ability is to learn how to handle every aspect that comes with it."

Lenora's thoughts went immediately to the sedative she bought for herself a while ago. She exhaled, thankful that she hadn't taken it. "But, my dad disagrees with your opinion," Lenora repeated.

"Yeah, but he's just trying to—"

Ian was interrupted by an adamant "No" coming from the living room. Ian and Lenora glanced at the door and back at each other. Lenora got up and went into the living room; Tom and Rose were standing in the middle of the room facing each other, Tom with a stubborn look on his face.

"Lenora, what are you doing up?" Tom asked sternly, shooting a disapproving glance toward Ian.

"It's not Ian's fault, Dad, I was already awake. I can't sleep."

"See?" Tom addressed Rose. "She can't sleep; all the more reason to give her a sedative. She's only seventeen years old, she can't—"

"No, Dad," Lenora interrupted him. "They're right, I need to face this thing. If I don't learn now, I'll never be able to control my abilities." She walked over to her dad and touched his arm reassuringly. "I don't want to take a sedative, Dad—it won't help me deal with any of this. It'll only make things worse for me in the future."

Tom sighed heavily and nodded his head. "It's your choice, Len. I just want you to get some sleep." Defeated, he patted her shoulder and walked to the kitchen. "Anyone else want a drink?"

"Yes, I'll take one," Rose answered.

Ian lifted his finger to agree with Rose, but looked at Lenora and stopped himself. "No thanks, Tom."

"No drink?" Lenora asked, skeptical.

"No drink," Ian affirmed. "I intend on being present for you tonight to help you through this."

"Thank you," Lenora whispered.

"That's what friends are for." He smiled at her, sat on the couch, and patted the seat next to him.

She sat next to him and rested her head on his shoulder. "Yep, that's what friends are for," she agreed sleepily and then closed her eyes. Two hours later, she woke in Ian's arms as he carried her to the bedroom.

"You fell asleep," Ian whispered, gently laying her down on the bed. He situated himself next to her, propping himself up on a pillow. Lenora leaned into his chest and smiled at him weakly. His expression was worn. "I'll stay with you tonight. You might dream… and it might not be good. But, I'll be here to get you out of it immediately. Trust me?"

"My dad…" she shook her head in protest.

"Your dad went to bed an hour ago. I know he disagrees with me being in here with you like this, but too bad—he has no choice tonight, and this is for your protection." Lenora nodded, yawning. "Get some sleep." He kissed the top of her head and squeezed her firmly to him.

She fell asleep immediately. And dream, she did.

The blackness swirled about inside his eyes, little red dots floated in the darkness like tiny snowflakes. There was a buzzing in his ear as if an insect were hovering above his head. He quickly opened his eyes and looked around the darkened room, confused.

He lifted his head and saw that night had long since cast its shadows in his long hall, the light from the lamppost illuminating the paintings, showing tiny, odd flecks of red paint on the walls. He rubbed his eyes and sat up, still dazed.

Looking around, he could tell he was in a different part of the house— one he wasn't accustomed to sleeping in. Confused, he tried standing up, but the dull, throbbing dizziness in his head prevented him from standing. He placed a hand on the back of his head where the pain was coming from and winced. The dull throb turned sharp as he pressed a large bump that had formed on his head.

He frowned. Could he have been hit? He must have.

He waited until the throbbing subsided and then slowly rose to his feet, grabbing on to a table next to him for balance as his sight faltered in the black swirling dizziness that overcame him. He held on to the table and took a breath before getting his bearings. He took another look around the room and still felt that confusion of place, until he followed the moonlight and saw illuminated upon the floor a desk leg, in a shape he was very familiar with. He was in the salon.

He gathered his strength and walked to the desk, where he knew would be a small lamp that would provide dim, yet efficient light to aid in his ability to see without blinding him or causing more pain. He switched on the light and squinted until his eyes adjusted to the muted light. The room looked the same as usual, except that the wall he looked at earlier, where the moonlight illuminated tiny flecks of red paint, was now more visible. The tiny flecks were not paint, but blood. He frowned. Where could the blood have come from?

He pressed his hand against the bump on the back of his head and then examined his hand. No blood. He looked his hands and legs over, and touched his face. Still, no blood.

He scanned the room and saw, behind the settee, two bare feet on the floor. He walked over to the side of the settee and gasped aloud and then groaned. It was her. She was lying on the floor, blood all over her body, which was badly beaten and bruised. There were scrapes and deep cuts along her skin, where the blood was still oozing from her wounds. He knelt beside her and carefully turned her body so that it was face-up. He covered his mouth as he involuntarily issued a high-pitched screech at what he saw. Her eye sockets were blackened and red, and her eyes had been removed.

Horror-stricken, he wept uncontrollably, holding her hand and rocking to and fro, as he shook his head in disbelief. "No, no, please, no!" He knew somehow that he did this, but he couldn't believe it—he loved her too dearly to inflict this kind of pain on her...and to remove those eyes. What kind of monster could do such a thing?

I could, he thought. I am a monster. He fought back the urge to smile as a sickening feeling of delight swelled within.

He shook his head violently from side to side, ignoring the deep, dark voice from within.

He bent next to her and kissed her lips, lingering for just a moment to smell her sweet lavender perfume, mixed with the coppery rust smell of blood on her skin. He inhaled deeply and felt a profound pleasure rise within and he smiled, and then relaxed. The deep darkness enfolded him.

He needed to get rid of it.

He picked her body up off the ground and carried it to his bedroom, where he gently laid her in the tub and washed her skin and hair. He placed her on the bed and dried her skin and applied lavender lotion and perfume. Knowing that her clothes were too bloody to present her in, he went into the closet and retrieved a dress from the trunk within. He unfolded the dress and held it in front of him. He hesitated. It was her dress—her favorite—he remembered the way she looked in it and held it close to him, inhaling the stale scent of the cedar chest within which it was held. It no longer smelled like her, so he supposed it would be alright to put it on this new one.

He quickly dressed the body and then carried it into the living room, where he laid the body down on the couch so that he could find a way of safely carrying it to the place. Thankfully, he kept the potato sack from the last one—that proved very handy. He stuffed the body into the potato sack and then hauled it over his shoulder, proceeding out of the flat and along the alleyways to the place. He gently laid the body down upon the bench, positioned her hands, and then kissed her full on the lips before parting.

Once he got back to the flat, he cleaned up the mess, which took him into the wee hours. He took a brief break to drink a cup of tea as he watched the sunrise, and then continued. While cleaning, he found something precious: a delicate white handkerchief with the initials FWC carefully hand-stitched in purple thread. He held it to his heart, sighed, and then noticed something in the corner of his eye. He looked to the floor and picked up the silk purple ribbon that she had tied in her hair for their special evening. She left it here for him!

Quickly, he ran to the cupboard where he kept all his treasures and laid them out on the table before him. He spread the handkerchief out and then examined each treasure separately. First, the porcelain thimble. Then, the tortoiseshell butterfly comb. He held the comb up to the window, the wings glittering brilliant color from dawn's light. His eye drifted to the gold band, the name etched within still legible: Hope. Finally, he lifted the beautiful gold locket and let it glisten in the early morning sun before his eyes. It was still so beautiful—as lovely as the one who wore it. He put the locket over his heart and closed his eyes, thinking of her, and then gently laid it with the other trinkets. He closed the handkerchief over the objects, creating a little makeshift satchel, and then enclosed it with the silk purple ribbon.

He exhaled slowly and then picked up the satchel, placing it in the special spot in the salon, where no one could find it. This was all he had left of them. These trinkets were his and his alone.

TWENTY-FOUR

She woke with a start, her mind still in a haze, neck stiff and sore. Feeling confused, she craned her head to see that she was still leaning on Ian, who was fast asleep next to her. She smiled and sat up, poking Ian in the arm to wake him—if her dad saw them, he'd be livid.

Ian's eyes fluttered open and he frowned, looking thoroughly confused. "Is it morning?" he asked, sounding dazed.

Lenora looked at the clock. "Yeah, it's almost nine o'clock."

"Um-hum," he uttered and then sat up quickly. "Nine o'clock!" Ian nearly shouted. "I have class at nine-fifteen!" He started rushing about the room, frantically pulling on socks, smoothing his wrinkled clothing. "I have to go!" He ran into Lenora's bathroom and splashed water on his face and hair. He looked in the mirror and tousled his hair to its normal disheveled look, grabbed his book bag, and headed out the door.

Stunned by what just happened, Lenora just stared at the door. Suddenly, the door flew open and Ian ran back in.

"Did you forget something?" she asked amused.

"Yep!" Ian said as he ran over to her. He placed his hands on the sides of Lenora's head and tilted it up toward his face. "I forgot to say good morning!" He kissed the top of her head, gazed at her for a moment, and then ran back out the door. "Bye, Love!"

"Um, bye," Lenora said too late.

After a few minutes gathering her wits, Lenora finally got up, stretched, yawned, and walked into the kitchen to find something for breakfast. She rummaged through the cupboards before settling on cereal.

She sat down at the table with her bowl of cereal and looked through the newspaper. A hand-written note lying on the table caught her eye. She could recognize her dad's scrawl anywhere.

Len,

Sorry that I didn't wake you, but I didn't want to disturb you after your rough night. Don't worry about coming in to work today, it can wait until tomorrow. As you know, tonight is my night for working late, so I won't be home for dinner. I'll see you later tonight, but please call if you need anything.

Love,

Dad

Lenora smiled as she read the note, feeling a bit choked up. She missed her dad—she had been spending so much time with Nicholas lately that she had neglected her dad.

This weekend, I'm going to make an effort to spend more time with Dad, she thought.

However, tonight, she and Nicholas were going out for dinner with Ian and Sue. The idea of the four of them together made her feel extremely nervous, but she also felt incredibly excited. And, it was something she could do to take her mind off the previous night's events. Her eyes became transfixed on the newspaper as she recalled visions from the night before. She shivered. She shook her head and focused on the newspaper article, determined not to dwell on the visions.

She needed to focus on tonight.

Nicholas was going to pick her up at the apartment—they were walking to the restaurant together. This was the first time she and

Nicholas were going somewhere together, rather than just meeting. And, this was their first evening date.

Lenora twirled in the mirror, admiring her new dress for tonight. The soft teal complemented her creamy skin and brought out the green in her eyes. She felt proud of her purchase—a pleated halter dress, cut just above the knee, an empire waist, accentuated with a little silver buckle with rhinestones. She also bought silver strappy sandals—and to complete the outfit—white, iridescent gloves that, when worn with the silver bangles, looked almost invisible from a distance.

For the first time in her life, she actually felt beautiful. She couldn't wait to see Nicholas's expression.

Lenora glanced at the clock. Nicholas was a few minutes late. She started to worry. What if he didn't show?

A knock at the door.

She sprinted to the door, feeling a gush of elation to see Nicholas standing there, looking stunningly handsome in a black suit and teal-colored tie.

He smiled widely at her. "You look absolutely beautiful," he beamed. His arm moved out from behind his back and he presented her with a bouquet of wild flowers. "For you."

She smiled and took the flowers. "These are beautiful, thank you!" She walked into the kitchen, grabbed a large glass, filled it with water, and put the flowers in it, displaying the bouquet on the table. She smiled at him slyly. "I was beginning to worry—you're a little late."

"Sorry about that," Nicholas apologized, "Actually, I *was* early, but I caught a glimpse of you in the window. You look absolutely radiant in your dress, so thought you might appreciate if I complemented your attire with a matching tie. I ran down the block and purchased this," he pointed to the tie he was wearing, "and got rid of the old one." To prove his point, he produced a burgundy-colored tie from his pocket. "I hope you don't mind."

"Mind?" Lenora exclaimed. "I don't mind at all – that was really thoughtful!"

Nicholas glanced at the clock and winced. "We had better leave now or we'll never make it." He offered his arm and they walked together to their date.

Ian stood up quickly from his chair, gaping.

"Lenora! You-you look...absolutely..." he paused, slack-jawed, eyes wide, "...beautiful." The last word was whispered almost inaudibly. He walked around to the other side of the table and held a chair out for her.

"Here, I've got it," Nicholas intercepted Ian. "I wouldn't be a very good date if I couldn't offer my girl a chair."

Lenora heard him say it, but she couldn't believe it. *My girl.* It made her feel lightheaded. She giggled and took the seat that Nicholas offered her and waited for the men to take their seats. But they weren't moving—they just stood there, sizing each other up.

Lenora began to feel uneasy. "Nicholas?" she uttered quietly, trying to deflect the moment.

Nicholas started and seemed to come out of a stupor. "Oh, sorry." He returned focus to Ian and extended his hand. "Pleased to finally meet you, Ian. I'm Nicholas."

Ian quickly shook Nicholas's offered hand. "Nice to meet you too, I'm sure."

They took their seats. Lenora glanced from one to the other, uncertain of what to say or do. She scanned the restaurant, noticing its quaint, intimate environment. "This is a nice place," she said to no one in particular, "I've never been here before."

Nicholas admired the surroundings. "Yes, Ian, my compliments for an excellent selection."

"It wasn't my choice," Ian admitted. "It was Sue's."

"Where is she, by the way?" Lenora asked, looking around. "Is she coming?"

Ian pursed his lips together. "No, she's not coming. We broke up yesterday."

"Oh, Ian! I'm sorry!" Lenora reached across the table and touched Ian's arm.

Ian patted her hand. "Thanks, but it was an amicable split. She told me that I was no good. I agreed with her and left." He smiled at them, feigning amusement, but neither returned his smile. "Either way, no big deal."

"Why didn't you tell me?" Lenora asked, ignoring Ian's attempt at indifference.

"Because you had too many other things to worry about," Ian explained. "Besides, I didn't want to call off the night—I was looking forward to a night out with you two." He smiled half-heartedly.

This was the first time Lenora saw Ian when he wasn't annoyingly cheerful, and frankly, she didn't know what to do. An uncomfortable silence passed as they looked over the menu. Once they ordered, the same quiet tension seized them as each nervously surveyed the restaurant décor.

The stress was too much for Lenora. She nudged Nicholas, looking at him pleadingly.

"Oh, right," Nicholas said, as if he completely understood her. "So, Ian, Lenora tells me that you are at university earning your doctorate. What is your main interest of study?"

"Psychology," Ian answered abruptly.

"Good, good." Nicholas's response was awkward. "So," he continued, "what is your plan after university?"

"I don't know," Ian answered, "I suppose I'll have to find a job of some sort. I figure that maybe I'll try for teaching at university or starting my own practice."

"Wow, that's very ambitious," Nicholas responded, trying to sound interested.

A dark look passed over Ian's expression. "Was that sarcasm I heard in your tone?"

"No, not at all," Nicholas explained, "I admire people who earn higher degrees. I could never do it."

"Oh," Ian said somberly, eying Nicholas. "So, what do *you* do?"

"Oh, well I sell books,"

Lenora was surprised. In the time that she had known him, she never asked what his job was—it never came up. "I didn't know that! What type of books do you sell?"

"Rare books," he answered softly, smiling at her.

"You didn't know that?" Ian asked Lenora, incredulous.

"No," Lenora replied, cheeks flushing. "I guess it never came up."

"That's sort of an important question, Lenora. Don't be so daft—"

Nicholas frowned. "Don't be so hard on her. We never talk about work when we're together."

Ian glared at Nicholas and then focused on Lenora. "I know you were taught better than that. Your dad didn't raise you to be stupid about strangers."

"Hey, wait a minute," Nicholas interrupted, "Lenora is anything *but* stupid. Our relationship has strictly been literary—we read books together and talk about them. Occasionally, we discuss personal things—like she's told me all about you and her dad, but—"

"But, what do you know about him?" Ian asked Lenora, completely ignoring Nicholas.

"Well, I—" Lenora felt utterly choked. Why was Ian getting so angry? She began feeling so dismayed that she could hardly speak. Her gaze shifted downward, tears falling to her lap.

"Oh, God, I'm so sorry Lenora!" Ian ran to her side, knelt down, and then grabbed her hands. "Please forgive me—it's been a horrible week, and it's not your fault!"

Lenora nodded her head. Nicholas handed her a handkerchief and she wiped her eyes.

"Are we okay? Can we start over?" Ian sounded sincere.

"Sure," Lenora whispered, nodding.

Ian got up and lifted her chin. "I'm sorry, Love." He kissed her forehead and went back to his chair. He peered at Nicholas, who looked uncomfortable. "I apologize, Nicholas—this is no way to meet you. I hope I haven't ruined the evening for you."

"No, the evening's not ruined," Nicholas responded uncomfortably. "You're just being protective of Lenora, and I completely understand. Bygones."

The rest of the evening went downhill from there. At first, Nicholas and Ian engaged in superficially amiable conversation. Lenora knew that it was feigned, particularly on Ian's part. Nicholas seemed to make a genuine effort, asking Ian questions and trying to keep the conversation light and flowing. Occasionally, an uncomfortable silence ensued for several minutes, at which time she was thankful that they had food in front of them—the act of eating at least excused them from having to talk to one another.

But, Lenora knew that things were going in a terrible direction when Ian set his fork down forcefully onto his plate. "So, *Nicholas,* you asked a lot of questions about me—was that to avoid answering any about you?" The look on Ian's face was set, stubborn. Lenora knew this was bad news—Ian had no intention of being agreeable.

Nicholas put down his fork and sat back, a polite smile on his face. "Well, other than being genuinely interested in someone for whom Lenora holds such great esteem," he explained, "I was only trying to keep the conversation going. I'm sorry if that offended you in any way." He paused, seeming to wait for a response. "I would be happy to answer any questions you might have of me."

Ian raised his eyebrows, a crooked smile playing on his face. Lenora immediately felt uneasy. "Good, I have several questions to ask."

"Ask away!" Nicholas said in mock enthusiasm.

"Where are you from?"

"Originally? My family is from Germany—I was born there. However, I've lived in England for many years. I currently reside here in Cambridge."

"Really?" Ian asked sardonically. "I've never seen you around."

Nicholas laughed jovially. "Ian, Cambridge may not be as heavily populated as London, but the student population makes it impossible to know *everyone* that lives here!"

"I would have seen you…you stand out," Ian scowled as he scrutinized Nicholas's attire. "Your long black coat and black attire—in the summer, no less—stands out like a sore thumb."

"Ah, it's about the non-conventional clothing, then? So, my clothing offends you?"

"Yes…I mean, no," Ian faltered. "Your clothes don't *offend* me. I just find it…odd that you wear such heavy and dark clothing in the summer."

"Seasons might dictate the *amount* of clothing one wears," Nicholas offered, "but only to the degree of one's own comfort. And, change of seasons does not necessarily mean change of one's own personal style preference."

"I understand what you're saying, but I—"

"Assumed deviance because I wear clothes that are presumably unseasonable, and of a color that is generally considered non-conventional for the season?" Nicholas interrupted.

"I didn't assume anything—"

"You didn't?" Nicholas challenged. "But my clothing choice provoked negative language on your part, language that was unprovoked."

"How do you figure?" Ian asked angrily.

Nicholas smiled and leaned in closer. "At first, you asked a completely innocuous question about where I'm from, which led to an equally innocuous answer. But, you were dissatisfied with the answer, which is telling from the turn in direction you made in the conversation. Most would simply ask how long I've lived here, rather than assuming I was being untruthful. You, on the other hand, did not bother with the natural question, but instead badly transitioned into an inquisition about my clothes." He sat back in his chair and looked at Ian thoughtfully. "You're not interested in where I'm from or in my clothing choice. You have more of a personal agenda, don't you?"

Ian's eyebrows raised in surprise. "You're right, I do have an agenda. My agenda is to protect Lenora." He considered Nicholas for a moment. "How old are you, exactly?"

Nicholas burst out laughing. "How old am I? I'm twenty-two."

"You don't seem twenty-two—you seem older than that."

"How so?" Nicholas asked, interested.

"Your speech is so…antiquated. Guys our age don't talk like you."

"Oh, so because my speech is not parallel with the common twenty-two year-old male's vernacular, I can't be your age?"

Ian sat forward, looked at Lenora, and pointed at Nicholas. "You see? Guys my age don't talk like that—'not parallel…common vernacular' – who says that?"

"Someone who's had an education and upbringing like I have," Nicholas interjected.

"Really? I'd like to hear more about that," Ian said, arms crossed.

Nicholas sighed and smiled weakly. "I was raised by my grandfather, who insisted that I have the highest degree of education. I went to Europe's most prestigious schools, and my grandfather was a disciplinarian—if I did not use proper language, I was punished severely. So, I approached my education rather dogmatically, earning a Master's degree by the time I was eighteen and then moving as far away as possible."

Nicholas stopped, raising a brow at an incredulous Ian. "Well, I *am* twenty-two, I assure you." He handed over his wallet, which was open to his driver's license. "See? It says right there on my government-issued ID." He smiled at Lenora, who looked at his picture and screwed up her face. "Yes, not a very good picture, is it?" he said, smiling. Lenora giggled.

"Well, anyone can fake an ID," Ian said tersely.

"No doubt," Nicholas responded.

Ian turned to Lenora. "He's too old for you."

"How do you figure? He's the same age as you are, Ian." Lenora felt a lump in her throat.

"Exactly. And you're not quite eighteen...and still in *secondary school*. And, someone your age dating a twenty-two year old is just... wrong."

"Why?" Lenora asked, eyes welling with tears.

"One, you're just a little girl. Two, I question a guy his age dating someone so young." He turned to Nicholas. "So, what's your angle, dating a girl so young?"

"Angle? What do you mean—" Nicholas began, visibly amused.

"I am capable of making my own decisions," Lenora rejoined. "Besides, if you had taken a genuine interest in my life, you would know that Nicholas and I *aren't* dating." She looked at Nicholas uncomfortably. "At least, we haven't discussed it yet."

Ian looked genuinely surprised. "Well, it's only a matter of time before he starts to—"

"To what, Ian, treat me like garbage the way that you treat your girlfriends?" she snapped. "Nicholas has been nothing but a gentleman. He takes more of an interest in my life than you do, and he certainly treats me more like an equal. He treats me with a lot more respect than you do." Lenora stopped because she noticed that her voice was raised and people were staring.

"Lenora," Ian pleaded, "I do respect you, it's just that—"

Lenora stood up, preventing Ian from finishing his thought. "I've had enough. This was supposed to be a fun night out with two of the three most important men in my life. Instead, it was a disaster. Thanks, Ian. Thanks a lot." She looked at Nicholas, who returned a look of unease. "Let's go."

Nicholas nodded uncomfortably at Ian while quickly helping Lenora to her feet. Ian rose to follow them out. Lenora stepped in front of Ian, holding a finger to his chest. "No, Ian. Don't you *dare* follow."

Ian moved forward, touching her shoulder. "Lenora, please, we have to talk about this—"

Lenora took Ian's hand off her shoulder. "No, we don't. Now, leave me alone," she whispered, tears spilling down her cheeks. She took Nicholas' arm and walked out, leaving Ian standing there, a crestfallen expression on his face.

"Sorry about that," Lenora said, as she angrily swiped tears from her face.

"Don't apologize—it's not your fault. And, don't be so hard on Ian, he's just trying to—"

She held up a hand to stop him. "I know what you're going to say, and I don't want to hear it."

"I understand." Nicholas agreed, squeezing her hand reassuringly.

Lenora and Nicholas sat on a small stone wall near the Silver Street Bridge, overlooking the Cam. They watched in silence as couples floated by on a romantic evening punt along the river. Street lights glimmered off the river's surface, and the rush of the little dam nearby had a calming effect. People seemed unaware of their existence—as if they were two ghosts watching life pass them by.

Couples strolled by holding hands; students huddled in groups, laughing and talking; and others sat on the green near the river, some on blankets, watching fire twirlers. For anyone else, this would be magical. For Lenora, it was disappointing. She couldn't even enjoy the excitement around her. Instead, she felt like going home, curling up in a ball, and crying herself to sleep.

Seeming to sense her mood, Nicholas squeezed her hand once again. "Would you like me to walk you home now?"

Lenora sighed. "Yes and no. Yes, because I am just not in the mood to watch people being happy. And, no, because I want to spend more time with you." She looked at Nicholas and a tear slipped down her cheek. "This was supposed to be a great night, Nicholas. It just went so terribly wrong. I'm just so....*mad* at Ian right now."

Nicholas looked at her sympathetically and put an arm around her shoulder. "I know. It didn't go well. But, it was just a terrible start…a series of misunderstandings. How about if I talk to Ian and get this all sorted out?"

Lenora perked up. Would he really be willing to subject himself to more scrutiny for her? She thought for a moment, and then shook her head. "Thank you, Nicholas, but no. I need to get this sorted out on my own. It's not your fault that Ian behaved the way he did. He's my friend—or is supposed to be anyway—and I'll talk to him. Just not right now."

"Well, don't let it go on too long, Lenora. We all need friends in our lives—they keep us grounded." He stood up and offered her his hand. "Come, let me walk you home."

Lenora took his hand and they walked together in silence until they reached the borrowed apartment. Nicholas pulled her toward him. "Thank you, Lenora, for a wonderful evening." Lenora shook her head in protest, but he put a finger to her lips. "Regardless of how dreadful you thought it was, just spending time with you is lovely for me."

"You're welcome. And thank you for being so understanding."

"No need to thank me for that. Isn't that what friends are for?" He smiled at her warmly. "Lenora, are you free tomorrow evening? I'd like to speak with you about something."

"Sure. But, does that mean that we're not meeting for tea?"

"Yes, I'm afraid so—I have a pressing matter to take care of tomorrow afternoon." Noticing Lenora's concerned expression, his face softened and he smiled. "Boring work stuff that I don't want to bore you with. But, to make up for it, I'd like to see you tomorrow evening. And, I'll pick you up here, if that's alright with you."

Lenora smiled widely. "It's a date!"

Nicholas smiled wanly, lifted her hand, and kissed it gently. "Until tomorrow, then."

Lenora walked up the stairs, stopping half way to catch another glimpse of Nicholas. He was there, staring up at her, unsmiling. She smiled brightly at him and felt relief when he grinned and waved. Once she reached the top of the stairwell, she turned to wave goodbye again, but he was already gone. Disappointed, she opened the hall door and walked slowly toward the borrowed apartment.

She paused before entering—she didn't want to go in, thinking Ian might have come home. But, there was no use in delaying the inevitable. She quickly unlocked the door, turned the handle, and walked in.

The apartment was quiet and most of the lights were out. It appeared as if no one was home. She tiptoed in and chuckled at her dad, who was sleeping in the recliner in front of the T.V., which was off.

She walked quietly into the kitchen and helped herself to a glass of water.

"Where have you been?"

Lenora nearly screamed and dropped her glass. She composed herself and then turned toward the dinette to see Ian, sitting in a dark corner.

"None of your business," she said tersely.

"Humor me."

"Ian, I'm really tired and don't feel like talking to you right now. We can talk in the morning." Lenora turned around and walked toward her bedroom. Heavy footsteps sounded behind her. She hurried the pace, opened the door to her bedroom, and quickly entered. But she wasn't fast enough—Ian put his foot in the door before she was able to close it.

"Ian, don't!" she whispered loudly. "Leave me alone!"

"Not until we've talked—we need to resolve this, Lenora." Ian kept his foot in the door, despite the fact that Lenora pressed all of her weight against it. She could see him wince as she pressed harder.

"I said that we could talk tomorrow. Can't this wait?"

"No, it can't," Ian said resolutely.

"I think it can." Lenora pushed harder, trying to get Ian to remove his foot. Her hold was weakening, however, and she could feel her grip on the door loosening. The glass in her hand shook, spilling water onto the floor.

Water.

Her reflexes took over before she could even think. She threw the water from the glass, splashing Ian in the face.

"Ach! Lenora! What the—"

Once the water hit him, he moved his foot, which gave Lenora the chance to shut her door and lock it. She leaned up against the door and took deep breaths, her heart beating wildly. She heard Ian lean on the other side of the door, pounding softly on the wood with his palm.

"Lenora? Love? I just wanted to talk, that's all. For what it's worth, I'm sorry." He paused at the door, listening for a response. Lenora heard him hold his breath, waiting for her response. Part of her wanted to open the door and let him in, hear what he had to say. Mostly, she just wanted to go to bed—she was too tired to argue.

"Good night, Ian. We'll talk in the morning."

Lenora flung herself on the bed, turned on some classical music, and opened the Bartholomew folder.

FINAL NARRATIVE OF BARTHOLOMEW BOOTH

PART IV

Doctor's Notes:

    The client indicated that the baroness didn't appear disturbed by the murders in her home. She made a small fuss about cleaning the carpets and finding new help, but never shed a tear for her loyal servant Graham. The next morning, Bartholomew was sent off to boarding school without a word from her.

    The next few years were relatively mundane. Bartholomew concentrated on his studies at the academy and kept mostly to himself. His endeavors to remain invisible were in vain—he was still verbally and physically abused by the other boys in the school, which is documented by the school's psychologist.

    He never asked the baroness about that night. What he knew was gleaned from eavesdropping on the servants' conversations. Archer did not believe the baroness when she told him that Miss Brown ran away. He spent a vast amount hiring a private investigator to find Miss Brown. Little did Archer know that Lady Fitzhugh paid that investigator handsomely to abandon the search. Eventually, Archer gave up, and last anyone had heard, he had graduated from medical school and was engaged to be married.

Bartholomew went to university, quickly moving up the ranks as top student, eventually earning a PhD in Psychology. Though his time was consumed by study, he did find time for brief romances. One young woman, by the name of Sarah Cartwright, captured his interest for nearly a year. Bartholomew nearly married the girl. The relationship ended when Miss Cartwright had an affair with another man while she was on summer break.

After university, Bartholomew accepted an immediate position with Barnes and Smyth, a highly esteemed firm specializing in psychological and psychiatric treatments for the wealthy. However, this position lasted only a few short months. His colleagues found it difficult to work with him, and his inability to connect with clients led to quick termination. He tried to start his own firm, but it failed within the first few months.

Finally, Bartholomew quit the psychology business, soon joining the J.P. Dunning Employment Services, where he assessed people's talents and abilities and matched them with fitting employment.

He enjoyed the job well enough, staying with the firm for fifteen years. This is where he met his next victim.

Bartholomew heard the bell ring, indicating that someone had entered the agency. But, having grown so accustomed to routine, he didn't bother looking to see who it was.

"Pardon me? But, I'm looking for employment."

Bartholomew was startled by the honeyed voice. Typically, the employment agency's clientele was male.

"Fill out the form to your left," he said, gesturing to a stack of papers. "When you are finished, put it in the slot marked 'Inbox' and wait until you are called."

"Yes, sir, thank you." She picked up a form and sat at the small corner table.

He picked up the folders of new potentials. It was Monday, which meant that several people were awaiting interviews. He called each name chronologically. She was last.

Bartholomew started when he saw the name: Hope Anne Millar. Surely he knew her, the name sounded familiar. He gasped quietly when he saw her come around the corner. Her eyes were what first captured his attention—they were a bright turquoise, and looking into them was like gazing into a cloudless summer sky. She took the seat across from him and smiled warmly.

He tried asking the pertinent questions, while struggling to ignore the other thoughts swirling around in his head.

"S-so, Mrs.—"

"Miss," she corrected, "it's Miss Millar."

"Ah," he said, thrilled. "So, Miss Millar, it says here that you are looking for a clerical job?"

"Yes."

"What are your skills?" Bartholomew barely listened as she described the skills learned while residing at St. Adelaide's, an alms-house for women. He couldn't help focusing on the clarity of her eyes and how the soft brown curls fell down her back. He wanted so badly to touch those curls.

"Sir?"

Bartholomew started—apparently she was through talking, and was now looking at him strangely. "I'm sorry," he apologized, "but I was just thinking that we have a fitting position for you here. Please, excuse me a moment." He rushed down the hall and knocked on his boss' door.

"Come in!"

Bartholomew walked into the office, closing the door behind him.

J.P. glanced over the top of his glasses. "Well? Do you have something for me, Bart?"

Bartholomew winced—he hated being called Bart. "Yes." He handed the file over to J.P. "This girl should suit us fine as a file clerk."

J.P. Dunning reviewed the file, clearing his throat several times in the process. Bartholomew found the incessant throat-clearing annoying. In general, he found Dunning's appearance rather disgusting. Dunning's greasy, silver hair was slicked back to conceal his balding pate, and bushy, grey eyebrows hung over his beady, brown eyes. His bulbous nose supported wire-rimmed, pince-nez glasses, and suspenders were stretched across his corpulent figure.

Though Bartholomew thought Dunning physically repulsive and abrupt, he did prove an astute business man and was well-liked by his peers. In addition, he trusted Bartholomew's judgment and was noninterfering, for the most part.

"So, go hire her—what do you need me for?" Dunning's tone revealed his impatience.

"I just thought I'd check with you first," Bartholomew responded, blood rushing to his cheeks.

"No need, Bart—I trust your judgment." J.P. grunted, handed the file back to Bartholomew, and then resumed his work. Bartholomew took the hint and left immediately.

Bartholomew rejoined Miss Millar, who was waiting patiently. "I've checked with Mr. Dunning, the agency owner, and we both agree that you would make a fine candidate for the file clerk position, should you want it."

"Yes…yes I would!" she exclaimed. "When may I start?"

"Tomorrow, if that works for you," Bartholomew replied, heart racing. She shook his hand vigorously, thanking him for the opportunity. He was speechless—he couldn't believe his fortune in finding someone so…perfect.

Bartholomew found sublime joy being around Miss Millar, and in such close proximity. Each morning, he greeted her at the door with a hot cup of tea and pastries from Dominick's Patisserie. Miss Millar was always so appreciative, expressing sincere gratitude for his generosity.

Afternoon teas were his favorite. At two o'clock, he closed the office doors, and J.P. left to have tea with his wife. This meant that Bartholomew had Miss Millar all to himself. Every day, they enjoyed their tea and biscuits, talking about everything under the sun. Mostly, Bartholomew listened—her voice was so soft, like a gentle breeze on a warm summer day. And, she was so timid—her eyes often downcast, delicate fingers nervously tracing the cup's rim.

After nearly two months of patient and careful interaction, Bartholomew decided to take things to a new level.

"I-I've been meaning to ask you…" he paused anxiously. "Would you accompany me to dinner this evening?"

"Dinner?" she asked, fidgeting in her seat.

"Yes, dinner," he affirmed, chuckling nervously.

"As friends or colleagues? Do colleagues do that?"

"No, silly girl," he chuckled, "not as *friends*…as…something more."

Hope's eyes immediately shifted downward. "I'm sorry, Bartholomew, but I can't."

He frowned. "Why not?"

"Because we're colleagues, and it's not professional for colleagues to go out on dates."

"I could have you fired," he said in a feeble attempt at a joke.

Hope did not find his joke particularly amusing. She forced a smile and then rose from her chair. "I have a lot of work to do… thanks for the tea." She walked out of the reception area and started working on a stack of files.

Bartholomew stared in disbelief. Things were going so well, how could it have turned so quickly? What did he do wrong?

For the remainder of the day, Bartholomew avoided eye contact with her.

Several days went by in total silence. Then, one day, she sat down in the chair directly across from him and smiled. He inwardly rejoiced—perhaps she had a change of heart! He tried a serious approach. "Yes, Miss Millar?"

"Bartholomew, I cannot continue working in this silence. I miss our teas—it's the bright spot in my day." She smiled warmly. "My answer still stands to your previous question. But, please don't take it personally. My mentor at St. Adelaide's has always advocated a strict guideline of professionalism, which I feel is a commendable one to follow."

Bartholomew softened. At least it wasn't a personal rejection. "Tea at two, then?"

Hope's eyes widened. "Yes! That sounds lovely!"

She smiled all morning, which made him feel…good.

Their tea time was just as it was before. And, the rest of the week got progressively better. Eventually, Bartholomew reformulated a plan: take it slow, become close friends, and then find her another job. He would still invite her to afternoon teas, and in due course, she would fall in love with him.

It was a perfect plan, until one rainy Monday morning.

Bartholomew returned from running a few errands for J.P., when he heard laughter. He walked through the office to their tiny lunch room, where he saw her talking and laughing with another man. Anger welled inside of him—who was this intruder? Bartholomew glared at the back of the gentleman's head.

Hope noticed him standing there and smiled brightly. "Oh! Bartholomew! You're finally here! There's someone here to see you." She motioned to the gentleman, who turned around and grinned.

"Hallo, Bart!"

Bartholomew frowned, unable to recognize the man.

The man held out his hand. "You don't recognize me, then?" Bartholomew shook his head. "It's me, Nathaniel Parker. We went to school together at Cambridge!"

Bartholomew thought for a moment—the man looked familiar, but he couldn't quite put his thumb on it. "Did we have class together, or—"

"Yes, psychology—you spent hours helping me after school. Remember?"

It finally dawned on him—Nathaniel was in his psychology program, and was completely daft. No threat. "Oh! Yes!" he took Nathaniel's hand and shook it enthusiastically. "I do remember! How are you?"

"Terrible, actually," Nathaniel admitted. "As you know, I wasn't particularly one of the brightest students, but I did—believe it or not—actually get my degree."

"In psychology?" Bartholomew was amazed that Nathaniel even graduated.

"No—the university wouldn't allow me a degree where I could potentially damage people," he jested, to which Hope laughed cheerfully. Bartholomew glanced at Hope, feeling a bit peeved.

"Actually," Nathaniel continued, "I have a degree in business, but am having a terrible time finding a job. I came here to see if you could help me—just like in the old days." He smiled enthusiastically at Bartholomew, who nodded and flashed a weak smile.

"Follow me," Bartholomew led Nathaniel to his desk. He pulled out an employment form. "Fill this out—I'll look for openings while you do that." He was anxious to get Nathaniel out of there. He occasionally caught Nathaniel staring at Hope, which Bartholomew found annoying.

Finally, he found fitting employment for Nathaniel. He handed the folder over. "This firm is highly respectable and fits within your skill-set. Tell them to call me. I will give you with a highly favorable reference."

Nathaniel looked over the job description. "This *is* a respectable firm!" He shook Bartholomew's hand vigorously. "I don't know how to thank you, Bartholomew!"

"Well, wait to see if you have the job first," Bartholomew responded, smiling wryly as he walked Nathaniel to the door.

"Thank you, again!" Nathaniel said, craning his neck to look over Bartholomew's shoulder. "Good-bye, Miss Millar! Thank you for entertaining me!"

"You're welcome! Good luck!" Hope shouted as Bartholomew practically shoved Nathaniel out the door.

Bartholomew watched Nathaniel as he walked out of sight. He hoped he was hired—the firm was at least five blocks away.

Several weeks later, just as Bartholomew was growing comfortable, Nathaniel showed up at the firm. Bartholomew was deeply annoyed. "What, did you lose your job already?"

Nathaniel laughed merrily. "No, I still have the job, and it's a great fit, thanks to you."

"No need to thank me," Bartholomew set his pen down. "So, what can I do for you now?"

"Since I am now a man of income, I mean to take my friend Bartholomew out for dinner to thank him for helping me!"

"Really, Nathaniel, there's no need to thank—"

"Nonsense! I will not take no for an answer." Nathaniel plopped down in the chair across from Bartholomew, helping himself to a peppermint candy.

Just then, Hope walked into the room, appearing pleasantly surprised to see Nathaniel. "Oh, hello, Mr. Parker," she said, offering a warm smile. Bartholomew scowled.

"Hey, my good man," Nathaniel whispered, "how does a man go about asking the lovely Miss Millar out for dinner? I mean, assuming she's free, of course." He smiled. "Unless you've staked a claim, you old devil!"

Annoyed, Bartholomew sighed. "No, I have not 'staked a claim,' as you so crudely put it."

"Have I offended you?" Nathaniel looked startled.

"You didn't offend me," Bartholomew lied, "it's just that...Miss Millar deserves respect."

"Oh, oh yes...absolutely!" Nathaniel agreed. "But, is she free? I mean, if you don't mind me asking?"

"No one is free in this country, Nathaniel," Bartholomew retorted acerbically.

Nathaniel laughed, overlooking the tone. "I hear you, old boy! What I mean is—"

"I know what you meant," Bartholomew interrupted. "To answer your question, Miss Millar is not currently attached to anyone...as far as I know."

"Did I hear someone say my name?" Hope walked toward the men, smiling.

Bartholomew cringed. "We were just—"

"I just asked the old boy here how one goes about asking a beautiful woman like you to dinner," Nathaniel boldly interjected.

Hope lowered her gaze, smiling timidly. "Well, I suppose you would just...ask."

Nathaniel walked over to her, picked up her hand and kissed it. "Miss Hope Millar, would you do me the honor of accompanying me to dinner this evening?"

Hope smiled and blushed. "Yes, I would love to."

Bartholomew gaped. "But, you hardly know him, Miss Millar, I hardly think that—"

"A friend of yours is someone worth knowing," she stared intently at Nathaniel, who kissed her hand and walked toward the door.

"I'll drop by the office after work," he said on the way out.

Bartholomew wilted, feeling completely disheartened.

Hope's incessant chattering about her date didn't help—in fact, it made Bartholomew feel nauseated. When Nathaniel arrived, he didn't bother coming into the office, which made Bartholomew happy. He didn't want to see the jubilance in Nathaniel's face as he walked away with his prize.

Each day thereafter, he was forced to endure the constant details of their courtship. As if he didn't know. He followed them, so was most certainly aware of the repulsive details. But, he suffered the accounts ad nauseam just to be near her. The inflections of her voice and the luminous way her eyes shone in their remembrances made Bartholomew wish it was all for him. But, patience was a virtue, and he knew that Nathaniel would soon be out of the picture. Besides being an idiot, Nathaniel was a proven scoundrel.

He didn't have long to wait.

Hope was unusually late for work one morning. Bartholomew was just shrugging into his overcoat to go check on her, when she walked in the door. Her clothes were disheveled, imprints from bed sheets lined her face, and she wore the same clothes from the previous day.

His fists clenched. He knew her honor had been sullied. He rushed toward her, angry, awaiting explanation. But, to his surprise, she wrapped her arms around his neck and sobbed uncontrollably. Confused, he patted her back, trying to soothe her.

When she seemed to settle down, he pushed her gently away. "What did he do to you?"

Her eyes were red and swollen from crying. "What? No, it wasn't...we broke up." She burst into tears again.

Bartholomew led her to his desk and lowered her into his chair. He ran into the back room and retrieved a cool cloth, which he immediately pressed to her forehead. "Would you like some tea?" She nodded, thanking him.

"I should have known something was amiss," she began when he returned. "He has been neglectful the past two weeks. Twice he forgot our date. Last night, he was two hours late, and when I went to his flat to make sure he was alright, I found him with another woman!" Fresh tears flowed down her cheeks.

"You're better off," he offered, trying to soothe her. "He was a complete moron in University—how could one expect him to be smart in any other part of his life?"

She frowned at him, and then burst into hysterics. Unsure of what was so humorous, Bartholomew laughed as well. "He *was* a bit daft," she added, catching her breath.

"In University, he spelled his own name wrong all the time—even the professors thought he was an idiot." Hope burst into peals of laughter, which prompted him to expound on Nathaniel's proven stupidity.

Hope laughed until doubled over, and then finally put her hand out to stop him. "Okay, I'm sufficiently cheered up now—thank you, Bartholomew." She hugged Bartholomew tightly. "Thank you. You're such a great friend."

"Sure, any time." He sunk. *Friend.*

His success at cheering her up opened new doors for him. In addition to afternoon teas together, they were now going for walks after work or meeting for lunch on Saturdays. The other girls at St. Adelaide's Almshouse teased Hope, referring to Bartholomew as her boyfriend, which she gently corrected. He knew it was only a matter of time before she stopped correcting them.

One Saturday afternoon, Bartholomew led her to a bench in the park, asking her to sit with him a moment.

She gazed at him intently. "Bartholomew, before you say anything, I would like to speak."

"Absolutely!" He wondered if she also felt that these past few weeks were wondrous, magical.

"I know what it is you would like to ask me. I would like to stop you before things get...uncomfortable...between us."

"I don't know what you mean." Bartholomew frowned, taking hold of her hand.

"What I mean," she said, removing her hand from his grasp, "is that I know you are going to ask if you may begin courting me. But, the answer is still no, Bartholomew." A single tear trickled down her face. "You are one of my dearest friends. But I don't think of you... that way. Do you understand? I really don't want to hurt your feelings." She pursed her lips, looking worried.

He smiled, seeming to look right through her. "I understand that you feel that way *now*, but in time—"

"No, Bartholomew. I won't feel that way...ever." She pressed his hand. "You are a dear friend, and I know you have feelings for me. But, it wouldn't be fair to mislead you or give you false hope. You deserve someone who will love you the way you deserve to be loved."

Bartholomew looked at her patronizingly. He smiled, placing a hand alongside her face, caressing her cheek. He leaned in and kissed her gently on the lips. She struggled against him, but he only pressed harder. She pushed against his chest, trying to break free, but when she couldn't, slapped him…hard…on his face.

He recoiled, putting his hand on the place where she hit him. "What did you do that for?"

"I'm sorry, but you weren't letting me go." She reached out, examining his face. "Did I hurt you?"

"See," he said, grabbing her wrist, "you care about me! That means you could love me! Just give me a chance! You don't think that you love me now, but over time—"

"*No*, Bartholomew!" She declared emphatically. She wrenched her wrist free and got up from the bench. "I'm sorry, but this is good-bye." She ran away without looking back.

Bartholomew stood up, shouting for her to return, but she caught a carriage, which took her swiftly off. He ran after the carriage calling her name, but she didn't look back. He sunk down in the grass and sobbed.

The following Monday, Hope didn't show for work.

According to J.P. Dunning, she showed up on his doorstep on Saturday and turned in her resignation. Dunning was confused, but Bartholomew knew why.

Bartholomew went to St. Adelaide's, but no one would let him in—those who were once friendly to him were now unwelcoming and cold. He tried sending letters, which were all returned, unopened. He tried all avenues to gain access to her and was thwarted at every step. His mood grew heavy and his body was weak from depression.

Bartholomew simply felt that they just had their first lovers' quarrel, that it would pass in time. He was willing to give her the time she needed to forgive him. Meanwhile, he redecorated his flat. He wanted to have something visually pleasing for her—a place she would be proud to one day call home.

His days soon became filled with activity. He rose at five o'clock in the morning, followed Miss Millar to her new job as secretary at an accounting firm. Then, he was off to work. At tea time, he watched Miss Millar as she ate her lunch in the park. After work, he followed Miss Millar back to St. Adelaide's—to ensure that she got there safely. Then, he walked home, where a new project awaited.

The first project was to put a fresh coat of paint on the walls and then polish the floors. New furniture soon arrived that—as the salesperson assured him—was appealing to women. Then, he purchased several landscape portraits to give the flat a spacious, international feel.

While hanging one of the portraits, his hammer went straight through the wall. Bartholomew peered into the hole, discovering an entire room on the other side. Despite the fresh paint job, he demolished the wall. When he finished, he walked into the strange little room. It was still furnished as if someone were occupying it.

A couch and a chair sat in one corner of the room, and a small writer's desk stood along one wall—it still had papers and pen situated on it. The papers appeared to be an inventory log of sorts. He knew that at one time a general store occupied the now vacant spot beneath him—this could have been the owner's office. Rummaging through the desk, Bartholomew found documents indicating that this was indeed the office for the Hodgekins Mercantile, all logs and correspondence signed by John Hodgekins, proprietor.

He cleaned the dust off of the furniture and swept and polished the floors. A quick glance around the room, and an idea formed in his mind: this could be Hope's salon! Fresh paint, luxurious tapestries, silk wall paper, and reupholstered furniture was all he needed to transform this into a room she could call her own. He immediately drew up plans, which he instigated the following day. He knew that once she arrived, she would be pleased with his work.

Once finished, Bartholomew admired the transformation. The walls were lined with pale pink, silk damask, the furniture a dark dusty rose. A French country corner daybed sat in the corner, where she could lounge and read in the daylight. The daybed had no head or foot rests, so he provided many plush pillows for her comfort. He refinished the desk himself, lovingly sanding and polishing it, and then placing delicate stationary for her writing pleasures. The freshly white-washed window was adorned with dark pink lace curtains and a pale pink shade, creating a warm glow in the room. The room was fresh, bright, and feminine—a room any woman could be proud of.

Bartholomew set out the next day to find her and bring her home. He was sure that one look at the room would change her mind about loving him.

She was exactly where he knew she'd be: sitting at the park bench. It was Saturday evening, and she was in her spot, reading and watching as the sun set over the trees near the river.

He sat next to her, reading the paper, listening to her breathing in the crisp spring air. He smiled.

London Chronicle

Cambridge, Oct. 8, 1910   Last Thursday Night, about Nine o' Clock, one Jacob Smith, a Lawyer at the Firm of Privy & Kator, was walking along the Cam River, when he noticed the Body of a Woman lying in repose upon a Bench near the Shore. Mr. Smith, thinking the Woman was asleep, and thinking it an unsavory time for a Woman to be out, tried to wake the Woman. After receiving no response, and determining she was therefore dead, he immediately dispatched to the Authorities; upon which, Hon. Inspector Gen. William Rood inspected the Body, determining that the Woman, one Hope Anne Millar, was barbarously murdered; her Body having been stabbed in the chest, and the Eyes were missing.

Insp. Rood has contacted Ms. Millar's Employer and is looking for the B___d that committed the barbarous Murder.

TWENTY-FIVE

Lenora got up and showered before sunrise to avoid having to talk to her dad or Ian. She knew this was the coward's way out, but she just needed some time to think things through...alone.

She wrote a quick note to her dad and then quietly snuck out of the house, heading toward Trinity Bridge. It was her full intention to drink coffee, watch the swans, and relax by the Cam. Trinity Bridge was *her* place—it wasn't as popular as Clare Bridge or the Bridge of Sighs at St. John's, so she could be alone here and truly think—especially in the early morning hours before the sun came up. She thought Trinity Bridge was just as beautiful, and the swans swimming gracefully underneath gave her a feeling of calm.

Lenora found a spot to sit under the bridge, near the river, and settled in, closing her eyes as she inhaled the strong aroma of coffee. She made it extra strong this morning, and was fairly certain that it would wake her dad up shortly. She was just thankful that Dr. Harvey's coffee machine wasn't as loud as the one they had at their own apartment.

She opened her eyes and watched the swans gliding gracefully under the bridge. Resting her back on the bridge's cold stone, she thought of the previous evening's events. She could still see Ian's face in her mind and hear the brazenness in his voice as he questioned...no *interrogated* Nicholas. Her pulse raced as she became angrier at Ian's audacity.

No doubt, she needed to talk to him, but right now, she wanted to think about how she left Nicholas—how his smiled looked so forlorn. Though she wasn't going to see him until later tonight, she wanted to mentally prepare herself for the worst—the look on his face as he left made her nervously aware that bad news was coming.

A rustling in the trees across the river averted her attention. She supposed it was the ducks coming in for a swim or perhaps a rabbit or two. However, when she looked closer, a human shape appeared to be stumbling around in the brush.

Oh, great, a drunk.

Annoyed at the thought of having to move, Lenora stood up and walked up the embankment. Once she reached the top, she paused to see where the drunk had passed out. She stepped onto the bridge to catch a better glimpse, and was shocked at what she saw. It was Nicholas, sitting on a rock, holding on to a black cane, and panting as if out of breath.

Without thinking, she ran across the bridge to the other side. Nicholas didn't see her coming, and looked completely taken by surprise when she approached him, out of breath.

"Nicholas! What are you doing here?"

"Lenora! I-I didn't expect to see you...here...so early."

"I couldn't sleep, and this is my thinking place."

"*Your* thinking place?" he asked.

"No one comes here, so I take advantage of the quiet to—" Nicholas winced and buckled over in pain, interrupting her. "Nicholas? Are you okay?" She rushed to his side and put a hand on his shoulder, concerned.

"Yes, I'll be fine," he said, trying to sound convincing.

"No, I don't think so," she said, hearing the pain in his voice. "I think you need to go to the doctor."

"No! No doctor," Nicholas protested loudly. He calmed himself. "Please, just sit down next to me, Lenora. I'll be fine—the pain will pass, as always."

Lenora's brow furrowed. "You have this pain often?"

"Every once in a while," he explained. "It's a childhood affliction that has followed me into adulthood." Noticing Lenora's worried expression, he smiled weakly. "Don't worry, it's nothing serious. It's just...annoying."

"How often do you have the pain?"

"Oh, three to four times monthly, on average. Sometimes, the time between bouts is longer."

"Isn't there anything the doctors can do for you?"

"No, I'm afraid not. But, like I said, it isn't anything serious or deadly—just bothersome, inconvenient. So, I try to walk it off...distract myself with beauty." He fixed a steady gaze on her. "This place is quite special to me too."

"How so?" Lenora asked, intrigued.

"This was the place I first saw you."

"Really? But, I thought the first time you saw me was at the book store."

"Oh, right—so this is where I saw you for the second time. I forget about the bookstore."

Lenora giggled. "How could you forget that? I passed out—that's a moment I'll *never* forget!"

Nicholas laughed and then winced in pain, holding his side.

"Oh! I'm sorry, I forgot." Lenora touched his arm again, which he promptly removed and patted her hand.

"It's alright," he chuckled softly, "if you just refrain from making me laugh and touching me, I'll be fine."

"It hurts if I touch you?"

"A little—I just need to be quiet and breathe some fresh air."

"I'll just sit here—quietly, not touching you, then. If you don't mind." She smiled at him sheepishly.

"It would be a pleasure." Nicholas smiled and patted the vacant spot on the stone next to him.

Lenora took his cue and quietly sat next to him. A tranquil quiet soon enveloped them as they sat together along the shore. After nearly an hour, their quiet repose was interrupted as the college burst to life—students were out and about, coffees and pastries in hand, walking to their early morning classes.

Nicholas turned toward her and touched her hand. "Shouldn't you be off? Don't you work today?"

Lenora looked at her watch. "Yeah, I should really get going." Her tone betrayed the disappointment she felt.

Nicholas grinned. "I'll see you tonight. Remember? At your apartment?"

"Can't wait!" Lenora got up from her seat, and started on her way.

But, rather than watching where she was going, she looked at Nicholas instead, missing the enormous tree root protruding from the ground. She tripped, falling to the ground and hitting her head on a rock. She lay there, stunned, for a few seconds before Nicholas came to her side. He picked her up in his arms, grimacing in pain. He carried her over to a large tree and propped her up, taking out a handkerchief to tend to her wound.

Gradually, Lenora recalled what happened and was mortified.

How stupid! He's going to think I'm such a klutz!

She groaned, held her head in her hands, and promptly burst into tears.

Nicholas laughed softly, gently moving her hands away from her face. He placed both of his hands along the sides of her face. "Are you alright?" He moved in closer and looked at her wound. "Perhaps it's much worse than I thought…you might have a concussion. I should take *you* to the doctor."

"No, I don't need a doctor. I'm so….so….embarrassed!" She burst into tears again.

"Oh, sweetheart, don't be embarrassed—it's just an accident!" He held her head to his chest and laughed softly. "You have nothing to be ashamed of. People fall every day." Lenora couldn't respond, crying softly into his chest. He stroked her hair and kissed the top of her head. "It's alright, have your cry out—"

"What are you doing to her, you son-of-a-bitch!"

Lenora and Nicholas turned in time to see Ian running across the bridge, enraged.

"Let her go!" Ian shouted, rushing toward them. Nicholas moved in front of Lenora protectively. Ian shoved him out of the way and then punched him in the face.

"Ian, no!" Lenora shouted, but it was too late—Ian had picked Nicholas off the ground and pressed his face forcefully up against the tree, binding his arms behind him. Nicholas' face was contorted in pain. Lenora got up and ran over to stop Ian, but she must have got up too fast, because everything started to go black.

Lenora woke up in Ian's arms as he ran across the bridge, away from Nicholas.

"Ian, put me down, you big dumb jerk!"

"No, I'm taking you to hospital."

"No, you're not! I'm fine—put me down!" She struggled in his arms, which only made him squeeze tighter.

Looking over the top of Ian's shoulder, Lenora saw Nicholas, standing near the tree, leaning on his walking stick and looking helpless.

"Nicholas!" Lenora called out. Nicholas opened his mouth as if to say something and then shook his head and looked down at the ground. Lenora's body drooped weakly as she gave in to Ian's stronghold and put her head into his chest, weeping softly.

"I'm fine, Dad. I fell and hit my head on a rock. Nicholas was just trying to clean up the wound when Ian started throwing punches. It was awful!" Lenora winced as the ice pack shifted on her head. She was just thankful that hospitals don't allow non-family members in the examination rooms. That meant Ian had to stay in the waiting room, where she couldn't yell at him.

"What were you and Nicholas doing there together at that early hour?"

"Didn't you just hear what I said? Ian *punched* Nicholas—without reason!" Lenora nearly shouted, angry that her dad completely ignored what she just said.

"Yes, I heard that, but I would like the complete story first before I make assumptions about anyone's actions."

Lenora relayed the entire story, starting from the previous night in the restaurant, and ending with Ian forcefully carrying her to the hospital. When she finished the story, Tom nodded his head in consideration.

"Well? Aren't you going to say something?" Lenora was growing more angry by the minute.

Tom spent a few moments in contemplative silence. "Well, Lenora, it just looks like Ian made a mistake—one I'm sure he's sorry about. But, you can't get too angry with him—he's trying to protect you."

"Uh," Lenora uttered in frustration. "I am so sick of people using that word as an excuse to act like a moron. Protect me from *what?*" Lenora asked, incensed.

"From *whom*, is the question," Tom responded. "He doesn't trust Nicholas—he's told me that already."

"Why?"

"Ian said that he just had this nagging feeling about him. That, and he's twenty-two, Len—that's a little too old for you."

"Too *old* for me? What about Ian? He's the same age, Dad!"

"But you and Ian aren't dating—he's just a friend and colleague."

"I'm not dating Nicholas, either—we're just friends!"

"But, I don't know Nicholas from Adam, Len. He could be anyone."

"Dad, if you met him, you'd change your mind."

"Possibly. Which is what I'm going to do."

Lenora sat up, suddenly excited. "You want to meet Nicholas?"

"Yes." Tom gently eased his daughter back onto the pillow. "And, I don't want you to see him until I do. After that, you won't be allowed to see him unless I'm around. After that, who knows? We can talk about it when the time comes."

"Dad! Don't punish me for what Ian did," Lenora pleaded, tears filling her eyes.

Tom laughed softly. "I'm not punishing you, just setting boundaries—boundaries that can be lifted once I'm satisfied that Nicholas is a good guy."

"This isn't fair," Lenora mumbled, wiping a tear that trickled defiantly down her cheek.

"It's the best I can do, for now," Tom offered.

Lenora was about to protest, when the doctor walked in, checked her bandage, and told her it was alright to go home. When they got out to the waiting room, Lenora saw Ian sitting in a chair, bouncing his leg erratically. Once he caught sight of them, he bounced up, looking worried.

"Dad, can you please tell Ian to go away?" Lenora didn't feel like talking to Ian, the anger still fresh.

Tom frowned. "Most certainly not. Why would I do that?"

"Because he's a big jerk, Dad. Do I have to tell you again what he did to me?"

"What he did was protect you. I know you're tired of hearing that, but it's foremost on our minds right now. I'm not going to remove him from our lives because you see things differently. You should be thankful that you have someone looking out for you."

Lenora started to object, but then thought better of it — she didn't want to argue with her dad in the hospital. "Fine."

"Good, and you are going to treat him with respect when you see him—he's really worried about you, Len."

"Fine," Lenora snapped.

Tom sighed and gently pushed Lenora along.

Ian seemed so ecstatic about Lenora's clean bill of health that she thought his head was going to pop off. She just rolled her eyes and said nothing as Ian and Tom talked about her "unserious" condition. Ian suggested that they all grab lunch together, a suggestion that her father thankfully declined, saying that he had papers to grade. Tom drove them both home, and then told Lenora that she was, under no circumstances, to leave the building—an order she was only too happy to follow.

Once they reached Dr. Harvey's apartment, Lenora ran upstairs and then locked herself in her room. Ian came in shortly after and knocked on her door.

"I'm making lunch, Lenora," he said cheerfully. No response. "Come on, Love, you've got to eat some time." He paused for a moment. "I'll come and knock on the door when lunch is ready, then."

Lenora waited to hear him leave, turned her music on, and went to sleep.

The air is quiet and shrouded in a heavy mist. The stillness is eerie, a foreboding presses heavily upon her. Fearing to move forward, she stands motionless, scanning the viscous blanket enveloping her. The sound of trickling water invites her, piques her curiosity. Stepping tentatively forward, she flinches at the cold surrounding her feet. Looking down, she grimaces in disgust as thick, black sludge seeps between her toes. An urgent need presses her forward until she finds herself along a stream. She bends down and lets the water run between her fingers, the silky coolness caressing her skin.

Strange footfalls sound ahead, and she stands in eager anticipation. A tall figure appears, the mist swirling around his billowing cloak. He walks toward her and stops, just as he nears. He holds a hand out to her.

"Lenora, come to me, my love."

She moves to take his hand, but the stream quickens and begins to flood the embankment. Her feet begin to sink into the cold mire. Grabbing for him, they brush fingers, and she catches a glimpse of his familiar eyes.

"Nicholas?"

"Yes, my love?"

"Is it you?"

"It's always been me." He drew nearer, his face becoming distinctive until she saw the familiar contours.

It was him. Her love. Her forever.

She sunk further into the mud. "Nicholas, I can't—"

*"Use the bridge my love." She followed his gaze and saw a bridge con-
necting the two sides of the stream. She couldn't run fast enough, as the ooze
pulled her in, slowing her step. Finally, she reached the bridge and took a step
upon the invitingly warm boards, keeping her eyes on the prize.*

*Halfway to her goal, she stopped. Another figure stood in the middle of the
bridge, preventing her from crossing. He held a knife. The figure lunged for
her, grazing her side. She halted as she felt the warm liquid oozing down her
side, a pool of red forming, staining her white gown. She put a hand to her
side; it came back stained red with blood.*

She looked to Nicholas in confusion and fear, reaching for him. "Help me!"

Nicholas slowly shook his head. "I cannot—you must cross to me."

A familiar, menacing laugh froze her. She knew that laugh. "You?"

"Yes, it is me, and I've come to claim you."

"No, you can't."

"Ah, but I can, you're mine."

*She shook her head. "No, I'm his now," pointing to Nicholas. "He will
save me from you!"*

*The figure barked an hysterical laugh. "He can't save you—he's already
dead!"*

Lenora bolted upright in bed, a heavy knock waking her. She looked
around the room, confused. It was dark.

I've missed Nicholas!

She jumped out of bed in a hurry and rushed to the door, only
to discover that it was her dad who waited for her, and he looked
very angry.

"I'm taking that lock off of your bedroom door," Tom said
abruptly.

"You can't—this is someone else's apartment," Lenora
responded, still drowsy.

"Perhaps not, but I can remove the door, if you keep this up," he
responded, visibly angry.

"What do you mean, if I 'keep this up'?"

"Locking your door and not answering, that's what."

"Well, I only locked it because I didn't want Ian to come in when I was changing," she lied. "Also, I didn't hear the knocking because my music is on," she pointed at her earbuds. "And, I was *sleeping*, for a change."

Tom studied her face briefly, eyes narrowed; he sensed the fib. "Yes, but you need to understand that you suffered a head injury, which requires monitoring. If anything were to happen to you…" he paused, drawing in a long breath. "Well, if it weren't for your incessantly loud snoring, I would have told Ian to knock that door down."

"I *snored?*" Lenora was mortified.

"Yes," Tom laughed, "Ian said you sounded like a freight train. When I called earlier to check on you, he held the phone up to your door. I could hear it…even through the door." Tom laughed.

Lenora crossed her arms, aggravated. "Are you done?"

Tom wiped the tears from his eyes and snickered. "I suppose—it was funny though." He smiled and tousled her hair. "I made dinner."

She peered out of the doorway, looking down the hall toward the kitchen.

Tom nodded, knowing what she was scanning for. "Ian isn't here—he has a seminar tonight."

Lenora grabbed her robe and slippers and padded down the hall. She was starving, and her growling stomach gave her away. The table was set for two, a hot bowl of spaghetti waiting in the center of the table. Lenora sat in her usual spot, dished up, and ate ravenously. Halfway through her plate, she remembered Nicholas.

"Dad, what time is it?"

Tom looked at the clock on the wall above Lenora's head. "It's nine o'clock."

"I've missed him!"

"Who did you miss?" Tom asked.

"Nicholas—he was going to come over at seven-thirty," Lenora felt panicked, her heart beating furiously.

"I was here at seven-thirty, no one showed up. Would he have knocked?"

Lenora frowned, thinking back to date night. *Did* he knock? Yes, he did.

"Yes, he would have knocked," Lenora responded, sinking. He didn't show. "Are you sure no one came over?" Lenora asked, now becoming skeptical. "I mean, was Ian here at seven-thirty?"

"Yes, I'm sure no one came over—I think I would know that. And no, Ian was not here—he left at seven," Tom sounded slightly irritated. "Also, if Nicholas came over, I would have invited him in—it would have been a good time to get to know him and ask his side of the story." He eyed Lenora. "I'm not a bad guy, you know, Len."

Lenora sighed. "I know, Dad...sorry. I just don't trust Ian anymore, that's all."

"Now, Lenora, Ian's—"

Lenora held her hand up to interrupt. "Save it, Dad, I know what you're going to say. Can I just enjoy my dinner?"

Tom agreed, resuming with his own plate.

After dinner, Lenora watched a little T.V. with her dad and then went to bed around midnight. It took every ounce of strength she had not to cry. Why didn't Nicholas show? She looked out the window at the unusually dark night sky, wondering what happened.

"Ian, if you ruined this for me, so help me..."

"*Ian meant no harm,*" came Thad's whisper from the corner of the room.

"Hi, Thaddeus." She was in no mood to visit with anyone. "No offense, but can you go away?" She sighed and then moved toward the bed, and then stopped in her tracks. "Did you just say that he meant no harm?" Realization struck. "Thad? Did Ian say something to Nicholas? Did he tell him not to come?"

"*Forgive him. He protects you.*" Thaddeus' voice sounded weak. Lenora wondered if it was because he spent so much time moving between her and Ian.

"I'll talk to him later, Thad. Don't worry about it. You can go back to Ian now." She planned on talking to Ian about this later—and she was determined to get a straight answer this time.

"*He told me to stay here.*"

"Then stay here, but let me sleep, please," she snapped.

"*Okay. Sorry.*"

"Good night, Thaddeus. And, thanks." Lenora felt bad about being short with Thaddeus. "I'm sorry…it's not your fault that your brother is a jerk."

Lenora sat on the bed and looked out the window. The street was completely dark—even the street lights were out. She lay her head down on the pillow. Hot tears streamed down her face.

FINAL NARRATIVE OF BARTHOLOMEW BOOTH

PART V

Doctor's Notes:

Yesterday, the patient became inconsolable after recounting Hope Anne Millar's death, so I had to leave him for the day. Today, I have returned to hear the next victim's story, though it took much prodding to get it out of him.

The patient said that after Miss Millar's death, he was determined to never love again, which explains the two-year gap between Miss Millar and the next girl. He was also daily plagued with fear of discovery. However, the detective's trail soon grew cold, and Bartholomew began to relax.

I asked the patient how he obtained the sleeping draught, chloroform, and needle; I didn't understand how an office worker could gain access to such items. He reminded me that, as a trained psychologist, he was still acquainted with former colleagues. He visited one former colleague, complained of sleep deprivation, and was immediately prescribed the sleeping draught. The chloroform and needles were stolen.

~~~~~~~~~~~~~

Temperance Jefferson Jones came into the agency on a fine Tuesday morning with her fiancé Albert Lynch. It was Mr. Lynch who sought temporary employment so he could afford Temperance's expensive engagement ring, not to mention the impending ostentatious wedding.

Bartholomew didn't like him. He found Albert Lynch arrogant and haughty, like those repulsive Donnerhill boys.

Temperance was another story.

She was a petite girl and terribly shy—a budding beauty. Soft ringlets the color of butterscotch wove softly down her back. She always wore a turquoise butterfly comb in her hair. Her eyes were a mesmerizing amber, almost gold.

Eyes were always the first feature he noticed. As they say, eyes are windows to the soul. To have eyes look upon you with love was to possess them—to him, it was like possessing the soul, the shining light within.

Bartholomew smiled placidly, listening to the detestable Lynch prattle on, and placing a hand discreetly over his breast pocket. He lovingly patting the two stones he always kept there. His keepsakes. One stone was a tiger's eye, the other, turquoise. Colors reminiscent of *their* eyes.

Constance and Hope. He closed his eyes as his heart ached for them.

During Mr. Lynch's frequent visits to the agency, Bartholomew noticed Lynch's cruel treatment of Temperance, ordering her about like a personal assistant, calling her inept. Bartholomew reckoned that Mr. Lynch was only marrying her to obtain his inheritance, which he would only receive upon marriage.

Bartholomew got Lynch a temporary job at a law office near the agency so he could keep an eye on him...and her. He couldn't get her off of his mind.

Presently, Bartholomew began following Miss Jones. It didn't take long to learn her routine. Every morning, she escorted Mr. Lynch to work, browsed the shops, met Lynch for lunch, walked the university grounds, and then sat in a tea shop, reading, until Lynch finished for the day. The couple dined out almost nightly, and then Mr. Lynch escorted Miss Jones to her parent's home, where he visited a few minutes and then left to hail a carriage home.

Their routine was like clockwork—it made his job so much easier.

One lovely Sunday afternoon, he followed them to an ice cream social held by Mr. Lynch's new employer. He watched in disgust as they walked hand-in-hand, wearing their matching, sickeningly white crisp linens—she looking radiant. Bartholomew was glad that Miss Jones was unaware of Lynch's roving eyes.

Bartholomew started taking tea at a different time so he could watch Miss Jones wander about town in the afternoon. She surprised Bartholomew with a change in routine one afternoon. As usual, she spent the afternoon walking about the university grounds, enjoying the sunny day. But, rather than stopping at the tea shop, she meandered to Silver Street Bridge, peering over the side at the punters floating lazily along the river. Bartholomew stood beside her, trying to appear unaware of her presence.

She turned and looked at him, surprised. "Mr. Booth? Is that you?"

He feigned ignorance. "Yes, I'm Booth. And you are?"

"Oh, of course, I shouldn't expect you to remember. I'm Temperance Jones. My fiancée worked with your agency to find employment? Mr. Albert Lynch?" She waited for his recollection.

He frowned, stroking his chin, waiting several seconds before showing recognition. "Oh! Yes, I do remember. He's employed with...Prevy & Kator law firm, correct?"

"Yes!" she exclaimed, smiling.

Bartholomew shook hands with her. "So, what are you doing on this fine afternoon?"

"Oh, it *is* a fine afternoon! I usually have tea right now, but I just had to be out to enjoy the lovely day."

He smiled at her. She was so charming. "I usually have tea now as well, but the lovely day called to me."

"Well, it appears as if we are kindred spirits, Mr. Booth."

His smile faded. *Kindred spirits?* He studied her expression, finding a rare earnestness. "Perhaps," he said quietly, "we could enjoy the day together. Join me for tea…in the gardens?"

She pondered a moment. "Yes, that sounds lovely."

Bartholomew felt great elation as she took his offered arm without hesitation. Could the happiness he sought be found in this girl? He hadn't felt this happy since…

He shook his head, refusing to ruin the moment.

They walked along the river path until stopping at a garden. Picking a bench near an aromatic rose bush, they sat and visited so long that he was nearly late for work.

They met that way, every day, for several weeks. He asked Temperance not to tell Mr. Lynch of their meetings since he may not understand. At first, Miss Jones balked at the idea. Then, Bartholomew reminded her of Mr. Lynch's jealous nature.

"You think him cruel?" she asked quietly. Bartholomew nodded and looked away, not wanting to cause her further discomfort. "Yes, he can be, I suppose. But, it's not always that way. I think he just feels…helpless." She looked imploringly at Bartholomew, as if trying to convince him. "You see, his inheritance is being withheld until we marry. He desperately wants to marry me and be able to give me everything I dream of. But his lack of funds prevents him from doing so. I told him it does not matter to me." She wiped a tear from her eye. "It's created a terrible strain between us."

Bartholomew softened. "I didn't mean to bring up such delicate matters. I just think you are a lovely girl and deserve kindness."

She nodded. "I know there was no bad intent in your query. Albert is under a great deal of pressure." He nodded and took her hand, squeezing it. She made no attempt at moving her hand. "You are a good friend, Bartholomew."

Color rose to his cheeks and he smiled timidly. "You know," he said hesitantly, "I think I may be able to help you. I have a lawyer friend who might help in the inheritance matter." He gave her a sidelong glance. There was a definite change in her demeanor.

"You would help out? Who is your friend? I mean, I would love to know who—" She frowned in contemplation. "Don't you think that the law firm with which Albert is employed might find—"

"No," Bartholomew interrupted abruptly, "they deal with criminal law—my friend works strictly with inheritance issues and such."

"Oh! That would be lovely!" she exclaimed, grabbing his hand and giving it another tight squeeze. "When do you think you could look into the matter?"

"Well, he's out of town this week, but next week, I could ask."

On the way home that night, Bartholomew's mind churned. *This time has to go right. No more mistakes.*

This time, more preparations were needed to help him succeed. The following week, he made himself unavailable to Miss Jones, informing her that he was swamped at work. He used the time organizing his plan.

Bartholomew built a bookshelf, stocking it with romance novels. He also purchased a phonograph and discs that played soft, romantic chamber music. Through his research, he discovered theories asserting that certain environments evoked specific emotions—a romantic environment evoked romantic feelings. The environment would help her fall in love with him, he just knew it.

The following week, he met her for tea in their usual spot. He smiled excitedly at her. "It's found!" he exclaimed. "My friend found the loophole!"

"Oh! You brilliant man!" she exclaimed. "Please thank your friend for me."

"You can thank him yourself," he replied. "He will meet us at my flat to give you the papers." He held his arm out for her to take.

She hesitated, looking uncomfortable. "At your flat? Why not here?"

He fought to keep his smile sincere. "Because...my friend wants to remain anonymous—he did this as a favor. He will get fired if his boss finds out."

"Oh, I see," she responded apprehensively. "Could you just bring the paperwork tomorrow? I would rather you just bring it to me...here."

"But, why?" Bartholomew's arm fell, he was growing impatient. "What's the issue here? Do you not trust me?"

"Oh, of course I trust you," she said unconvincingly. "It's just that it is... improper for a single woman to enter a single man's home..." she trailed off.

He exhaled. "I'm sorry you feel that way. I just thought it would be a place of neutrality where you can meet my friend and sign the papers in the presence of someone you know and trust." He pointed to himself and smiled. "Otherwise, I think it would appear imprudent to meet *two* single men in public. What would Albert think should someone see you and report the meeting to him?"

"Oh, I didn't think of that." She nodded, taking his offered arm.

The walk back to the flat took entirely too long, in his opinion. His heart drummed loudly, and he talked too fast, which made him nervous—he didn't want to give himself away.

When they arrived at the flat, he led her into the living room and offered her tea, which she immediately accepted.

While Bartholomew made tea, Miss Jones looked around the room. "I really like the pictures. The landscapes are lovely. Where are they from?"

"All over the world, really, but mostly France," he answered from the kitchen.

"I really want to go there one day," she replied, glancing at another picture. She wandered about the room, looking at diverse decorations, running her hand along a cabinet that contained assorted tea cups. "Where do these tea cups come from? Were they your mothers?"

"No," he answered, carrying a tray into the living room, setting it down upon the table. "The tea cups are various ones I've collected through my travels."

"Oh, your travels? Where have you been?" She sat in the chair opposite him, looking interested.

"France, Germany, Ireland, Italy…everywhere." He lied, pouring tea and offering her a cup.

She hesitated. "Shouldn't we wait for your friend? I thought he was going to meet us here."

"No, he said to start without him, that he'd be here shortly." Bartholomew looked at the clock. "Yes, he should be here in about fifteen minutes, if you don't mind waiting."

"No, not at all," she responded, glancing around the flat. "Your home is charming—it has a real woman's touch."

"Thank you," he said, blushing. "I hope it isn't too feminine… it's only me here."

"Oh, no, not at all," she replied. "It has just the right amount— any girl would be happy to call this home!"

He smiled. "I'm glad you said that."

"Was there a Mrs. Booth at one time?"

"No, just a thought of one…" he trailed off in thought.

"I'm sorry, did I touch on a sensitive subject?"

"No," he responded carefully, "she just…she died two years ago."

"Oh, I'm sorry!" She reached over and touched his hand. "Please forgive me." He shook his head and patted her hand. "What was her name, if you don't mind me asking?"

"Hope," he responded distractedly.

"That's a beautiful name…" she frowned. "You said she died two years ago and her name was Hope? It wasn't the girl who was murdered and found in the park, was it?"

His heart lurched. He should have been more careful. "No, they're unrelated. It's just a coincidence." He took a sip of tea and swallowed loudly, feeling his face became flush. Beads of sweat formed on his forehead. He had better set things in motion before losing his nerve. "Would you like to see the salon I built for her?"

"I would love to…if you don't mind."

He led her to a corner of the living room, placing a hand alongside the wainscoting. "I created a hidden room for her—somewhere that she could retire to read or write in private. This flat is so small—I wanted her to have a place of her own." He opened the paneling, exposing a secret door that led to the salon. He opened it.

"Oh my," she exclaimed under her breath, taking a step in. "This room is lovely, Bartholomew!"

"I'm glad you approve." He grinned intently at her, instantly checking himself as she threw him a cautionary glance.

Miss Jones took a turn about the room, glancing at the books on the shelves. "Hope must have enjoyed romance novels," she observed.

"Um-hum," Bartholomew replied distractedly. He walked behind her, trying to usher her toward the desk. Getting her to sit at the desk was altogether too easy.

It was time—he would make his move now.

Bartholomew could not believe that she almost escaped. He had to be more careful. This time, he closed the door, tightened the straps, and stayed awake. When Temperance woke up, she tried to scream, but he quickly stopped her, explaining that if she screamed, the straps would get tighter and he would have to hurt her. He was not interested in causing her harm, but she didn't know that. She simply nodded her head and quieted down.

His rules were simple: she was to be locked in her room all day, reading silently. At the end of the day, they would dine together. He explained that if she listened, and did as he instructed, that she would eventually gain more freedom.

After several weeks had passed, he showed her the newspaper articles that were written about her disappearance. He pointed out how it was her parents, not Mr. Lynch, who alerted the authorities. She sobbed upon discovery that the search had discontinued because the trail grew cold. Bartholomew assured her that learning the truth now would enable her to focus on a man who really loved her, rather than worrying about Mr. Lynch, who had already moved on.

Bartholomew forced Temperance to read the romance novels daily, providing him a written synopsis and details of how it made her feel. Each day, he returned to find the same response sealed in an envelope:

Synopsis: Romantic drivel

How I feel: I miss my family. I want to go home!

His plan wasn't working—he needed a new tactic.

Bartholomew brought in the phonograph and played romantic, soft music. He poured wine and tried persuading her to dance with him, which was met with disdainful resistance and a painful slap to his face. He was growing weary of her.

The darkness crept slowly in.

On the seventh week, he questioned whether she was truly his intended. Long walks and fresh air every evening helped him gain perspective. One night, upon his return, he opened his front door to a surprised Temperance, who again attempted to escape. He quickly forced the door open, knocking her to the ground. He grabbed her and dragged her over to the salon. The door was closed, which meant he had to try and open the panel while holding on to her. She yelped in pain as he grabbed her by the hair.

Temperance thrashed about, slapping him and kicking him in the shins. Bartholomew winced in pain, shouting at her to keep quiet, or he would punish her severely. She screamed wildly for help.

Panicking, he let go of the door and grabbed at her. She struggled in his arms as he frantically tried to subdue her. She kicked her heels at him, causing him to double over. He increased his hold on her and shook her about to subdue her, but her struggles only increased. He grabbed her head and turned violently. A dull crack was heard before her body grew limp.

Bartholomew froze, loosening his grip. She fell to the floor, motionless. He dropped down on his knees and felt below her nose—no breath.

He let out a groan. He had killed another one.

His shoulders slumped in disappointment. Feeling about to cry, a soothing voice calmed him.

Get rid of it....more to be had...it was not right for you...

Bartholomew grinned, rose, and dragged her body over to the couch. He had to wait until late to dispose of the body. Hungry, he made a sandwich and sat on the floor beside her, talking as if she could hear him. He went into the salon and picked up the mess she had made from struggling with the lock on the door, which he would have to fix.

He finished cleaning the salon, grabbed one of the romance novels off the shelf, and then went into the living room. He sat next to the body, reading aloud until two o'clock in the morning.

Bartholomew wrapped the body in a blanket, hoisted it over his shoulder, and carried it out into the night. He walked the back alleys, past Silver Street Bridge, and then lay the body down upon a bench along the river. He situated her arms just so, fixed her collar, smoothed out the wrinkles on her dress, and then pressed his lips to her forehead. He sighed deeply, removing the butterfly comb from her hair, placing it in his breast pocket. One last kiss on those soft lips, and then he walked away.

London Chronicle

Cambridge, Nov. 15, 1912   Another murder has occurred in Cambridge. This Morning, about Six o' Clock, one Percy Newman, a Baker for Dominick's Patisserie, was walking near the Cam River, on his way to work, when he noticed the Body of a Woman lying in repose upon a Bench near the Shore. Mr. Newman called out to the Woman, and then tapped her Shoulder to try waking her. Having no response, Mr. Newman immediately dispatched to the Authorities.

Hon. Inspector Gen. William Rood discovered, upon investigation, that the Woman suffered a broken neck, allowing him to determine that she, one Temperance Jefferson Jones, was murdered. Insp. Rood is certain that Miss Jones was murdered by the same person who murdered Miss Hope Anne Millar, a Woman found dead in a similar manner two Years hence. We at the Chronicle have dubbed the culprit in these crimes the "Gentleman Killer" because of the way in which both women were found. Miss Jones' family has been notified.

Insp. Rood welcomes contact from anyone who may have information connected to the murders.

London Chronicle

Cambridge, Dec. 01, 1912   Murderer Captured! Hon. Inspector Gen. William Rood, lead investigator on the case of the "Gentleman Killer," has announced the capture of one Albert W. Lynch, who is being charged with the murders of Hope Anne Millar and Temperance Jefferson Jones, two women who were found brutally murdered. Both women were found lying in repose upon a park bench along the Cam River.

Insp. Rood commented that the investigation discovered that Mr. Lynch, who was formerly engaged to Miss Jones, raised suspicion when he became engaged to another woman three weeks after Miss Jones' disappearance. Insp. Rood stated that Mr. Lynch has denied having anything to do with the murders, but other evidence suggests that he is connected to both. Rood would not comment on the connection, saying that the evidence is being held for fair trial in one month.

London Chronicle

Cambridge, Jan. 12, 1913   Murderer Accused! Sentenced to Death by Hanging! Mr. Albert W. Lynch, the man accused of being the "Gentleman Killer," has been tried by a jury and found guilty of murdering both Hope Anne Millar and Temperance Jefferson Jones. Though Mr. Lynch continues to declare his innocence, the court has found irrefutable evidence that led to a unanimous ruling of guilty. Mr. Lynch is sentenced to death by hanging, which will occur one week from today.

TWENTY-SIX

Nicholas was gone for good.

Lenora obsessed over his absence for the past month, wondering where he was, what he was doing, and why he hadn't called. Every day, like clockwork, she waited at their tea shop, clinging desperately to the hope that he would show. But he never did.

She even tried looking for him at their favorite spots—along the Cam, Silver Street Bridge…Trinity Bridge. Sometimes, at night, she thought she could see a figure hiding within the shadows of the buildings beneath her bedroom window. Once, she called out his name.

There was no sign of him anywhere—he was gone.

Each day, Lenora grew more despondent, losing interest in what formerly gave her pleasure. Nothing appealed to her anymore. Food seemed to lose its flavor. She discontinued cooking for her dad, choosing now to purchase frozen meals that she barely ate.

She didn't read anymore.

Although Percy had sent her postcards announcing new arrivals, she refused to set foot in Barton's Books, choosing instead to stare out her window at the passersby, chancing that one of them might be him, coming back for her.

A deep misery weighed down upon her, making her feel suffocated, out of breath.

The dreams got worse.

She grew tired…worn.

She stopped leaving the apartment altogether. She blamed Ian.

TWENTY-SEVEN

"Len? You have a visitor."

"Nicholas?" She lifted her head from the pillow, eyes red-rimmed and glossy.

Tom sighed, with mixed frustration and concern. "No, I'm sorry, it's not Nicholas."

"Then, tell whoever it is to go away." She pressed her face back into the pillow, pulling the covers over her head.

The door creaked open. The sound of slow, gentle footsteps approached. Lenora uttered something inaudible.

"Lenora, dear?"

She knew that voice. But she couldn't bring herself to look into his face. He drew a chair near the side of the bed. She could hear his watch chain clink against the chair's wooden spindles.

He said nothing, but simply placed a warm hand on her arm. After several minutes, he cleared his throat and commenced reading poems by Edgar Allen Poe: "Annabel Lee," "Lenore," "The Raven," and then ending with "A Dream Within a Dream."

When he finished, she heard him close the book and place it carefully on her nightstand. He placed a gentle hand on the side of her head. "We must all suffer pain and loss to truly know great joy."

Lenora lifted her head from the pillow and looked into the kindly blue eyes that gazed upon her with compassion and worry.

She sat up, and in one swift movement, clung to him, collapsing into heavy sobbing. He wrapped arms around her, patting her on the back, soothing her.

Percy Barton glanced at Tom, who was leaning on the door jamb. Tom squeezed his eyes shut and exhaled in relief.

Lenora glanced at the clock and put on her shoes. The CSP meeting was about to start—it was time to leave. Unsure of where she was going, but knowing full well that it wasn't to the meeting, Lenora left the borrowed apartment and hurried along the street.

After Percy visited her that day, Lenora started feeling better. But, it was a slow process, and she still didn't feel completely restored. Occasionally, she drifted into melancholy whenever she was reminded of Nicholas. However, she resumed cooking for her dad, took long walks, attended the last of the summer concerts, and was back to reading. Actually, she couldn't take her eyes out of books and frequented the library at least twice per week.

She went to Barton's Books every day. Percy hired her as a clerk, and she rather enjoyed recommending books to customers, stocking the shelves (even cleaning them), and opening new arrivals. Since she mostly worked the front of the store, Percy was able to work in the back with the rare books, which was what he preferred.

Two things she still couldn't bring herself to do: attend the CSP meetings and talk to Ian. Obviously, attending the meetings meant a run-in with Ian, who she had managed to avoid without issue, though he lived in the same apartment. He knocked at her door every day, hoping she would respond. Sometimes, he even sat outside her door, reading to her or telling her about his day. Other times, he sent Thaddeus.

She turned her music up to block them both out.

The CSP team had no new information at the last meeting, and her dad rarely spoke of it, so she assumed they were fine without her. She did, however feel guilty about receiving paychecks from Walter for doing CSP work. She *was* reading the file, but that was the extent of her actual work. Lenora vowed to go in one of these days and talk to Walter—straighten things out.

Sitting along the wall in front of Kings College, she tilted her head back, soaking in the warmth of the bright August afternoon, and watching crowds of tourists as they passed by. After a while, she continued her walk along the streets, window-shopping and sipping on an iced latte.

Lenora heard the familiar chimes of Percy Barton's grandfather clock and decided to detour into the store and see what he was up to. Per her father's request, Lenora took Sundays off to attend CSP meetings. Tom held hope that she would attend a CSP meeting one of these days. Actually, now that she thought about it, she had a vague recollection that he expected her to attend today's meeting. She shrugged her shoulders. Nothing she could do about it now.

When she walked in the store, Percy looked over the top of his glasses, raising his eyebrows. "Not going to the meeting today?" Tom had explained everything to Percy—her abilities, CSP, what they do, and when the meetings were held. He felt that if Lenora had at least one trustworthy person to confide in, it would ease her burden.

She never talked about it.

"No, not today. Maybe next week." It was her canned response, and she wasn't fooling Percy, who gave her a reproachful look. "I know, I know, I say it all the time. Maybe this time, I mean it."

"You have to talk to him some time," Percy reminded her. Lenora was uncertain at times whether having Percy know was a good idea.

"On my own time." Lenora pursed her lips together, indicating her disinterest in continuing the conversation. "Get any new books in?"

"Not today," Percy answered, "and all the chores are done for the day, so I have nothing for you to do."

Lenora sighed. "Alright. I'll just hang out for a while and then get out of your hair."

"Hang out all you want," Percy responded, smiling kindly.

When the clock chimed five-thirty, Lenora closed the book that she was perusing, put it back on the shelf, and waved at Percy. "I have to go. See you later!" The CSP meeting had been long over, she was sure, and Tom was more than likely home by now. Her stomach tightened in a knot as she drew closer to home.

Ian wouldn't be there—he rarely spent time at the apartment the past couple of weeks. But Tom would be, and she knew he'd be thoroughly angry.

"Where the *hell* have you been?" Tom bellowed as Lenora opened the door.

"Hi to you too, Dad," Lenora said, trying to sound cheery as she closed the door.

"Don't even try it with me right now," Tom said crossly. "Everyone was worried about you. We stopped the meeting—at Ian's request, mind you—and started a search party."

"Well, you didn't look hard enough—I was at the bookstore." She smirked, but her smile faded once she saw her dad's incensed expression. Lenora wilted. "I'm sorry, Dad. But, I told you this morning that I didn't feel like going."

"Yes, and what did I tell you?"

Lenora didn't respond; she knew it was a rhetorical question.

Tom took her firmly by the arm and led her into the living room, where most of the CSP crew was sitting, a look of disapproval on all of their faces.

Lenora swallowed hard and walked into the room. "I'm sorry, guys. I guess I should have left a note or something."

"What you *should* have done," Tom interjected, "was come to the meeting or *stay home*, like I told you to." He motioned for her to sit in the recliner so that she was facing her condemners. Lenora felt uncomfortable sitting there, everyone staring at her. She looked at Emily, who screwed up her face in a half-amused smile. Okay, so not everyone hated her. She could hear Tom on the phone, telling someone on the other end that she was found.

This is getting worse by the minute. Lenora sank lower in her chair, heart caught in her throat.

Tom came back into the room and gave her a reproachful look. "You and I can talk about this later. We have something more important to address right now." He looked over at Amelia. "Amelia, go ahead and tell her what you told us earlier...and I apologize that you have to repeat it." He glanced angrily at Lenora, who sunk even further.

Amelia nodded. "What we found, Lenora, was that after your visit to the flat with Ian and Rose, things started to really happen." She turned the video on and motioned for Lenora to join her on the couch. Amelia hit the "play" button and Lenora instantly saw what the excitement was all about. She could actually see furniture moving on its own, covers being thrown off her bed, and the pictures on her desk being knocked off. The scariest part was seeing a shadowed, human figure walking around in the apartment. But, when the shadow stopped in front of a picture of her in Tom's study, Lenora could feel the hair on her arms rise, and a chill went through her spine.

"We captured EVPs at this part," Amelia continued, pausing the video at the spot where the shadow stopped in front of the picture.

"What's an EVP?" Lenora asked.

"Electronic Voice Phenomena," Phillip answered. "They're noises that are captured electronically. The noises can be static, voices, radio transmissions—anything audio related, really."

Amelia produced a mini-recorder and pressed "play." All Lenora could hear were ticking sounds from her father's desk clock. Then, what sounded like breathing, coming closer to the recorder. A faint sound, almost like a word, was murmured. Lenora couldn't tell what it was, so she leaned in closer to the recorder, narrowing her eyes in concentration. Amelia played it back again, this time with the volume turned up, and Lenora still hadn't a clue.

Lenora shook her head, indicating that she didn't understand what was being said. Amelia motioned for Joe to join them. Joe brought over a laptop and plopped himself between the girls. He immediately turned the equipment on and then explained.

"So, you can see here," Joe pointed at the screen, where the line was thicker and spiked higher than the rest of the lines, "that this is where the entity speaks. I'll press play, and see what you think." He turned the volume up and pressed play.

Lenora could still hear the clock ticking in the background, and the breathing was much clearer, since Joe singled it out for her, and this time, the murmur was more of a loud whisper that said what sounded to Lenora like "lended."

"What is that, 'lended'?" Lenora asked, frowning—she still didn't get it.

"Okay, I'll increase the volume and slow it down for you," Joe responded. He pressed play and they all waited for the whispered word. This time it was much clearer: 'Len dead'."

Lenora was frozen in fear—chills ran through her body's core, then traveled to her limbs and up through her head. "Did it say 'Len dead'?"

Joe looked at her and nodded. "Yeah, that's why we were trying to find you."

"That's why it's so imperative that you do as you are told until we can get rid of this thing, *Lenora*." Everyone turned to see Ian standing in the doorway, looking infuriated. He strode in, stopping mere feet from her. "You need to realize how vital it is that you *listen* for once." His eyes narrowed. "When we—and I mean *anyone* in this group—tell you to stay, go, come along—whatever— do it. This is serious. It's your life we're talking about. This isn't a stupid little schoolgirl game."

"Okay then!" Emily interrupted Ian's rant. "So what we need to share with Lenora now is our investigation plan." She looked around the room. "Who's in charge of that?"

"I can take it from here," Tom responded, focusing on Lenora, who was in tears. "We've already laid out the plan, so I can tell you the details later. But in a nutshell, equipment will be reset, and then Emily, Ian, and Rose will enter the apartment and do their thing. Emily will bring her dowsing rods; Ian and Rose will try to communicate with the entity. After that, we'll reconvene to discuss removal of the entity from the apartment." Tom noticed the color begin to drain from Lenora's face. "It's complicated, I know, but we'll coach you through the entire process, don't worry. For now, however, everyone can go home and get some rest. We'll meet at the apartment on Friday evening."

A low murmur issued from around the room as everyone packed up their things. Lenora felt thoroughly ashamed that she wasted everyone's time.

"Hey, can you all hold up a second?" Everyone stopped what they were doing and turned toward Lenora. "I-I just wanted to say that I'm really sorry for making you all so worried and for wasting your time today." All eyes were on her, expressionless.

She swallowed hard and continued, tears welling in her eyes. "It's just that I've had a terrible few weeks. I think my boyfriend…or the guy I've been seeing…broke up with me…he didn't say anything, he just…disappeared." She looked over at Ian, his eyes narrowed. "And…I lost my best friend. Life has just…sucked lately, and I didn't feel like being around people. I know it's no excuse, but I'm sorry…I wasn't thinking." Tears spilled down her cheeks as she stood in the middle of the room, feeling exposed, judged.

Emily ran over and hugged her. "It's alright, Lenora—you have every right to feel…heartbroken." She eyed Ian and then squeezed Lenora tighter. "Now, get some rest, and I'll see you Friday night!" She kissed the top of Lenora's head and walked out the door.

Lenora felt like a small weight had been lifted as everyone reiterated Emily's sentiments, hugging her or touching her arm reassuringly. Everyone, that is, except Ian and her dad, who both just stood in the corner of the room, looking cross.

Lenora was unsure of what to say to Ian, or where to begin. She was still mad at him for potentially driving off Nicholas. Maybe he had good intentions—she just wasn't quite sure whether she wanted to forgive him yet. Of course, it had been over a month, and maybe there was a limit on how long a person should be mad. Either way, she was tired of not talking to him or having him in her life.

Once everyone had left, Lenora turned to Ian and her dad and smiled. "Well, I think I'll be going to bed now." She started walking toward her room, when her dad stopped her.

"I don't think so. We have some things to discuss."

Lenora's eyes flicked between the two men, who still wore disapproving looks. Feeling a bit anxious, she walked slowly back to the living room and plopped down on the couch.

Tom sat down on the recliner, as usual, and Ian sat at the opposite end of the couch from Lenora. She kept her eyes down—the harsh looks were making her feel uncomfortable.

"Lenora, look at me," Tom said, knowing that his daughter was avoiding eye contact. Lenora's eyes slowly found her dad's, whose look was softer—more like the dad she always knew. "First of all, I would like to say that I'm proud of you." Lenora straightened, surprised. "I'm proud of you for taking responsibility for your actions. Apologizing to everyone was a step in the right direction—it shows me that you have remorse for what you did, which will help you out in the long run."

"Help me out?" Lenora was confused.

"Yes, help you out in the punishment I will be dispensing in a second." He raised one eyebrow, giving her the "you-know-better-than-that" look.

"Oh." Lenora was expecting punishment of some kind, but hoped the apology would offset the castigation.

"First, when I tell you to be somewhere, I expect you to be there...whether you like it or not. Second, if you do go somewhere, leave a note and tell me *where* you're going. You need to understand that you have responsibilities to me, Ian, the CSP group—and to yourself—to help us protect you. Everyone was upset because they feared for you. You were being very inconsiderate of everyone's time and feelings."

Lenora lowered her head, feeling ashamed. "I'm sorry I put you through that, Dad. I honestly didn't think anything was wrong."

"I know," Tom said softly, "that's why your punishment will be light...this time." He leveled a gaze at her. "Next time, it won't be so fun." He leaned forward in his chair. "For the next few weeks, you are grounded. You will go to school and then come straight to the university because I have a project for you to work on, and then you will come right home. If you need to go anywhere–and I mean *need*– you call me first. No friends, no boyfriends, no T.V.–unless it's with me–and no wandering about on your own. Are we clear?"

"Yes," Lenora replied dolefully. "What about my job at the bookstore?"

"I've already talked to Percy. He'll only schedule you for the weekends until I've said otherwise."

"Oh. Okay." Lenora wasn't shocked—her dad thought of everything.

"Well, since you seem to understand, your old man is going to hit the sack. I have classes to teach, and you two need to chat." Tom rose from the chair, stretched, and then walked toward his bedroom. Before he got to the door, he turned around. "Oh, and don't stay up too late, you have school tomorrow."

Oh, school, I forgot about that.

TWENTY-
EIGHT

The first days of school were dismal. Lenora was the new girl, and everyone made sure she was aware of it. No one talked to her—just treated her like an alien.

She felt like one.

And, if that wasn't enough, she was instantly labeled a weirdo on the first day because of an incident in homeroom.

Lenora groaned just thinking of it.

All eyes were on her as she walked in to homeroom and made her way to the only available seat. She tried not to draw attention to herself and slunk down in her seat.

"Hi," came a cheerful voice next to her. "My name is Kate. What's yours?"

Lenora glanced at the girl and smiled. She was just about to introduce herself, when she froze.

And then screamed.

Kate looked exactly like the girl in the sketch that Emily had drawn that summer—the one that Ian saw in his visions…the one that the entity would go after if he couldn't have Lenora.

Startled, Kate jumped back and then frowned. "What was that about?"

Lenora didn't know what to say—she was speechless.

And then, she did the unthinkable: she took out her phone and snapped a picture of Kate.

"What the?" Kate screeched.

But, Lenora didn't have time to answer—the homeroom teacher quickly confiscated her phone and remonstrated Lenora in front of the class.

Ian thought the scene uproariously hilarious. However, when he compared the picture to the sketch that Emily drew, his smile faded.

"Uncanny resemblance," he said distractedly. "I'm glad you're a bit socially awkward."

"Gee, thanks," Lenora responded sourly.

"This gives us proof that the entity isn't fooling around," Ian continued, ignoring her. "I'm going to take this to CSP." He sent the photo to himself and then handed her phone back. "You'll need to stay away from this girl."

"Well, that's an understatement," Lenora responded sardonically.

"I'm not joking," Ian retorted.

Lenora exhaled in irritation. "What I meant was that there's no need to tell me twice—Kate avoids me like the plague. Everyone does."

Ian's expression softened. "Sorry. That would be tough…especially in high school." He chuckled softly. "But, it's to your advantage until we can get rid of this entity. Then, maybe we'll have to rework your image. I'll come up with something."

Lenora froze. "No, I don't want any help, thank you."

Ian laughed heartily and ran to get them sodas.

Lenora was glad that she and Ian were talking now. It was still a bit awkward, but they were making progress, nonetheless. Ian denied having anything to do with Nicholas's disappearance, but she didn't quite believe him yet. She kept that bit to herself, hoping to one day give him the benefit of the doubt.

She did make an attempt at being *somewhat* open with Ian. Though, she refrained from telling him that she was irrevocably in love with him.

Ian came bounding through the dungeon door, sodas in hand. He plopped one down on the desk for her, sat on top of the desk, and opened a soda for himself. "So? What are the plans for tonight?"

Lenora pondered a moment. The past few nights, Ian had stayed home and seemed genuinely interested in spending time with her and Tom. She wasn't complaining, but it was just...odd. "I have homework, and Dad has his late lecture."

"Oh, that's right—it's Thursday."

"Don't you have a class tonight?"

"Nope. Both of my classes are on Tuesday morning—back to back."

"Nice being you," Lenora mumbled.

Ian sat back in his chair, grinning. "Maybe you and I should go out for dinner and a movie tonight."

"That would be great, except I'm grounded," Lenora reminded him. "And, it's a school night."

"Oh, right," Ian said thoughtfully, getting up from his chair. "Hey, I forgot that I have something to do." He rushed out the door without another word.

"Hey!" Lenora shouted after him, confused. *Ugh! He can be so... flakey.*

An hour later, Ian peered around the corner. "I talked to your dad," he said, smiling broadly.

"And?" Lenora asked unenthusiastically.

"And, my pessimistic little friend, he said that dinner and a movie out with me was fine, providing your homework is done." He sidled into the room, closed the file she was working on, grabbed her hand, and yanked her out of the chair. "We must get you home *immediately* so you can finish your homework. Ian's hungry."

"Talking about yourself in the third person isn't very cool, Ian."

"Ian doesn't care!" He sang at the top of his lungs, arms out-stretched above his head.

Lenora looked around, embarrassed, and then rolled her eyes.

Ian and Lenora had dinner at a little café that she had never heard of. The waitress knew Ian by name, which wasn't surprising.

They chatted all through dinner—it was as if they hadn't skipped a beat. And later, even though the movie was terrible, she and Ian enjoyed mocking the horrible acting and storyline. They should have known that a movie entitled "Love Shackles" would be terrible.

Lenora was glad to have things back to normal; she missed Ian terribly, and the night had been fun. On their walk home, Ian chose the side streets that took them along the river Cam. He held her hand as they walked along the river and watched the punters glide idly by.

Lenora's thoughts drifted to the night when she and Nicholas sat on the stone wall together. A dark look crossed her face.

Ian took notice. "Hey! What's the matter, Love?"

"Absolutely nothing," she lied.

"You're lying...I can tell." He stopped walking and led her to a bench that overlooked the river. "Come on, tell Ian what's the matter. Remember, we promised to be completely honest with each other."

"I know, but it's just that..." She inhaled, feeling hesitant. "Nicholas and I spent time here together last summer." She glanced at Ian nervously. "I know you didn't like him. But I did...a lot."

Ian pursed his lips together. "I'm sorry that things didn't work out for you." Lenora opened her mouth to argue, knowing Ian's feelings toward Nicholas, but Ian held up a hand to stop her. "I know what you're going to say, and you can save it. I don't like the bloke, but regardless of what you might think, I do want you to be happy— just with someone else. I had this bad feeling whenever I was around him. I trust my gut, Lenora–it's never steered me wrong."

Lenora didn't respond, but nodded, looking out at the moon's silvery reflection rippling atop the river.

Ian tilted her face up to his. "I apologize for the pain I caused you, but you are important to me, and the last thing in the world I want is for you to be hurt. That would absolutely kill me. You understand, don't you?"

Lenora was so taken in the moment that she couldn't answer. His blue-grey eyes glittered in the moonlight, and she was becoming lost in them, as she once did not so long ago. Her heart fluttered, which caught her breath.

"Lenora? You understand, don't you?" Ian frowned and removed his hand from under her chin.

Lenora shook her head. "Yes...yes, I understand. Sorry." She blushed and looked away from him, embarrassed.

"Are you sure? It took you a while to answer me." He frowned, appearing frustrated. "Your hesitation tells me something completely different."

"No, I do understand. That's not why it took me so long to answer." She was searching for a reason—anything—so that she didn't have to tell him why.

"Then, what happened to you just then?"

Lenora shook her head, trying to find a plausible reason for her hesitation. *Come on, Lenora—think!*

"Well?"

"Fine!" Lenora snapped. "I hesitated because you..."

"Because I what?" Ian sounded annoyed now.

"Because you're... gorgeous," she blurted out dreamily—immediately regretting her proclamation.

"Oh!" Ian responded, surprised. He leaned his back against the bench. "Oh," he whispered again.

Horrified at her sudden confession, Lenora wanted to get up from the bench and run as far away as she could, but Ian slid his hand over to hers and grasped it tightly. He looked at her affectionately.

"You are such a lovely girl, Lenora. I don't deserve such a great friend."

Oh. So, he doesn't get that I'm completely infatuated with him. That's... good. She nodded and smiled wanly. "Can we go now? I'm getting cold." She really wasn't, but her need to get away was much stronger than her desire to stay.

"Oh, sure." Ian helped her up from the bench. To her great comfort, they walked the rest of the way in utter silence.

TWENTY-NINE

The old apartment was a mess. The entity had completely destroyed what it could. Covers were thrown off beds; glasses and vases broken; cupboards open, their contents tossed out; and there was a smell that Lenora couldn't identify, but was sure it was rotten food...or so she hoped.

She kept her distance as the CSP team worked their magic.

The technicians set up equipment and refreshed batteries, while Amelia walked around with recorders to catch more EVPs for analysis, and Phillip tried to capture thermal readings.

Emily brought two L-shaped, brass dowsing rods to help her detect spirit activity in the apartment. She drew a crude map of the apartment and fastened that to a clipboard, which she stuck under her left arm. While walking around the apartment, Emily held the dowsing rods out in front of her. Whenever the rods crossed, she took out her clipboard, found the correct room on her map, and then recorded the location by marking an X on the spot.

Ian and Rose wandered about the apartment separately, trying to make contact with the entity. Though, it appeared as if neither had any luck, because both simply wandered from room to room, looking lost.

Once the team finished their initial sweep, everyone gathered in the living room. Ian snuggled in next to Lenora, giving her a quick squeeze before taking on a serious expression.

"So, what's the verdict?" Tom asked once everyone had settled in.

"Phil and I checked the recorders—no EVPs or thermal readings were detected," Amelia reported.

"I got nothing—it won't talk to me," Ian added.

"Me, neither," Rose offered, shaking her head.

"The dowsing rods told me where the entity most frequents," Emily explained, "but I think we all know where the most activity resides." Everyone glanced surreptitiously at Lenora. "Personally, I think we should use a Ouija board to induce the entity to react to us," she suggested.

"I think that's a bad idea," Rose responded emphatically. "Ouija boards invite trouble."

"How so?" Lenora asked before Emily could respond.

"Ouija boards can help people interact with spirits," Rose explained. "However, it can also act as a portal, inviting evil spirits to physically unleash their evil into the human world. Ouija boards can be dangerous, and I'm skeptical of their use."

"True," Emily replied, "however, we're trying to drive the spirit out into our world—getting it here will help us remove it."

"I'm with Rose," Lenora responded, feeling uneasy. "I don't want it here. It's already done enough damage." She could feel the scar burning on her leg.

Everyone turned to Walter, who was deep in thought. After a few minutes, he nodded. "I'm with Emily on this one." Emily gasped, her expression one of shock.

"But, Walter!" Rose shook her head. "Ouija boards aren't toys—they shouldn't be tampered with…the results could be—"

Walter held up a hand. "I realize what you're going to say, Rose. And, usually, I agree with your assertions. However, we're all professionals here, and this will be done as such. None of us here are interested in treating the Ouija like a toy…and none of us will. Besides, the entity has already unleashed its evil on Lenora—let's challenge it to take us all on. Collectively, we might be able to get rid of it."

Rose nodded, conceding. "If you don't mind, then, I'll just stand by in case I'm necessary."

"Fair enough," Walter agreed.

Emily set the Ouija board in the center of the room, lighting two candles on either side. Then, she lit four more candles, placing them at strategic positions around the board. "I'm setting these candles north, south, east, and west to draw a circle around the board," she explained. "Those who are participating in the session will sit inside of the drawn circle."

Emily then instructed everyone else to light the entire apartment with candles, since spirits found candles inviting. Once the room was ready, Lenora, Ian, and Tabitha sat within the drawn circle with Emily, who sat in front of the Ouija board. Rose sat on a chair outside of the circle so that she could monitor the situation, and Tom sat close behind Lenora. The tech crew—Joe and Maggie—were in the kitchen, looking at video screens; Amelia and Phillip were holding still with their equipment to capture EVPs and thermal images.

"Everyone needs to keep silent and still now," Emily instructed. "Lenora, remove your gloves." Lenora did as she was told and then watched as Emily placed the planchette in the middle of the board. "To begin the session, everyone in the circle should hover their hands over the planchette and chant 'Ouija, Ouija, Ouija, are you there' simultaneously. When the planchette moves and answers YES, then we can begin." She glanced at everyone in the circle before focusing on Lenora. "Ready?" When Lenora nodded her assent, Emily nodded for everyone to hover their hands over the planchette. Once everyone was situated, Emily nodded and took a deep breath.

"Ouija, Ouija, Ouija, are you there?" everyone chanted.

Lenora held her breath, watching the planchette carefully, fear trickling down her spine. Lenora jumped as the planchette seemed to move on its own around the board.

It stopped at YES and then moved back to the center of the board.

"Good, then we can begin," Emily replied. "Are you a good spirit?" she asked the board. The planchette jerked forward and landed on NO.

"What kind of spirit are you, then?" Emily repeated. The planchette slid across the board and landed on the moon.

"What does that mean—" Lenora began, before she was stopped by Ian, who simply shook his head. Lenora exhaled and refocused on the board.

"No, questions are good," Emily responded, "Lenora is learning." She glanced at Lenora. "The sun means it's a good spirit; the moon means that it's evil."

"Evil?" Lenora started shaking her head. "I don't think I want to—"

"It's alright," Emily reassured her, "we're in the sacred circle—it can't touch you." Lenora nodded, but felt little relief.

"Are you a male?" Emily continued with the questions.

YES

"Are you old?"

NO

"Between the ages of 25 and 35?"

YES

"Did you at one time live in this apartment?"

YES

"In what year did you die?"

The planchette slid slowly to 1, then 9, then 1, and then quickly flew to number 7.

"Okay," Emily responded. "You died in 1917. Of natural causes?"

NO

"How did you die?"

Lenora held her breath. For what seemed like several seconds, the planchette remained, unmoving, in the center of the board before it slowly began spelling out a word.

H-A-G-I-N-G

"Haging? Is that even a word?" Lenora asked, exasperated.

Emily shook her head. "Spirits oftentimes misspell words. A letter is missing." She returned her gaze to the board. "Did you mean hanging? Were you hung?"

The planchette flew over to the word YES.

Emily nodded. "Death by hanging usually means that you committed a crime. Did you rob a bank or commit some form of robbery?"

NO

"Did you murder someone?"

YES

"How many people?"

The planchette whirled around the board, stopping at each number before quickly moving on and hovering over the number 6.

Emily removed her hands from the planchette. "Okay, now I'll ask it some specific—"

The planchette began moving around the board on its own. Everyone sat frozen, watching in shock as it started spelling words over and over again.

L-E-N-O-R-A L-E-N-O-R-A L-E-N-O-R-A

Lenora's heart froze in terror.

Emily quickly moved and poised her hands over the planchette, which wrenched away from her and flew immediately to the word NO. Emily glanced at Lenora, her eyes wide with fear. "I think it wants to talk to you, Lenora." No sooner had she spoken, than the pointer flew to the word YES. Emily removed her hands from over the board and rose. "We need to switch spots."

Lenora glanced nervously at her dad, who shook his head and put a hand to his forehead. His silence spoke volumes—against his better judgment, she was to submit. Slowly, Lenora rose and took Emily's place. She stared at the board, her entire body shivering in fear. She didn't know where to begin. She glanced at Emily, who nodded at her. "We're all here if you need us."

"I don't think this is a good idea—"

The planchette began to move swiftly around the board… unaided.

S-H-U-T U-P I-A-N

"Oh, so you know who I am," Ian stated.

K-N-O-W A-L-L

H-A-T-E A-L-L

L-O-V-E L-E-N-O-R-A

"You can't love her—" Ian began, but Lenora cut him off, shaking her head.

"How can you love me? You don't know me?" As if more relaxed, the pointer moved slowly, methodically, around the board.

K-N-O-W L-O-V-E W-A-N-T T-A-K-E

"Where do you want to take me?" Lenora asked, not wanting the answer.

W-I-T-H M-E

"But, what if I don't want to go?"

M-U-S-T

"Why?"

S-E-V-E-N-T-H

"Seventh? What does that mean?" Lenora was confused. She glanced at Ian in bewilderment and then noticed that the pointer moved quickly around the board, spelling the same thing over and over again.

S-E-V-E-N S-E-V-E-N S-E-V-E-N

"Stop!" Lenora shouted. The planchette immediately obeyed. Lenora placed a shaking hand over her forehead. "Okay, think. Seven what?" Realization dawned on her face and she glanced into Emily's knowing expression. Lenora nodded. "You killed six…so I'm the seventh?"

The planchette moved slowly across the board and stopped at YES.

Lenora's shoulders slumped as a knot formed in her throat. She straightened, deciding to face this thing head-on. "How can you take me? You're dead…I'm not. What if I refuse? What could you possibly do?"

The planchette moved swiftly around the board, spelling the same word continuously.

C-A-T C-A-T   C-A-T

"Cat? What in the world—" Ian began, utterly confused.

"I think he means Kate," Lenora interrupted. She looked back at the board, watching the continuously moving planchette. "Do you mean Kate? The girl in my class? What do you want with her? What does she have to do with anything?"

The planchette immediately stopped in its tracks, made a small circle in the middle of the board, and then slowly moved toward the bottom, hovering over the words GOOD BYE. Then, it stopped altogether.

"Sorry, but the spirit has closed our session," Emily informed her apologetically.

"Hey!" Lenora shouted. "I'm not done yet! Come back! Tell me what you're going to do to Kate!" She hovered her hands over the pointer, but nothing happened. Emily leaned forward and hovered her hands over the board as well.

The planchette shook and then flew off the board, hitting the wall and nearly missing Tom's head. Everyone stared in disbelief.

"I've never seen that happen before," Emily whispered distractedly. "Never."

"Well, there's got to be some explanation," Tom replied.

"Perhaps the video footage will tell us more," Phillip offered. He turned and walked toward the kitchen, Amelia hurrying closely behind as if she didn't want to be left alone.

Everyone got up from the floor, except Lenora, who still felt detached from her body. This experience left her feeling numb, disoriented. As the rest of the group filtered into the kitchen to see the video footage, Lenora stared at the board for several minutes. She reached her hand out and touched the board with the tip of her finger.

Bright light flew from the board like sparks, sending an electric current through her finger. The shock surged through her body, causing it to tremor uncontrollably. Painful white-hot flashes blinded her, and she couldn't move.

She lay in a heap in the corner of her room, afraid to sleep. Too long had he tormented her after his death—the whispers in the dark, hot breath on her neck, hearing her name whispered in the deep darkness…the dreams.

The sedatives were no longer working, but only seemed to make it worse. She looked down at her arms and legs—bruised and bloody from the invisible attacks. Her parents thought she was going crazy…her uncle was growing tired of her. An overwhelming urge to go home filled her breast, and she began to cry.

"Don't cry, my dearest Prudence."

She started at the words and then sobbed. It was him, coming for her.

"Do you want my visits to stop? Do you want the pain to end?" he asked soothingly. She nodded, wanting that more than anything. "Good, then do as I say, and I promise your suffering will end."

She rose at his will, walking toward the door, past her sleeping family. It was as if she was in a dream, walking along the cold cobblestone of her new town, so late at night…so dark. He led her to his home.

She didn't want to go back in, but he was no longer there— what harm could become her?

She entered without issue, stepping into the vacant flat, hearing the creaking floorboards echoing.

He led her to the salon—the room she was kept in. She gasped as she walked in, noticing there was no change—everything was still in place, and it made her shiver. Gingerly, she stepped forward, taking the awl he said she would find. She pried the boards loose.

Inside, was a delicate satchel tied with a silk purple ribbon. Instinctively, she took the satchel and placed it in her pocket, as instructed.

She walked back home, meeting him on the rooftop of her uncle's estate. He waited for her, a menacing stare, his lips stretched into a sneer. Her body trembled—the air was cold, snow had recently fallen, blanketing the rooftop terrace. Moonlight sparkled on the newly fallen snow, which usually delighted her—particularly since it was Christmas Eve— but today, it did not.

Though everything within her shuddered against the idea, she approached him, showing the satchel.

"Open it—it's your present."

Fingers shaking from the cold, she tentatively loosed the ribbon and watched as the filmy material fell gently onto the palm of her hand. Tiny little trinkets were revealed to her—a thimble, gold locket, and a tortoiseshell butterfly hair comb.

"They're beautiful," she said in disbelief.

"You may have them, if you do one thing for me," he uttered. She nodded, having an inexplicable desire to have the trinkets. "Pluck a hair from your head."

"What?" She felt confused.

"Pluck one hair from your head, add it to the trinkets, and then retie the satchel."

Frowning, she did as she was told, then looked at him expectantly.

"Now, you are part of my collection," he explained, sneering.

"Your collection?"

"Those are the precious treasures of my girls." She stared at him in confusion, and then realization dawned on her face. "Yes, I see you understand." He flashed a hungry smile.

Waves of nausea surged through her until she purged what little she had in her stomach. "I will not be part of your collection!" she screamed, "And I will not be part of you!" She ran to the edge and hurled the satchel over the side. Once it hit the ground, she heard him laughing and whirled on him. "What's so funny?"

"You just sealed your fate," his voice becoming deep, sinister. "Now you will be mine forever."

She felt dizzy. Something hit her hard on her chest. She stumbled backward, over the rail, and plummeted downward toward her death.

Lenora stood on the snowy ground, watching the scene... watching as the girl fluttered to the ground as if a mere feather caught in a gentle breeze. She watched as the light drifted from the girl's eyes.

A shadowy figure stood by the girl, touched her hair, caressed her face. He brought his lips just above the girl's, a smoky tendril wafted from her mouth into his. He breathed it in, smiling.

Lenora knew what it was. He was taking her soul. She felt repulsed. "Leave her alone!"

The figure glanced at her, baring teeth. "She's mine now. My sixth..." He stood and walked toward her, the light catching his face. Lenora knew this face somehow... somewhere.

"Seven," he whispered, as if calling her by name. "Seven... seven...seven."

Lenora put her hands over her ears. "Stop saying that!"

"Seven, seven, seven..." His whispers grew louder, raspy, menacing.

"Leave me alone!" Lenora started backing away, but the man was quick—he was beside her in a flash, grasping her arm, pulling her to him. She struggled against him, but the more she struggled, the tighter his hold grew.

He pressed his face into her neck, inhaled her scent, and rolled his eyes. "I can't wait to make you mine."

Lenora was repulsed by the sickening stench of his breath, his icy touch. She tried pushing him away, but he grabbed her more firmly and pressed her face closer to his.

He slaked an icy tongue across her cheek; her stomach roiled. "Please, no..." She felt the strength draining from her body.

"Leave her alone!"

Lenora turned and saw Ian standing beside them, his body wavering out of view. Ian spoke again, but the words drifted; she could barely hear him. He reached for her, but his hand went straight through her arm. Ian looked at his hands in shock.

The entity laughed. "She's under my control now!" He started pulling Lenora in the direction of the dead girl; Lenora struggled against his grip. She opened her mouth to scream, but nothing came out. She turned to Ian, his silhouette barely visible.

Her body felt weak, numb, floating. The entity dragged her closer to the girl. She had no strength for resistance.

"NO!"

Ian ran toward them, his figure a luminescent glow—it was as if he was the ghost in her dream's reality. The entity let go of Lenora and she fell limply to the ground. She could no longer hold herself up.

The entity walked furiously toward Ian. "You want her, come and get her, boy!"

Ian launched himself at the entity and went right through him. The entity looked at him, at first with incredulity, and then with anger. It began running toward Ian, who was in a full sprint toward Lenora.

Ian grabbed at Lenora, his hands going right through her body. He clawed at her, letting out frustrated and desperate gasps. The entity drew nearer, his face contorted in rage.

Lenora was fading.

Suddenly, a bright light shone behind Ian. His form became more solid, and he grabbed for her, shouting in triumph as he finally grabbed hold of her, hauling her into the brightness.

Lenora and Ian lay on the floor, out of breath. Ian rolled on his side and stared at Lenora, a terrified look on his face.

"Good grief, Lenora! I almost lost you!"

"What on earth happened?" Tom nearly yelled, running to Lenora's side. "What's wrong with her? She's not moving!"

Tom tried to gently rouse his daughter. Then, without a word, Ian moved Tom aside, sat on top of her, and slapped her hard on the face. Tom shouted at Ian to stop, but halted when Lenora finally moved.

"What happened?" she asked, feeling weak and disoriented.

"You went into another trance," Ian answered as he repositioned himself. "This one was tough, though—I nearly didn't get you on time."

Lenora burst into tears. Emily rushed to Lenora's side and held her. "It's all right, Love, it may have almost got you this time, but it will be the last, if I have anything to do with it."

"What does it want with me? Why did it choose me?"

"I don't know," Ian answered honestly. "But, if we don't find answers soon, I'm truly afraid for you."

THIRTY

The walk back to their borrowed apartment seemed to take an eternity. Lenora felt exhausted and numb, and she wanted nothing more than to go home, take a hot bath, and go to sleep.

After everyone left the haunted apartment, Tom went to the CSP conference room with the technical crew to go over the findings. He asked Ian to walk Lenora back to their borrowed apartment and stay with her. Ian walked with his arm held tightly around her shoulders the whole way, which generally would have her thrilled beyond belief. But now, she just wanted to get home, she was so drained.

As they neared the apartment, Ian stopped and bristled.

"Ian? What's wrong?" Lenora uttered, concerned. She followed his gaze to the doorway that led to their apartment staircase. A tall, dark shadow stood near the doorway, a figure that Lenora recognized.

"Nicholas!" Lenora screamed. And, before Ian could stop her, she darted off and ran into Nicholas's arms, which felt strong and warm. She inhaled his familiar scent and squeezed him tightly. She couldn't believe he was actually here.

Nicholas kissed the top of her head and gently pushed her away from him, looking deeply into her eyes. "My sweet Lenora," he whispered, stroking her cheek, "Oh, how I've missed you!"

"I've missed you too, Nicholas," Lenora returned affectionately, lingering in his scent, an instant feeling of well-being washing over her.

She then pushed away from him, frowning, remembering the pain and anguish she suffered over his disappearance. "Where have you been? You never called or came to see me! I thought you left for good. I was so…" The tightness in her throat stopped her, eyes filling with tears.

"I'm so sorry about that. Work called and there was an emergency—I had to leave immediately. The emergency was a bit more… challenging than I originally thought."

"What do you mean? You're a rare book seller. What kind of emergency—"

Nicholas placed his finger to her lips, stopping her thought. "Perhaps I will have a chance to explain later. However, I have a train to catch in a few minutes. I just came by to say goodbye."

"Goodbye? What do you mean?" Lenora felt hysterical. "You just got here! You're coming back, aren't you? Please tell me you're coming back!" She looked pleadingly into his eyes.

Nicholas shook his head sadly. "No, I'm afraid not. My work is taking me elsewhere and I have to leave Cambridge," his brows furrowed, "and regrettably, you."

"No, you can't leave me! I need you!" Lenora grabbed his arm in protest.

"Believe me, leaving you is the last thing I want, but it's for the best." He removed her hand from his arm and kissed her forehead. "Thank you, Lenora, for the most wonderful time in my life. I will never forget you for as long as I live."

He turned away from her and walked down the street. Lenora stood, watching him go, and then without thinking, began running after him.

"Nicholas, please!" she shouted, gaining ground. She caught up and ran in front of him, blocking his ability to move forward. "Please don't do this–don't write me out of your life completely—you mean too much to me." She looked up at him, pleading.

Nicholas sighed and shook his head. "I'm sorry, Lenora, I shouldn't have come. But, I couldn't bear leaving without seeing you one last time." He shook his head, tears welling in his eyes. "I can't expect you to wait for me. I'll be too far away. You need to live your life...move forward...without me. Go back to your flat. Enjoy school, make friends, and have a life. It has to be over between us... for your own good." He gently moved her to the side of the building and held her shoulders firmly. "Goodbye, my sweet Lenora." He started to walk away and Lenora moved to follow, but Nicholas held up his hand. "No."

Lenora stopped in her tracks. Nicholas gave her a furtive glance and swiped at a tear on his cheek. She watched as he walked away, his figure becoming enveloped in the night's shadows. She leaned up on the building and slid her body down to the cold ground, sobbing uncontrollably.

A warm hand on her shoulder startled her. "Nicholas?"

"No, Ian." He crouched down in front of her and put both hands on top of hers. "I can't believe the nerve of him...coming back." He exhaled deeply. "You just started getting over it...and now?"

Lenora looked into Ian's concerned face. "He's gone, Ian. He's really gone!" She started to sob again.

"I'm sorry Lenora. I really am." He rubbed her arms, trying to console her. "Let's go home." He gently pulled her up and put his arm around her. Wordlessly, he led her to her room, pulled the covers over her shoulders, and stroked her hair. He kissed the top of her head and then turned off her bedside lamp and left the room.

Lenora did not sleep that night.

THIRTY-ONE

Losing Nicholas now had an unexplainable finality to it that made Lenora feel dazed. Though she didn't sink into a depression like she did when he went missing, she lapsed into a haze, like she was a functioning zombie.

Tom told her she was being overly dramatic—after all, they had only been seeing each other for a couple of months, and it wasn't that serious. Ian avoided the discussion—trying to cheer her up every time she tried talking about it. But, she didn't want to be cheered up or have her feelings invalidated—she wanted someone to understand how devastating it was to lose him—for the second time.

She certainly didn't feel like being at the CSP meeting today, which no doubt showed in the sour expression on her face.

"Hey, you." Lenora was startled out of her reverie by Emily, who was looking at her sympathetically. "Ian told me about you and your man breaking up." She tilted her head contemplatively and then put her hand on Lenora's arm. "You don't have to talk about it if you don't want to, but I'm here if you need a friend."

Lenora warmed at Emily's thoughtfulness. "Thanks, Emily. I might have to take you up on that."

"Anytime," Emily said before they were interrupted by Phillip and Amelia, who had just entered the CSP conference room, talking animatedly. Rather, it sounded more like an argument.

"We can't do that now!" Amelia asserted.

"We have to," Phil replied, just as adamant.

"Well, it's wrong, that's all," Amelia responded, sounding deflated.

"What's going on, guys?" Emily asked.

"Uh," Phil hesitated, looking at Lenora. "Nothing. We can talk about it later." He took a seat and pulled out the chair next to him for Amelia, who scowled at him and plopped down in a different chair.

Lenora sat in silence as everyone else came in. Ian showed up last—late as usual—and took his seat across from Lenora. She loved it when he sat across from her—they had this silent communication that usually resulted in her having to stifle a laugh. Today, however, he was trying hard to not make eye contact. In fact, no one was making eye contact.

Now what? Lenora sighed. These surprises were tiring. *What would it take to have a normal life?*

Tom entered the room and closed the door behind him. He gave Lenora a quick nod and then went over to shake Walter's hand. No one had seen much of Walter since his retirement at the end of summer. He felt that Tom would have a better transition as supervisor without him there. Walter's presence at the meeting today made Lenora nervous.

Quiet chatter ensued around the room. Lenora watched as everyone whispered with their neighbor, stealing glances in Walter's and Lenora's direction. Her heart thudded as she wondered what was happening. She fought an incredible urge to run out of the room.

Finally, Tom stopped chatting with Walter and turned toward the group, raising both hands in the air to get everyone's attention. "Okay, okay. Let's all quiet down now so we can get down to business."

Everyone quieted down and moved their chairs to face Tom. Lenora looked to Ian for a reassuring glance, but he didn't meet her gaze—he faced his chair toward Tom and then shifted his eyes quickly to steal a sidelong glance at Lenora.

Lenora felt a sour taste in her mouth as a feeling of dread swept over her.

What could possibly be wrong?

Tom cleared his throat as if in preparation for a long-winded speech. "No doubt, you're all wondering why Walter is here. I'll not waste anyone's time and get right to the point." He glanced over at Lenora and gave her a faint smile. "As it turns out, we're going to have to pull out of the investigation of my and Lenora's apartment."

Lenora sat bolt-upright in her chair. "What? Why?"

Tom held his hand up. "Calm down, Lenora, until you've heard everything. Okay?"

She nodded and sat back in her chair, but not before shooting an inquiring look at Ian, who shook his head sympathetically. *So, he knows? I wonder how long?* Her mood soured. *Why didn't Ian say anything?*

"As I was saying," continued Tom, "the investigation will need to stop—for the time being—for a couple of reasons. First off, upon intensive investigation, we have discovered that the entity is too powerful for our group. We're going to need an expert to perform a spiritual cleansing." Wild whispers circled the room, which caused Tom to pause, making him visibly frustrated.

"I know, it's more than what we thought," he affirmed, "but that is what we've got, nonetheless. The expert that usually performs spiritual cleansings for this group is currently on a retreat and won't be available for a few weeks. Consequently, it's completely unnecessary for us to keep investigating, so as of today, all equipment will be removed from the apartment." He looked directly at Maggie and Joe, who both slumped in their seats; this meant hours and hours of work—on a Sunday night.

"But why are we pulling all the equipment?" Maggie asked, sounding frustrated. "We're going to finish the investigation, aren't we?"

"Yes, however, we have another investigation that's come up—a paid investigation that will take up our equipment and time."

Tom picked up a stack of papers on the table and started handing them out to the group. "This is the new investigation. Included in your packet is the background information and assignments. I expect that you will all read the documentation and then when we gather next week, we'll all be on the same page." Tom stopped as there were chuckles around the table. "Sorry. No pun intended."

Lenora was the only one not laughing. She was also the only one who did not receive a packet. "Dad? I mean…Tom? I didn't get a packet."

"That's because you aren't part of this assignment," Tom responded.

"Why is that?" Lenora demanded.

"You aren't experienced enough to be involved in the investigation." Tom gave her a hardened look that told her to stop pursuing the questioning.

She refused to take the hint. "But, I'm a *paid* member of this team, am I not?"

"Yes, you are, but–"

"But what, exactly?" Lenora interrupted Tom before he could finish his thought. "How am I supposed to learn if I'm not included? Can't I just hang out and watch?"

"Lenora," Tom began sternly, "we can talk about this later."

"When?" Lenora challenged. "When we're home—in an apartment that's not ours?"

"Lenora," Tom warned firmly, "this is not the time or place to argue—"

"Why? Because I'm your daughter?" Lenora rose out of her chair and stood, challenging Tom. "I am part of this team. If anyone else asked this question, you wouldn't be so dismissive. If I wasn't your daughter—"

"If you weren't my daughter, I would take you aside and talk to you about it in my office, privately." Tom uttered, now visibly angered. "Look, Lenora, you need more training and time before getting into a big investigation of this manner. When a smaller case comes up, you will have the opportunity to take part. At this point in the game, you'll just get in the way."

Get in the way?

Lenora heard a gasp and felt everyone's eyes on her. A lump formed in her throat, catching her breath, and her eyes welled up.

Don't cry! Don't cry!

But it was too late—tears started streaming down her face, she was so humiliated.

Before her dad could continue, she ran out of the room. She ran to their borrowed apartment, slammed the door shut, and locked herself in her room. She opened the Bartholomew Booth file, more determined than ever to solve this on her own.

FINAL NARRATIVE OF BARTHOLOMEW BOOTH

Part VI

Doctor's Notes:

Admittedly, Bartholomew did not feel remorse about an innocent man being hanged for his crimes. He felt a certain delight in the idea that such a selfish, conceited person "got his due."

It took little time to get over the loss of Miss Jones. She meant little to him—she gave him too much trouble. Since someone else was hanged for the murders, he knew no one would be looking, giving license to begin the search for his "next true love."

~~~~~~~~~~~~~~~~~~~~~~~~~~

When Justina Smith first walked into the employment agency's office, Bartholomew was captivated by her striking features. She was slender, with an athletic build, and had deep copper hair worn in long curls. Her lime green eyes reminded him of fresh new spring grass.

She came from St. Adelaide's Almshouse, looking for clerical work. Bartholomew immediately hired Miss Smith as office file clerk.

To his surprise, she had the office in top condition before the end of the week. He struggled to find things for her to do the following week—he couldn't lose her now. Multiple times, he tried unsuccessfully to engage her in conversation. But, she seemed disinterested, offering cordial but curt responses. She even declined when he brought in breakfast and his offer for afternoon tea.

She narrowed her eyes, quickly zeroing in on his intentions. "I know what you're up to, and I'm not taking the bait." Bartholomew tried looking oblivious, but she stopped him. "Please, don't insult my intelligence—I can tell if a man is interested. Let me be clear: I am not interested in starting any sort of relationship with you. We are colleagues—that, and nothing else."

Bartholomew felt foolish. "Sorry," he said under his breath.

"Don't apologize, just stop."

He nodded, face flushing, and focused on his work, avoiding her as much as possible. And, after hours of complete silence, he decided to have her reassigned—she wasn't the one after all.

Later that week, J.P. informed them that he had received a call from government compliance and that they were to be inspected the following day. He requested that Bartholomew and Justina stay late that night to help get the office in tip-top condition. Justina immediately began cleaning the office and reorganizing files, while Bartholomew ensured that all files were complete. They worked late into the evening, only stopping once for tea. Mr. and Mrs. Dunning delivered dinner for them later that evening.

After the Dunnings left, Bartholomew and Justina sat a few minutes more, enjoying Mrs. Dunning's famous plumb pudding.

Bartholomew was finally able to engage Justina in conversation. He refrained from being overly personal, which she seemed to enjoy. He launched into stories about his days at University—the same stories he shared with Miss Millar—the ones that were not his to share. Justina seemed highly amused by the stories, often erupting into fits of laughter. At one point, she placed a hand on his arm, laughing at the absurdity of one story.

He looked down at her hand, feeling a stirring in his stomach. His laugh died down, his smile faded. Emboldened, he leaned in and kissed her.

She immediately pushed herself away from the table. "What was that?" she asked him, wiping her mouth.

"N-nothing...I—"

"What did I say earlier, Bartholomew?"

"You said that you weren't—"

"I said that I wasn't interested. I thought you understood that!"

"But, you laughed...you touched my arm—"

She looked at him incredulously. "So, because I laughed at your story and touched your arm, you took it to mean that I was interested?"

He shrugged his shoulders. "Well...yes." He wasn't sure what she was so angry about—she was the one who touched him.

She stared at him in disbelief, shook her head, and then sighed. "Let's get back to work. I want to go home."

Bartholomew followed her in to the office, where they continued working in silence. After several minutes, he heard her sigh heavily. She pulled a chair near his and studied him a moment. "You really did misinterpret me, didn't you?" He nodded, avoiding eye contact. She put a hand on his arm. "I'm sorry. I didn't mean to take that tone with you—I'll just have to be clearer next time. I'm sorry for the confusion—"

Encouraged, Bartholomew grasped her face, forcefully pulling it into his, kissing her full on the lips. She struggled, which only urged him to tighten his hold. He kissed her face and neck, and then stood up, picking her up in his arms and laying her on the desk. She struggled and kicked at him, trying to tell him no, but his weight bore down upon her—all that came out were inaudible gasps. His lips moved excitedly on hers, as he ignored her pleas to stop.

Finally, she kicked her knee hard, thrusting it into his mid-section, crippling him. The white-hot pain shot through his body, causing him to double over. He fell off of her, landing hard on the floor. She instantly got up off the desk, grabbed her coat, and ran out of the office. He lay on the floor for several minutes, crippled in pain. He had never experienced such violence from a woman before, and wasn't sure what to think of it. What he did know, was that he was becoming very angry.

The next morning, he noticed a note on his desk. It was from J.P., asking Bartholomew to report to his office immediately upon arrival.

Bartholomew gingerly opened the door and peered in. "You wanted to see me, sir?"

"Come in and close the door." J.P. kept his eyes on the newspaper, while Bartholomew sat across from him, waiting. Dunning finished the article, and then looked over the top of his glasses. "I suppose you know why I called you in here."

"Actually, I haven't a clue," Bartholomew answered honestly.

"Well, I'll tell you, then." J.P. gave Bartholomew a disapproving look. "Do you know what I had the pleasure of sitting through last night?" He looked expectantly at Bartholomew. After no reply came, he continued. "Last night, my wife and I had to calm an hysterical girl because she was attacked."

"Oh my, attacked?" Bartholomew sat forward, looking concerned. "What happened?"

J.P. frowned, staring at him dubiously. "You really don't know what I'm talking about?" He shook his head. "Unbelievable. I was talking about Miss Smith—she said you attacked her last night. Care to divulge?"

Bartholomew, visibly taken by surprise, thought for a moment. Finally, realization dawned on his face. "Oh, that," he said, nearly whispering. "It's not what you think."

"No?" J.P. sat back in his chair, folding his arms in front of his chest. "I'm listening."

Bartholomew took a moment to formulate. He cleared his throat. "She and I were sharing stories, she laughed and touched my arm, and I thought she was expressing interest. So, I made a pass at her." He nodded once, indicating his satisfaction with the explanation.

J.P. sat forward. "So, let me get this straight. She laughed at your stories, so you took that to mean that she was interested? I don't understand—"

"...and touched my arm," Bartholomew added.

J.P.'s eyebrows rose. "Uh-huh. I see," he replied, resting his chin on a hand in contemplation. "I just don't know what to do with you..."

Bartholomew felt a lump in his throat. Was he losing his job?

J.P. drummed his fingers on the desk. He reached into a drawer and pulled out a piece of paper. Bartholomew watched nervously as his boss filled out the form, writing furiously. Dunning placed the paper in a folder and then looked up at Bartholomew. "Miss Smith quit her position here, and I have reassigned her to another location."

"W-where did she—"

"Never you mind," Dunning responded curtly. "You no longer have access to Miss Smith's files. Understand?" Bartholomew nodded and shifted his gaze downward. "Bartholomew, I talked to an acquaintance of mine who runs a large company and shared our predicament. Do you want to know what he suggested?" He paused, not waiting for a response. "He said that you should be immediately sacked."

Bartholomew's heart dropped.

Dunning smiled stoically. "But, I'm not going to do that. You're a good employee, and you don't seem to have a clue as to what you did to Miss Smith."

"Thank you, sir—I really don't know what came over me...maybe it was the long hours." He smiled at Dunning.

"Get back to work, Booth," Dunning said, eyeing Bartholomew.

Bartholomew thanked him again and walked toward the door, when J.P. hollered at him.

"Hey, kid, one more thing: stop touching the girls, alright?"

Bartholomew, deeply embarrassed, reddened. He closed the door behind him, went back to his desk, and slumped into his chair.

Bartholomew felt lost without Miss Smith in the office. He missed her smile and laughter...the way she smelled, like the scent of daffodils on a cool spring breeze. One day, when Mr. Dunning was out of the office, Bartholomew snuck into his desk and retrieved her file. She was placed as secretary to the president of England Royal Bank.

Bartholomew set out the next morning to make things right with Miss Smith. He watched through the bank's front window as she worked, marveling at her efficiency. She had spent most of the hour filing, when the bank president called her into his office. Bartholomew went to the side of the building, pressing his face against the pane for a better view. Miss Smith spotted him and stood up, pointing at him, talking animatedly to the bank president.

Alarmed, Bartholomew backed away from the window and started walking swiftly down the street, when someone grabbed his arm. It was the bank president, who looked quite angry. He hauled Bartholomew to the police station and filed a report against him.

An incensed J.P. Dunning came to the station and brought Bartholomew back to the office.

"You've put me in a difficult position," he said, shaking his head sadly. "What made you do it? Why did you follow Miss Smith to her place of employment?"

"I just wanted to apologize, that's all."

"Well, regardless of how good your intentions were, I will have to put you on two week's suspension—without pay. I will place Miss Smith with another agency in the meantime. You are to have no further contact with Miss Smith. Understand?" He spoke as if talking to a slow child.

Bartholomew felt ridiculous. He slowly rose from his chair. "See you in two weeks?" Once he received Dunning's silent affirmation, he quickly left the office. On his walk home, he pondered his actions. After some thought, he still didn't understand what he did wrong.

He spent the entire two weeks following Miss Smith at a safe distance.

One morning, she didn't emerge from her building at the appointed time. Bartholomew waited for hours, watching the front door. Miss Smith was nowhere to be seen. The next few days came up with the same results—Miss Smith seemed to have vanished. Concerned, he decided to go into St. Adelaide's and inquire after her.

The minute he walked in the door, he noticed a foul odor that hung in the air, making him cringe inwardly. He held his breath and asked for Miss Smith.

"Which one?" The woman at the main desk was grossly overweight and gruff-looking.

Judging by her appearance, Bartholomew didn't doubt that she was the source of the odor. "Oh, uh, Miss Justina Smith," he answered, scowling. He pointed to the registry. "Justina Smith? Is she in?" He held his breath and looked away.

"Oh, of course."

Bartholomew's face twisted in disgust as he watched the woman lick her fingers to page through the registry, her thick, gray tongue slaking across rough, sausage-like fingers. Globs of saliva stuck to the top of each page, leaving a trail of goo along the edges. His stomach turned.

"Yes, here she is." She offered nothing further as she read through the log. Bartholomew was becoming agitated. "She doesn't live here anymore." The woman nodded, satisfied that she found the answer.

"Doesn't live here anymore? Where did she go?"

"Oh, let me look." The woman opened the log book and browsed. "Oh, here it is." She glanced up and smiled at Bartholomew, who was just about bursting. "She lives on the corner of None of Your Business and I Can't Tell You." She sneered at him and slammed the book shut.

Bartholomew scowled at her and turned on his heels. He'd just have to do this the hard way.

The next day, he stood outside of St. Adelaide's and waited for a woman he knew to be a friend of Miss Smith's. Once the woman emerged, he followed for two blocks and then caught up to her.

"Excuse me, are you Beatrice? Justina Smith's friend?"

"Yeah. Who wants to know?"

"I do," he said, frowning.

She gave him a sidelong glance. "What do *you* want?"

"I'd need to know where to find her." He was having trouble keeping pace. "Can you slow down?"

"No," she said adamantly, "I am almost late for work." She noticed his earnestness and stopped. "Okay. You want to know where Justina is. Last I heard, she…wait. Why do you want to know, and who are you?"

He sighed heavily. "I'm…John Carter. I worked with her at the bank. She left something there and I wanted to return it to her." He watched Beatrice, hoping she believed the lie.

"Sure. I guess I can believe that." Beatrice exhaled impatiently. "Justina moved in with Oliver Hollingsworth."

"What? Who?" Bartholomew's head started to spin.

"The president of England Royal Bank?" She shook her head. "I can't believe you don't know your own boss."

"I just started there…mail room," he offered distractedly. "Did they get married?"

She stared at him incredulously. "No, you idiot. Mr. Hollingsworth is already married. Justina was hired as personal chef to Mr. H and his wife."

Relief washed over him. "I didn't know she could cook," he said with a crooked smile.

She laughed. "She's a great cook, actually."

"Thank you, Beatrice." He placed money in her hand. "Here, for your trouble."

She glanced at the money and grinned. "Any time!"

It was easy—finding Hollingsworth. He only had to follow the old man home. For three days, Bartholomew peeked in the windows, watching Miss Smith cook and serve meals to the Hollingsworth family. She looked well, wearing newer and cleaner clothing, smiling. He loved her smile—it lit up her face and made her eyes luminous.

On the forth night, he waited near the back door for her to finish cleaning after the meal. He knew that moments from now, she would open the back door to remove the trash. When she emerged, he stood in her path.

"Bartholomew! You startled me! What are you doing here?" Her expression grew serious. "How did you find me?"

"It doesn't matter," he said, smiling sedately.

"You shouldn't be here," she said nervously, backing up toward the house.

Not wanting to frighten her, Bartholomew held out a hand, smiling warmly. "I know. I didn't come here to scare you or make you uncomfortable. I simply came to offer my sincerest apologies and to ask your forgiveness."

"Oh, well, that's nice of you," she said appreciatively.

He stepped forward and took her hand. She recoiled, making him chuckle. He kissed her hand and bowed. "I wish you a good evening, and a lovely life—this job suits you." He smiled amiably. "Good-bye, Miss Smith."

"Good-bye, Bartholomew," she said softly as he walked away from her. He avoided turning to look at her. No doubt she was staring after him, a look of astonishment on her face. It was a good start. Soon, her look would show affection and love. He grinned.

~~~~~~~~~~~~~~~~~~~~~~~~~~~~~~~~

Bartholomew examined the damages in front of the mirror in his wash room. Deep gashes ran down his cheek from just below his eye down to his jawbone. The marks would be difficult to hide. A mistake she would pay for.

Miss Smith's reaction to the sleeping draught wasn't nearly what he had expected. She woke up an hour after he gave her the first shot, which was terribly unusual. Generally, the sleeping draught lasted nearly a whole night, sometimes a bit longer.

He hoped that the second dose wouldn't prove harmful, but he couldn't take any more chances with this one. She had unexpectedly overpowered him, and he was prepared not to let that happen again.

The snoring from the salon affirmed that she was completely under. He had time to tend his wound, get her into the restraints, and then rest before she woke and discovered her situation. He dressed the wound, knowing that a trip to the hospital tomorrow was necessary to avoid infection.

Bartholomew walked into the salon and secured Justina's restraints. He placed two filled syringes on the table near her and the bottle of chloroform with fresh cloths—this time, he'd be prepared. He covered her with blankets and then tied a cloth over her mouth. He checked the rest of the room to ensure that all was secure, locked the inside door, slid the paneling closed, and then collapsed onto his bed, falling instantly asleep.

Three o'clock the following afternoon, he finally walked back into his flat—tired, hungry, and incredibly angry. He waited at the clinic for over two hours, and then had to convince the pharmacy to stay open just so he could purchase his medication and salve. He briefly glanced in the salon's direction. She had been alone all day.

She'd have to wait.

He threw the pharmacy bag on the table and fixed himself something to eat. He took his medication, applied the salve, and was just about to lie down for a nap, when he heard a dull *thunk* in the salon.

He flew toward the salon, fumbling with the lock. He opened the door to see Miss Smith, awake and looking enraged. She screamed angrily the second she saw him.

He smiled placidly, sitting next to her on the settee. "Good afternoon Miss Smith! I hope you enjoyed your rest. Would you like something to eat?" Her reply was muffled. "Now," he continued, "I am going to remove the cloth from your mouth, but you have to promise to be quiet, alright?" She nodded and he removed the cloth.

She flexed her jaw, flashing an irate glance.

"You're going to be sore from the cloth and the restraints." He spoke softly as if speaking to a small child. "But, if you behave, you will eventually gain more freedom." He grinned, stroking her hair. Her eyes narrowed and she spit in his face. He wiped his face and then shook his head. "You see, this is what I'm talking about. This behavior will get you nowhere." He picked up the cloth and replaced it on her mouth, tying it tighter than before. She grimaced in pain and then issued loud, muffled protests.

He patted her arm. "Well, because of your behavior now, and this," he pointed at the bandage on his face, "you will have no food today."

He walked over to the side table and picked up another syringe. She started to shake her head violently side-to side, tears streaming from her face. "Don't panic. This is only a mild sleeping draught. If you can't behave and be quiet, then you'll just sleep. Tomorrow morning, I will come back and check in on you, and we'll see just how much you change your tune."

He inserted the needle and gave her another dose of the draught, waving at her as she drifted. "Nighty-night!"

Miss Smith's behavior didn't improve. She remained in her restraints without food, lying in her own stench, for several days. Whenever he walked in the room, he gasped—the smell from her urine and excrement flooded his nostrils and nearly took his breath away.

The day when he smelled the odor upon entering his flat was when he decided that something needed to be done. He again drugged her, washed her clothing and body, and then cleaned the room. Restraining her to the couch wasn't working, so he purchased heavy rope and bolts, and tied her to one spot in the room. She had freedom to roam about, but her wrists were tethered together so she couldn't injure him further.

When Miss Smith woke, she discovered her newly washed body and clothing. She looked at Bartholomew and flushed in embarrassment. "You *bathed* me?" She scowled in disgust.

"Don't worry, I tried not to look...much." He grinned slyly.

"Don't you touch me...ever again!"

"Sorry, but I had to. You smelled rather foul." She screamed at the top of her lungs. He merely chuckled. "Scream all you like—no one will hear you. This place is completely insulated for sound." She ran at him, only to be jerked back violently by the rope. He laughed hysterically.

He walked closer to her and grabbed the collar of her dress, pulling her in to him. "You will do as I say, when I say, and how. You are mine now." She kicked him and spit in his face. He fished a handkerchief from his pocket and wiped his chin. "Fine, then, you will go without food again today." He spun on his heels, closing the door to riotous screaming behind him.

The next morning, Miss Smith seemed to have calmed down. She didn't scream when he entered the room, and she asked, very sweetly, if she could have something to eat. The rest of the week, he brought her meals and cleaned up after her. Gradually, they exchanged a few terse, but polite words. He was pleasantly surprised when she began reading the romance novels. Eventually, they visited about the books. Encouraged, Bartholomew started playing music for her to set the mood. He figured that she was gradually breaking down—he just needed to move slowly with her.

Bartholomew came into the salon one day to find her sobbing. He sat next to her and tried holding her hand, which she refused. He pried until finally getting her to talk.

"I want to go home!"

"But, you *are* home," he reassured her.

"No! This is *not* my home! Let me go!"

He shook his head sadly. "I'm sorry, but I can't do that."

She stopped crying and stared at him in disbelief. "You mean, I'm being held prisoner here?"

He shook his head. "You're not a prisoner—I'm merely restricting your movement until you realize your love for me. Or die... whichever comes first."

She screamed and kicked him hard in the groin, sending him reeling to the floor. She kicked him repeatedly in the stomach, head, and chest until he rolled away from her reach. She struggled against the ropes and screamed piercingly loud. Though the pain was excruciating, he rolled himself off the floor and used the desk to help him stand.

He took several gasping breaths before speaking. "You will no longer eat until you love me or I kill you." He strained to walk out of the room, locking the door behind him. He didn't go back for three days.

On the third day, he was preparing a large pot of broth and had just baked bread to bring to Miss Smith, when a knock came at the door. He opened the door to someone he had seen before—but only in the newspapers.

"Hello, are you Mr. Bartholomew Booth?"

"I am," Bartholomew answered, heart beating hard and fast.

"Hello, Mr. Booth, I am Inspector William Rood here on official police business. May I come in?"

"S-sure," Bartholomew answered, opening the door for the inspector. He looked down the hall to see if anyone saw and then closed the door. The inspector strolled around the room and looked at his pictures. Bartholomew's eyes narrowed. "So, can I get you anything? Tea?"

"No, no thank you." The inspector waved his hand distractedly. He pointed at the painting in front of him. "Is this Tuscany?"

"Uh, no, it's southern France," Bartholomew replied. "That one's Tuscany." He pointed at the painting hung by the door.

"Ah," the inspector nodded and continued browsing the room.

"Can I offer you a seat?" Bartholomew led the inspector toward a chair away from the salon. He took a seat across from the inspector. "So, what can I help you with?"

"Oh, yes," the inspector tried a tone of indifference, but Bartholomew knew better. "A girl has been reported missing. Her name is Justina Smith. Do you recognize the name?"

Bartholomew put a hand to his chin, feigning having to recall. "I think so...a girl named Justina Smith worked at my firm a while back."

"Yes, she was a file clerk at your firm several months back, as I am told by Mr. J.P. Dunning."

"Then, why did you need verification from me? We have all of that in our records...in the office."

"Yes, I've already been there...nice office you've got there!"

Bartholomew narrowed his eyes. "I'm sorry, but I don't remember seeing you there, and I see everyone that walks into that office."

"I was there three days ago," the inspector responded, "you weren't in."

"Oh, yes, that's right, I was home, ill."

The inspector nodded slowly, eyeing Bartholomew's face. "That's one awful bruise you have there." He pointed at Bartholomew's right eye.

"Yes, I fell down the stairs the other day. In fact, that's why I called in sick—I was in a lot of pain."

"Mhmm." Inspector Rood smiled, his blue eyes glittering in the late afternoon sun. "Is that how you got the scratches on your face?"

"No." Bartholomew sat rigid. He didn't like this inspector and wanted him gone. He exhaled loudly as if irritated. "I was watching my neighbor's cat, and it doesn't like me too well..."

The inspector sat forward and examined the scratches. "Looks a little big for a cat scratch. Are you sure that's where you got them?"

"Of course I'm sure," Bartholomew replied, now becoming angry. "Why would I lie about that?"

"Not sure," the inspector said, sitting back in the chair and scribbling something in his notebook.

"What are you getting at?" Bartholomew challenged, now tiring of the inspector's game.

"Well, your boss allowed me full access to your firm's files to help in the case. I stumbled across a note indicating that you made a violent pass at Miss Smith."

"It was hardly violent," Bartholomew replied, smiling benignly. "Miss Smith exaggerates."

"Then, why did she file a complaint and quit?" the inspector prodded.

"I can hardly guess at someone else's motive."

"After some checking, I found that you were caught spying on her at her place of employment." The inspector looked at his notes. "At the English Royal Bank. It says here," he pointed to his notes, "that the president of the bank...Mr. Oliver Hollingsworth...not only saw you, but took you to the police station himself." The inspector paused, glancing though his files. "Oh, yes, I see here that he pressed charges."

Bartholomew stared blankly; he felt sweat dripping out of every pore. He had to clasp his hands together to stop the shaking.

The inspector narrowed his eyes. "So, my theory—and mind you, it's just a theory—is that you didn't get those scratches from a cat. You got those scratches when you kidnapped Miss Smith from her home, and when she fought you—and fought hard by the looks of it—you killed her."

Bartholomew's eyebrows rose—he was shocked at how close the inspector was to the truth. "I think your theory—though well formed—is terribly incorrect."

"Really?" the inspector said with a feigned level of curiosity. "And, why is that?"

"You *are* correct on many things. Yes, I made a pass at Miss Smith—though I would hardly consider it 'violent.' She gave me the impression that she was interested. I became passionate. When I went to the bank, it was for the sole purpose of offering my apology." Bartholomew tried to look sincere. "It was all a terrible misunderstanding. I would never harm Miss Smith. She is a lovely girl and I hold no grudge."

The inspector stared at Bartholomew for several seconds and then wrote something in his notebook. "So, when was the last time you saw Miss Smith?"

"That day at the bank was the last time I saw her."

"Umhmm," the inspector wrote again in his book, "and, where were you on the night of September 6?"

"That was over a month ago," Bartholomew responded. "How can I possibly remember that?"

"Try, please." Inspector Rood gazed at him expectantly.

Bartholomew frowned and searched his mind frantically. He was coming up blank. "What night of the week was it?"

"It was a Friday."

Bartholomew felt hysterical —he just had to think of something!

"Do you keep a calendar?" The inspector asked. "That might help."

A calendar!

"Yes," Bartholomew replied, walking into the kitchen to retrieve the calendar off the wall. He felt instant relief as he looked at the day. On September 6 was scribbled "Mozart Tribute Orchestral Concert. 7 - 9 p.m., Cambridge City Gardens." Lately, he had developed the habit of writing down cultural events around the city—particularly ones that promised a lot of people. He thought it might be helpful at one point.

When he got back into the room, the inspector was standing by the wall, looking at the picture of Tuscany. Bartholomew didn't like him there. He went over to Inspector Rood and pointed at the calendar. "I went to a concert that evening."

The inspector nodded his head. "Did you go with anyone?"

"No."

"Did anyone see you there?"

"I'm...unsure."

"So, no one can confirm that you were in fact at the concert that night."

Bartholomew frowned. Beads of sweat formed on his forehead. "No, I guess not."

"Do you have ticket stubs from the concert?"

"No," Bartholomew replied, "I'm afraid you'll have to take my word for it."

"How was it? The concert, I mean? What was your favorite piece?"

"The concert was wonderful, and the Requiem—"

A thump on the other side of the wall interrupted Bartholomew. Both men glanced at the wall.

"What was that?" The inspector asked.

Bartholomew shrugged his shoulders. "Not sure."

"It came from the other side of this wall," the inspector said, pointing to the wall.

"That's impossible—there's nothing on the other side of this wall," Bartholomew reasoned.

Ignoring Bartholomew's reply, Inspector Rood walked closer to the wall and pressed his ear up against it. He frowned and then knocked on the wall. "Well, there's no hollow sound."

"Why would there be? There's nothing there." Bartholomew's hands shook; he shoved them in his pockets.

The inspector frowned. "Did you know that this flat at one time was connected to an old mercantile below?"

"No, I was not aware." Bartholomew's heart raced.

"Yes, several years ago, there was a general store below, and this upstairs area was used for storage. The store owner had a room off to the side—on the other side of this wall, in fact—for his bookkeeper's office. Strange how it was just walled off."

Bartholomew nodded. "Yes, strange. Don't you think you might be mistaken about the location?"

"No, I worked here when I was a boy and went into the office often."

"Perhaps they walled it off for a reason, then," Bartholomew offered.

"Perhaps. They did have a rat infestation…at one time."

"Well, that might explain the thumping sound. Maybe I should have my flat checked for rats." Bartholomew laughed softly.

Inspector Rood frowned at the wall for several seconds before checking himself and then turning to Bartholomew. "Well, I've taken up enough of your time. Thank you." He shook Bartholomew's hand. "Oh, but before I go, I should let you know that I may return at another time for more questioning should the investigation require it."

"Yes, I'm glad to help." Bartholomew smiled and waved as he closed the door. Once the inspector left the building, Bartholomew collapsed onto his couch and sobbed with relief. He needed to be more careful.

Bartholomew began to panic. He feared that the inspector was following him around. At first, Bartholomew thought he was simply being paranoid; however, the inspector appeared everywhere he went. Whenever he glanced out the window, the inspector was there, standing a small distance away, staring at the front door to his office.

Every night that week, he lost sleep pacing about his flat in the dark, trying to figure out the next move. Finally, he decided to get rid of the girl—there was no way around it.

Begrudgingly, he opened the salon and was shocked at what he saw.

She was sitting on the floor, in her own filth, and appeared emaciated, weak.

He frowned and scratched his head, confused by her condition. Then it dawned on him: lost in the paranoia brought on by the inspector's trailing him, he had forgotten about his little captive. When he thought about it, she had gone over a week without food. He felt a pang of regret—he never wanted her to suffer.

Bartholomew gently touched her arm. She flinched and struggled to move away from him, using her arms to slide across the floor.

"I'm not going to hurt you," he said quietly, trying to calm her.

"Go away! Leave me alone!" She positioned her back against the wall, drawing her knees to her chest, staring at him with mixed fear and loathing.

Bartholomew slowly approached her, holding his hands out in front of him. He sat down next to her and noticed her hands immediately. The wrists were still bound, and the rope had rubbed the skin off, dried blood stains caked the rope and stained the skin around her wrists.

He exhaled deeply and shook his head. "I'm really sorry that you had to suffer. If it wasn't for the policeman, I would never have forgotten you."

"Policeman?" Her voice was raspy, and her throat made a dry clicking sound as she tried to swallow.

"Yes, he came here and asked me too many questions and I got nervous. Plus, you made a noise in here, which almost tipped him off."

"A policeman was here? Looking for me?"

"Yes, I'm afraid so."

Barely a sound came from her as she quietly sobbed, her shoulders shaking, body trembling.

"There, there," he said quietly, patting her arms. "It'll all be over soon."

She quit crying and looked up at him, eyes wide. "Are you going to…k-kill me? Oh, please, no!" She shook her head violently from side to side, the sobbing becoming louder, more frenzied.

"Shh, quiet now," he said, trying to calm her. "I'm not going to kill you."

She looked up at him in disbelief. "You're not?"

"No, of course not! Silly girl!" he laughed. "No, what I'm going to do is give you another shot of that sleeping draught. Once that takes effect, I will carry you back to Mr. Hollingsworth's home, drop you off at the back door, and then knock loudly so that someone will find you."

"I don't believe you," she said with uncertainty. "How do I know you're telling the truth?"

"Because," he responded, lifting her chin with one hand and stroking her hair with the other, "I never brought you here to harm you—I just wanted you to love me." He smiled affectionately and kissed the top of her head. "Now, you have to promise me something. If I promise to bring you back safely, you must vow not to alert the authorities about me. If you do as I ask, I will never bother you again. Agreed?" She nodded her head vigorously in agreement. "Good, because if you don't," he grabbed her arm and squeezed— she winced and gasped in pain, "if you don't, I will hunt you down and torture you until you scream for mercy. Do you understand?"

"Yes, yes, please! I-I won't tell anyone…ever!"

He released her arm and smiled. "Good. I'll go get the syringe and we'll say our farewells." He went into the other room and prepared the syringe. When he came back, she was smoothing down her hair and smiling at him weakly.

Bartholomew grabbed a pillow off the settee, and then knelt down next to her. He brought the pillow toward her and she flinched. He smiled and placed the pillow behind her head. "You look uncomfortable." Her body seemed to relax with his reassurance. He adjusted the pillow and then kissed her forehead. "Okay, just a little sting, and we're done."

She looked down at her arm and winced as the needle pierced her skin. As he pushed the plunger to deliver the medication, she smiled at him warmly. "Thank you, Bartholomew—this is the kindest thing you have done for me...I'll not forget it."

He flashed a weak smile and then loosened the rope around her wrists. "I will miss you."

The sleeping draught took immediate effect, as her body grew limp and relaxed. He waited until her breathing became steady and then lifted her from the floor and carried her to the settee, where he laid her down. He took the pillow from the corner where she just lay and put it tenderly over her face, pressing until the breath left her.

He waited several minutes and then removed the pillow. He checked for breathing and heartbeat—there were none. Carefully, he undressed her, washed her body and clothing, and then waited. When the time came, he carried her down the stairs and out the door, walking the usual route through the back alleyways to the river. He placed her gently on the bench and positioned her properly.

A small clinking sound diverted his attention. A porcelain thimble had fallen from Miss Smith's pocket. He picked it up, noticing the Hollingsworth family name inscription—it must have been a welcome gift. He smiled and then placed it in his breast pocket.

He pushed his finger into her cheek, watching the head loll to the side, and then walked away.

London Chronicle

Cambridge, Oct. 28, 1913   Another Girl Found Murdered! Early this Morning, Cambridge Police verified the finding of another Woman, Justina Smith, who was found lying dead on a Bench along the Cam River. This was the same Bench that Police found murder victims Hope Anne Millar and Temperance Jefferson Jones, who were both brutally murdered and found lying in repose upon the same bench that the latest victim was found.

Hon. Gen. Inspector William Rood would not comment if this may be another attack by the Gentleman Killer, stating that it is too early in the Investigation to decide. If this is yet another victim, then the Gentleman Killer is still out there, threatening the young Women of Cambridge, and Albert Lynch, the man originally accused and sentenced to death by hanging for the murders of Misses Millar and Jones, was innocent and wrongly accused.

THIRTY-TWO

"**H**eya, Love!" Ian peered around the corner at Lenora, who was working in the dungeon on a project for her dad.

She briefly glanced up and then forced a smile. The past few days' events had left her in a despondent mood. Nicholas' abrupt departure was depressing, and she felt like a total reject at school. Not to mention that CSP—the only group that made her feel like she belonged—decided not to let her in on the newest case.

Everyone on the CSP team was so busy with the new case that all she got lately was a hurried "hello" in passing. Even Ian and her dad were too busy for her. Ian and Tom spoke for hours about the new case—behind closed doors. Ian was constantly in Tom' office at the university, or they locked themselves in the den at their borrowed apartment.

"What do you need?" she asked Ian, not in the mood for company.

"Need? Nothing! I thought you might like a quick break." He strolled in and put a cola on the desk in front of her.

"Thanks," she said, unconvincingly.

"Aw, come on, Lenora!" Ian said, giving her a measured glance. "You're still upset about not being on the case?"

Lenora shrugged, keeping her eyes on her work. "I'm kinda busy here, Ian."

Ian chuckled softly, placing a hand over the paper she was looking at. "Doing what? Transferring your dad's lecture notes onto a transparency? That lecture doesn't happen for another term!" He laughed and opened her soda, pushing it toward her. "Don't bother pretending, Lenora, I know better."

She rolled her eyes and took a sip of her soda, turning away from him, arms folded.

Ian wasn't going to let her pout. He grabbed a chair and set it behind her, swiveling her chair so that she faced him.

Stupid swivel chairs, Lenora thought, sulking.

Ian put his hands on Lenora's knees. "Look, Love, it's not the end of the world. So you don't work on this case—there will be many more, believe me. Tom was right, and you were out of line for confronting him in front of the group like that." He pinned her with his gaze. "I know this sucks, and I know you're tired of it all. But, you need to have patience and give it time—we'll solve your case soon. And, stop distancing yourself from the ones who care."

He looked at her with sincerity and then smiled. "I'm done lecturing now. Let's have a break." He reached in his pocket and produced two chocolate bars. "There's no way you can refuse chocolate!"

Lenora took the chocolate, feeling somewhat cheered, despite her best efforts to remain depressed. She savored the silky chocolate on her tongue while listening to Ian's animated explanation of his Developmental Psychology seminar. She didn't understand half of what he talked about, but thought he looked particularly handsome in his academic robe and scarf.

Suddenly, he grew silent and glanced at her thoughtfully. "Still upset? You're not saying much."

"No, I'm over it…I think," she replied. "I was just thinking about our case and wondering if you could tell me—"

"Lenora, it'll be solved—you need to have some patience. And you know I can't—"

"No," Lenora held her hand up to stop him, "I was wondering if you could tell me what a spiritual cleansing is."

"Oh," Ian sat back, smiling. "That. I can somewhat tell you what it is. Generally speaking, it's a spiritual healing of sorts.

People seek out a spiritual healer to help with negative energies that stem from divorce, financial difficulties, or stress. The gifted ones can help with unusual or persistent spiritual disturbances, such as yours."

"Can he…or she…get rid of it?"

"Some can, yes. My conviction rests on our guy's abilities—he's incredibly gifted."

"What will he do? I mean…what will happen?"

"Sorry," Ian shook his head, "that's about all I know. Usually, our guy works alone. But, you'll want to ask the guy himself. It would be more…interesting…coming from him." Ian smirked.

"Why do you say it that way?"

"He's…unique." Ian grinned widely. "Now, don't get me wrong—the guy's not only incredibly gifted, but he's bloody brilliant. Formerly, he was a neurosurgeon, but got his calling as a spiritual healer soon after he began his practice. I love it when we need him—he is definitely a character, that's for sure." Ian chuckled to himself as he reminisced.

Lenora shook her head in confusion. "So, are you going to share? What's so amusing?"

"No, I'll wait until after you've met him—you'll find the stories that much more amusing." Ian smiled—Lenora could tell he genuinely liked the guy.

"So, since I can't be a part of the current case, can you at least tell me about it?" Lenora regretted asking the question—Ian's face turned grave, and his mood became somber.

"No, I can't…and you know it. So please stop asking—you're taking advantage of our friendship when you ask that of me."

"I'm sorry," Lenora looked at him apologetically. "I just want to feel part of something."

Ian nodded, taking her hand in his, tracing the tip of his thumb along the back of her hand. Lenora's heart fluttered. Ian gazed into her eyes, his face taking on a serious expression. "Lenora, I was wondering if—"

"Hello?" Ian was interrupted by a female's voice in the doorway. They both looked up to see an attractive girl in her mid-twenties, her eyes sparkling as she beamed at Ian.

"Clare?" Ian exclaimed, immediately dropping Lenora's hand and running over to the girl. Lenora drooped, her stomach churned.

"Hello, you!" Clare said excitedly as she ran across the room and jumped into Ian's arms.

Lenora sat, dumbfounded, as she watched Ian and this Clare person, hug and kiss each other. After several minutes of this, Lenora cleared her throat loudly.

Ian stopped kissing Clare, looked at Lenora and flinched, evidently forgetting that she was in the room. "Oh, sorry about that!" He released Clare and grabbed her hand, pulling her toward Lenora's desk. "Lenora, meet Clare, my girlfriend."

"Your girlfriend?" Lenora didn't try hiding her confusion.

Ian explained that he and Clare had been dating since last year, but she'd been in Paris the past eight months, studying for her PhD in French Literature.

Clare beamed at Ian and then smiled at Lenora. "Well, I don't know if I should be insulted that you don't know who I am, but I know all about you," she said with a touch of affection. "Ian's written me several lines about his little sister Lenora."

Lenora flinched when Clare said "little sister." Ian noticed and corrected Clare. "Sorry, she doesn't like to be called 'little'—makes her feel like a child. It's just 'sister' now."

Lenora rolled her eyes at him and extended her hand to Clare. "Nice to meet you," she said through gritted teeth, a heavy feeling enveloping her.

Clare shook her hand, smiling. "Likewise." She turned to Ian. "Now, if you don't mind, I think we need to be off to get reacquainted."

Ian smiled at her knowingly and then nodded. "I'll just finish up here and we can go."

"Okay," Clare responded, "I need to run to the French Studies department for my mail and then I'll be back down to get you."

Lenora watched Clare leave and then turned to Ian. "Girlfriend? So, you were dating her while you went out with all those other girls?"

"It's complicated, Lenora," Ian uttered, color rising to his cheeks.

"How so?" She questioned, eyes narrowed.

"You wouldn't understand," he replied, trying to avoid the question.

"Try me," she challenged. She watched as Ian shifted his stance, looking like he was searching for the right words to say. When he didn't respond, Lenora crossed her arms in front of her and tilted her head. "Does she know what you are?"

Ian frowned instantly, looking incensed. "What do you mean 'what I am'?"

Lenora shook her head and held up her hands. "Sorry, it came out wrong. What I meant was, does she know that you're a medium?"

"No, she doesn't," he replied, still sounding irritated.

"Are you going to tell her?"

"I didn't plan on it."

"I think you should."

"What does it matter?"

Lenora was taken aback. "It matters a lot. If you're serious about her, she needs to know. It's an important part of who you are."

"You never told Nicholas about you," Ian argued.

Lenora winced—hearing his name stung a bit. "Nicholas and I weren't together that long. You and Clare have been together for over a year. I think that constitutes serious, Ian."

Ian frowned at her. "That's really none of your business—"

"I'm back!" Ian was interrupted by Clare, who walked quickly into the room and grabbed Ian's hand.

"Talk to you later, Len." Without looking back at her, Ian walked out of the room, hand-in-hand, with Clare.

Lenora stood in stunned silence, unable to move.

FINAL NARRATIVE OF BARTHOLOMEW BOOTH

PART VII

Nearly two and a half years passed after Miss Smith.

The inspector's visit made Bartholomew overly anxious. The strange men following him everywhere didn't help.

Bartholomew knew he was a suspect. As a result, he tried living a mundane, predictable life: up before dawn, to work an hour before opening, home after work. On the weekends, he went to the market, then the library, and spent time reading in the park. Eventually, the men no longer followed him and he began to relax.

The next girl showed up unexpectedly.

When he saw her walk in the door of the employment office, Bartholomew's heart skipped a beat. Everything about her exclaimed fashion and society—from her silky, mahogany hair, which was swept back in curls, to her perfectly crisp and pressed dress, to those expressive violet eyes. She had a beautiful smile, and her manners were a perfect combination of amiability, refinement, and modesty.

She did not come from St. Adelaide's.

When she shook Bartholomew's hand and introduced herself, a thrilling tremor ran through him. "Mrs. Clarke, lovely to meet you."

"Oh, please, call me Faith." She smiled brightly, taking the chair across from Bartholomew.

"Faith…that's a beautiful name," he said dreamily. "So…Faith… what can I do for you today?" Bartholomew, though delighted to see her, wondered what a woman of her fine breeding was doing in an employment agency. "Are you seeking employment?"

She issued a lovely, soft laugh. "No, the work is not for me. I am looking to hire."

"Oh," Bartholomew responded, his shoulders slumping. "Then, you want to speak to Mr. Dunning, the owner of this agency—he works strictly with employers. Could I have Mr. Dunning contact you…or Mr. Clarke?" His eyebrows rose in anticipation—perhaps there was no Mr. Clarke in the picture.

"No, I'll deal with this directly. There's no need to bother the Admiral."

"Admiral?"

"My husband, Admiral Joseph K. Clarke. He's with the Royal Navy."

Bartholomew nodded, suddenly feeling a nervous twitch in his stomach.

"I'm having a rather large dinner party and fundraiser next month. I need to hire servers and cleaning staff. Do you think your agency can help?"

"Yes, I believe we can. But, let me take you to Mr. Dunning's office." Bartholomew led Mrs. Clarke to J.P's office, introduced her, and then left the room. He leaned against the door, listening to their conversation. Her voice was soothing. He liked it.

When he heard them finish their conversation, Bartholomew dashed to his desk, pretending to be busy.

Mr. Dunning tapped a pen on Bartholomew's desk. "Booth? I've arranged a contract with Mrs. Clarke, and am assigning you as overseer on the entire project."

"I'm sorry?" Bartholomew was never allowed to oversee a project of this magnitude. Usually, Dunning took these projects himself.

"Admiral Clarke is a personal friend. It's imperative that this job is done well," Mr. Dunning explained. "And, since I'm attending the banquet, I want my best man on it." He nodded at Mrs. Clarke. "Faith will discuss the details with you." He bid Mrs. Clarke good day, and then went back to his office. Bartholomew turned to Mrs. Clarke and smiled faintly.

The entire month was a frenzied blur. Bartholomew interviewed nearly one hundred potential employees, hiring forty to cover serving hors d'oeuvres and meals, and others for cleanup. Mrs. Clarke expected over one hundred attendees, with the goal of fundraising for St. Adelaide's. Bartholomew was surprised to learn that Mrs. Clarke was a benefactress for the almshouse.

Mrs. Clarke was a lovely woman, and being around her made Bartholomew feel happy, contented, and alive.

At first, he thought Mrs. Clarke perfect for him, but then changed his mind. She was too highly visible in the community—not to mention married—and taking her would be a great risk. Instead, he decided to focus on a girl named Charity Smeeton, whom he hired to work as a server at the dinner. He planned to work closely with Charity at the event, and then on pretense of walking her home, capture her on a side street and take her home.

The charity event went according to plan. Bartholomew was excited to see everything run like clockwork. Mrs. Clarke came to him several times throughout the evening, expressing her gratitude and congratulating him on a job well done—a sentiment she shared in a toast at dinner. Bartholomew never had such laud, and he could feel the color rising to his cheeks as she raised a glass in his honor.

Charity, his new girl, worked tirelessly and the guests found her charming. Bartholomew was proud of her. He smiled, patting his breast pocket to ensure the chloroform, cloth, and syringe were still there for later. After the event, she would be his completely.

At the end of the evening, Bartholomew stepped out on the back porch for a breath of fresh air. The moon was full and the summer evening was pleasantly warm, with a cool gentle breeze. He sat on the stoop, trying to calm his angry nerves. Though the event went according to plan, his later plans were foiled. As a gesture of gratitude, Mrs. Clarke hired coaches to drive his hired staff home. Charity was on one of those coaches, along with several of her friends.

It was not his night. He would have to bring his girl home another time. He sighed and inhaled the fresh air, the garden's floral scent permeating his lungs, making him feel dizzy.

"There you are!" Mrs. Clarke stood in the doorway, smiling at him. She joined him on the stoop and closed her eyes, taking in a deep breath. Bartholomew marveled as her pale skin glowed in the soft moonlight. "What a beautiful evening, don't you think, Bartholomew?"

"Yes, it most certainly is," he agreed, feeling enraptured.

She chuckled softly and handed a piece of paper to him. "Here, for your hard work and dedication to my cause."

He took the paper and unfolded it. It was a check for his services, but it was made out for twice his fee. He refolded it and offered it to her. "Thank you, Mrs. Clarke, but I can't take this."

"Why not?"

"Because, it's too much."

She shook her head and pushed his hand away. "No, you must take it—for going above and beyond. This evening would not have been such a success if it weren't for you. I made five times more than what I had hoped for St. Adelaide's. I couldn't be more thrilled!"

Bartholomew shook his head and put the check on her knee. "I appreciate your gracious compliments, however, I did not perform them alone. The entire staff worked diligently for the cause. Please, pay for the services as contracted and then donate the extra to St. Adelaide's."

She studied him at length and then smiled. "You surprise me, Mr. Booth. The world needs more men of integrity like you." She placed a hand on his arm, gave it a squeeze, and then stood up. "Now, I need to find Lloyd. There's a leftover sack of potatoes that I want to donate to the almshouse."

Lloyd the butler.

Bartholomew scowled—he hated that man. Since the start of the event planning, Lloyd scrutinized everything Bartholomew did. He stared at Bartholomew all night as if he were a miscreant...it was infuriating.

He got up from the step and opened the door for Mrs. Clarke. "Thank you, Mr. Booth, for everything." She shook his hand and then kissed his cheek. Bartholomew, teemed with excitement, grabbed her arm and pulled her to him, pressing his lips to hers. She grew limp in his arms and returned the kiss, and then gently pushed him away. "Good night, Bartholomew."

He grabbed her wrist. "Wait! Where are you going?"

"To bed, Mr. Booth, I've had a long day and need to rest."

"But, can't you stay here with me a little longer?"

"Why would I want to do that?" She tilted her head in curiosity.

"Well...you...we just kissed." He raked his hand through his hair. "I thought that—"

"You thought *what?* That there would be more than that?" She laughed softly. "I'm a married woman, Mr. Booth. Our interaction will go no further than that kiss. You're a handsome man, but you are remiss to think that someone of my station could ever...fraternize with...well, let's just say this will go no further."

She started to walk away, but Bartholomew ran in front of her, pressing her into a corner. She looked up at him and laughed. "You sure are persistent!" He tried kissing her again. She didn't bother to move, but simply looked amused, and then started to laugh.

Rage boiled inside of him. What was so funny?

"Stop laughing!" he shouted. She laughed harder. "I said, stop laughing now!" Enraged, his hands balled into tight fists, and before he could stop himself, he punched her in the face. Startled, he backed away from her, staring in disbelief. She covered her mouth and started to move away from him slowly.

He couldn't let this go. She would tell someone, and then that pesky inspector would find a new excuse to snoop around his place again. He couldn't let that happen.

Suddenly, he flung her to the ground. Bartholomew pinned her with his knees, stuffing an old dust rag into her mouth. Her cries were muffled as he pressed his knees into her shoulders and dug in his pocket for the chloroform. He held the drugged cloth firmly to her mouth until she went limp. Then, he removed the syringe and delivered the sleeping draught.

Ensuring that no one was around, he walked gingerly into the kitchen and grabbed a full sack of potatoes and an empty sack. He put her body into the empty sack and then dragged it out the back door, placing it in the shadows just by the steps. Then, he went back in to the hall and took the full sack of potatoes, carried it outside, and stuffed it in the bushes along the side of the house—he would be back for this later.

Bartholomew carefully lifted the sack that contained Mrs. Clarke and hauled it over his shoulder. He walked from the back stoop and through the garden path that led to the side street, when a deep, booming voice shouted at him. He turned to see Lloyd, running at him. His first thought was to run, but he thought better of it and merely stopped in his tracks and awaited Lloyd's approach.

"Stop!" Lloyd shouted out of breath. "Where do you think you're going with that?"

"With what, this?" Bartholomew nodded his head toward the sack over his shoulder.

"Yes, that," Lloyd panted irritatingly. "Mrs. Clarke's home is not a free-for-all. The missus would not look kindly to your stealing from her."

"Oh, I'm not stealing," Bartholomew tried looking sincere. "Mrs. Clarke said that she wanted to donate this leftover sack of potatoes to the almshouse. She was going to ask you to do it, but I volunteered to take it, since I will be going there tomorrow anyway."

Lloyd raised an eyebrow. "*You* are going to St. Adelaide's tomorrow? Whatever for?"

Bartholomew gaped. "Why wouldn't I?" He tried looking cross. "Mrs. Clarke has done a great deal for the women in that home. Through her, I've come to see it as a cause most worthy. I planned on making a monetary donation tomorrow."

"What I mean," Lloyd interjected, "is that St. Adelaide's is normally closed to donations on Saturdays—that's the day they reserve to cook for the Sunday church services."

Bartholomew was surprised that Lloyd knew so much about almshouse. "So, how do you know this?"

"Because, I help Mrs. Clark," Lloyd issued an irritated sigh.

"Oh, of course," Bartholomew nodded.

"So, since the missus originally wanted me to take the donation, I shall take it off your hands and take care of it."

"No," Bartholomew insisted. "After I volunteered, Mrs. Clarke expressly asked that I not allow anyone else to take care of it. She's counting on me."

Lloyd's eyes narrowed. "Really? Well, then you won't mind if I go in and ask her then?"

"N-no, go ahead." Bartholomew stammered, feeling his resolve weaken. He had to think quickly. "You'll have to wake her, though. She told me that she was going straight to bed."

Lloyd scowled and walked toward the house.

Bartholomew felt a wave of panic sweep over him. He decided to take the tough approach. He caught up with Lloyd and pointed at his chest. "Listen here, I've already discussed this with Mrs.

Clarke. I am dropping this donation off tomorrow. End of discussion." He glared at Lloyd, who crossed his arms defiantly. "But, if you're so hell-bent on taking it, then be my guest. Though, I hope Mrs. Clarke doesn't berate you for openly defying her orders, simply because you don't like me." He took a firm stance, expecting a challenge.

"Fine, take it, then." Lloyd leveled his gaze. "But, if you fail to bring this to the almshouse, then I will hunt you down and make sure Mrs. Clarke knows who's to blame."

Bartholomew rolled his eyes and sighed. "Fine, then. Check if you will." He hesitated. "But, there's no reason to distrust me. Mrs. Clarke is a gracious and benevolent woman. Working with her was a pleasure, and I would never do anything to harm the professional rapport we've established."

"Bah, take it then!" Lloyd waved him off and skulked toward the house. Bartholomew held his breath until Lloyd entered the house. Once Lloyd was inside, Bartholomew exhaled in relief.

Taking her home was easy—this time, he had an explanation for what he was carrying. No need to hide or prowl in dark alleyways. She made no sound, but the sack was heavy, and he had over a mile to go.

By the time he got home, his arms were screaming at him, and his legs were rubbery and shaking. He set the sack down for a small rest before pulling it into the salon. When he opened the sack, she was still sleeping deeply. He placed her limp body on the settee, tethered her firmly, and then placed a cloth in her mouth.

At two o'clock in the morning, he snuck out into the shadows of his familiar back alleyways. No one was around, except the occasional staggering drunk. He ducked behind buildings, waited in darkened doorways, and crept along the dark shadowed walls until he came to Mrs. Clarke's mansion. All the lights were off, except for one—Mrs. Clarke's bedroom. No one would notice that she was gone until tomorrow.

He crept over to the hedges that bordered the property and found the full potato sack. He heaved the sack over his shoulder, grunting as his muscles strained against the pressure of the weight. This sack was heavier—he knew the next eight miles would be a challenge.

She was still sleeping soundly the next morning. Regardless, Bartholomew administered another dose of the sleeping draught to ensure that she would continue sleeping while he was away. He stood up, feeling the stiffness in his back from the night before. He was not looking forward to lugging the potato sack again this morning. But, he had to establish an alibi.

When he rang the doorbell at St. Adelaide's, a pretty young woman answered. She flashed him a comely smile. "May I help you, sir?"

"I would like to make a donation." He pointed to the sack of potatoes at his feet.

"Oh! How generous of you, Mr.—"

"Booth, Bartholomew Booth. But, this is from Mrs. Faith Wells Clarke. It's left over from last night's fundraiser."

"Mrs. Clarke is such a gracious lady!"

"Yes, she is," agreed Bartholomew. "Say, would it trouble you to write a receipt for me? Mrs. Clarke needs it for her records."

"No trouble at all!"

Bartholomew waited while the girl filled out the receipt form. When she was through, he examined the form, noticing that his name, the type of donation, and the date and time were all present.

He smiled. It was the perfect proof he needed.

He took a carriage home, where he made himself a hearty breakfast, caught up on his monthly bills, and then lounged on the sofa with a book until he fell asleep. When he woke, it was nearly three in the afternoon. Realizing that he had Mrs. Clarke in the salon, he swiftly got to his feet and opened the salon door.

She was awake and looking quite terrified.

Bartholomew stepped carefully into the room to avoid frightening her. She frowned in confusion. She spoke his name in a muffled, confused tone. He sat next to her and smiled warmly.

"Please be calm, Mrs. Clarke. I have absolutely no intention of hurting you. Do you believe me?" She blinked several times and then slowly nodded. "Good. I had actually intended on another girl, but she went home in the carriage you so graciously offered. But, that's not why I took you." Her brows creased and eyes grew wide in fear. "You laughed at me. For that reason, I had to hit you. I can't have you telling on me and alerting the authorities…that's the last thing I need."

She shook her head, trying to speak.

"I'll remove the gag, but on one condition." She nodded vigorously in agreement. "You mustn't make any noise. Otherwise, I'll have to do something to quiet you down." He waited for her nod of assent and then removed the gag.

She flexed her jaw for a moment and then looked at him pleadingly. "I won't tell anyone, Mr. Booth. I was being incredibly rude, and you did such a lovely job for me. You didn't deserve that poor treatment, and I sincerely apologize." She smiled benevolently.

He ran a finger along her cheekbone. "You are so beautiful! It's like you were meant for me: that face, your name…those eyes…." He gazed dreamily into her eyes. She moved her face away from his touch and twisted around in her tethers. He snapped out of his reverie and grabbed her face roughly. "Now, now, Mrs. Clarke. You need to stay still and listen. Otherwise, the last thing you will ever see is this room, just like the other girls…" he trailed off, staring into space.

Mrs. Clarke whimpered and eventually let out peals of horrified shrieks. Bartholomew quickly stuffed the rag back into her mouth. Frustrated, he got up from the settee and left the room. He returned with a filled syringe. Noticing what Bartholomew had in his hand, Mrs. Clarke began thrashing about to try freeing herself from the ropes, but with no luck.

Bartholomew sat next to her, smiling lovingly. "It's alright, sweetheart. There's nothing to worry about. This is just a sleeping draught and it will help you rest until you decide to be a good girl for me." He inserted the needle and administered the draught. Mrs. Clarke's eyes flashed a brief look of terror before her body went limp.

Faith seemed to have a change of thought when she woke up the next morning. She was compliant and polite, and never screamed or caused Bartholomew pain or stress. They spent a lovely Sunday together, laughing and talking, and he even unbound one of her arms so that she could feed herself.

Monday morning, he prepared her for his departure by binding her hands and feet and placing a gag in her mouth. He was just locking the interior salon door, when he was startled by a knock at the door. Quickly, he repositioned the paneling and ensured it was secure. He smoothed out his hair and jacket and then opened the door.

He wasn't surprised. It was Inspector Rood.

"Hello, again, Mr. Booth," the inspector said, feigning amiability. "Here we are again."

"What can I do for you, Inspector?"

"May I come in?"

Bartholomew smiled wanly and let the inspector in, scowling behind his back.

The inspector didn't skip a beat. "Unsurprisingly, I have another missing person."

"Well, that doesn't bode well for the Cambridge Police, does it?" Bartholomew chided. "Losing people is bad for business, eh?"

The Inspector was unaffected. "It isn't the police department that's losing people, Mr. Booth."

"Well, I haven't lost anyone," Bartholomew retorted.

"Have you taken anyone?" the inspector asked, point blank.

Bartholomew was taken aback by the inspector's candor. "N-no, why? W-why would I take anyone?"

"Just thought I would ask the obvious question," the inspector smiled politely.

"Well, no, I haven't taken anyone, and I don't have the faintest idea of what you're talking about."

"Do you know a person by the name of Faith Wells Clarke?"

"Yes, of course I know her—I worked for her charity event on Friday evening. Why?"

The inspector nodded, ignoring his question. "And, you saw her all evening?"

"Well, most of it, I guess," Bartholomew shrugged.

"So, when was the last time you saw Mrs. Clarke?"

"Has something happened to Mrs. Clarke?" The inspector gave him a blank stare. "Uh, I guess it was around midnight…right before I left for home."

"And in what capacity did you see her?"

"What do you mean by that?" Bartholomew was beginning to feel defensive.

"What was your conversation about?" the inspector clarified.

"Oh, well, she thanked me for a job well-done, she handed me a check for my services, and then I left."

The inspector raised an eyebrow. "Is that all, then? Nothing else you discussed with her?"

"No, that's it!" Bartholomew frowned, feeling the blood rush to his cheeks.

"Alright," the inspector said reluctantly, "then if that's all, I will thank you and be on my way." He nodded to Bartholomew and turned to leave, when Bartholomew rushed at him.

"Wait! There's one other thing." The inspector looked at him expectantly. "She wanted to donate a leftover sack of potatoes to St. Adelaide's. I volunteered to take it for her, since she looked tired." Bartholomew walked over to the table and picked up the receipt. "Here," he said, handing it to the inspector, "I brought the donation in this morning, and this is the receipt. I was actually planning to bring this to Mrs. Clarke this morning."

The inspector examined the receipt and then nodded slowly. "Do you mind if I take this receipt?"

"Well, I need to give it to Mrs.—"

The inspector shook his head. "I'll keep it safe, don't worry. When I see Mrs. Clarke, I'll give it to her personally." Bartholomew acquiesced, feigning disappointment, but inwardly rejoicing that the inspector fell for it. The inspector paused in the doorway on the way out. "Please stay in town—I might need to ask more questions later."

Bartholomew nodded, trying to look concerned. "I am glad to be of service. Mrs. Clarke is a lovely lady." Bartholomew waited to hear the door close at the bottom of the stairs before running to the window. He watched the inspector walk down the street, turning only once for another contemplative glance at Bartholomew standing in the window.

Bartholomew took great care in the ensuing weeks to ensure that he lived the life of a dull solitary. He wasn't sure if he was being tailed, but he took no chances. He only went between work and home, stopping only at the market to buy single-portion meals to avoid detection. Rationing single portions into two servings was difficult, but necessary until he was sure the police no longer suspected him.

Faith quickly became his best ward. She responded well to the romance novels, providing him with adequate synopses in the evenings, including character comparisons between the hero and Bartholomew, the heroine and Faith. Eventually, he loosened her tethers, especially after she agreed to dance with him to romantic tunes on the phonograph. She even showed delight upon his arrivals from work in the evenings, and often laughed enthusiastically at his jokes.

At one time, when they were dancing together, he asked if she missed her husband. She discontinued dancing and became despondent for a few seconds.

"Have I offended you?" he asked, terrified that their studies would have to start over again.

"No," she whispered. "The admiral is frequently away. I am left alone most of the time. That is why I am benefactress of the alms-house—it keeps me busy." She turned to face him. "The admiral doesn't love me…he never did. It was the money he loved."

Bartholomew placed a hand on her arm. "I'm sorry, Faith. He doesn't deserve you."

"Thank you, Bartholomew, I appreciate that you see what he does not."

"You say you do not miss him, but yet, I hear you cry often."

She smiled weakly. "I shed no tears for my husband. The tears are for the poor women of the almshouse. What is to happen to them when I am gone?"

"When you are gone?"

"When you kill me, Bartholomew," she added. "I am afraid for them—they would surely parish without my help."

Bartholomew looked earnestly at her. "I am not going to kill you!"

"You won't?" she asked, incredulous.

"No, you silly girl!" He held her close. "I only want to love you!"

"You want to…love…me?"

"Yes!" He held her out at arm's length, placing a hand along-side her cheek. "Reading the romance novels, dancing to romantic music—it's all to woo you!"

Faith frowned. "You're keeping me here—"

"So you can fall in love with me," Bartholomew finished.

"What happens to me after I fall…in love…with you?"

"Freedom" he answered, shrugging, "first within your salon, then in my flat, and then eventually, we shall marry and move elsewhere… start anew."

"What about the almshouse?"

"We will make generous annual donations—anonymously, of course."

"How is that possible?"

"I have money," he responded. "My family is incredibly wealthy. I inherited millions upon my aunt's death."

"Then, why do you—"

"Work?" That was just to keep me busy until I found my soul mate!" He smiled enthusiastically.

"Oh, I see." She nodded her head slowly. Hot tears streamed down her cheeks.

Alarmed, Bartholomew immediately produced a handkerchief. "Please don't cry, my love! Loving me is not such a bad thing, is it?" He grabbed her shoulders, squeezing so hard that it brought fresh tears to her eyes.

"N-no, B-Bartholomew," she cried, struggling against his powerful grip, "it's not a bad thing! That's the reason behind my tears—I could never have imagined anything so...wonderful!"

Bartholomew released his grip, staring at her in disbelief. "Could it be true, then? Are you falling in love with me?"

Faith cried, her shoulders shaking. "Y-yes, Bartholomew! I am... falling in love with you!" He held her close to him as she sobbed uncontrollably.

"Then, why are you crying, my love?" He caressed her hair.

"B-because, I-I'm...married...Bartholomew! Falling in love with someone else is...it's a sin!"

He pushed her slowly from his embrace and stared lovingly into her eyes. "Not if you change your name, my love—then you will be another person in the eyes of the law! Eventually, they will stop looking for Mrs. Faith Wells Clarke—the Admiral will have her declared legally dead. Thereafter, you will be known as Mrs. Constance Booth!"

Fresh tears sprung to her eyes. "What a beautiful name."

"I'm glad you like it." He kissed her fully on the lips, and then released her from his embrace. "However, until then, we must keep a low profile. Once that annoying investigation closes, we will be free to marry. Then it will be just you and I—my beautiful Constance."

She closed her eyes and nodded as Bartholomew tightened her ropes once more. He walked from the salon and blew her a kiss before locking the door behind him.

Over the next few weeks, Bartholomew began allowing Faith her freedoms—first in the salon, and then out in the flat while he was present. Evenings were spent with him telling her about his day while she cooked. After enjoying a delicious meal, they danced and held deep, romantic conversations. It was as if they were already married. It was a dream come true.

Bartholomew also noticed that the police were no longer shadowing his daily movements. In fact, Inspector Rood came into the agency one day saying that he could use Bartholomew's help in the investigation. Bartholomew excitedly agreed, providing names of those who worked at the charity event, and details about Mrs. Clarke's character and acquaintances. Bartholomew felt his help would enhance the inspector's trust in him.

After five months, Faith's disappearance was downgraded to a small mention on page ten. The police admitted that the trail had grown cold, and that she was no longer considered a missing person. She was declared dead shortly thereafter. A week later, the newspaper reported that Faith's mother had died of a broken heart in mourning for her daughter.

This news sent Faith into a fit of tears. Bartholomew tried consoling her, but she just wept hysterically until growing limp in his arms.

He wiped her tear-streaked face and smiled affectionately. "There, there, my love! All will be better soon."

"Better? How can it be better? My mother is dead!"

"W-well, this means that no one is looking for you! We can marry now!"

She gaped. "Married? How can you talk of marriage after telling me that my mother has died?"

"B-because…I thought it would cheer you up." He tried pulling her to him, but she pushed him away.

"No, Bartholomew!" She withdrew, pointing a finger in his direction. "This is your fault, and I want nothing to do with you!" She ran into the salon and slammed the interior door. He wanted to run after her, but thought better of it. She'd come to her senses soon.

He was right to wait. Sunday morning, everything was back to normal, except that she was slightly melancholy, which he allowed for. When he came home from work the next day, he unlocked the padlock to his flat and found Faith sitting in the center of the room with a certain trunk open.

He thought he hid that.

She had something in her lap. Bartholomew smiled at her. "Hello! How was your day?"

"What's this?" she asked, motioning toward the trunk.

"A trunk," he answered sarcastically, smiling crookedly.

Her eyes narrowed. "This is no time for jokes, Bartholomew. Whose trunk is this?"

His eyes flickered to the trunk. "It belongs to…someone I used to know," he stammered.

"Would it be…" she picked up the garment in her lap and looked at the collar, squinting. "Constance Brown's trunk?"

"Yes," he answered, bracing.

"Who is she?"

"Now, Faith, don't be jealous—"

"Who IS she?" Faith stood up. Bartholomew could now see that Faith was holding *her* dress…the one she wore the night that he…

His eyes widened, forgotten feelings returned. He snatched the dress from Faith and threw it back in the trunk. "Constance," he replied angrily, "was my nanny."

"What happened to her?" Faith asked, looking stunned.

"She…went away…" he trailed off, gazing into the distance.

"What do you mean 'went away'?" Faith's tone spoke of her increasing alarm.

He grinned wanly. "She died. This trunk is all I have left of her." He caressed the top of the trunk.

Faith watched Bartholomew caress the trunk, feeling terror rise within her. She felt flooded in panic. "Bartholomew?" she asked gingerly. "Did you...did you...kill...her?"

Bartholomew hugged the trunk and then immediately got to his feet, straightened his jacket, and gave her a cheerful smile. "Don't be silly. I didn't kill her. Why would you assume that?"

"I just thought—"

He shook his head, wagging a finger at her. "Don't lie, Faith— it's unbecoming. Why do you ask me these things?"

"I...I think you are what the newspapers are calling the 'Gentleman Killer,'" she blurted, scooting to the opposite end of the couch.

He laughed maniacally. "The Gentleman Killer? How amusing!" He continued to laugh boisterously, making her feel uneasy. "Well, Mrs. Clarke, you have most certainly provided me with my laugh for the day! Gentleman Killer, really!"

She chuckled softly, uncomfortably. "Sorry, Bartholomew, but I just had to ask—"

He patted her shoulder. "You've been under a lot of stress lately." He carried the trunk back to his bedroom closet. When he returned, he made a pot of tea for the two of them and joined her on the couch.

She took several sips of her tea, staring in his direction. Finally, she set her cup down and looked at him earnestly.

"What now?" he asked without looking at her.

"I would like to attend my mother's funeral."

"No, absolutely not!" he barked, spilling hot tea on his trousers.

"But, Bartholomew! She was my mother and I loved her very much—"

"What part of no do you not understand? We'll be discovered!"

"N-not if I go in disguise!" she got down on her knees and put a hand on his. "If I put on one of those dresses in the trunk and a heavy veil, I can sit where no one can see me!"

Bartholomew considered a moment. "I'm sorry, Faith, but my answer is still no."

She hung her head and cried. "Please…please…she's my mother…"

He removed her head from his knee and stood up. "No, it's just too risky." He walked into the kitchen to clean the spill on his trousers, when she issued a loud, frenzied scream. Immediately, he sprinted to her, put a hand over her mouth, and forcefully carried her into the salon. He threw her upon the settee and strapped her in, stuffing a rag into her mouth.

Tears streamed down her face, and her shoulders shook as she cried. He sat next to her, shaking his head. "I'm sorry, sweetheart, but it's too risky. Besides, it's quite a depressing sort of thing, a funeral, isn't it?" He flashed a patronizing smile and patted her hand.

She stayed that way for two weeks, when she finally came to her senses and returned to her former pleasant self. Bartholomew was glad, for he was tiring of her fits and tantrums. Soon, they fell effortlessly to their normal routine, where she wandered about the flat freely and they enjoyed meaningful conversation and romantic, cozy evenings.

Then, he slowly became ill.

At first, it was a mild dizziness that stole over him at night before bed. Then, he began losing his appetite. When the violent bouts of vomiting ensued, he began to worry.

One evening, as he lay in bed recovering from a recent bout of violent heaving, he ruminated aloud about calling the doctor.

"But, my love, we'll be found out!" she said, alarmed.

"I know, I know, but what if I'm dying?" he asked.

"Shh, my love," she murmured reassuringly. "I read in the newspaper that a common ailment is going around. This will soon pass. You're not going to die!"

He smiled and nodded, returning to a slumber that was interrupted continuously by violent illness.

A week later, he felt much better, and was in high spirits. During his lunch break that day, he went into a jeweler's and picked out a suitable engagement ring. That night at supper, he asked Faith to prepare an exceptional meal tomorrow night for a special occasion. He laughed as he had to wave off her constant begging to know the details. He couldn't believe his luck—he was so in love.

The following evening, he walked home to a veritable feast, complete with a lovely cake soaked in dark sugar and rum. The table was set in his aunt's fine china, burgundy wine sparkled from crystal glasses, and candles were lit. He couldn't help but gasp when he saw how beautiful Faith looked in the candlelight. He walked to the table, her violet eyes sparkling in the amber glow, and kissed her softly. She smiled sweetly at him, caressing his cheek with her own.

"Welcome home, dear," she said, her voice raspy.

His body flowed with love. Unable to wait, he immediately got down on one knee and produced the ring. "Will you, my dear love, marry me?"

"Yes!" she exclaimed, flashing a radiant smile. "Yes, I will marry you, Bartholomew!" She threw her arms around his neck and hugged him tightly. His heart swelled as he returned her embrace, squeezing her affectionately, excitedly. He released her from his embrace and kissed her tenderly.

"You've made me the happiest man on earth," he beamed.

"That's because I am the happiest woman," she cooed.

They enjoyed a romantic meal, talking animatedly about their wedding and where they would live afterward. They settled on Paris, since she spoke French fluently, and no one knew them there. After the meal, they adjourned to the living room, where he doubled over in severe pain.

She grabbed his arm. "Bartholomew, my love? What's wrong?"

He opened his mouth to speak, but instead vomited forcefully onto the living room carpet. Immediately, Faith escorted him into his bedroom and laid him down upon the bed.

"Here! Lie down!" She helped him get under the covers, and then fetched a cool cloth, which she pressed lovingly to his forehead. "My poor dear! I'll go clean up in the other room and will be back to tend to you presently."

Bartholomew smiled and sighed, grateful for his loving fiancée. He started.

Fiancé.

The word sounded strange to him. Stranger still, was the fact that he was soon to be married, and would leave this miserable life in Cambridge behind him. He sat up and watched as Faith busied herself in the kitchen. The candles flickered on the table, giving off a warm amber glow. The color reminded him of Constance's warm bronze eyes. Tears stung his eyes as he thought of the life he and Constance could have had together.

He mustn't cry…mustn't remember *her.*

His loving fiancé stood mere feet from him, and he needed to focus on her. He smiled, thinking of his approaching nuptials. Closing his clammy hands into tight fists, he tried to ward off the cold waves of nausea that overcame him. No longer able to fight it, he purged his supper and rolled over into the bed, moaning in pain.

Faith pressed a cool cloth to his forehead and whispered soothingly in his ear. He comprehended nothing of what she said, but as he drifted, he thought he heard "finally got what's coming…"

Bartholomew woke with a start. He looked around the room in utter confusion. It was his bedroom—that much he knew. Nothing was out of the ordinary, except that when he glanced in the corner of the room, Faith was there, slumped over in a chair, slumbering.

He smiled.

This was the girl—the one who would rescue him from the depths of despair and bring him into the bright, shining light. He watched her chest rise and fall evenly in slumber. Her dark eyelashes graced the soft pale skin of her cheek. He inhaled to invite her scent, but instead grimaced at the stale stench of sickness.

Now he remembered: he spent the night violently retching. He wilted, remembering the beautiful meal she had made in celebration of their engagement. The dining room table was still set, reminding him of the moment she said yes. He couldn't believe his dream was finally coming true, though it took him five times to get it right.

He propped himself up, rubbing his face and eyes. He slipped out of the covers, dressed himself, and then walked over to steal a glance at his future bride. Tenderly, he lifted her from the chair and carried her into the salon, where he lay her down upon the settee, covering her gently with a blanket. He tiptoed out of the room, taking one last glance before softly closing the door.

Bartholomew sent word to his office that he would not be in that day. He feared for his job—he had been out ill quite often lately, and hoped he would not lose it. Though he didn't need the employment, being fired might pique the inspector's interest.

He glanced at the table and noticed that the spiced rum cake was left out. A wave of nausea overwhelmed him. He grabbed the cake and tore it into small pieces, then threw the pieces out the window for the birds and squirrels.

Despite feeling nauseous, Bartholomew knew he had to eat something. He made a quick gruel, leaving some for Faith, once she woke up. After finishing breakfast, he noticed that the room had grown quite cold. Since he felt the apartment was sufficiently aired, he walked over to the window to close it.

He looked out the window, expecting to see several birds and rodents snacking on the cake, and gasped at what he saw instead. Several of the birds were lying, face up, on the ground, and two squirrels appeared dead. Another squirrel approached to eat a piece of the cake, but soon after struggled to walk, eventually dropping over dead.

Bartholomew frowned. He doubted that a small bit of rum could cause this much damage. He ran downstairs, scooped up the cake, and brought it back to the flat to examine it. It looked and smelled fresh. He put the cake in a small bag, stuffed two more bags in his pocket, and headed outside. Once out on the street, he put a bird in one of the spare bags, and a squirrel in the other, and made his way down to the chemist's.

The chemist frowned as Bartholomew explained what had happened. He asked the chemist to analyze the contents of the bags and apprise him of the results immediately.

Bartholomew waited at the chemist's…all day…for those results.

The chemist finally finished and nodded solemnly. "These animals, I am afraid, have been poisoned."

"By what?" Bartholomew asked, visibly shaken.

"I couldn't identify the type of poison, but it was in the cake. I fed it to a few of my laboratory rats and they all perished within seconds."

Bartholomew didn't wait for a response, but fled the chemists.

He doesn't remember the trip home.

London Chronicle

Cambridge, Feb. 17, 1916 Police Still on the Lookout for Gentleman Killer! City Still Mourns Death of Mrs. Faith Wells Clarke!

Local police are still searching for the Gentleman Killer, one who is suspected of murdering several young women in Cambridge, including Mrs. Faith Wells Clarke, a well-respected patroness of St. Adelaide's Almshouse. Several inhabitants of said almshouse have gathered by Candlelight last Evening to honor the Memory of Mrs. Wells Clarke.

"She meant so much to all of us," stated Emily Roark, resident of St. Adelaide's, "Without her constant help and care, we're afraid of losing our home and well-being. She will be sorely missed."

Miss Roark, along with the other Inhabitants of St. Adelaide's were reduced to tears and bouts of heavy weeping at their loss.

Mrs. Wells Clarke's Husband, Admiral Joseph K. Clarke, has stated that he will continue to support the Cause that was so close to his Wife's Heart, but that the Love and Care she gave the Inhabitants to the Almshouse could never be replaced.

THIRTY-THREE

"How long are you going to be gone?" Lenora asked Tom as he was packing a suitcase.

"A week," he answered, distracted.

"Well, what am I supposed to do?" Lenora asked, not wanting her dad to leave. He had just found out that day that one of the Psychology professors at Oxford University needed someone to substitute for him immediately—his wife died in a car accident that morning. The professor was able to cancel classes for the remainder of the week, but needed someone there for the following week.

"Ian's here—he can watch you."

Lenora sighed and rolled her eyes. Ian had been absent since Clare showed up; Lenora and Tom hadn't seen him in over a week. "Yeah, okay…reliable Ian. Dad, I don't need a babysitter."

"That's not what I meant," Tom responded, taking a long breath. "You have plenty of people around to help if you need it. I know that Ian hasn't been around, but he knows I'm leaving and said he'd be around if you need anything. Otherwise, I expect that you'll behave in a trustworthy manner while I'm gone." He gave her a stern look and then continued his packing.

"What about your classes?"

"I'm having one of the graduate students take over for me."

"Couldn't the professor from Oxford do the same thing? Have a grad student take his classes, I mean?"

"No, Ron doesn't have any seasoned grad students this year that he can rely on. Besides, I have given many lectures on the topic he's covering next week." Dr. Ronald Baker had been trying to coax Tom into making a guest appearance in his Psychodynamic course. Tom was one of the leading experts in that field, but he was never able to get away from his current obligations. Now, however, because it was a serious matter, Tom felt compelled to help.

After Tom finished packing, Lenora walked with him down the stairs and watched as he drove off in the taxi. She slowly trudged up the stairs and made her way to the kitchen to scavenge for something to eat.

Alone on a Friday night—how pathetic.

She did not look forward to spending an entire weekend alone, and she knew that Ian wouldn't be around to goof off with. She wasted a half an hour looking for something to eat before finally deciding to order pizza. Just as she reached for the phone to dial for delivery, it rang.

It's probably Dad, checking up on me.

"Hello?"

"Lenora?" a familiar female's voice inquired.

"Hi Emily!"

"Hey girlie! Your dad just called me and said he's going out of town for the week."

"And let me guess," Lenora said with a sigh, "you're supposed to check in on me."

"No, he didn't ask me to do that—he asked me to offer my phone number in case you need anything."

"Uh-huh." Lenora didn't believe her.

Hearing the disbelief in Lenora's tone, Emily giggled. "Okay, you don't have to believe me, but it's the truth. If your dad asked me to check in on you, I'd tell you as much. You're not a little kid, Lenora, and you deserve the truth—even if it sucks."

Emily was always candid with her, so Lenora decided to give her the benefit of the doubt. "Sorry—I know you're about the only one who thinks that way." She reached over and picked up a pen and tore a corner off of an envelope lying on the counter. "What's your number then?"

Emily recited her number to Lenora and then paused to give her time to write it down. "So, what are your plans while your dad's out of the house? Any big parties? Because if there are, I had better be invited!"

Lenora chuckled. "No parties. You have to have friends for that."

"You have friends, Lenora," Emily said unsympathetically.

"Yeah, like who?"

"Like me!" Emily said enthusiastically. "Listen, if you don't have any plans for the weekend, why don't you come to my place? Bring a couple days' worth of clothes—we can have a slumber party!"

"Slumber party?" Lenora rolled her eyes. "Isn't that what little girls do?"

"There's no age limit," Emily explained. "Besides, it's a great excuse for us to get to know each other better, eat junk food, and talk nasty about boys." She paused, and then when she had no response, continued, "Maybe I can show you a couple of fun spells, if you want."

Lenora smiled—it actually sounded like fun. "Okay, sounds great. How do I get there?"

"I'll call you a cab. Go pack!"

Lenora began to say something, but the line went dead. *Um, okay, I guess she hung up.* Lenora stared at the phone for a bit, and then realizing that she had little time, ran to her bedroom to pack a bag.

No sooner had she finished packing and written a note to Ian to let him know where she was, when a horn sounded downstairs. She looked out the window to see a cab sitting there, waiting for her. The ride to Emily's was short—she lived on Panton Street, not too far from the Fitzwilliam Museum. Emily was standing on the front lawn, waiting for her, a big smile on her face. Emily paid the cab driver and then took Lenora's bag out of her hand as she stepped out of the cab.

"Come with me!" Emily said excitedly as she grabbed Lenora's hand and led her inside.

Lenora gasped aloud as she entered Emily's apartment. She should have expected as much, considering the way that Emily dressed—but it was surprising nonetheless.

"A bit surprised, are we?" Emily asked, amused.

"Yeah...I mean—" Lenora was embarrassed and didn't know what to say—she didn't want to insult Emily.

"It's okay—I've had worse reactions, particularly from my mum." Emily took Lenora's hand and led her in. "Here, I'll give you a tour."

Emily led Lenora around the apartment and talked about the various places she found the different vintage items that decorated the apartment.

The living room walls were covered in a deep burgundy, heirloom damask, velvet-flocked wallpaper. Mahogany tables were placed tastefully around the room, all decorated with vintage table lamps, vases filled with dried rose petals, candlesticks, table scarves, and antique books. The sofa and chairs were covered in a heavy paisley tapestry, all topped with many lush pillows in deep shades of various colors. Antique silver picture frames dotted the walls, some with ancestral pictures. It was a bit cluttered for Lenora's taste, but it was cozy. Emily called it "Victorian gothic" style.

Emily's bedroom continued the theme with a dark blue, ivy velvet-flocked wallpaper, wrought iron bed frame and candelabra, black satin bedding, and black sheer voile curtains.

Once they got to the spare room, Emily stopped and held the door open. "This is where you're going to stay."

Lenora looked around, touching the soft velvet of the gold matte Empire flocked wallpaper. The room was simply decorated with rich mahogany furnishings and a simple cream-colored bedspread and matching curtains. This room was more minimalistic than the others, which made Lenora frown.

Noticing Lenora's perplexed expression, Emily chuckled. "This is my minimalist design. It's for my mum, so she is comfortable in this room at least." Emily turned to leave and then looked back, smiling. "She won't even go near the altar room."

Altar room?

Lenora turned to ask, but Emily had already left. She set her bag atop the bed and walked down the hall, opening the door to the room she thought was the altar room. The room was luxurious and dark, decorated in a red acanthus, velvet flocked wallpaper. Vintage lamps with red, tasseled lampshades provided an amber glow, and the altar was a simple table with multiple candles that were currently unlit.

Lenora quietly closed the door and went to find Emily, who was already in the kitchen, pouring them tea from a red and white damask teapot.

"I thought we could have a bit of tea before deciding what to do tonight." Emily looked up at Lenora and smiled. "Sugar?"

"Yes, please," Lenora answered absentmindedly as she browsed through Emily's eclectic collection of tea cups–none were the same style or design.

"I like having such a differentiated collection–that way, everyone gets a different style and color according to their own personal taste," Emily offered as if Lenora asked. "For example, for you, I chose this simple white cup with the delicate purple lilacs. I thought simplicity for you." She looked up at Lenora with apprehension. "I hope that's okay."

"No, it's great–the cup's perfect." Lenora took a seat next to Emily, where she enjoyed nearly an hour of silly small talk. The chiming of Emily's clock alerted Lenora to the time, which also caused her stomach to growl.

"Oh! Where are my manners?" Emily asked apologetically. "I imagine you're starving by now. Want to order pizza?"

"That's exactly what I had planned!" Lenora was glad she took up Emily's offer to stay the weekend.

Emily ordered pizza and they both sat, talking and laughing, into the early morning hours, finally going to bed sometime after three that morning.

Lenora awoke the next morning, feeling groggy but in a great mood. Not only was the night with Emily fun, but Lenora didn't have any nightmares for a change—Emily had put a protection spell around the apartment. Last night, Emily showed Lenora how to put a good dreams charm around her bed. It was fun...and seemed to work. Lenora put her robe on and padded out into the kitchen, where Emily was already up, dressed, and cooking breakfast.

"Good mornin'!" Emily looked chipper and wide awake. "How'd you sleep?"

"Great," Lenora replied, yawning. "Best sleep I've had in a long time. You should show me how to put that good dreams charm around my bed at home." She smiled at Emily, who nodded distractedly. "When did you get up?" Lenora asked.

"At dawn," Emily replied, "as usual."

"I can't believe you got up so early considering the late night we had." Lenora couldn't fathom the idea of how Emily could be so cheery with such a small amount of sleep.

"Well, I get up at dawn everyday—regardless of how late I'm up. I can always nap later." Emily removed a pan from the oven and placed its contents on a plate. "I've made scones, in case you're interested."

Lenora was famished and the scones were delicious—much better than her attempt at making scones, which always turned out dry. After they finished breakfast, Lenora helped Emily clean up, and then showered and dressed for the day. When she finished, she found Emily sitting on the couch, reading a book and drinking tea.

Without looking at Lenora, Emily motioned to a book on the table. "A book to occupy yourself with today. I have some reading to do for my research."

"Oh, sure." Lenora picked up the book. The title read "Vampyre Hallows" by Mischa LaRue.

Emily looked amusedly at Lenora. "It's a gothic tale—I thought I would submerge you in my world for the day." She chuckled and continued reading.

"Actually, all I ever read is gothic fiction," Lenora informed her.

Emily's eyebrows raised in surprise. "Well now, my first surprise for the day—that's great!" She smiled. "Oh, before I forget, I hope you don't mind, but I invited some people over tonight."

"Oh?" Lenora's stomach started to tighten as she wondered who Emily invited and what kind of evening it would turn out to be.

"I asked Ian, Tabitha, Amelia, Phillip, Maggie, and Joe. Everyone's been working so hard on the latest case that we all need a bit of fun."

"Are they all coming?"

"As far as I know. Why?"

"Well, Ian's been so busy with Clare lately that he hasn't really had time for anything else." She paused, trying to figure out how to ask the question she really wanted to ask. "Or, is his girlfriend coming too?" she asked sheepishly.

"No, Clare's not coming," Emily said, eyeing her.

Lenora noticed the look on Emily's face and decided to discontinue the conversation. "Sounds like fun," she said, trying to sound nonchalant. Without looking at Emily or waiting for a response, she settled in to the cushy wing-backed chair and started reading.

Lenora didn't notice how dark the room had become until Emily switched on the lamp over her head.

"It's getting a bit dark for the eyes," Emily explained. She hovered over Lenora's shoulder. "You're nearly finished with the book? It's over 400 pages, girl!" She laughed, seeming pleased.

Lenora glanced down at the page—she hadn't noticed that she had already reached page 307. "Yeah, I read fast...especially if it's an interesting story."

"Well, if you finish that one tonight, I'll give you the sequel tomorrow."

"When is everyone coming over?" Lenora asked, closing the book and stretching.

"Not until after ten tonight," Emily answered. "We're having sushi for dinner, by the way."

Lenora screwed up her face in a scowl. "I don't think I like—"

"If you say you don't *think* you like it, then you've never tried," Emily said, giving her a reproachful glance. "Sushi does not imply raw, either—I'm making you all cooked rolls just to try."

Lenora watched as Emily made various types of sushi, feeling a nervous twinge in her stomach—this was definitely out of her range of acceptability in trying new foods. Little did she know how much she would like it.

Once they devoured the sushi, Lenora helped Emily decorate the apartment—which she thought needn't be done; it was already decorated enough in her opinion. But, Emily wanted more candles, creating a warm, yet somewhat ominous ambiance. They made a variety of hors d'oeuvres together, and then Emily excused herself to get ready for the evening.

Lenora went into her room and plopped down on the bed to finish reading her book.

An hour later, Emily woke her.

"Wake up, sleepyhead," Emily said, shaking the bed with her foot. "It's time for you to get ready."

Lenora stretched and yawned. "I *am* ready," she responded. She showered and changed earlier, and felt a jeans and t-shirt were fine for tonight—she knew everyone and didn't feel the necessity to dress up. Besides, she brought nothing along that was party-worthy.

"Uh, no you're not," Emily responded, throwing some clothes on the bed. "Wear this—tonight's theme is Goth"

"There's a theme?" Lenora frowned, not expecting a theme.

Emily sighed. "When you come over here for a party, it's always Goth—it's just a way for me to expect society to conform to me for a change." She smiled. "I'll do your hair and makeup when you come out."

Emily left, and Lenora inspected the clothing. The top was a filmy black material with three-quarter length sleeves and satin laces aligning the bodice. She picked up the black mini skirt, which was adorned with buckles and satin lace. She looked around for the rest of the skirt—it was more mini than she was comfortable with. Thigh-high, black leather boots, black lace gloves, and a black velvet choker topped off the outfit.

Not really her taste—she went for more simplistic fashions. But, she giggled as she pulled on the shirt and skirt, feeling almost giddy with excitement. When she exited the bedroom in her full gothic attire, Emily squealed with delight, spinning her around a few times and then pulling her into the bedroom to finish the hair and makeup.

Emily pulled Lenora's hair into two high pigtails, adding multiple red satin ribbons that she tied in bows, allowing the remaining ribbon to stream softly down her back. Emily only gave Lenora a soft, smoky eye makeup and then dark burgundy lip gloss—she said she didn't want to overdo it. Lenora thought she looked great.

When everyone arrived, they seemed stunned and pleasantly surprised by Lenora's transformation. She was equally excited to see everyone dressed up in gothic style—even Phillip, who did his best in all black attire and spiked hair, which was no doubt Amelia's work.

When Ian arrived—in black leather pants, vintage rock t-shirt, and red streaks in his overly-gelled hair—Lenora stifled a surprised laugh. His expression betrayed his discomfort—he was truly out of his element. He couldn't have been more shocked by her look, pausing in the doorway to give her an appraisal. His grin said it all—that he highly approved of her look. He squeezed her tightly and whispered that she looked fabulous…borderline delicious, which left her thrilled for the rest of the evening.

The party was a success. Everyone mingled about, savoring the hors d'oeuvres, playing silly games, and dancing. Ian asked Lenora to dance several times, though Lenora had the impression that

Emily wasn't thrilled as a look of disapproval crossed her face several times...particularly when Ian seemed overly affectionate.

He never left Lenora's side...that is, until the doorbell rang and ruined Lenora's fun. It was Clare, who was disinterested in joining the festivities, and after several moments of discussion, refused to come in, pleading for Ian to go home with her...after changing his clothes, of course. Ian came back in looking defeated, said his regrets, and then left without a second glance.

Lenora felt the sourness creeping in. The party ended for her soon after that.

THIRTY-FOUR

Lenora was reluctant to go back to the borrowed apartment— her time with Emily was entirely too enjoyable. However, she had school, and Emily had work. She did, however, meet Emily for dinner a couple of nights during the week, since Ian was mostly unavailable.

Thursday night was supposed to be movie night, but when Lenora came home from school, she noticed that Ian had left a note, telling her not to expect him because he and Clare were going out.

She was getting tired of hearing about Clare.

Disinclined to stay at home sulking, Lenora walked to the library and got a book for the weekend, and then decided to stop somewhere for takeaway. When she got to Trinity Street, she stopped directly below her old apartment and looked up into her bedroom window. She sighed, wishing she was back at home. Just wanting to get that "home again" feel, Lenora climbed the stairs and sat at the very top, trying to pretend it was a normal day—that her apartment wasn't haunted and she was just passing the time in the stairwell as she used to.

Hunger finally got the best of her, so she went around the block and bought herself a sandwich. Not wanting to return to her borrowed apartment, she walked back to the old place and sat on the top step, reading and enjoying her meal.

Then, she started getting curious.

What if she just walked around the apartment? If she didn't touch anything, what could be the harm?

A thousand scenarios ran through her head, and none of them really turned up entirely negative. Besides, she missed home, wanted to be in her own bed.

She left her book on the stair and turned the key in the lock, feeling a moment's trepidation before slowly walking in.

None of the mess was cleaned up from the previous CSP visit, which meant that when this was over, she had lots of work to do. Lenora walked around, tracing her gloved hands along the walls, sitting on her bed, feeling the softness of her grandmother's quilt, all while bemoaning the disgusting state of her home.

That's it! I'm cleaning this place!

Lenora rose from the bed, ran into the kitchen, donned a pair of cleaning gloves so that her lacy gloves wouldn't become soiled, and then went to work—picking up, rearranging, sweeping, dusting, and scrubbing. The place was filthy, which was evident in how much time it took for her to clean. When finished, she stood in the middle of the living room, sweating, and admired her work.

"There! Back to normal!" She sighed, feeling good about the work she just put into the place. She was positive that Tom would be thankful...but she wouldn't tell him until things settled. She knew telling him now meant trouble.

Lenora put the cleaning supplies back and removed the cleaning gloves. Then, she padded into her bedroom to use her own sink to wash up in. She washed her face twice, it felt so refreshing. As she dried her face in a fresh towel, she glanced up in the mirror, her cheeks still flushed from all the hard work. She felt a momentary dizziness sweep over her, which she dismissed as dehydration—she hadn't anything to drink the entire time she cleaned.

Her reflection in the mirror grew hazy, disoriented. She squinted, trying to regain focus and reprimanded herself for not paying attention to her fluid intake. Then, the mirror grew dark, the reflection behind her growing elongated and nebulous. Taking a closer look, it appeared as if the environment behind her was altering to another state.

She looked behind her, and the room looked as it always did. But, when she returned her glance to the mirror, it was different. The décor was antique, Victorian. Pale, pink damask lined the walls. The floors were a darker stain, and the furniture was a velvety, dusty rose color. Dark pink lace curtains flowed in the breeze. This was not her room.

She turned around, and the room wasn't her own—it had altered to what was shown in the mirror. A foreboding flooded within her as she looked around at the foreign furnishings.

Movement in the corner of the room caught her attention. There was a woman lying on a settee, her arms and legs bound in leather straps. Slowly, against her will, Lenora moved forward toward the woman, who was wearing early twentieth century clothing, and had a gag in her mouth. Lenora quickly rushed over to her and removed it.

"Are you okay?" she asked, feeling as if in a dream.

"No," the woman answered softly. "He's taken me. It's too late for me, but you can save yourself."

Confused, Lenora began to ask how, when she heard footsteps behind her. She turned in time to see a large object being hurled at her head. She quickly ducked out of the way and ran to the other side of the room.

The man hovered over the top of the woman on the settee. "This is what you get for overstepping your bounds." He brought the large metal object over his head and brought it down swiftly, hitting the woman over the head with a loud crunch. Lenora winced and began to sob.

Blood splattered the man's shirt and face, and he stood unmoving over the woman as if making sure he did the job. Then, he slowly fixed his gaze on Lenora and sneered. "I knew you'd come to me," he said, his voice sonorous, raspy. "They always come to me."

His lips stretched across his teeth in a sickening grin that made Lenora feel like retching. She slid along the wall, thinking that if she just worked her way slowly to the side, she could escape out the bedroom door.

He moved quickly and positioned himself between her and the door—she had nowhere to go. Panic surged within—her throat closed, her breath became hitching sobs within her chest.

He put a finger over his lips and shushed her. "There, there, little girl! I won't hurt you. I love you…I would never hurt what I love."

Lenora shook her head violently, trying to regain her strength. "You don't love me! You can't have me!" she shouted, still sobbing.

"Aw, now that's no way to talk to the future love of your life," he said in a threatening tone. "I think I need to teach you better manners."

Before she could react, he grabbed her arm, throwing her down to the ground. He positioned the metal pipe above his head and she rolled quickly, avoiding a blow to the head. She scrambled to her feet and ran to the opposite side of the room near the window. But, she realized her mistake too late—she had backed herself into a corner.

He smiled, tapping the pipe on his opposite hand as he came toward her.

"RUN!" a voice shouted from beside her. She turned to see Thaddeus standing in between her and the man, yelling at her to run. Lenora shot a quick glance at the man, who jumped back, looking startled and somewhat afraid, unmoving. Did Thaddeus have that much power?

Lenora quickly spun on her heels and ran out of the room. She bolted out the door and ran down the street as fast as she could go.

And she never looked back.

Emily opened the door, looking surprised and a bit frightened at Lenora's sudden appearance. She let her in without a word, allowing Lenora to catch her breath before recounting what had happened.

"Oh God, Lenora! What a terrible mistake you've just made!"

Lenora bowed her head. "I know. I-I just wanted to be home again…"

"I know," Emily replied, empathy in her voice, "but you really put your life in danger. You were told not to—"

A sudden pounding at the door stopped Emily short. Frowning, she rose and opened the door to find an out-of-breath and enraged Ian.

"Where is she?" he shouted. Emily opened the door wider, not saying a word. Ian burst into the room and grabbed Lenora, pulling her to her feet and shaking her wildly. "What did you think you were doing? You could have gotten yourself killed! What was going through your head!"

Lenora started to sob. "I'm sorry! I didn't mean..." She collapsed to the ground, weeping. Ian stood over her for several seconds, and then grabbed her arm and forcefully pulled her up. "Get up, we're leaving...NOW."

Emily put a hand on Ian's arm. "Ian, maybe you should settle down first. Don't be so hard on her."

"You think this is being hard on her? Believe it or not, this is restraint!" Ian's lips pursed tightly and his fists clenched. He glanced angrily at Lenora. "I was in the middle of a date, thank you very much, when Thaddeus came and told me what happened. I had to leave Clare at the movie theater—ALONE—so I could come and knock some sense into you!" He reached into his jacket and retrieved Lenora's library book. "Here, you left this at the apartment on your way out. Grab it, and let's go."

Lenora did as she was told, glancing at Emily for support. But she got none. Emily just shook her head and led them out.

Ian grabbed Lenora roughly by the arm and escorted her home. She felt like a petulant child being reprimanded by an angry father, and she was becoming angrier at his roughness the further along they went. She could feel bruises forming underneath her arm, and each time she tried to keep up, he would walk faster, causing her to lurch forward, intensifying the pain of his grip. About halfway home, she decided she was sick of it and wrenched her arm free from his grip. When he moved forward to grab her again, she staggered back and he stumbled.

"Ah!" Ian shouted angrily, as he turned and tried grabbing for her again. Lenora took off running, only to trip over a cobblestone, sending her sprawling onto the pavement. She felt a sharp sting as the skin scraped off of her knees. She winced in pain, but had little time to gain her bearings, because Ian ran at her in full force. He tried to grab her arm, but she rolled and swept a foot under his. He fell to the ground hard, issuing a loud grunt as the wind was knocked out of him.

They caused quite a scene as they struggled on the ground. Lenora tried getting to her feet, but Ian grabbed hold of her. She crawled forward, grabbing onto the cobblestone for leverage, as he scrambled forward to grab hold. Finally, he leapt on top of her, sending the breath out of her lungs. She felt fuzzy as he rolled her over, holding her down with his knees, pinning her arms to the ground.

Ian and Lenora stayed that way for several minutes—Ian pinning her to the ground, both exchanging angry glances and trying to catch their breath.

Lenora's resolve began to give way as the pain increased from Ian's knees digging into her thighs. "Ian, get off me," she said breathlessly, defeated. "I give up—I'll go home quietly…just get off me."

"No, not until you understand what it is that you did," Ian responded angrily.

"I get it," she replied, struggling under his grip. "Just take me home. I'll stay there…I've learned my lesson. Go back on your date with Clare. I'm sorry I messed up your date."

"Messed up my date!" Ian yelled, then stopped himself, calming down. "We can talk about that later. Don't you get what you did? You could have *died*, Lenora. Don't you get that? What needs to happen for you to get it, huh?" Lenora could now hear the fear in his tone. "You put your life in danger. You put Thad's *soul* in danger—ever think of that?"

Lenora's heart sunk. She hadn't thought of that. Thaddeus had become such a permanent part of her life now that sometimes she didn't think of him at all. Hot tears streamed down her face.

"God, Len! That entity in your flat wants to kill you! You thought of nothing...no one...tonight! You didn't even think of me!"

Lenora's tears streamed steadily. "I'm so sorry...I didn't think about Thaddeus...you could have lost him!"

"I could have lost you!" Ian cried. "What the hell would I have done if you died back there, huh? How am I supposed to go on without you?" He put his arms around her, nestled his head into her neck and sobbed. He brought his head up, gazing into her eyes, stroking her hair. "My world would be colorless without you." He kissed the top of her head, then her cheeks, and then sniffed, wiping tears from his face.

Ian released his grip and helped her up, smoothing out wrinkles in her clothes, wincing at the large scrapes on her knees behind the fresh holes in her jeans. "Sorry about that," he said, chuckling with embarrassment.

Neither said a word the rest of the way home.

Ian spent the rest of the weekend looking after her and helping tend to her wounds. But neither spoke of the incident, nor did they exchange much more than pleasantries. Lenora was thoroughly confused, and by the look on Ian's face, so was he.

FINAL NARRATIVE OF BARTHOLOMEW BOOTH

PART VIII: INSPECTOR FILES

Doctor's Notes:

I read aloud the newspaper article detailing Mrs. Wells Clarke's death. The patient grew calm, his eyes expressionless. He turned from me and refused to speak to me any further. I waited for nearly an hour before finally giving up. I'll return tomorrow, when we can revisit the subject.

It is the following day, and I was refused entry into the patient's cell. Bartholomew has now refused continuation of our discussions. He is greatly stressed at his impending execution. The patient has discontinued eating and drinking, and refuses to see anyone but the jailer. My fear is that yesterday was the last I will ever hear him speak. Though he must pay for his crimes, his story has greatly contributed to the study of the criminal mind.

From here on, I am relying on the thorough account taken by Hon. Gen. Inspector William Rood. The following are excerpts from his personal and unpublished accounts of the investigation. These continue where Bartholomew left off.

Inspector Wm. Rood: Personal Notes on Gentleman Killer Murders
February 15, 1916

I have just returned from interviewing Bertram Mills, the young officer who found the body of Mrs. Wells Clarke. Constable Mills is quite shaken. This is his first sight of a corpse, and it took a great deal of time to console him. However, I was able to extract his findings.

Mills indicated that Mrs. Wells Clarke's body was found much like the other Gentleman Killer victims: laid upon a bench, neatly dressed, and missing eyes. One peculiarity was that she appeared badly beaten about the face and torso. She had deep cuts and scrapes lining her arms, neck, and face.

Admiral Clarke, the husband of the deceased, also acted curiously. Rather than acting as grieving husband, he has taken to shouting orders, as if aboard one of his ships. The entire department is up in arms. Admiral Clarke was particularly vexed over his wife's attire. He insisted that the "dismal, hand-sewn frock" was not her own, and asked for it be removed immediately. He produced a silk gown and ordered several female employees to dress her. The admiral forced the entire department to swear an oath not to reveal the state of her attire. I reluctantly agreed, being it was an unimportant matter in police business.

The clothing has been placed in the evidence locker.

While at the evidence locker, I withdrew the files from the Gentleman Killer case to review the victim profiles. The similarities between the victims are that they were all found along the Cam, all with eyes removed.

But the differences are baffling, making profiling the murderer difficult. Name, age, features, date found, and social status all differ (personal note attached).

Thus far, nothing connects the victims. Three had associations with St. Adelaide's: two were residents, Mrs. Clarke was a benefactress. However, Temperance Jefferson Jones does not have connection with the almshouse whatsoever.

I placed the chart on the wall above my desk to keep them in my thoughts daily. I must catch this murderer before another young woman perishes.

Name	Age	Found	Description
Hope Ann Millar	17	Oct. 8, '10	hair: dk. brown, curly build: tall, thin status: low Address: Ft. Adelaide's
Temperance Jefferson Jones connection?	19	Nov. 15, 1912	hair: dk blonde build: petite status: mid-upper class Note: Father owns banks in town
Justina Smith	24	Aug 28, 1913	hair: copper, red build: med height, strong status: low, poor Address: Ft. Adelaide's
Faith Wells Clarke	27	Feb 15, 1916	hair: black build: med height, small frame status: upper class Note: Wife to Admiral Clarke

Patty Tea
- flour
- butter
- bacon

450

February 17, 1917

I must profess frustration at my wife Patsy's uncanny ability to see through that which daily clouds my mind. Today, as she brought in my lunch, she simply glanced at the wall and noticed something I had not before.

"Why do you only have part of the seven heavenly virtues listed on the wall?"

"What do you mean, by seven virtues?" I asked. Then, upon closer inspection, it came to me. The seven heavenly virtues are: prudence, temperance, justice, fortitude, charity, hope, and faith—I had four of those virtues on my wall!

That was it! A possible connection!

I immediately hugged my wife and left to brief the other investigators. I'm unsure of how the clue will play out, but it's a break at any rate.

Observation: Only four of the seven virtues are mentioned. Who is next?

February 18, 1917

After briefing the other investigators on the case, we agreed not to publicize the detail about the seven virtues; it might cause mass-hysteria with the general public. Moreover, it could serve to alert the murderer to change his modus operandi.

I went to St. Adelaide's to interview the staff and residents, but came out with information no different than what I already had. None of them knew Temperance Jefferson Jones, all had good things to say of Mrs. Clarke, and none knew of anyone with motive to murder the women.

Thereafter, I went to the J.P. Dunning employment office, where Mr. Dunning gave me explicit access to his files, particularly the staff list for Mrs. Clarke's charity event. He then deferred me to Mr. Bartholomew Booth, who was apparently the sole contact for Mrs. Clarke, and in charge of all staff that evening.

I excused myself from detaining Mr. Dunning, adjourning to the main office, where I could observe Mr. Booth. He seems an amiable fellow, but something about his mannerisms piques my curiosity. His eyes are shifty, and he made me feel uneasy. There is more to this fellow than meets the eye.

During the Justina Smith case, I did have Mr. Booth followed. I had a hunch that it was necessary. Though all sources reported no suspicious mannerisms or activities, something still tugged at me in regard to his character. Even so, I still had to dismiss the investigators.

My instincts tell me to keep Mr. Booth close. Though I have a general mistrust of people because of my occupation, my instincts are typically correct.

March 28, 1917

I seem to have reached a dead-end in the staff interviews. The charity event staff had nothing of significance to add regarding the evening. All admitted that it was a beautiful event and that Mrs. Clarke was indeed generous. All had an alibi, corroborated by the carriage service, who took everyone home immediately following the event. The records at St. Adelaide's also indicate that all returned simultaneously and remained at the almshouse for the rest of the evening.

I have no reason to suspect the accuracy of the records at the almshouse. The woman who manages the front office, though extremely odious, is thorough and strict. None of the residents at St. Adelaide's would have gone past her without knowledge. This, I believe.

I did employ Mr. Booth to help during the interview process. He was industrious, helpful, polite, and direct. However, he is still not above suspicion.

April 02, 1917

This morning, I went to Mrs. Clarke's home and interviewed the butler, Mr. Lloyd Compton. Since he was present the night of Mrs. Clarke's disappearance, he is listed as an official suspect.

However, I do not believe him to be the culprit; I found his sorrow deep and sincere.

Additionally, Mr. Compton has been with Mrs. Clarke's family since before she was born. He followed Mrs. Clarke to serve her after marriage, stating that he would do so "until my dying day, as she was my little 'un, and I loved her like she were mine own." Mr. Compton loved Mrs. Clarke like a daughter. No one with such affinity could inflict such horrible atrocities.

This I know.

Nothing Mr. Compton told me differed from what I heard from the staff and attendees of the charity event.

One thing of note: Mr. Compton did not particularly like Mr. Booth. When I mentioned his name, he scowled as if he just bit into a lemon.

Mr. Compton admitted that he remembered him well and remarked at Mr. Booth's industriousness when working with Mrs. Clarke, which Compton admitted was (and I quote) "His only saving grace."

I asked him what he meant by that last statement.

Compton replied that he noticed early on that Mr. Booth was strange—that he lurked in corners, and leered at one of the event staff. He wasn't sure which one, but his ogling made Compton feel sick to his stomach. He watched Mr. Booth closely all night.

His next statement I have to note verbatim: "There was something about him I didn't like or trust. Can't put my finger on it, but I trust my intuition."

I asked Compton if he could identify the ogled woman by sight. He vigorously agreed, saying that he committed her face to memory *should something happen to her.*

This statement heightens my curiosity and suspicion of Mr. Booth.

May 18, 1917

Early this morning, Mr. J.P. Dunning burst into my office, declaring that his niece went missing. It took three large officers to subdue the frantic Dunning enough to get the story from him.

His niece, Prudence Elizabeth Dunning, came to live with him and his wife to care for their children. She had been living with the Dunnings for the past few months. He made the following statement:

> "This morning, Mrs. Dunning became concerned when Prudence did not turn up for breakfast. Thinking her ill, Mrs. Dunning went to Prudence's room to check on her, only to find the room empty, and the bed never slept in. Mrs. Dunning enlisted my help, along with our children and staff, to search for Prudence. Not only did we not find her, but we became more alarmed when finding blood near her window pane."

Mr. Dunning is fully convinced that this was the work of the Gentleman Killer. I assured him that I would put my utmost and immediate attention to the matter.

After he left, I wrote her name in large block letters and pasted her name up on the wall next to the others. Her name fits the puzzle. He struck early this time.

I think he's becoming desperate, which is good for me—it means I could be closer to catching him.

May 19, 1917

Yesterday, after Mr. Dunning left, I immediately sent for the evidence boxes for each victim in the Gentleman killer case. The file clerk, Daniel Harvey, brought them immediately and helped me go through the details of each case. The last box I opened was for Faith Wells Clarke.

I held up the dress that Mrs. Clarke was found in, noticing for the first time that a name was stitched into the collar: Constance Brown.

I asked Daniel to go back into the evidence logs to see if names were sewn into the collars of the other dresses. Daniel looked through the logs, reading off the names that were sewn into the other dresses: Hope Anne Millar and Justina Smith.

This is something—another connection to at least two of the girls!

Just then, my wife Patsy came in with a basket of dinner for Daniel and me. I asked her if there would be any reason for a woman to sew her name into the collar of her dress. She confirmed that women at the almshouse sew their names into their garments to prevent them from being stolen or mixed in with another woman's clothing on wash day.

I showed her the back of the dress that was found on Mrs. Clarke, asking if it could possibly be the tailor's name, rather than the owner. She examined it closely and said that it would be neatly embroidered if it was made by a tailor. But, since the name was crudely sewn, it had to be the owner.

There was no time to lose—Daniel and I immediately made for St. Adelaide's.

When we arrived at St. Adelaide's, I had to bite my tongue from laughing at Daniel's face as he first glanced at that odious woman, Malvina Herbert. I elbowed Daniel in the ribs to silently reprimand him. His incessant sarcastic grin made my work quite difficult.

I asked Miss Herbert to look up the name Constance Brown. She found that the young woman had lived at St. Adelaide's many years hence. I asked for the file, which she assured us would take a while, so I informed her that was alright, since Daniel needed to look through the logs from the evening of the Clarke Benefit anyway.

Miss Herbert exhaled heavily several times whilst retrieving the log book, which I immediately gave to Daniel so that he could copy the names and compare them to our records from the J.P. Dunning agency. I took a chair near Miss Herbert's desk and waited while she retrieved the file on Constance Brown.

I couldn't help but notice Miss Herbert's appearance. Especially her thick, grey tongue that she used to wet her fingers to leaf through papers, leaving heavy streaks of slime on the papers as she went along. Her skin was an ashen color and hair was a wiry dark grey. Protruding from her sunken, beady eyes were bushy eyebrows that met in the middle of her forehead. She appears sickly and unhappy.

After much groaning and carrying on, Miss Herbert retrieved the file, which recorded Miss Brown's comings and goings, various employments, and a few letters of recommendation from former employers.

Miss Brown was fifteen when she came to live at the almshouse after her father committed suicide. Her two sisters, Charity and Prudence, were immediately adopted by a wealthy couple from America. Constance was not informed of her sisters' good fortune. The late headmistress of St. Adelaide's decided to spare her the heartbreak that she was considered "too old to adopt" by the couple. Instead, the headmistress personally trained Constance for employment as a governess. Most of Constance's assignments were short-lived, until she was hired at age seventeen by the baroness, Lady Fitzhugh, as nanny to her young nephew.

According to the records, Lady Fitzhugh was greatly pleased with Miss Brown's education and demeanor. The nephew was not identified, so I made a note to have Daniel conduct research to find this nephew so that I might interview him.

Shortly thereafter, Daniel ran over and showed a newspaper clipping from the file. Miss Brown was reported missing, and the Lady Fitzhugh was quoted in the article:

> "I don't know what happened to the dear girl. She was my nephew Bartholomew's nanny. We all loved her greatly, and she will be sorely missed. My maid informed me that Miss Brown was searching for her two missing sisters. I assume she went to search for them. That would be the first place I would look, if I were conducting the investigation."

Daniel looked as shocked as I felt. I immediately ordered Daniel to research Lady Fitzhugh's background and find any information that might connect her to Bartholomew Booth.

This could be the break we were looking for.

May 23, 1917

Daniel has come through for me again with a wealth of information on Lady Fitzhugh and her nephew.

He interviewed dozens of the baroness' acquaintances, all who remember her nephew, particularly Eugene and Francis Donnerhill, who were school mates of Bartholomew. Both referred to him as Booth several times throughout the conversation. Neither seemed terribly fond of Booth, and both eventually admitted (though reluctantly) that they abused him, both verbally and physically, on a regular basis. They mentioned that the abuse stopped once Lady Fitzhugh found out, but he was also abused by the other boys at school. The Donnerhills indicated that Booth was neither well-liked nor one to be well-remembered.

Eugene and Francis knew of Miss Constance Brown and mentioned that she was a beautiful girl. Both were quite aware of Mr. Booth's infatuation with her. They said that Bartholomew became jealous of anyone who talked to her, and often privately lashed out at anyone who did. They commented that they often teased him about her. Both expressed regret for their abuse of Mr. Booth, but stated that he brought it on himself. Deeper sorrow was offered at the disappearance of Miss Brown, stating that it was odd, especially since she was engaged to be married and appeared to be happy.

Daniel then went to Mr. Booth's former school and questioned the Dean, who did recall Mr. Booth. The Dean indicated that Mr. Booth was a recluse and often steered away from activity or socializing with the other boys because of the abuse he often took. However, he did indicate that Mr. Booth was incredibly intelligent and felt that the other boys were jealous of him—a fact that neither Daniel nor I agree with.

Daniel found Miss Brown's former fiancée, one Mr. Theodore Archer, who was more than willing to discuss Miss Brown's disappearance.

<u>Daniel's interview with Mr. Archer</u>

After identifying myself, Mr. Theodore Archer immediately led me into his parlor, where sat his wife Annie and two daughters, Pearl and Constance (a namesake I was surprised to learn).

I engaged in polite conversation with the family, then commenced with my business, starting with a blunt question to Mr. Archer.

> *Daniel: Did you know a Miss Constance Brown? (At the mention of Miss Brown's name, Mr. Archer became visibly saddened.)*

> *Mr. Archer: Yes, I was once engaged to Miss Brown.*

Since his wife was in such close proximity, I asked if we could speak more privately.

> *Archer: No, that's not necessary. Annie knows about Miss Brown. In fact, they were good friends—Annie's father was the private detective that helped search for Miss Brown's sisters. After Constance disappeared, Annie volunteered in the search. We fell in love a year later and named our first daughter after the lovely angel we adored.*

> *Daniel: You believe that Miss Brown disappeared, rather than simply left?*

> *Archer: Without a doubt. We were to be married the next day. We were deeply in love.*

Daniel: I mean no disrespect, but perhaps Miss Brown had a change of heart.

Annie Archer: Impossible. Constance confided to me how in love she was. She talked of her dress, the rings, the honeymoon, and their future children—notions that a woman who was about to have a change of heart would not entertain.

Daniel: Could she have run off to find her sisters?

Annie Archer: No. We found them living in America with the couple that adopted them. Constance decided it best that they live a happy life with their new family.

Mr. Archer: Yes, that's true. Constance wanted her sisters to live a life filled with love and happiness. But, we did agree that after a few years, we would write them and visit.

Daniel: If she didn't leave of her own volition, then what do you suppose happened to her?

Mr. Archer: I firmly believe she was murdered.

Daniel: But, the police found no hint of foul play in her disappearance.

Mr. Archer: That was the baroness' doing, I'm sure—to cover up for her nephew.

Daniel: Do you recall her nephew's name?

Mr. Archer: Bartholomew Booth. That boy was infatuated with Constance. He watched her from his window. Once, he gave me an evil look and drew his finger across his neck like this."

(Mr. Archer drew his index finger across his neck in a slicing motion.)

And he then mouthed the words "you are dead" at me.

Daniel: Why didn't you notify the authorities or talk to the baroness?

Mr. Archer: I urged Constance to speak to someone. But, she refused out of love for the boy. Eventually, she saw him watching her every move, questioning her, becoming violent and moody. He scared her. That's when she spoke to the baroness.

Daniel: What did the baroness say?

Mr. Archer: She thought the boy harmless, but still made the decision to send him away. She then dismissed Constance, telling her that Booth was too old for a nanny. The baroness said that to make up for the early dismissal, she would pay for our wedding and provide Constance a year's salary.

Daniel: It sounds almost too good to be true.

Mr. Archer: I thought so, too, at first. But the next day, Constance found a year's salary deposited into an account for her, and a tailor waiting to take measurements.

Daniel: How did the baroness behave after Miss Brown's disappearance?

Mr. Archer: She refused my admittance. She sent her maid—not her sidekick Graham—to tell me that Constance had gone missing. I didn't believe her, or the baroness' explanation. I was nearly arrested trying to enter the gates to the mansion. I suspected something foul and brought my theory to the police, but no one looked into the matter. I'm afraid someone was bought off.

Daniel: What was your theory?

Mr. Archer: I firmly believe that Bartholomew, upon hearing of Constance's engagement and dismissal, murdered my dear, sweet girl. I hold firm to the idea that he murdered her so that no one could have her.

End of interview.

I asked Daniel about the baroness' "right-hand man," Graham. Daniel discovered that Graham Hargrave, personal attendant and butler to the baroness, died two days after Miss Brown's disappearance.

I quickly signed an exhumation request for Graham Hargrave and a search warrant for Bartholomew's premises.

My next task was to scan the staff listing from the charity event that Daniel and I obtained from St. Adelaide's. When comparing that list with the one we received from the J.P Dunning agency, I immediately noticed a discrepancy. The J.P. Dunning list was missing a name: Charity Smeeton. I rechecked both lists twice and then paid another visit to St. Adelaide's, where I was informed that Miss Smeeton was currently at the J.P. Dunning agency for placement.

I ran back to the station and sequestered the help of two other officers. We then went directly to Mrs. Wells Clarke's former home, where I asked the butler, Lloyd, to accompany us for further questioning.

The carriage stopped near the agency. The officers stayed with Lloyd to record what he had to say. I went into the agency on pretense to see if Booth had further information for me. I waited while he conducted an interview with the young lady, who I assumed to be Miss Smeeton. I listened carefully to determine if it was Miss Smeeton, and when I didn't receive confirmation, dropped a pen upon the floor. When the young lady passed, I picked up the pen and caught up to her.

"Your pen, Miss, I think you dropped it," I offered.

The lady shook her head and assured me that it was not her pen.

I introduced myself, and she shook my hand, introducing herself as Miss Charity Smeeton. Having positive identification, I offered to escort her out. I excused myself, telling Mr. Booth that I had urgent business and had to leave. He did not seem suspicious.

I walked Miss Smeeton to the end of the block and then returned to the coach. Lloyd, the butler, seemed highly agitated, stating that the girl I had escorted out of the office was the very one that Mr. Booth ogled the night of the charity event. I asked if he was absolutely certain, to which he replied (and I quote):

"Yes, most certain—one cannot mistake the paleness of those blue eyes…they're unforgettable."

I ordered the carriage turned round, and we stopped Miss Smeeton, informing her that she was in grave danger and that she was to accompany us. She at first was reluctant, but upon seeing my officers, consented. We secured her at the home of a good friend, who assured me that Miss Smeeton would be cared for until the danger passed.

I asked Miss Smeeton about Mr. Booth. She had nothing but good things to say of him, stating that he was helpful in her search to find gainful employment. I ceased that line of questioning should she become curious and report to Mr. Booth. Instead, I carried on a polite conversation about everything under the sun, and then excused myself, but not before telling her she was not to leave until further notice.

May 25, 1917

Today, there was a blow to our investigation. The magistrate says that there isn't enough information to gain a search warrant for the premises of Bartholomew Booth. I have enlisted Daniel's help to search through our files and find evidence of something more concrete for the judge. I am getting more nervous by the day. Prudence Dunning has been missing for eight days, and the trail grows colder daily.

I am going to instigate a search-party for her tomorrow morning and involve J.P. Dunning and his family. I will extend an invitation to Mr. Booth so that I might observe him for the day.

May 26, 1917

We conducted a search of the area for traces of Prudence Dunning. Though I was certain we would not find her, it was an opportunity for me to observe Bartholomew Booth.

Yesterday, I went to the Chief of Detectives and gained permission for the search, telling him of my suspicions and plans. The chief felt that this was a wasteful use of his forces, but agreed to it nonetheless—he was feeling the pinch from the public as well.

J.P. Dunning took less time to convince. I urged Dunning to enlist the help of all the men he could find. Taking the cue, Dunning asked Mr. Booth to help in the search. Mr. Booth replied that someone needed to man the office, which he was glad to do. To my great relief, Dunning became incensed, insisting that his niece's disappearance was more important—that the office would be closed for the day, and threatened immediate dismissal should Booth refuse. Booth looked defeated.

As I suspected, the search rendered nothing. Dunning left disheartened, so I tried reassuring him that not finding her in the fields or near the river was a good sign.

The search did allow close observation of Mr. Booth. Daniel and I included Booth on our search team. At first, Booth appeared skittish and afraid. I knew that for us to glean any information from him, we needed to gain his trust. So, I enlisted Daniel's help. I introduced Booth to Daniel, stating that I knew no one as thorough and efficient as Booth—that his service today was invaluable. The praise seemed to puff Booth up a bit, and he was affable all day.

Since Booth had trust issues with me, Daniel's task was to befriend Booth to gain his trust. Once Booth became comfortable with him, Daniel asked what he knew of Prudence Dunning. At first, Booth was enigmatic, offering little information. But, when Daniel mentioned (offhand) that no one even knew the color of her eyes, Booth immediately offered "gray, with flecks of pale blue." This distinction made Daniel and I exchange curious looks.

I wrote it down for future reference.

As we took a break mid-afternoon, we each sitting atop three separate stumps alongside a farmer's field, I mentioned my need to ask Dunning what color his niece's hair was so that we knew what to look for.

Booth, who was sitting not too far from us, said nonchalantly that her hair was "a soft honey brown that shimmers in the sun like waves of golden wheat."

Daniel's look of concern caused me to instantly change the subject (for I didn't want Booth to catch on to us). I quickly jumped off of my seat and declared that Booth's mention of wheat reminded me that I was starving. I invited both to join me for ale and bread.

Booth nearly declined, but Daniel (the good boy) clasped his arm around him and said that I knew a place that served the best ale and bread in town.

We three took refreshment together in town. The entire time, I thought of how this man could potentially be the one who has murdered all of these young women. I couldn't help thinking of my daughter and how I would feel...what I would do...if something like this would ever happen to her. These women were someone's daughter, sister, or wife. I was taking refreshment with a man who potentially took a beloved life from someone.

I've never felt so sick in my life.

May 26, 1917

Daniel came to my office early this morning, looking haggard and tired. He said that after sharing a pint with that sick Mr. Booth, he couldn't sleep. So, he came to the office last night and poured over the evidence trays.

He claimed to have found the information needed for the search warrant for Mr. Booth's flat.

If ever I felt like hugging a man, it was right then.

Prior to yesterday's search, Mr. Dunning brought in all of his personal backlogs from the past ten years. He forgot to consult Mr. Booth, and thankfully so. On a whim, Daniel decided to look only at the records for the years that our victims were murdered.

- Hope Anne Millar—employed through J.P. Dunning agency.
- Temperance Jefferson Jones – fiancée, Albert Lynch, employed through J.P. Dunning agency. The file noted dates that she came into the agency with Mr. Lynch.
- Justina Smith—employed through J.P. Dunning agency.
- Faith Wells Clarke—used J.P. Dunning agency to employ staff for her charity benefit.
- Prudence Elizabeth Dunning—niece to owner, J.P. Dunning.

I couldn't believe my eyes! Every victim had a connection of some kind to Mr. Booth through the J.P. Dunning agency.

Daniel already drew up the paper requesting a search warrant, which he immediately dispatched to the magistrate.

Additional news today: the body of Graham Hargrave was exhumed. The coroner's report indicated that Mr. Graham died of a stab wound to the neck. We may not have connection to Mr. Booth on that murder; however, it does open a new investigation.

May 27, 1917

We got him! We captured the Gentleman Killer!

Once I had search warrant in hand, I immediately assembled a team and briefed them on the case. Since Mr. Booth was at work (where I had posted two men across the street to watch him), we had the landlord let us in. We began our search, and at first, turned up nothing. Booth's flat was clean—it was neat and tidy, and there was no evidence to incriminate him.

I felt a near sense of defeat, until one of the men saw an oddity in the wall near the east window. He felt along the paneling and discovered a latch. The officer depressed the latch, which popped the paneling open, exposing a door. There was a lock on the door, which meant we were not able to enter, according to the search warrant parameters. However, we were in luck. One of my men, being ever so clumsy, accidentally fell upon the door, his hatchet running clean through it. We looked in the gaping hole and saw Prudence Dunning, tied to a chair, gag in her mouth, terrified expression on her face.

We tore down the door and retrieved the terrified girl, taking her immediately to the hospital.

My men and I immediately dispatched for the J.P. Dunning agency, where Mr. Booth was working quietly at his desk. He had no idea.

He greeted me cheerfully, to which I replied by ordering my men to apprehend him. Booth screamed, sending Mr. Dunning out into the office.

At first, Dunning was confused and demanded to know what was going on. I explained that we were arresting Mr. Booth and why.

Mr. Dunning looked as if he were about to faint. He stood for several seconds, silently staring at Mr. Booth, mouth agape. Then, he quietly walked over to him, and punched him square in the jaw. Then, he asked to see his niece.

My men took Dunning to hospital, where he and his family were reunited with Miss Prudence.

In the meantime, I had the distinct pleasure of escorting Mr. Booth to headquarters, where he was formally charged with the kidnapping of Miss Dunning.

Now I must get him to confess to the rest of the murders, which I know him guilty of.

May 28, 1917

This morning, I went to see Miss Dunning to inquire about her general health, and to ask for her statement. Upon first appearance, one would never know that she had been through a full week of torment. Surprisingly, she offered her story without hesitation.

Miss Dunning's Account

> *I met Mr. Booth when visiting my uncle at his agency. I begged my uncle for a small job around the office, but he refused. It was Mr. Booth who vied for me, saying that the experience would enrich my life and strengthen my character. Uncle J.P. finally relented, saying I could work two days each week.*

> *Mr. Booth trained me in various jobs and always treated me kindly.*

> *One day, Mr. Booth said that I had made a gross error on several forms. He showed me the error and then put me to work to fix the forms since they were due the next morning. It soon became apparent that I would have to stay late. Mr. Booth offered to escort me home, to which my uncle agreed.*

> *When we finished our work, Mr. Booth hailed a carriage, which drove directly to my uncle's home. Mr. Booth walked me to the door and saw me safely inside. I spoke with my uncle briefly and then retired to my room. Just as I started*

drifting to sleep, I heard tapping at my window. It was Mr. Booth.

I lifted the window pane, cutting my finger in the process and getting blood all over my gown and the floor. I asked Booth the reason for his visit.

He said that I left my parasol at the office, and he had come to return it to me. It was the parasol I borrowed from my aunt, and I knew she would be angry with my negligence. I hastened quickly to meet Mr. Booth at the back door by the kitchen.

Mr. Booth stood at the bottom of the steps, refusing to come up. He said that it was improper for a gentleman to enter a lady's home so late at night. In addition, he did not want to anger his boss. I joined Mr. Booth at the bottom step, where we had a pleasant enough exchange. He ripped a portion of cloth from his own shirt to attend my wound.

When I went to take from him my parasol, he moved it back, and I tripped forward. He caught me in his arms and then placed something over my face. Everything went black.

I awoke in the dark, in a foreign place. I tried moving, but my arms and legs were tied, and I had something stuffed in my mouth that had a foul odor to it. I had lay there for several hours, in my own filth, until the next morning when Mr. Booth entered.

At first, I was relieved to see him, thinking that he would help me. However, I knew by the look on his face that he would not. I tried to scream, but the cloth in my mouth prevented it. Mr. Booth said that if I was quiet, he would take the cloth out and explain the situation. I immediately complied—the rag tasted and smelled quite foul. He removed the cloth, which was a great relief.

Mr. Booth told me that he loved me and knew that in time I would love him. He said that after a while, as I grew to love him and accept my station, I would be granted small freedoms. When he trusted fully that I loved him, we would marry and live life anew.

I became frightened and started to cry. He became angry and hit my face very hard several times. I vowed thereafter never to cry in his presence again. I think that saved me.

Though Mr. Booth took good care of me, I was daily afraid for my life. He fed me good meals and treated me with kindness. However, it was humiliating when he attended me to my toilet and dress. He forced me to read romance novels, after which he would quiz me—asking for my feelings on the plot, and if the hero reminded me of him. I never connected the hero to Booth, but I dared not say so. After my fourth day of captivity, I began comparing the hero to Booth, which seemed to satisfy him.

Mr. Booth never struck me again. Nor did he instigate violence against me during the rest of my captivity. There was an entire day that I was left alone, which he later informed me was because he joined a search party, who was looking for me. That evening, I did cry bitterly for my family, whom I missed terribly.

Shortly thereafter, I was happily rescued.

Miss Dunning has agreed to testify against Mr. Booth. Despite the fact that he treated her kindly during her captivity, it will not help his case.

I am still certain that Mr. Booth is the Gentleman Killer, and am determined that he will confess. Daniel discovered one of Booth's previous professors, a Mr. James Theodore Kirkland, who teaches psychology at Cambridge University and is a practicing psychologist.

Professor Kirkland feels that he can use his familiarity with Booth to obtain the confession. I hope he is right.

THIRTY-FIVE

The air was grey, misty, and heavy. Droplets of moisture ran down the window pane like tears, carving rivers on the hazy window. Leaves, covered in mist-laden dew, draped unmoving and heavy on the trees.

It had rained non-stop for the past three days and Lenora was growing weary of the grey wetness. She sighed and shifted in her seat, not wanting to watch the movie adaptation of Shakespeare's "Othello." They had been studying the play for the past two weeks and now the teacher was showing the film version as a post-exam treat. But, she had already seen this version and wasn't in the mood to see it again.

Lenora was having difficulty concentrating; her mind drifted between subjects. She was still confused about what happened between her and Ian when they scuffled on the pavement. His eyes seemed to express more than what he conveyed. She thought of talking to him about it when they were alone, but there was a different sort of tension in the air that prevented her.

Tom's return was definitely welcome—his presence eliminated the uncomfortable glances and thick silence that passed between Lenora and Ian for three days. Once Tom came home, Ian immediately left to see Clare, which Lenora had mixed feelings about. It was great to have Ian gone for a while, but she felt ill whenever thinking about him with another girl. She had to accept it and move on, she knew, but it wasn't easy.

Then there was the apartment entity. Ian did make Lenora tell Tom what happened, and he was furious, as she knew he would be. However, Ian downplayed the situation and it eventually boiled down to nothing.

She blamed her sudden bravery on her reading of Bartholomew's story. Reading about his human side made it difficult to be afraid of him. At the apartment, the entity was scary, but his life story was compelling. Fundamentally, he was just a human thirsting for love and affection from someone…anyone. She empathized with that part of him. Her dad argued that Bartholomew's circumstances and treatment by others nurtured the monster within—that had he been treated with love and kindness, Bartholomew would not have been lead down a path to murder. Ian disagreed.

Lenora spent the better part of Sunday listening to the "nature versus nurture" argument between the two men. She wasn't sure what to believe.

The recent revelation in her reading about the seven heavenly virtues seemed significant, however. She brought this to Tom's attention, who then brought it up at the following CSP meeting.

"That makes sense!" Amelia exclaimed. "I did some digging after Ian told us about your picture-taking fiasco at school." Lenora blushed. "Kate's real name is Charisse Katherine. She goes by Kate to avoid confusion in her family. She's named after an aunt that's still living. Cherisse is a form of the name Charity." She smiled apologetically. "I'm sorry, Lenora."

"So, the entity appears to want to possess the seven heavenly virtues," Ian added. "As it appears, he 'possessed' only five of them," he glanced at the inspector's notes that Lenora had brought in, "six, if you include Prudence, who died after Bartholomew was hanged. So, that leaves charity as the virtue he's missing."

Lenora nodded. "Yes, but I don't understand what that has to do with me. My name is Lenora, not Charity."

"Your name means 'light'—but part of the name meaning is charitable, giving," Tom explained, groaning.

"So, it's either me or Kate that dies to complete his collection?" It was a rhetorical question that no one answered. Lenora already knew what her choice would be.

One good that came from the meeting was Tom's announcement that the spiritual cleanser would be available this coming Saturday.

It couldn't be soon enough.

Lenora exhaled loudly.

"Bloody boring, isn't it?"

Lenora started from her reverie and looked at the girl sitting to her right. It was Kate, who was, surprisingly, smiling at her. Lenora figured after the picture-taking and screaming debacle, Kate would want nothing to do with her.

Lenora smiled weakly. "Yeah, I saw this lame movie last year."

Kate laughed quietly and extended a small box, gesturing for Lenora to take it. Lenora opened it and found an array of chocolates. She looked hesitantly at Kate, who nodded at the box. "Go on, take one," she offered quietly.

Lenora took a chocolate and handed the box back to the girl. "Thanks," she whispered.

"You're welcome—"

"Kate! Lenora! Pay attention or you'll be after school!"

"Yes, ma'am," Lenora and Kate replied simultaneously to their annoyed teacher.

Kate smiled surreptitiously at Lenora, rolled her eyes, and faced the front of the room.

Lenora did the same, smiling as she tried to pay attention to the movie. But, it wasn't long before her smile faded. She knew that Kate was reaching out to her—an unspoken olive branch for Lenora's past behavior. Lenora wanted so badly to accept it—to welcome Kate's friendship.

But associating with Lenora would prove too costly for Kate. The entity would use Lenora to get to Kate, hunt her down, and destroy her. And, without the backing of CSP, Kate would unquestionably perish.

The sound of rustling paper on the desk caught Lenora's attention. She looked down in time to see Kate slipping a folded piece of paper on the desk. Lenora unfolded it and read the short note Kate had written: *Wanna hang with me -n- Olivia after school?*

Lenora glanced at Kate, who motioned toward her right. Olivia nodded enthusiastically.

*Of course, if I was with Kate, I **could** keep her safe.*

And, against her better judgment, Lenora nodded her assent, agreeing to meet them on the front steps of the school, after last bell.

After school, Lenora sat on the top step, in front of the school, waiting for Olivia and Kate to show. She had been waiting a while and began to wonder if this was just a joke…a way for Kate to get back at her for being such a moron.

Did they trick me? Was this just a joke to them? A prank on the weird girl?

Lenora sighed, picked up her books, and stood up. She should have known. Perhaps this was better, since it would put Kate in danger anyway.

Just as she was leaving, Kate caught Lenora's arm. "Wait!" She worked to catch her breath. "I'm sorry we're late, but Olivia and I were kept after in Biology for passing notes."

Lenora looked at Olivia, who was nodding in agreement. "Oh." Lenora felt a bit guilty that she didn't give them the benefit of the doubt. "No problem. I was just studying for the English quiz on Friday," she lied.

"Cool, because we really wanted to—" Kate paused mid-sentence, gazing past Lenora's shoulder, smile fading. "Hey, that guy standing over there? He's the reason we were passing notes."

Lenora followed Kate's gaze, seeing a shadow of a figure through the fog. Something about the figure seemed familiar to her.

"Nicholas?" Lenora whispered, incredulous.

"You know that guy?"

"Yeah, he's sort-of my ex-boyfriend..." she trailed off, feeling hazy, as if she were in a dream.

"Oy! Earth to Lenora!" Olivia waved a hand in front of Lenora's face, interrupting the spell.

Lenora shook her head. "Sorry. He left almost three weeks ago... for a job in another town." She frowned. "He said he wouldn't be coming back...I don't know what he's doing here."

"We should go find out," Olivia said, taking Lenora by the arm and dragging her toward Nicholas.

As they approached, Nicholas held his gaze on Lenora. A knot formed in her stomach, but she steeled herself, determined not to let his unannounced visit get to her.

"What are you doing here, Nicholas?" Lenora asked, trying to sound indifferent.

"Well, hello to you too!" Nicholas replied, visibly amused.

"I wasn't expecting to see you here," she shrugged, still feigning disinterest. "You said you weren't coming back." Lenora felt a sudden triumph. She was not going to let him weaken her resolve—especially after the pain he caused when he left her. But even now, she felt that delicious giddiness she always experienced in his presence. She inwardly cursed herself for even allowing it.

"I'm here on business," he explained. "My company sent me here to set up a book fair. I'm only here for a couple of weeks." Nicholas smiled warmly at her, and then turned his attention to the two girls standing behind her, each with silly grins on their faces. "Are you going to introduce me to your friends?"

"Oh," Lenora blushed, "Nicholas, this is Olivia and Kate." Without looking at them, she motioned to both girls behind her.

Nicholas moved around Lenora and shook both girls' hands. "I'm genuinely pleased to meet you both. Any friend of Lenora's is a friend of mine," he said politely.

Olivia giggled uncontrollably and Kate snorted, both unable to respond. Lenora rolled her eyes, not knowing whether to be embarrassed at their silliness or irritated at him for getting to them too.

Nicholas touched Lenora's arm, sending a warm vibration through her. "I was wondering if you had time for tea this afternoon?" he whispered in her ear.

Lenora's heart pounded heavily—she felt warm, lightheaded. Instantly, she wanted to run into his arms and tell him how much she'd missed him.

"Lenora?" Nicholas asked, interrupting her stupor.

"Sorry," Lenora blushed again, inwardly remonstrating herself. "Actually, I already have plans with Olivia and Kate."

"Oh," Nicholas sounded disappointed. "Perhaps tomorrow, then?"

"Maybe," Lenora responded indifferently. "I'll have to look at my schedule."

"Oh," Nicholas replied, sounding bewildered. "Yes, I'm sorry….I didn't think— "

Lenora nodded and turned slowly around, walking away from Nicholas. She couldn't continue the conversation—any longer, and she would have given in. She felt numb.

What does he want with me? What if he just wants to be friends? I don't think I can take that. I just can't let him hurt me again.

"Bye, then," Nicholas uttered, sounding confused.

Without looking back, Lenora lifted her hand and waved.

After they had walked a few paces in silence, Olivia ran out in front of Lenora, stopping her. "Are you daft?"

"What do you mean?" Lenora asked, confused.

"You turned *that* down for us?" She nodded her head in Nicholas's direction.

"But, we had plans," Lenora reasoned. "And, he just can't come back, waltzing in, and thinking I'm at his beck and call."

"Go with Nicholas—we can hang out tomorrow." Olivia responded. "Besides, the guy looks heartbroken…like he has something important to say."

Lenora looked back at Nicholas, who wore an expression of misery.

"Yes, go!" Kate chimed in. "We'll meet up tomorrow."

"And, you had better share every last detail!" Olivia added, pushing Lenora in Nicholas' direction.

Lenora smiled at the girls. "Fine, I'll go. I'll see you tomorrow then," she said as she walked gingerly toward Nicholas.

"No skimping on details!" Olivia shouted, joining Kate in a fit of wild giggling.

This is so awkward.

Lenora looked across the table at Nicholas, who gazed at her intently. He looked like he had something to say, yet said nothing, and it was making her uncomfortable. She shifted her gaze away from him and looked out the window at the people in Market Square.

The entire walk to the tea shop was silent—he was uncommunicative, and she didn't know what to say. She asked him how he was and he muttered that he was fine, but offered nothing more. And, when she asked him what he had been up to, he started to say something, but shook his head and stared straight ahead. Lenora withered—he just wasn't the same, and she wondered what she did wrong.

Finally, unable to take the silence, she sat up and stared directly at him. "So, did you ask me out to tea to ignore me the whole time, or are you actually going to talk to me?"

He lowered his gaze and shook his head. "I'm sorry. I've been wavering all afternoon, and I'm still unsure of how…. wise …it is to be with you."

"What do you mean by that?" Lenora challenged.

He smiled at her softly. "Not that being with you is regretful—I want nothing more." He paused, sighing heavily. "It's just that breaking my promise may prove unwise."

"Promise?" She asked, thoroughly confused. "What promise? And, to whom?"

He shook his head. "I really shouldn't say—and it isn't important. What's important…"

"What do you mean, not important?" she asked, furious. "Who said that you shouldn't be with me?"

"Please, Lenora, I didn't come here to point fingers. I came here to—"

"Tell me!" Lenora pounded her fist on the table, sending her spoon flying. They both watched, shocked, as the spoon landed unnoticed on someone else's table. They both looked at each other and burst out laughing.

"I'm sorry," Lenora said after the laughter had subsided. "I'm sorry for the outburst," she corrected, "but I do have the right to know who told you not to see me anymore."

Nicholas's smile faded as he leaned back in his chair, carefully deliberating on whether to tell her or not. "For the record, I don't think any good can come of me telling you." Lenora began to protest, but he held his hand up to stop her. "However, I will tell all if you promise that this stays between us. Okay?"

He waited for her silent assent and then continued. "After that little ordeal in the park with Ian, I went to talk to him—to smooth things out. I'll have you know that he was completely civil and we had a good discussion. He apologized for jumping to conclusions in the park, but assured me that it had everything to do with trying to protect you rather than expressing animosity toward me."

He looked at her briefly and smiled affectionately. "I don't blame him, you know. I would protect you with every fiber of my being, if I could. So, I understand where he's coming from, and told him as much. I assured him that I had nothing but good intentions and that I cared for you deeply—that I was not interested in taking advantage." He paused and took a sip of tea. "I also promised him that I would take things slowly. Altogether, our conversation was congenial, and we both left with a better understanding of one another."

"When did this discussion happen?" Lenora asked.

"Immediately after he brought you to hospital–I hid around the corner of the waiting room until I saw that your father was in with you and Ian was alone. I sat next to him, figuring that a public place would help keep his temper in check. I was right." He chuckled and told her how Ian looked visibly angry, but kept looking around at all the people, causing him to lower his tone to avoid a scene.

"We were supposed to meet that night—you never showed up!" Lenora said, visibly upset.

"I know, and I'm sorry for that," he said remorsefully. "Remember in the park, how I was limping and in pain? Well, I had such terrible pain that day that I had to go to hospital myself. And, I was so hazy with all the drugs they gave me that I slept through the night and into the next day. Monday, I had to board the train at five in the morning and travel to London for work."

He looked at Lenora, who still appeared upset. "I would have called or sent a note, but I don't have your number or address. And, I was too ill to chase either down—a mistake that, believe me, will never happen again." He tilted his head and smiled—she didn't seem to buy it. He laughed softly. "I see that I have some work to do to earn your forgiveness."

"You still haven't explained the promise you made to stay away from me."

"Oh, that." He exhaled in frustration.

"Yes, *that*." She crossed her arms and sat back in her chair. "I'm waiting. Please, explain."

"I came back from London that following Thursday," he began.

Lenora frowned. "Thursday, but you didn't—"

He held up his hand. "Please, just let me get through this." Lenora pursed her lips, nodding. "Thursday evening, I was heading to your place—with flowers, a card, and a gift. I was intercepted by Ian, who asked me—very rudely, by the way—where the *hell* I had been. He told me that you were incredibly depressed and thought that I had left you. I gave him the same explanation I just gave you, and he didn't buy it…just like you."

He shook his head and raked a hand through his hair. He told Lenora that Ian described to him how devastated she had been all week—how his absence had completely broken her heart. Ian explained the level of Lenora's depression, and berated him for not calling or sending her a note of explanation. Ian pointed out that if Nicholas had a brain, he would have gone to hell and back for her. Ian ended his rant by telling Nicholas that he didn't deserve someone as special as Lenora.

"That really stopped me cold, Lenora," Nicholas said sadly. "He was right. How could I claim to love you and endeavor to deserve you if I didn't even bother trying? I spent the week thinking about it, and decided that I needed to let you go so that you could be happy. That afternoon, I went to your apartment to explain. Ian was there. I told him what I had decided. He said that if I did let you go, I was to stay away from you—permanently."

"That...jerk!" Lenora nearly yelled. "As soon as I see him, I'm going to—"

"You'll do nothing," Nicholas argued. "Ian is just trying to protect you. Don't be angry at him for being your friend." He leaned forward and put his hand on hers. "Feel as you will, but he did nothing but point out the obvious and try to protect you from future sadness."

Lenora, still reeling, sighed and nodded her head. "Alright, I won't say anything. But, if he starts in, I'm going to let him have it!"

Nicholas laughed and squeezed her hand. "Still the same girl that I fell in love with."

Lenora started to say something, but checked herself. *Wait a minute.* "Did you just say that you *love* me?" she asked incredulously.

His smile faded and his face took on a serious expression. "Utterly, infallibly, completely—in love with you," he said, tears filling his eyes. "I have never loved anyone as much as I love you, and it's so overwhelming that I can't bear to be without you. That's why I've come back—because I am lost without you." He gazed deeply, imploringly, into her eyes.

Lenora felt completely stunned—and superbly happy at the same time. Her eyes filled with tears as she stared into the eyes of the man she loved. She knew—from the moment she laid eyes on him—that she was in love with him. But, she said nothing for fear of scaring him off. But now, she felt completely elated.

"Lenora, your silence is killing me."

Lenora started from her daze. "I'm sorry Nicholas! I am just so happy. I've loved you for so long. Your telling me that you love me seems...surreal."

Nicholas came around the table, pulled her out of the chair, and held her tightly. "It's going to be different from here on, I promise," he whispered, kissing her cheeks.

They stood like that–hugging and kissing each other—until the waitress came by and let them know that they were causing a scene. They returned to their seats, laughing and wiping tears.

THIRTY-SIX

"**G**et out of here!" Olivia exclaimed in disbelief. "That only happens in movies."

"Well, believe it or not, that's what happened. I'm so happy!" Lenora couldn't help spilling the beans about what happened with Nicholas—this was the first time she had friends to confide in since moving to Cambridge, and it felt good.

"That's so romantic!" Kate clasped her hands together in front of her. "And, he's so positively gorgeous!"

"Yeah," Olivia agreed, "where did you meet him, and does he have friends or brothers?" All three girls burst out laughing.

Kate and Olivia were there after school, waiting for Lenora and eager to learn about the previous day with Nicholas. They went to Market Square, bought coffees, and sat along the rock wall in front of King's college, gossiping and laughing, until Kate's watch went off in a series of strange and erratic beeps.

"What in the world is that?" Lenora asked, covering her ears.

"It's my watch," Kate said matter-of-factly and then stuck out her right arm to show them. It was an eclectic watch, with a multi-colored, bejeweled band. The large, round clock face was bordered with multi-colored rhinestones, and the clock face was orange with oversized numbers and showed different moon phases, the half-moon currently glowing. "It's a moon-phase watch," she explained, "my mum is Pagan, and the moon phases are important. Mum used her synthesizer to record the chimes in my alarm. I like it, actually."

Lenora was stunned that she hadn't noticed it before, it stood out like a sore thumb. "It's definitely different," she said, trying to sound complimentary.

"Thanks," Kate responded appreciatively.

The girls started walking toward the middle of the square. Once they reached the center, they said their adieus and walked separate ways.

"Where have you been?" Ian asked angrily, hands on hips, as Lenora walked in the door.

"Out with friends," she said in an equally angry tone. "What's it to you?"

"Tonight's the spiritual cleansing," he explained.

"Oh," she said apologetically, "I forgot, sorry. I went with Kate and Olivia to Market Square—we had coffees and just chatted—it was fun!" she tried to sound cheery so that Ian changed his tone with her.

"Oh, hey, that does sound like fun!" Ian's demeanor softened. He sat listening, hand resting on his chin, to Lenora's recount of the afternoon. He seemed genuinely interested in her story, laughing at the right spots, asking the right questions—it was unnatural.

Of course, she left out the part about seeing Nicholas—she did not intend to bring it up until absolutely necessary. She was still angry at Ian for interfering in her personal life, and felt it best to talk to him after she'd cooled off. Nicholas was right—he was only trying to protect her, and she promised that she would try to be mindful of that.

They made dinner together and set the table in preparation for Tom's arrival after work. The plan was to eat a quick dinner and then assemble at their old apartment. Lenora couldn't wait—tonight the apartment would finally be rid of the entity. She couldn't wait to sleep in her own bed.

In the meantime, Lenora lay on the couch, reading the last bit of journal she had left. Though she was excited to get rid of the entity, she felt slightly sorry to leave Bartholomew Booth.

FINAL NARRATIVE OF BARTHOLOMEW BOOTH

Part IX: Death of a Madman

Doctor's Notes:

It took several days to obtain the confession from the patient, Bartholomew Booth. I was able to gain the confession that Inspector Rood needed to charge Booth with the murder of one man and five women: Graham Hargrave, Constance Brown, Hope Anne Millar, Temperance Jefferson Jones, Justina Smith, and Faith Wells Clarke. He was also charged with the kidnapping of Prudence Elisabeth Dunning.

I informed Mr. Booth that he almost got his seven virtues, but only ended with five.

After several moments of tension-filled silence, he smirked. "I will have my seven."

"How? You are sentenced to death, Bartholomew," I reminded him.

"Death cannot impede my cause."

"What cause is that?" I asked.

"Putting an end to false virtue," he said. "None merited the virtuous names they were given."

"But, I thought you only meant to love them—not to determine their merit."

"Yes," he chuckled, "I wanted to love them, and I wanted them to love me. Loving me would have cured them of their imperfections, restored their virtue."

"But they already loved their families, friends, and fiancées—isn't that enough?"

"No, they need to love the unlovable for their sins to be forgiven."

~~~~~~~~~~~~~~

Bartholomew Booth stood trial and was found guilty. He was sentenced to death by hanging, which will take place tomorrow afternoon. The patient refuses to speak with me or anyone else, and has asked to remain in solitary confinement for the duration of his sentence.

June 23, 1917

Today, Bartholomew Booth was hanged for the crimes he committed. He said nothing as he walked on the gallows, but simply closed his eyes while they placed the black hood over his head. His death was quick, but his torment, I am sure, will follow his soul.

December 24, 1917

I have just read some disturbing news. Both girls—Charity Smeeton and Prudence Elisabeth Dunning are dead. They both died last night.

I saw the article for Miss Smeeton, which indicated that she had committed suicide by hanging. I immediately dispatched to St. Adelaide's and interviewed her close friends. They said that after the hanging of Mr. Booth, Charity had become depressed to the point of no return. The ladies also mentioned that they noticed Charity diminishing into insanity—walking the halls at night and talking to the air invisible.

The ladies admitted to keeping watch of her, and noted that she constantly entreated them to make "him" stop—that "he" was trying to kill her. Being that Miss Smeeton never left the almshouse, they were utterly confused and simply placated her momentarily by promising to help.

Miss Prudence Elisabeth Dunning's story differs. The papers mention that she was found lying in the street by J.P Dunning. She was clutching a purple silk ribbon.

I visited with Mr. J.P. Dunning, who told me that Prudence had been acting strange as of late—walking in her sleep and talking aloud in her room to no one. Her diary contained what Dunning felt was proof of her delusional state. She wrote daily that "he" was there, haunting her, telling her evil things, and asking her to commit acts against her moral spirit.

Inspector Rood said that Mr. Booth's former flat was broken into the previous night, and that nothing of note was taken. However, he firmly believed it to be Miss Dunning—a torn piece of fabric matching the dress she wore the night of her death was found in the flat. He said that victims often revisited the scene of the crime, particularly if they are plagued with it.

There is a bit of insecurity gnawing at the back of my mind. The deaths of these women occurred exactly six months to the day that Mr. Booth was hanged to death. Both women would have been the sixth and seventh victims. Coincidence? Did Mr. Booth acquire his seven virtues beyond the grave?

I am perplexed, and terribly troubled.

THIRTY-SEVEN

"I just feel badly for him, Ian. The poor guy didn't have a chance in life...at all."

"He had every chance in the world," Ian said unsympathetically. "Things could have come out differently for him if he would have made better choices. You can't just decide to kill someone because they refuse to love you."

He had a point.

Lenora leaned on the windowsill, surveying the activity in her old apartment. She felt incredibly nervous about tonight—not only was she going to be around the entity, she was also witnessing a spiritual cleansing for the first time. Lenora inhaled the crisp, cool autumn air that came through the window, trying hopelessly to relax.

"Is it painful for the spirits?" she asked no one in particular. "The spiritual cleansing, that is?"

Ian burst out laughing. "How old *are* you?" he chuckled and then noticed Lenora's hands balling into tight fists. "Sorry," he offered, pursing his lips tightly. "It's peaceful for them."

"Thanks," Lenora uttered tightly. "You could have just said that."

Tom's aggravated sigh and glare put a stop to further conversation, so Lenora continued watching in silence. Everyone from the CSP team had arrived two hours before Lenora and Tom. Lenora was impressed with the team's efficient system.

Maggie and Joe already had all the equipment set up, and were currently testing to ensure that all was running smoothly. Tom walked around with Rose and took notes as she gave her first impressions of each room, while Phillip, Amelia, and Tabitha tested EVP recorders and thermal detectors. Ian and Emily were huddled together in a corner, talking secretively.

Lenora didn't care for that.

Stop it, you have a boyfriend, she thought, unconvincingly. At that moment, she overheard someone speaking about the seven virtues and felt compelled to listen in on the conversation.

"...so he'll know how to use that bit of information?" Phillip asked Tom.

"I'm positive," Tom replied firmly.

"Can I ask?" Lenora interrupted, "Have you discovered the significance of the seven virtues, and what it has to do with me?"

"I'll tell you!" a booming voice roared from the doorway. Everyone turned to see a lofty figure standing in the entry. Lenora thought he looked like a biker. He was wearing all black from head to toe. He had on a long black leather duster jacket and a black leather cowboy hat. The hat was pinched up on the sides and had a wide black band adorned with a skull and crossbones concho. Dark brown, curly hair fell to the middle of his back, and his goatee was divided in two, like inverted horns.

He took his coat off in a flourish—reminding Lenora of an ostentatious magician—hung it on the rack, and then sauntered into the room. Removing his coat revealed a black leather vest, and to Lenora's surprise, a green t-shirt underneath. His jeans were black and a long silver chain hung on his side. His black leather boots made a sound as if he was wearing spurs (Lenora checked...he was not).

He took a turn around the room, stopping briefly in front of each person, surveying them with one eyebrow raised, murmuring to himself. He stopped in front of Ian and lingered at length. He leveled a gaze at him, the corners of his mouth twitching as if fighting back a smile.

"Petunia," he nodded, addressing Ian, "it's nice to see you." His Irish brogue was unmistakable and commanding.

Ian just smirked and nodded his head. "Nice to see you again, Dr. C."

Lenora glanced around the room, flabbergasted at everyone's silent regard. Everyone looked intimidated—everyone, that is, except for Ian, who wore an interminable smirk on his face. The man stopped in front of Lenora and chewed on a cigar stub as he surveyed her, eyes narrowed. He removed his hat. "Doctor Sean Cuddigan, spiritual healer, at your service!" He clicked his heels together and bowed, taking hold of her hand and kissing it.

The shocked look on Lenora's face was evident, as Tom abruptly stepped in and shook his hand, introducing himself. Dr. Cuddigan kept stealing glances at Lenora, narrowing his eyes suspiciously. Finally, he sidled around behind her, placing two hands on her shoulders. She was mystified.

"So," Cuddigan began, "will someone bring me up to speed?"

Tom nodded and opened his mouth to begin, when Cuddigan interrupted. "...and none of that long-winded nonsense you professors are wont to do—give me the skinny." He patted Lenora's shoulders as he spoke, sometimes a little too hard. She winced, but was slightly afraid to say anything.

"When Lenora and I moved in—"

"No, no, no!" Cuddigan interjected, drumming on Lenora's shoulders. "Please spare me the boorish details! Just tell me what happened!"

"Well, that's what I was trying to—"

"Good God, man! What's the problem?"

"Well, I—" Tom looked utterly confused.

"Cat got your tongue?" Cuddigan asked. "Go on, then, I'm listening." He squeezed Lenora's shoulders, shaking her back and forth like a rag doll.

"As I was saying—" Tom began, holding his breath, waiting for the interruption. When none came, he continued updating Cuddigan on the occurrences with the entity.

While Tom spoke, Cuddigan leaned in to Lenora. "I really got the old man flustered, didn't I?" he whispered conspiratorially. Shocked, Lenora looked up into his face, speechless. He winked and gently patted her shoulders. "Keeps his mind off the fear."

Lenora's shoulders relaxed. *Maybe there's more to this man than meets the eye.*

They all listened in silence as Tom recounted the story. Somewhere in the middle of his speech, Lenora felt something in her hair, and discovered to her utter shock, that it was Cuddigan's hand. And he wasn't caressing or stroking her hair gently, he was rummaging around as if looking for his misplaced keys...or lice. Lenora's head jostled about, and then she felt the sudden sting of a hair being plucked out.

She whirled around and gave Cuddigan a nasty look, but he was already off, holding the hair in his finger—twirling it about, looking mystified.

Tom stopped midsentence. "Ah, Dr. Cuddigan?"

"Sean, if you please," Dr. Cuddigan said with a dismissive wave.

"Okay...ah...Sean? Are you listening?"

"Not really," he admitted bluntly.

Tom looked confounded. "And, why not?"

"Because I already know all that drivel," Sean responded.

"Then, why make me go through all of it?" Tom sounded quite annoyed.

"Because, while everyone listened to you yammer on, I was able to assess the situation through the room's energy."

Tom's eyebrows raised. "Okay. You have my attention. What is your assessment, exactly?"

Dr. Cuddigan walked to the center of the room, drew in a deep breath, and pointed to Tom. "Your apartment. Haunted." He pointed to Lenora. "She's a retro-cog with outstanding abilities. Entity wants her." He pointed to Emily. "Occultist, mind reader, all around gifted." He winked and gave her a suggestive nod, causing Emily to blush—something Lenora had never seen.

He pointed to Amelia and Phillip. "Investigative team….oh, and lovers." Phillip and Amelia exchanged smiles, obviously impressed with the analysis.

Dr. Cuddigan pointed to Rose. "She's a clairvoyant with other hidden specialties." Again, he winked. "Those two over there are techno-geeks," he said, pointing to Maggie and Joe. He stopped at Ian. "And this guy sees dead people and is in love with…" he stuck his arm out, index finger pointed, and spun around in a circle. He stopped at Lenora. "Her." He sucked in a breath and nodded in a self-congratulatory way. "There…I think I've got it."

Not only was Lenora impressed with Dr. Cuddigan's ability to say it all in one breath—he got it all right. At least she hoped so. She looked over at Ian, who hung his head, his cheeks a flushed crimson. Lenora gushed at the thought. What if he was right? Was Ian really in love with her? Her head spun, and then she checked herself.

Nicholas.

Ian looked up and met her gaze with a troubled expression.

"So!" Cuddigan shouted so loudly that Rose jumped and issued an audible gasp. "Lenora. Let me sum this up quickly so we can get on with it. The entity is searching for the seven heavenly virtues, which are prudence, temperance, justice, fortitude, charity, hope, and faith." He ticked them off on his fingers as if reciting for a test. "The entity in question, a Mr. Bartholomew Booth, killed five women in his lifetime: Constance—which is a simile for fortitude—Temperance, Justina, Hope, and Faith. He killed one woman as a spirit, and that was Prudence. He has only one of the seven heavenly virtues left: charity."

"But, Charity Smeeton," Lenora interjected, a hopeful lilt in her tone. "She died—he got his seven."

"Nope," Cuddigan corrected her. "Charity committed suicide. She's the one that got away."

"Remember your choices, Len?" Ian interrupted quietly. "Either you willingly let him take your soul, or you commit suicide to escape him and he'll go after your friend Kate?"

Cuddigan shook his head sadly. "Yes, a terrible choice to make for someone so young."

Lenora nodded and inhaled, steeling herself. "Okay, so, what do I have to do?"

"*We*," Dr. Cuddigan corrected her, "get rid of it—together—that's what."

"How?"

"With a little cleaning," he answered again, just as enigmatically.

Lenora opened her mouth to ask something else, but Tom held up a hand, shaking his head emphatically. She decided to heed his caution.

"So, the first step in a spiritual cleaning," Dr. Cuddigan began, turning circles around the room as if searching for something, "is an investigative interview...and I already took care of that."

"You did? When?" Tom asked, still sounding unsure.

"Last week. I stopped in and talked to Walter." He sauntered over to Emily. "Strange man, if you ask me," he whispered and nudged her. Emily giggled like a little girl, and Lenora was somewhere between appalled and amused.

Cuddigan gave Emily a sidelong glance and smiled. "Hey, hotness, why don't you be a dear and get that Ouija board for me." Emily smiled and nodded, and then screamed as Cuddigan slapped her hard on the rear-end. "Pronto!" He chuckled, rocking back and forth on his heels, still chewing on his cigar stub.

Emily returned with the board and handed it to Cuddigan. "No, hotness, place it in the middle of the floor, would you dear?" Emily did as she was told, flashing Lenora a surprised grin.

Cuddigan moved to the center of the room and opened a box that Lenora failed to notice before now. He took out a large bowl and small hammer, a wooden tray, and a bunch of sticks, and then set them next to the Ouija board.

Lenora was perplexed. "What are those?"

Cuddigan pointed to the sticks. "These are incense, which attracts spirits. The bowl is twofold. The first is attraction: you tap it with the hammer, the gonging sound will attract the spirit. The second purpose is as a transfer agent. After attracting the spirit, we'll place things that were his into the bowl and ignite them. This turns his negative energy to ash, which I will later bury in sacred ground, rendering him unable to haunt you again."

"What's the wooden tray for?"

"To set these things on," he answered. "I don't want to start a fire in your flat." He chuckled, setting the Ouija board atop the tray.

"Oh." Lenora felt slightly embarrassed.

Cuddigan looked up at Rose. "Sugar Lips? Could you get me a light?" Rose looked startled. She nodded and then quickly moved to the kitchen and retrieved a lighter. She started to move away from Cuddigan, when he cleared his throat loudly. "Where you going, Sugar Lips? I would like you to sit here on the floor next to me," he patted the floor to his right, where she instantly took a seat. "Light the incense, please dear." Rose lit the incense and set it on the tray in front of her.

"Okay," Cuddigan looked around the room, "where'd hotness go?"

"She has a *name*—" Tom began, but Ian stopped him, shaking his head and frowning. Tom exhaled impatiently.

"Sorry," Cuddigan blurted, "but I don't have time to remember everyone's names, so I just go with what works." He glanced about the room. "Hotness?"

"I think he means you, Emily," Ian added with a grin.

"Oh!" Emily giggled and worked her way back over toward Cuddigan. She had just finished lighting the last of the candles that she had set in a wide circle around the Ouija board.

"Ah! Hotness! There you are! Come sit on my other side," he patted the floor to his left. "Hold the bowl and hammer, and hit it when I say 'gong,' got it?" Emily nodded, flashing an excited smile at Lenora.

Cuddigan nodded to Tabitha. "Honey Bun, will you take my vest for me?" Tabitha quickly moved forward and waited for Cuddigan to remove his vest. Once he did, she whisked it off to hang it up, looking bright and chipper as she did so.

"Okay, then," Cuddigan sighed as he removed something from his pocket—it was a piece of hair. Lenora squinted. It was *her* hair. He placed the hair in the middle of the board and then glanced at Lenora. "Come on over, Baby Doll—you're going to sit across from me." Lenora did as she was told. Cuddigan glanced around him, nodding in approval. "This is how I like it—surrounded by hot girls!" He let out a roaring laugh. No one else seemed as amused, particularly Tom.

Lenora had to stifle a laugh as she looked at what Cuddigan was wearing. His green tee shirt was mostly hidden by the vest, so she missed the gold trophy cup with the saying "Trophy Wife" written alongside. She pursed her lips together as she discovered that the shirt was a bit too short, coming just to the top of his belt buckle, which she noticed as she got a closer look, was a silver and black Batman emblem.

"You know, Baby Doll, it's not polite to stare at a man's private business," Cuddigan said stoically.

Lenora quickly looked up, embarrassed beyond all belief. "No, I was…it was your…" she stammered, trying to explain herself. She glanced at Ian, who looked highly amused.

"No need to explain, Doll, there's plenty of me to go around." He leaned in. "I have to say. Though it's not polite to stare, it sure makes a man feel wanted." He winked and then chuckled loudly. Lenora frowned and then realization crossed her face. He was jesting. This man was difficult to pinpoint.

"Now, I plucked your hair for two reasons," Cuddigan explained. "One, so that I could feel your energy—which is good and strong by the way…though not so confident." He leaned in again. "And, you have a secret or two of your own, my little friend, by way of…" he shifted his eyes in Ian's direction, "…someone…but your secret is safe with me," he whispered slyly.

Lenora felt the color rise on her cheeks as she tried not to look at Ian. *This guy does not know about tact.*

"No, I believe that honesty's the best policy, Baby Doll," Cuddigan said, as if he could hear her thoughts. "The second reason I pulled out a strand of your lovely hair," he continued, "is to avoid you having to touch the board or anything around it—this will eliminate the danger. If you touch something during a spiritual cleansing that the entity can use as a portal, it can drag you into the spirit world. But, using something like a strand of hair gives you connection without the danger."

"Now," he continued, "because this entity is so strongly attached to you, and because it wants nothing more than to kill you, it requires a bit more energy…from all of us…to get it out of here—to cleanse your spirits from his. Does that make sense?" Everyone nodded their heads. "Good. Now, everyone needs to sit within the circle of light around the Ouija board." Everyone scurried toward the circle and sat down.

The room grew quiet as everyone looked at Cuddigan expectantly. Lenora felt uneasiness rolling within her, forming a tight knot in her stomach.

Cuddigan looked at his watch. "Now, for the newbies, I'll just explain that the first task is to contact and then connect with the spirit. Once we have contact, we'll be able to move forward with the cleansing. No contact means no cleansing."

Lenora felt a lump in the back of her throat. "So, if you can't connect to the spirit, there's nothing you can do?"

"Not today, no," Dr. Cuddigan answered. "We'll start at midnight."

"Why midnight?" Lenora asked.

"It's what's called the 'witching hour' or the 'hour of the dead'—it's a time of day when spirits can roam freely about the earth," Emily explained. "It's the best time we have to connect with the spirit world."

"Very good," Dr. Cuddigan winked at Emily, who giggled and blushed.

"So, what do we do until then?" Lenora asked. It was ten minutes to midnight, and she really didn't understand how ten minutes made a difference.

"We wait...quietly," Dr. Cuddigan answered, leveling a gaze at Lenora, who immediately discontinued questioning.

He began precisely at midnight without ever once looking at the clock.

"Is there someone here in the room with us?" Cuddigan asked. Everyone sat breathless for several seconds, glancing nervously about the room, waiting for a response. "I know you're here," Cuddigan prompted. "Can you make a noise to let us know you're here?"

A heavy silence engulfed the room. Lenora held her breath, waiting for something.

A quiet knocking sound startled her. She glanced around the room to see if anyone else heard it.

Tom nodded. "Yes, I heard that," he whispered, turning toward the kitchen. "Maggie? Joe? Did either of you make a knocking sound?"

"No," Joe answered, "that came from neither of us."

"If that was you, spirit, make the noise again so we know it was actually you." Cuddigan paused, looking in the vacant darkness. Then, the knocking sound came again—but this time, much louder.

"He's here," Ian and Rose uttered simultaneously.

A small, involuntary whimper escaped from Lenora. She held a hand to her mouth. Cuddigan reached across and patted her hand. "You need to fight that fear—he feeds off of it."

"I feel him strongly," Ian said, sitting up. "I sense an intense anger...he doesn't like us here...I keep hearing a loud voice shouting at us to get out." He closed his eyes and sat silent for several seconds and then nodded, opening his eyes and focusing on Lenora. "I'm also sensing an intense satisfaction—he likes that you're frightened."

Chills ran up Lenora's spine, and the hair rose on her neck.

Cuddigan cleared his throat and nodded. "There's no need for you to instill fear in anyone here. We are here to do you no harm— we just want to ask you questions." He paused, glancing into the blackness, seeming to await an answer. "Did you live here in your human life? Can you affirm this by knocking for us again?"

Goose bumps formed on Lenora's arms as she heard the floorboards creak.

"Does anyone else hear footsteps?" Emily asked. Unable to speak, Lenora nodded and noticed that everyone else heard them too.

Phillip stepped forward slightly, showing Tom the thermal camera. "The temperature is dipping quickly. The mean temperature all evening has been 68 degrees—it's now 31...now 27....now 22."

"I can see my breath," Lenora observed.

"Of course you can, "Ian smirked, "it's below freezing."

Cuddigan cleared his throat and gave Ian a disapproving look. "Don't mock her...you'll only weaken her resolve, and that's what the entity wants."

Ian lowered his head. "Sorry..."

"Don't apologize to me," Cuddigan nodded toward Lenora, "direct it to her."

Ian glanced at Lenora and pursed his lips. "I'm sorry, Love—I don't really know when to turn off the sarcasm."

Angry at his sharp tongue, Lenora could only bring herself to nod at him and then look away. She glanced at Cuddigan, who offered a kind smile.

"Anger is always better than fear in these situations," he offered. "Just don't let it get the best of you." He returned focus and closed his eyes. "If you lived here in a previous life, could you be Bartholomew Booth? If so, make a sound to confirm."

Amelia gasped. "Did you all hear that?"

"No," Tom replied. "What did you hear?"

"I heard a distinctive laugh..." she looked over her shoulder, "from behind me." She rewound the recorder and pushed play. Everyone strained, hearing a faint chuckle.

"Was that you laughing?" Dr. Cuddigan asked into the void. He let several seconds pass before speaking again. "Why don't you quit playing games with us and make yourself known? So, I ask: is it Bartholomew we are speaking to?"

Eyes wide in anticipation, Lenora glanced about, trying to see in the darkness. Nothing appeared to move. The room was thickly silent, creating a tension that Lenora felt through her entire body.

She jolted at the sudden slam of her bedroom door. Everyone turned to look down the hall. The office door slammed shut.

Tom glanced at Lenora and then quickly looked over his shoulder. "Maggie?"

"Wasn't us, Dr. Kelley," Maggie answered.

Dr. Cuddigan chuckled. "Okay, so you're into theatrics, Mr. Booth. I get it. So, tell us—why are you here?" He rose and stood in the center of the room. "Come on out, you coward—face us and tell us what you want!" Dr. Cuddigan wore a determined expression as he challenged the entity.

"Don't provoke him," Rose uttered quietly. "It will only make him angry, and Lenora isn't the only one in jeopardy here."

"What do you mean," Tom asked.

Rose kept her eyes closed, lowering her head in concentration. "I'm picking up the spirits of other women. Two in particular are fighting to come through—Faith and....Justina...are their names." She looked up at Tom just as Lenora issued an audible gasp. "Do those names mean anything?" She glanced at Lenora.

"Faith and Justina were victims of Bartholomew's," Lenora answered, trembling.

Rose nodded. "Yes, they're showing me that. He's keeping them here—he holds their spirits captive. They can't get out."

"That's what he plans for Lenora," Ian added. "I can see what they're trying to say. He wants to possess them all."

Dr. Cuddigan approached Tom and put a hand on his shoulder. "Tom, you need to try fending the spirit off by being firm with him. Tell him that he isn't welcome here and needs to leave your daughter alone. Some spirits respond to assertiveness." Tom frowned at him, looking confused and uncertain. Dr. Cuddigan gently nudged him toward the center of the room. "Go on, then, protect your daughter."

Tom stood in the center of the room and cleared his throat. "Y-you need to leave," he stated faintly.

"You have to be more assertive than that," Dr. Cuddigan interrupted. "This entity wants to steal your daughter's soul and trap her in purgatory. Do you want that?'

"No, absolutely not!" Tom responded angrily.

"Then tell him!" Cuddigan urged.

Tom nodded. "Bartholomew, you need to leave my home immediately! And, leave Lenora alone. She's my daughter—mine—and you can't have her, so leave!" His fists clenched, Tom stood defiantly challenging the entity.

"Uh," Phillip uttered, "I just saw a form in the thermal camera—it went through Lenora's bedroom wall, into the hallway, and then it walked right through the wall on the opposite side to Tom's den."

Everyone turned to look down the dark hallway. Lenora felt an intense fear crawling through her body. She shivered, crossing her arms.

"What kind of form was it, Phillip—" Tom began to ask, but was interrupted by Phillip's surprised expletive.

"The form just walked out of the den and is now walking down the hall! It's a human form, no mistake." Phillip glanced away from the camera and glanced down the hall. "It's definitely paranormal—I see nothing down that hallway with the naked eye." He peered back into the camera and then looked up at Lenora. "It's heading straight for you."

Lenora jumped, turning to face the hallway once more. She strained to see in the darkness, but couldn't make anything out. "I don't see—" She stopped suddenly, her body shaking uncontrollably as a cold breeze blew forcefully through her, taking her breath away. "I think...it just went through me!" She whimpered, glancing at her dad in sheer panic.

Ian rushed toward her, but Dr. Cuddigan stopped him. "No, she needs to deal with this head on." He glanced at Lenora. "Face it, Baby Doll—it feeds off of your fear."

"I-I don't think that I can," she groaned. "I don't know how."

"You need to be brave—" Dr. Cuddigan explained, but stopped short, as he shifted focus to the Ouija board. The planchette was moving on its own. Everyone moved in closer, watching the planchette as it sped across the board, spelling the same thing over and over:

L-E-N... L-E-N... L-E-N... L-E-N

Ian shook his head and raked a hand through his hair. "No! I'm not taking this anymore! Either you communicate with us, or we resort to drastic measures to get rid of you! You aren't human—you can't hurt us!"

The planchette stopped in its tracks and then moved in slow circles in the middle of the board.

H-E-L-L-O I-A-N

Ian froze for a second, pausing. "Hello, Bartholomew. Instead of communicating through that board, why don't you talk to us like a real man?"

The planchette stopped in the center of the board for several seconds, then resumed its slow, circular motion.

NO   T-R-I-C-K-S
N-O-T S-T-U-P-I-D

"I didn't say you were stupid," Ian answered. "I'm just sick of this board." Ian watched the planchette make measured figure eights around the board. "Why don't you let the women go?"

NO

"What good are they to you?"

V-I-R-T-U-E

"You want to possess their virtue?"

YES

"I'm sorry, Bartholomew," Ian shook his head, "but no one can give you virtue—you have to earn that on your own."

NO M-I-N-E M-I-N-E M-I-N-E

"No, I'm afraid not—" Ian began, but was interrupted by Rose, who gently touched his arm.

"Don't provoke him," Rose whispered, "he's getting angry and the women are becoming agitated. If you provoke, we'll lose him."

Ian nodded. "What do you want with Lenora?" The planchette stopped at the outer edge of the board. Everyone waited for several long seconds, staring at the unmoving planchette. Finally, thinking that he wouldn't get a response, Ian opened his mouth to ask again, when the pointer began moving slowly around the board.

F-I-N-I-S-H

Ian frowned. "Finish *what?* What do you want to finish, Bartholomew?"

C-O-L-L-E-C-T-I-O-N

"You can't collect Lenora," Ian replied. "She's a human being."

N-O M-O-R-E

"What do you mean to do?" A choking sound emitted from Ian's throat, betraying his fear.

K-I-L-L K-I-L-L K-I-L-L

"Stop it!" Ian yelled. "You can't have her! If you harm her, we'll harm you. Get it?"

The planchette began moving in quick circles in the center of the board.

"Ian! Stop shouting at him—he's now dangerously angry!" Rose looked terrified. "The women's spirits have all left me—they've fled out of fear!"

Just then, the planchette began spinning rapidly and then flew across the board, landing on the word NO. It stopped only briefly before flying off the board and hitting Ian in the chest.

"Oof!" Ian fell backward into Rose, who caught him instantly. He quickly regained his balance and rubbed the center of his chest. "Whoa, that really hurt! This thing's got some strength behind it!"

"Tom?" Maggie shouted from the kitchen. "There's a figure heading right for Lenora—I can see it in the thermal imagery!"

Tom turned just in time to see Lenora struck from behind. She flew across the room and skidded on the floor, stopping herself before her head struck the wall. Tom ran to his daughter and turned her over. "Lenora?"

"I'm okay, Dad," she mumbled, groaning.

Tabitha ran over and held Lenora's face in her hands. "She's alright, Tom. I'm going into tech review to see if I can read the entity's aura."

Tom nodded at Tabitha and then helped his daughter sit up. He then looked at Dr. Cuddigan. "This is too much—she needs to get out of here."

Dr. Cuddigan nodded and knelt next to Lenora. "It's up to you, Doll. Do you need to leave?"

Lenora shook her head violently side-to-side. "No!"

"Lenora, I really can't—" Tom began.

"No, Dad, I need to face this thing." She rose from the floor and steadied herself. "This is my battle too."

Dr. Cuddigan steadied a gaze at her. "If at any time you need to leave, just leave, okay?" Lenora nodded. Cuddigan focused on Tom. "I'm relying on you to keep an eye on her—but it's her choice whether she leaves or not."

Tom didn't reply, but simply nodded once and then shifted his gaze downward. He was clearly not thrilled with Lenora's choice, or Dr. Cuddigan's support of it. He wrapped an arm around Lenora and squeezed her shoulders.

"He's back!" Ian shouted, eyes wide, searching. "Leave Lenora alone, you coward!"

"No, no, no!" Tabitha shouted from the kitchen. She ran into the room. "I just saw the entity's aura—he means to kill Lenora tonight! We need to get you out of here!" Tabitha grabbed Lenora's arm and started to pull, when a vase flew off of the mantle, across the room, and hit Tabitha on the head, knocking her out cold.

"Okay! Lights on!" Cuddigan shouted, running for Tabitha. Maggie and Joe quickly ran about the apartment, turning all lights on. Cuddigan took out a medical bag and examined Tabitha, who was not responding. Everyone waited, watching and holding their breath. Finally, Dr. Cuddigan nodded and turned toward the onlookers. "She's alright. She will have a nasty headache for a while, but otherwise, she's fine." He glanced at Emily. "I need you to close the Ouija session."

Emily nodded and quickly picked up the planchette from the floor, and then moved to the board. "Lenora?" She paused, glancing at Lenora, who was frozen in place, staring at Tabitha in fear. "Lenora!" she shouted, finally rousing Lenora out of her stupor. "Help me close the session."

Lenora moved forward and knelt down next to the Ouija board, wiping tears from her cheeks.

"At least two are needed to play," Emily explained, "and at least two are necessary to close the session. Understand?" Lenora nodded. "We're going to hover our hands over the board and chant the word 'goodbye' three times. Got it?" Lenora nodded again and did as Emily instructed, hovering her hands over the Ouija board.

Emily placed her hands on top of Lenora's and then nodded. "Goodbye! Goodbye! Goodbye!" both girls chanted together. They hovered their hands over the Ouija board until the planchette moved on its own, hovering over GOOD BYE.

Emily nodded and removed her hands. "Done." She gave Lenora a reassuring smile and then turned to Dr. Cuddigan. "The session is closed."

"Good. Keep the board in its place—we'll need to burn it with the rest of his things. " Cuddigan glanced at Tom. "We all take a break now. The spiritual cleansing will begin thereafter."

They took a break for a couple of hours so that Tabitha could recover. Everyone except Lenora reviewed the video footage. She just couldn't bring herself to look at it. Not yet, anyway. Tabitha slowly emerged into consciousness, but she still looked confused and winced whenever she turned her head. Lenora felt awful that Tabitha sustained any sort of injury because of her.

Once everyone had fully rested, Dr. Cuddigan called them back into the living room and instructed all to resume their former positions. Apparently, while most of the team reviewed video footage, Dr. Cuddigan set the room up again. Everything was ready. Lenora was not.

Cuddigan glanced around the room seriously. "Everyone needs to remain still." He turned to Emily. "When I say the word, you strike the bowl lightly with the hammer once…and only once." Then he turned to Rose. "When I lightly tap you on the arm, wave the incense toward Lenora."

Cuddigan leaned over the incense in front of Rose, waving the smoke into his face, taking deep inhaling breaths. He sat up, closed his eyes, and exhaled slowly. He chanted something in a foreign language that Lenora was not familiar with, repeating the same words over and over again, waving his hands over the top of the Ouija board. Occasionally, he would say the word "gong" quietly, and Emily would lightly hit the metal bowl, creating a quiet gonging sound. Then, Cuddigan continued his chanting, speaking it more rapidly, his eyeballs moving back and forth under his eyelids.

Then, he stopped all of a sudden, tapping Rose, who waved the incense in Lenora's direction. Lenora tried not to cough. The smell was nauseating and made her feel woozy, disoriented.

Cuddigan's chants started up again, this time the words seemed different…almost in a different language. He spoke rapidly, still waving his hands over the top of the Ouija. This time, Emily and Rose both had their eyes closed and appeared to be in a trance—their bodies swayed in motion with Cuddigan's hands; they no longer needed prompting for their work on the bowl and incense.

Lenora grew more frightened; her body started to tremble, head began to spin, and she could taste the bile in her mouth as her stomach churned.

Emily and Rose began to chant along with Cuddigan, as if they were familiar with the ritual. Lenora looked around, noticing that everyone had their eyes closed and appeared to be whispering the words along with Cuddigan.

Was he hypnotizing them? Did he cast a spell on everyone?

Lenora thought she could hear faint drums in the background, and everyone swayed in time with the beat, the chanting growing louder, faster. Her head grew heavy and the spinning was slow, deep, and encompassing. Her heart pounded loudly, her breathing grew rapid. The slow churning in her stomach increased and the coppery taste flowed in her mouth. Her body started lurching violently. She clapped a hand over her mouth as she could feel her stomach starting to retch. Horrified, she realized she was going to vomit and was unable to move.

Unable to control it, her hand flew from her mouth as she felt hot liquid rise from within. Her body violently heaved forward as the hot liquid disgorged. Shockingly, it wasn't vomit that issued from her, but a cloud of breath that was thick and black.

She coughed and sputtered as the last of it escaped her mouth, and then she drew in gulping breaths of fresh air.

The chanting stopped. Lenora's eyes closed uncontrollably. Dim light flashed behind her eyelids, appearing as if it was a television going out of focus; the form of a man materialized through the flashes. She felt a sharp jolt run through her body as she recognized who it was.

It was the man from her dreams—the one who tormented and hunted her—and he materialized before her, as if real.

He sneered at her, his eyes blazing with anger. "You can't escape me, Lenora—you are mine!"

Lenora opened her mouth to speak, but nothing came out. She looked at Cuddigan, who began chanting again in another tongue, the image of his body wavering, going out of focus.

The entity shrieked, putting his hands over his ears, twisting his head violently and unnaturally around to leer at Cuddigan. He hollered obscenities at Cuddigan, who didn't seem to hear him. The entity's head twisted back again, and this time, instead of leering at Lenora, his face changed to one of pleading.

She started as his face changed; it appeared to be getting younger by the minute. He looked like a young boy, the face of Bartholomew Booth, before he became a murderer. He stretched his arms out, imploring her to help him. "Please, miss, please don't let them hurt me!"

Lenora sank, feeling instant compassion for this poor boy who only needed help…a chance. She shook her head. "I'm so sorry, Bartholomew! I can't!"

"Oh, please!" He pleaded, tears filling his eyes. "I only want someone to love me! Please help me!" The tone in his voice became more urgent. "I'm running out of time! Please! Grab my hand! Help me! It huuuurts!"

Tears filled Lenora's eyes as she watched this poor young boy writhing, looking at her pleadingly as each sharp pain attacked him.

"I want my mom!" He shrieked and sobbed wildly

That's it! Lenora couldn't take it anymore—he was just a boy, after all. She reached forward, to touch his outstretched fingers, a feeling like an electric spark arcing between the two. A jolt of white-hot pain surged through her body and she felt herself instantly weaken.

She struggled to move her arm, but it wouldn't budge. Looking up at him incredulously, she saw his face contort and change, the sinister sneer reappearing. He was no longer the innocent boy, but the murderer. She tugged at her arm, but to no avail—he wouldn't let go.

Petrified, she realized that he was taking her with him—he tricked her!

Suddenly, she saw movement in her mind's eye. Cuddigan took the bowl from Emily, threw it down on the Ouija board, and then ripped the necklace off of Lenora's neck. She panicked as she saw that it was the very one her dad made for her—the amber stone on the silver chain.

"No!" she shrieked, but she wasn't heard. She tried moving forward to reach the necklace, but it was no use, she couldn't move; her body weakened by the second.

Cuddigan then removed something from his pocket and set it in the middle of the bowl next to Lenora's necklace. It was a satchel made of a flimsy material, tied together with a purple silk ribbon. Cuddigan untied the ribbon, exposing a tiny ceramic thimble, a gold locket, a butterfly comb, a tiny gold ring, a lock of honey-colored hair and one of auburn.

Lenora gasped. "That's Prudence's hair...and mine..."

Cuddigan ignored her, inhaled, and then resumed his task, pouring a thick, black liquid into the bowl and then setting it on fire. He then began to chant loudly and rapidly. Soon, everyone in the room but Lenora were entranced into the chanting, swaying in rhythm to the imagined drum beat that resounded throughout the room.

A white burst of energy forced Lenora back, hurtling her violently into the coffee table. The pain that traveled up her arm was searing hot—she glanced down at her arm at a traveling burn mark that surged up her arm along her veins, like black rivers cutting into dry earth. Noticing that she lost the spiritual connection to the entity, her gaze quickly shifted to the center of the room.

She saw the entity with her own two eyes—it was contorted in pain and appeared to be wavering in and out of focus.

She watched as its body grew indistinct, nebulous, like swirling black ash. A white mist streamed upward from the bowl, shapes emerging that resembled female human forms. Lenora thought she could see colors glowing around each form: a shimmering gold, bright aqua, deep amber, lime green, violet, and a pale grey.

Suddenly, Lenora felt an overwhelming sense of peace, calm. Once the mist dissipated, Cuddigan quickly covered the bowl.

The room grew quiet, as everyone looked around, confused.

"It's gone," Rose said with relief.

Ian nodded. "Yes, I feel it too." He looked up at Lenora and grinned.

Lenora felt an intense relief that she hadn't felt in a long time. It was gone.

She glanced at Cuddigan, who smiled knowingly at her. "Yes, it's power over you is completely *diminished,* and the spirits of the entrapped women have been released, but the entity is not *gone* yet."

Lenora frowned, a tight knot forming in the pit of her stomach. "What do you mean, not gone?"

"Well, this type of entity cannot be rid of in a night—it will take much more time to get rid of it completely." Cuddigan noticed that Lenora still looked confused. "Tonight's ritual only dispelled the entity from you, Lenora. It can no longer haunt you or this flat—it hasn't the energy. The ashes in this bowl are the remnants of your entity. I will take this bowl with me to sacred ground, and over the next few days, will perform additional cleansing rituals to send the entity where it belongs."

Lenora panicked. *Days? How many more days do we have to go through this?*

Reading her mind, Cuddigan chuckled. "You're done…. dealing with the entity, that is. It's paramount that I begin cleansing the entity's spirit immediately and persistently over the next few days so that it cannot regain energy. As it is, the entity has the energy of a low-grade virus that needs to be contained."

He sighed as if already bored with his explanation. "Though you're done with the entity, I still need to cleanse your spiritual energy to ensure that it's strong enough to ward off Bartholomew's spirit for good. That will happen on a weekly basis, when I expect to meet with both you and your dad. When we're through, you should be able to move back in here—but not until then."

"How long will that take?" Tom asked, immediately regretting the question from the angry look on Cuddigan's face.

"As long as it takes," Cuddigan responded, miffed. "These things don't go away overnight." He looked up at the ceiling and shook his head. "These people need to stop watching paranormal shows on the tellie…it brings unrealistic expectations. " He leveled a gaze at Tom. "You are fully aware of how much time it takes, however, aren't you?"

Tom's expression changed to surprise. "Uh…." He stammered, trying to find an answer.

Cuddigan raised his eyebrows. "Not ready to discuss that, then? You'll have to…sooner or later." His eyes flickered to Lenora and then back to Tom. "My secretary will contact you with dates and times." Tom nodded in agreement.

"Can I ask where you got the satchel?" Lenora asked tentatively.

"Ah, yes," Cuddigan replied, "Bartholomew's souvenirs from his kills." He nodded, seeming off in his own world. "You see, when I read the case file, I immediately recognized the inspector's name. The current lead detective for the Cambridge Police is one Billy Rood. He has worked with me on past cases and we've become good friends. I went to him a few days ago and asked his relation to Inspector William Rood, who as it turns out, is Billy's great-great grandfather."

"Apparently," Cuddigan continued, "after Booth's arrest and death, most of the evidence on the case went missing. So, to prevent from losing all the evidence, Inspector Rood kept this satchel locked up safely in his personal vault. He passed this down through generations. When I told Billy what was going on—he gave this to me for today's cleansing ritual in hope it would rid you of the spirit, and rid him of the cursed task of guarding it. Billy said it has brought nothing but trouble."

Dr. Cuddigan sighed heavily and then rose from the floor. "Well, I'm famished! Anyone up for a steak? I always crave a good steak after a ritual burning!" His booming laughter filled the room. He looked around the room at blank stares. "No one? Alright, then I guess it's steak for one tonight."

"Oh, *hell*, I'll go!" Emily held up her hand and pranced across the room. "Not sure if I'm hungry, but I could use a good drink."

"That's the spirit!" Dr. Cuddigan stopped by Lenora for a simple touch on the shoulder before continuing on to the door for his coat.

Lenora, sad to see him go, instinctively touched the spot where her necklace once resided. "Dr. Cuddigan?"

"Yes, Baby Doll?"

"Why did you take my necklace?" Lenora still felt the sting from when the chain was torn from her neck.

"It was his. That stone was the color of his first victims' eyes," he explained. "Since you've been wearing it all this time, you are a part of its essence. Destroying it along with him fulfills his desire to possess the seven heavenly virtues. He may not have had all of you, but he has part of your essence. Make sense?" Lenora nodded. "Good. Someday, a good-looking bloke will give you a new one." He eyed Ian and then chuckled softly.

Dr. Cuddigan threw on his vest, coat, and hat. He winked at Lenora, offered Emily his arm (which she took enthusiastically), and left without another word.

Soon after, Lenora heard a loud rumble on the street. She ran to the window just in time to see Dr. Cuddigan pulling away on an enormous motorcycle, Emily on the back squealing in delight. Lenora smiled. She looked over as Ian issued a soft chuckle nearby.

"He's bloody brilliant—I love that guy!" Ian shook his head, quietly laughing.

Feeling bold, Lenora stepped closer to him. "Who else do you love?"

Ian took a step back as if she invaded an invisible barrier. "I love all sorts of people, Len...in all sorts of ways." He eyed her with caution. "Cuddigan was right. I do love you...but not like a man loves a woman...more like best friends."

Lenora felt an instant surge of embarrassment. An uncomfortable moment passed between the two as they stood in silence, staring out the window. Commotion in the room startled both out of their separate musings, and they joined in on the cleanup, avoiding each other completely.

Tom, Ian, and Lenora walked to the borrowed apartment in silence. Lenora felt compelled to ask Ian a million questions, but kept them to herself, her heart aching the entire way. Once they arrived at the apartment, she stopped Ian and asked to speak with him alone. Tom gave her a wary look, exhaled, and then slowly made his way upstairs.

Once they were alone, Lenora turned to Ian, not exactly sure what to say. "So, since this is done, are you moving out?"

Ian nodded. "Yeah, but not until your sessions with Cuddigan are over. I'll move when you do."

Lenora felt a wave of relief rush through her. Good, she still had time. "And Thaddeus? Will I get to see him from time to time?"

Ian chuckled. "Of course—but only if you ask."

Lenora nodded, shuffling her feet, feeling the thick tension in the air. "Ian, I wanted to thank you—"

Ian quickly moved forward, grabbing the sides of her face, gazing into her eyes intently, their faces close. "Oh, to hell with it," he muttered, moving his face toward hers. Lenora's heart beat furiously as she felt Ian's breath on her face, her lips parting in eager anticipation.

"There you are!"

Ian immediately dropped his hands and quickly moved away from Lenora, glancing at her guiltily. He shook his head and sighed, turning around to see Clare down the street, waving and smiling. "I've got to go," he muttered. Ian opened his mouth to say something else, but thought better of it, instead deciding to kiss Lenora's forehead quickly, impersonally. "Sleep well. See you…later, I guess." His smile was mechanical, weak.

Lenora nodded, heart in her throat. She stood on the sidewalk, watching Ian walk away from her and into someone else's waiting arms.

EPILOGUE

She lounged on her bed and stretched, a patch of moonlight glowing on her pale skin.

It was good to be home.

Everything about her life was good right now. She no longer had nightmares or visitations from sinister ghosts, thanks to Dr. Cuddigan. It took three weeks of intensive work with Cuddigan to cleanse the apartment—equally so for his sessions to cleanse her and Tom's energy. She thoroughly enjoyed sessions with Dr. Cuddigan and hoped she got to work with him again in the future. He was funny and quirky, and he kept her on the edge of her seat. The three weeks seemed long, but looking back, it went by fast, and now she was sleeping in her own bed.

Growing tired, she curled up in her grandmother's soft quilt and inhaled the warm, clean scent—searching for that gentle scent of apples and cinnamon, which always reminded her of grandmother. Sometimes, she liked to pretend she was back in her grandmother's house, curled up on the couch, waiting for the first taste of hot apple pie. It made her homesick.

But, this was her home now, and she needed to get used to it.

It was getting easier now that she had made friends, and she was beginning to really enjoy Olivia and Kate's company. They seemed to accept her for who she was, and never really asked about the gloves, which Lenora found a bit odd, but somewhat comforting that she didn't feel compelled to fabricate a reason.

Then, there was Nicholas. She sighed, rolling over and peering out the window at the moon.

Now that everything with the entity was through, Lenora had a long talk with Tom, and he agreed to let her date Nicholas…supervised. This past month, Nicholas came over twice a week, having dinner and playing games with Lenora and Tom. Saturdays, he joined them at the market, spending most of the day with them, but leaving just before dinner out of respect for Tom's wishes to have quality time with his daughter.

Last week, Tom allowed them to meet for tea after school…alone. Next week was the dance—their first night out together alone. She couldn't wait.

Lenora bound out of bed, threw on her robe and slippers, and opened her closet to stare at the dress she bought specifically for the night. They were going to a faculty-only Halloween dance to raise money for a local charity. It was a black and white masked ball, and she couldn't be more thrilled.

Everyone she knew was going. Tom had asked Rose, which Lenora was unsure about, especially considering how soon it was after her mother's death. Tom assured her it was only two colleagues attending together because neither had an interest in taking an actual date. She wasn't sure she bought it. Emily was taking Cuddigan, and Lenora just couldn't *wait* to see what those two showed up in. Phillip and Amelia were going together, of course, and Maggie and Joe both had dates as well. The only one she wasn't sure of was Ian.

Her smile faded.

Since the night of the spiritual cleansing, Ian hadn't been around…anywhere. Tom said he was staying at Clare's. When they moved out of the borrowed apartment, Tom had Ian's things shipped to Clare's place. Ian never showed to the CSP meetings either, which Tom also reasoned was because Ian had just taken over teaching a course and needed that extra time to prepare.

That, Lenora did not buy—he loved going to CSP meetings. She tried calling…even leaving messages…but he never returned her calls. She wasn't sure if she should be terribly sad or incredibly angry at him. After all, they were friends, and he certainly wasn't treating her like one.

Mood now turning sour, Lenora trudged back to her bed, took her robe and slippers off, and crawled back under the still-warm blankets. She peered out the window again to take in one last look at the moon before giving in to sleep. Feeling a little warm, she opened the window and closed her eyes as the fresh, cool night air filtered in. She glanced down at the empty, quiet street and started, seeing a shadowed figure in a shop doorway across the street. Leaning in and squinting, Lenora tried to discern if her mind was playing tricks on her. The figure moved and walked swiftly down the street.

Perhaps it was someone taking a break from the cold autumn air. She wished it was Ian…she wished he would just come talk to her.

Thinking about Ian, wondering where he was, and the guilty pangs whenever Nicholas would enter her mind kept her wide awake for nearly three hours. Finally, growing weary of the questions and what-ifs, she began to drift into that deep, comfortable dizziness, letting it carry her off.

She stood in the middle of the road, the evening mist just gathering. A cool breeze wafted up, and she felt cool material fluttering against her skin. Mystified, she glanced down at her leg and wondered why she was outside wearing her nightgown.

Though she thought of going inside, her limbs would not carry her, feeling as if they were frozen to the spot. A piercing iciness rushed through her body, causing her to shiver. She crossed her arms in front of her, looking down the street for whatever it was she felt a compelling urge to wait for.

A figure pushed through the mist, his black cloak whirling about his quickened steps. No longer feeling the invisible tethers, Lenora quickly moved to the side of the street, sheltering in the doorway of a shop. The doorway was familiar, as if she had been here before. Instinctively, she looked up and across the street, seeing her bedroom window, curtains billowing out, fluttering in the evening's chilly breeze.

Looking back into the street, she could see the figure nearing. She huddled down, seeking shelter in the doorway to avoid being seen.

The sound of boots clicking on stone caught her attention, as she strained to discern where the soft ticking sound came from—it appeared to keep time with the figure's footsteps. Curiosity getting the best of her, she peered around the corner and saw where the sound came from—it was a cane. But, the figure didn't appear to use it to help him walk—he held it up, as if leading a parade.

Just as visions of parades crossed her mind, other figures appeared through the mist, shadowing the figure in black. The followers, all young boys, trailed behind their leader, stepping rhythmically to the click of the cane. The sound of the boys' marching steps grew intensely louder, as if it were an army approaching. Lenora clasped hands to her ears, muffling the noise. She strained to see the boys' faces and stifled a gasp. Milky black eyes spiraled hypnotically, sunken and stark against ashen skin. Their faces were expressionless, eerily calm. She stood frozen, noticing that their bodies were translucent, mere apparitions.

Heart pounding in sheer terror, she pressed against the wall, fearing she would be seen. Tremors ran up her spine, and through her body, fear holding her in its icy grip. She drew in a long breath, steeling herself for the glance she knew must be taken. Quietly, she turned again toward the street, peering at the leader.

He wore a black top hat, and his hair streamed down from it, matted and greasy. She blinked in disbelief as the hair changed different shades of color, alternating in nauseous, thick waves of black and blood red. The movement of the color made her stomach churn, a slow burn rising in her chest.

She swallowed hard, forcing herself to look into his face, which appeared distorted, bowing in and out of focus, as if she were looking at his reflection in a funhouse mirror. The eyes were sunken, black-rimmed, glowing red. A thick, black ooze wept from his eyes and stained the white pallor of his cheek.

As the procession drew near, Lenora again hunkered down in the shop doorway, hoping that she would remain unseen. As the leader closed in, he didn't seem to notice her, but one of the followers did. The boy slowly raised his arm, pointing in her direction. The leader stopped in his tracks, halting his legion. He stood in the center of the cobbled street, staring ahead for several seconds.

Lenora couldn't breathe—her heart thumped furiously in her chest. She pressed against the building's cold stone, slowly inching her way into the doorway's shadow. The movement caught the leader's eye. His head turned slowly, mechanically, to the side until his gaze found her—his eyes glowing in anger, lips stretched in an evil grimace.

Then, an abrupt look of astonishment.

The eyes lost their glow, instantly turning a dark chocolate brown... almost black.

A sudden fear washed over her, sending waves of sick revulsion through her body.

No... it can't be...

Lenora bolted up in bed, panting, terrified. "Nicholas?"

ACKNOWLEDGEMENTS

Without the help of some incredible people, this book would never have been completed.

Special thanks to my group of early book readers, particularly Alexis and Rachel, who gave me honest and thoughtful feedback… especially since they had no idea it was me (wink, wink).

My deepest appreciation to Sean and Tammie for their thorough reader response, enormous support, and encouragement during the early writing stages. Without the two of you, I would never have had enough courage to move forward. Immeasurable is my love for you both.

To my editor Kristi: what can I say that even compares to how grateful I am for your diligent and enthusiastic feedback? I am so very lucky to have had you as part of this process, but even luckier to have you in my life.

A heartfelt thanks to Janet for the endless support and laugh therapy, which got me through the toughest of times.

Finally, to my husband Dan. For the thorough reading and candid feedback, my sincerest appreciation. And, for your infinite patience, love, and support throughout the entire process, I thank you, my dearest, best, and most beloved friend.

About the Author

M.L. Harveland is a writer and editor who lives in North Dakota. After earning a Master of Arts degree in English literature, she decided to finally get serious and put her imagination to work. She resides with her husband, Dan, two Golden Retrievers, two cats, and a bossy parakeet. *The Seventh Soul* is her first novel.

Made in the USA
San Bernardino, CA
16 October 2015